SALTCROP

ALSO BY YUME KITASEI

THE STARDUST GRAIL

THE DEEP SKY

YUME KITASEI

SALTCROP

FLATIRON BOOKS
NEW YORK

This is a work of fiction. All the characters, organizations, and events portrayed in this novel are either products of the author's imagination or used fictitiously.

Printed in the United States of America. For information, address Flatiron Books, 120 Broadway, New York, NY 10271. EU Representative: Macmillan Publishers Ireland Ltd, 1st Floor, The Liffey Trust Centre, 117–126 Sheriff Street Upper, Dublin 1, DO1 YC43.

www.flatironbooks.com

Designed by Jonathan Bennett

Wave and ripple designs produced by the Japanese artist Mori Yuzan in 1903.

Library of Congress Cataloging-in-Publication Data

Names: Kitasei, Yume, author.
Title: Saltcrop / Yume Kitasei.
Description: First edition. | New York : Flatiron Books, 2025.
Identifiers: LCCN 2025003836 | ISBN 9781250380968 (hardcover) | ISBN 9781250380975 (ebook)
Subjects: LCGFT: Apocalyptic fiction. | Thrillers (Fiction) | Novels.
Classification: LCC PS3611.I8777 S25 2025 | DDC 813/.6—dc23/eng/20250221
LC record available at https://lccn.loc.gov/2025003836

First Edition: 2025

10 9 8 7 6 5 4 3 2 1

For my sisters

PART 1

SKIPPER

CHAPTER ONE

The day Skipper decides to go and find her oldest sister, Nora, all the mussels are stolen from Gull Gang Rock.

Skipper picks her way along the shore. The rocks are slick with wet seaweed and the retreating ocean tide. Everything gleams in the fading orange-yellow light. Soon it will pour, and she regrets not wearing her rain jacket. She is twenty-two and generally considers herself invulnerable to things as ordinary as weather.

Gull Gang Rock is a particularly large rock jutting out among the waves beneath a ruined wooden pier. Carmen, the middle Shimizu sister, gave it its name when they were younger, based on all the brassy-voiced laughing gulls that hang out there.

Carmen loves naming things. It's her way of claiming ownership, and it's annoying, but the names stick anyway.

For example, Skipper's real name is Rosa, but it's been many years since anyone has called her that. When they started fixing up their boat, Carmen began calling her Skipper as a tease, because it was all

Skipper wanted to talk about. The more annoying Skipper found it, the more Carmen used it. But the irritation rubbed smooth over the years, and now all that's left is the residue of affection.

Skipper is medium height and wiry, with short-cropped brown hair, thick eyebrows, and a hunch to her shoulders like she's trying to figure out the secret of evaporating. As that is impossible, she avoids most people instead, which is one reason she is down here by the beach at this particular moment.

As the familiar stink of rotting sargassum fills her nose, something glints in a tidal pool, warm from the afternoon. A half-crushed plastic bottle is caught in the rocks. She reaches out with a long-handled pincher and wrestles it free, tossing it over her shoulder into the sack on her back. It rattles with the few other odds and ends she's found: a comb, a sturdy aluminum bottle, and a doll missing a leg, a head, and most of its clothes. Selling a hundred pieces of garbage will cover a day of their grandma's medication.

A truck comes every other month to haul away plastic, metal, and glass painstakingly skimmed from a giant slurried patch a half day's sail from the harbor. The metal and glass get recycled, the plastic fed to vats of hungry little worms in giant factories up north in the city.

Skipper wishes she were out in the ocean, dragging her nets through gunky water, but a monster storm is on the way, and even Skipper knows better than to be caught out in it. Some people blame the government for overseeding rain clouds this season. On this point, Skipper agrees with Grandma: People should never have gotten into the business of trying to manage the weather.

She's come down to the beach to collect mussels. Guilt pricks her. It's Grandma's birthday, and she should be helping Carmen assemble the meal. But lately all she feels at home is a smothering, like she can't breathe. She doesn't know when it started. Perhaps she's lived her whole life this way and never noticed until now.

Skipper pries a translucent, tattered white bag free. It reads *Thank you* in purple letters, a polite desire transmitted across the fifty years since plastic bags were ubiquitous. Inside is a half-decomposed baby turtle. She shakes the bag until the fishy carcass tips out.

All morning at home, she waited for a knock, Nora appearing in the doorway just in time for the party. Nora would apologize for not letting them know she was coming home, but she wanted to surprise them. Not that Nora is good at keeping them informed anyway. She is a terrible letter writer.

Nora moved up the coast for college ten years ago. She used to come home for the holidays once or twice a year, greasy-faced from the city air and exhausted from riding in the front bucket seat of an automated commercial truck. It takes her twelve hours of sleep to recover, but it's the cheapest way to travel: a long ten-hour drive over broken highways, with only two stops to recharge. Nora dehydrates herself and abstains from food for a day beforehand and arrives home hungry and parched. Then Grandma fusses over her for a week in a way she never fusses over Carmen or Skipper, until Nora must do the reverse trip all over again.

Nora didn't move back home when she graduated. She got a job working for a Renewal lab testing agricultural products before they go to market. Since then, her visits home have become less frequent, and Nora has worn soft in Skipper's mind like a much-patched denim jacket.

Skipper fantasizes about sailing to the city, is even saving money for it, but it never happens.

Over a month and a half ago in late September, they received a message from one of Nora's colleagues—his name is John—saying Nora was gone. They hadn't heard from her in almost two months, and her last paycheck bounced. The colleague thought she'd returned home and wanted to know if they should mail her things from the lab: a thin, silk scarf, a yellow teapot painted with sunflowers, a chipped mug with bees on it, and several boxes of books.

For a brief, excited week, Skipper prepared for Nora's arrival. She stayed home and cleaned the house from top to bottom so thoroughly even their grandmother muttered something dangerously close to approval. She fixed the squeak to the guest room door. They planned a big meal.

Except Nora never arrived.

It took a week of agonizing back-and-forth to clarify that John-the-colleague, in fact, doesn't know where Nora is or anything useful, despite the *PhD* included prominently in his message signature.

At first, Skipper and Carmen thought maybe Nora took a detour—as if there is more than just one route from the city to the town. But another two weeks came and went, and they had to assume the colleague was wrong.

All messages to Nora prompt only the frustrating automated reply she's used for years: *Hello, I do not check this inbox often, as I do not believe in sharing my personal business with corporations. If you need to reach me, you know how to reach me. Thank you!*

Nora's quaint paranoia is no longer endearing or amusing.

"She just wants to be mysterious. It's selfish," Carmen says. Carmen and Nora don't get along.

This morning, as Carmen and Skipper were yanking onions in the garden for Grandma's birthday dinner, John-the-colleague, PhD, wrote again: *We'll need to dispose of Nora's personal property if you don't arrange for shipping in a week. We have a new staff member starting, and as I am sure you agree, he has a right to space for his personal things.*

The price he then quoted to freight her things back was enough to make Carmen's lip curl. "It's not worth that much," she said, ever practical. "She wouldn't have just left the stuff if it meant anything to her."

Except—except! It is the mention of the mug with the bees. Bees and boats. Skipper painted that mug herself back in art class. She gave it to Nora right before she went away. And it means something, that Nora's kept it, sipped from it, put it where she could see it for ten years. It must be more than chipped by now, maybe glued back together. Nora wouldn't have "just left" it.

"Do you think she's in trouble?" Skipper had asked for the thirteenth time this morning.

"She was always a little thoughtless," Grandma said, more lucid than usual. "I'm sure she's just gone off and forgotten to let anyone know."

Carmen wrote to the police and an old friend she knew in the city—Carmen has friends everywhere—without satisfaction. But it is a city, and cities are places a person can get lost. No one knows where Nora is. No one is even bothering to *look*.

Skipper has been hoping, deep down, Carmen will fix everything. Carmen is two years younger than Nora and four years older than

Skipper. And while Nora may be the one with big ideas, Carmen is the one who has woken up every day at six since she was twelve, earned a college degree and nursing license while working a full-time job, and still folds the laundry after all of that. Not much can fatigue Carmen, and Carmen's creeping failure now makes Skipper more anxious than anything.

Skipper reaches Gull Gang Rock and pauses to balance in its shadow, bracing herself for the freezing spray. Once, this beach was covered in white sand, before rocks were dumped to slow erosion. The rocks are perfect for a certain kind of mussel.

Last year, she seeded a long rope with mussel larvae and hung it down in the ocean water in the lee of Gull Gang Rock. The mussels are minimally engineered, which means they are cheap and more likely to die. In nature, baby mussels are born in the gills of adult mussels, and their larvae nestle in the tissue of unsuspecting fish until they're big enough to survive. Why would a fish put up with that?

There are never a lot of fish around, but she's recently noticed baby mussels budding beyond her rope in the cracks and crevices nearby. It's a reason to hope: nature returning, one step at a time. Maybe a sign of something more. It's not that Skipper believes in things like that, but she wishes she did, so she lets herself pretend, just like she pretends Nora is on her way home.

Skipper comes by this rock every so often to examine the mussels and their pretty black shells, shiny and expectant. The last time, there was maybe a bucket worth of big guys ready to collect.

Her mouth waters in anticipation, remembering how they tasted years ago: melted butter, salt, onions, several cloves of garlic, and the soft flesh parting between her teeth. Scarcity looms following a poor harvest year due to flooding, and the mussels promise a treat before a long march of cabbage, potatoes, and beets.

When she edges to the spot, though, the mussels are gone, and not just the big ones. She balances on one leg and leans around the rock to be sure, thinking at first maybe the rope just slipped. But no, there are a few tiny ones, that's it. Someone has been here, has taken her whole stash.

She is breathless from the violation of it. Then rage floods in, and she curses. It is enough to distract her from the danger of her surroundings. A wave comes up and slams into her, and on top of everything else, it's as if the whole world means to knock her down. Only a childhood spent on boats saves her from falling.

Her canvas shoes and the legs of her pants are soaked. Her anger flows out as quickly as it came, leaving instead a vast, familiar despair that isn't quite sadness so much as a cavity inside, like she will always be hungry. She tried to explain the feeling once to Carmen, when she was foolish enough to think it was something everyone felt sometimes.

Apparently not. And Carmen, with her unfortunate hawklike perception, has learned to spot it in the vacancy of Skipper's expression. She refers to it as Skipper's "empty face."

Suddenly, all Skipper wants is to be back in the kitchen drinking a hot mug of cider. She turns back to shore, overwhelmed by the distance. The thudding of her heart drowns out the rain, and her fingers tingle with the aftershock of terror. The sun sinks rapidly behind a sickly stand of palms designed to withstand mercurial weather patterns, and the rocky beach is swathed in shadows. Everyone else from town is safe at home. Skipper is alone out here, like a creature on the verge of extinction.

A bell tolls, breaking the spell. She feels more than sees the weight of sudden clouds thickening behind her, rolling in from the sea. She hurries.

Choppy waves lick her feet, nipping at her ankles as she scampers from rock to rock to rock. The faster she moves, the more fear rises inside her, until she is just a vessel in motion. She slips a couple of times, cries out, but there is no one to hear, so she keeps going, a scrape on her right knee stinging from the salt.

The first fat raindrops catch her a few feet from shore, and she slows so she doesn't fall again. She trembles in relief. A *ba-ba-BOOM* shakes her sternum. The sky tears open, and great sheets of rain wash down. She runs through the tall sawgrass, a half-empty bag of trash dangling off one elbow, toward a cluster of red cedar trees, but she is already drenched.

She dreads the heat of Carmen's temperamental gaze, the harsh cut of Grandma's voice as she asks Skipper what she was thinking, as if Skipper weren't a grown woman.

Lightning strikes behind her so close it smells like ozone.

Maybe this will be the day the ocean rises up and cleans their town off the face of the earth. She doesn't hope for it, so much as she's grown up expecting it: Grandma carried off by a wave, still in her chair with a blanket over her lap and her eyebrows bent in rage, Carmen treading water, lecturing everyone about how they should have prepared better for this.

Rain cuts Skipper's cheeks, and she runs along the muddy path by memory alone, past fallow fields stained burgundy with Amaranthine, the ubiquitous two-in-one fungicide weed killer that smells oddly like vanilla. A ghost from long ago touches her palm, Nora's slim fingers clutched against hers, Carmen telling them to hurry up, they are going to be late for dinner again.

Skipper arrives home, shivering uncontrollably, face so wet it's impossible to see her tears.

"Come in," Grandma calls from her chair. "Why were you out in this weather?"

A fire crackles in the fireplace, and a small chicken sits on the table, skin glistening and bronze. And it shouldn't be like this. It's wrong to celebrate when Nora isn't here.

Carmen sets the table. "What's happened?" she asks, but Skipper's teeth are chattering too hard to say: *Don't you hear the echo in our hollow house? There isn't enough inside to keep the roof up; any moment it will come tumbling down.*

CHAPTER TWO

In a dry change of clothes, clutching a mug of hot cider, Skipper huddles in the chair across from Grandma.

Her sister and Uncle Tot talk about the increasing price of seeds, whether Renewal's latest treatments have improved arugula production, and how a farmer they knew was fined for planting old seed. Carmen feels strongly about this: It's reckless and threatens the health of everyone else's crops, not to mention the risk of contamination for others if there's seed drift. Uncle Tot hates it: People should be free to plant what they want.

Skipper likes these conversations because they demand little of her.

The kitchen is open to the dining room table, so Carmen talks to them as she finishes the cooking. Skipper tries to help, but Carmen snaps that Skipper is in the way; she needed help earlier, but now it's mostly done.

"She's fine," affirms Uncle Tot, clapping Skipper on the shoulder. "Don't worry about your sister." This successfully unites both sisters in irritation, which may have been his intention. He flicks through a catalog of home gardening seeds as if he doesn't notice.

"We should order the new Soy 4X39," Carmen says. "It's supposed to be 15 percent more productive than the 4X30, 30 percent more resistant to blight, and grows great with Amaranthine."

"What, did you memorize the catalog?" Uncle Tot laughs, because that was something Carmen used to do when she was young.

There's plenty of room in this house, but Uncle Tot moved out at the first opportunity, before they were born. He lives in a half-empty four-story apartment building at the outskirts of town where the neighboring lots are so overgrown there are trees growing through the roofs.

Uncle Tot is a small man with a handsome face and thick black hair. He mumbles too much for Grandma to understand him half the time and drinks steadily from six o'clock to midnight on Mondays, Wednesdays, and Fridays.

"Where's Ollie?" Skipper asks, surprised Carmen's girlfriend of four years is not here. She wonders if it's because of her. Recently, Skipper confronted Ollie about the way Ollie conned their neighbor into buying a broken generator. Carmen doesn't know about that or their argument, Skipper's pretty sure. Carmen would have been on a warpath because Skipper didn't tell her about it.

Skipper *would* have, if she hadn't promised Ollie she wouldn't. Anxiety trickles down Skipper's spine.

Uncle Tot gestures too late for Skipper to drop the subject.

"We broke up," says Carmen, as if it is nothing, though the flutter of her eyelashes betrays subterranean emotion.

"You did?" Skipper waits to hear it's her fault.

"I'd like not to talk about it for four weeks while I process, okay?" says Carmen, bending over the stovetop, brown hair hiding her face.

Carmen is the tallest sister and the beauty of the family. Everything about her face is perfectly balanced, from the graceful parabolic arches of her slender eyebrows to the full curve of her lips and dimples on either cheek. The last are a courtesy of Carmen and Nora's father, a highway repairman who comes through town every year or so with gifts of boat parts, even though neither of his daughters sail anymore. Skipper is happy to accept the precious items on their behalf.

Skipper's own father is a blank space on her birth certificate. She credits whoever he is for her small, flat nose, straight dark brown hair, and large cheeks that make her look like a foreigner.

"Wow," says Skipper. "Not thirty-nine days?"

"It's a simple request." Carmen fetches a blanket from the living room and drops it over Skipper's head and shoulders so Skipper can't see. "Stop shivering."

"What did you say?" asks Grandma.

"Nothing, apparently," says Skipper, wrapping the blanket around her.

The house shudders in the wind. Their five-bedroom is old, from before times, when Grandma was young and there was such a thing as an upper middle class. When money had more meaning in this country. It is, in fact, Grandma's house, which is why Uncle Tot, then Nora, then Carmen had moved out.

Carmen lives in a stilted, skinny house down the street. Spring to autumn, she works full-time as an equipment maintenance worker for Renewal.

Renewal is a mega agriculture company. They sell seeds, equipment, contract labor, and soil treatment products, including their fungicide, Amaranthine. Decades ago, a blight appeared that devastated corn, wheat, and soybeans across the country. A million people died in the famine before Renewal developed Amaranthine to combat it, and the world was able to slowly recover. A few years later, when the wilting leaves and black rot spread to other crops, Amaranthine prevented further devastation. Today, food production is stable but precarious. Renewal is a leader in food production, and half of the people in town work for them in one way or another.

Carmen loves complaining about work, but she doesn't accept criticism of Renewal from people like Skipper. They deserve acknowledgment, she says, for rescuing the country from starvation.

Uncle Tot used to work for them too, until an accident with a sprayer convinced him of his own impending mortality. He retired to pursue, as he calls it, a "life of joy," which generally consists of playing cards with his friends, talking politics at the local bar, and inviting himself over for dinner at his convenience.

Only Skipper stayed behind with Grandma, and if the house continues to stand, someday it will be hers. Though she wouldn't put it past Grandma to leave it to some charity organization no one has ever heard of just to shock them.

Skipper doesn't want the house. She hates it, in fact, with its cheerful pink exterior and leaky roof, but she supposes she might die here anyway. For all her dreams of traveling to other places, a lack of momentum has plagued her since she was a child. The thought she might sail in circles from the harbor to the patch and back, day after day, makes her rigid with terror sometimes, and yet she continues, locked in the habits of her childhood.

The house is built into a hill, and it has withstood many storms before. Once, before Skipper was born, a cypress fell and crushed the porch and half of Grandpa and Grandma's bedroom while they were sleeping inside. Down it went, right through their marriage bed. Grandma survived, miraculously, because meanness is a survival trait.

Grandma fixed the house and the bed and went on living in that bedroom for many years, and the half newness of the façade faded with time.

Grandma sleeps downstairs these days so she doesn't have to manage the stairs. In the middle of the night, she sometimes wakes up not knowing where she is. She cries out for help, so Skipper, who remains in her childhood bedroom even though it is the smallest room in the house, must come down and lead her back to bed.

A few times, Grandma wandered straight out the door and down the street in her pajamas until a neighbor found her and brought her home.

So now Skipper locks the door and listens to Grandma haunt their house, searching for an exit. It is a part of their rhythm, like Grandma swallowing her parade of pills, or Skipper reading aloud to her from one of Nora's books before bed.

Once a year, in an arrangement negotiated by Carmen, Uncle Tot stays over, and Skipper sails her boat a short way up the coast for a few days' reprieve. She can never relax when she does this, sweating as she lies in her bunk, mentally ticking through all her neglected duties.

Carmen says this is ridiculous, that Uncle Tot is just as responsible for the old woman as they are, that Skipper should move out herself, and they should hire someone. But the few caretakers are overstretched as it is, and Skipper worries about leaving Grandma's care to a stranger.

Grandma's other needs are expensive too. Her hospitalization last year would have wiped them out if Nora hadn't come up with the money at the last minute. It was impressive Nora could do that. They didn't know Nora made that kind of money. Of course, Carmen found a reason to complain about it instead of being grateful. She thinks Nora should cover other things too, then, if she can.

Sometimes, Skipper does allow herself the sweet, mint dream of a future something else, of taking her boat and just sailing beyond the horizon to see if the world has become as bad as Grandma believes. But as hard as the woman sometimes was to them, they owe her for taking care of them after Mom died.

Fortunately, in weather like this, Grandma is peaceful, as if the chaos outside muffles the noise inside her brain. She sits at the table, face lit by candles, her napkin tucked under her chin as she waits for a fork to be placed in her hand.

"How old are you, then?" Uncle Tot asks her.

"What?"

Skipper repeats his question.

"Don't be rude," Grandma says, but then she tells him anyway, "I'm seventy." Which is not correct. She is eighty-six. Not that it matters. She will probably outlive all of them.

"Quite an achievement," says Uncle Tot, sitting down. His memories of his mother are softer than his nieces'. She was a super woman, the kind who worked a fancy job and still found time to also assemble elaborate class projects and throw big holiday parties. But by the time she took in the three sisters, she was old and explicit in her resentment.

"I didn't sign up for this," she used to say, and Skipper wondered what she *had* signed up for, because even as a kid, Skipper understood life wasn't a waiting list for a good time. It's hard not to resent Uncle

Tot's fond recollections of family travel and presents piled all the way to the door on holidays.

"Not really," says Grandma now. "It's not hard to get old. You don't do anything, and the years pass." She sniffs at the steam curling out from the warm dishes Carmen sets on the table.

In addition to the chicken, there's a pot of green beans covered in crushed walnuts the way Grandma likes, and a ceramic dish steaming with corn pudding—all for the four of them. It's extravagant to eat like this with a long winter ahead, but as a Renewal worker, Carmen gets a discount at the local store, and they agreed they should do something nice for Grandma.

At least this year the town was spared the worst of the blight. They've been through enough hard times to remember long stretches of gnawing hunger. This year, they lost broccoli rabe, which is fine with Skipper. She regrets the peas, though, which were infected: spiny and purple. Renewal claims they are safe to eat, but no one wants to risk it.

The image of the mussels returns with a pang, but worry over Nora overshadows anything else. Skipper pulls a napkin into her lap, then refolds it and puts it back on the table. An idea sloshes about her mind, and any moment, she will speak it aloud, spilling its contents down the white tablecloth like wine, and she won't be able to take it back.

"Happy birthday, Grandma," she says instead.

"What do you mean? Birthdays are never happy," Grandma says. "They're just days. I don't know why we count them."

Carmen snorts a laugh into the sink, which Skipper covers with a loud coughing fit.

"You aren't sick, are you?" Grandma asks. "You should sit over there." She points at the far end of the table.

"I'm not," says Skipper, but she gets up and switches her place, even though it's Nora's seat.

"It's a big storm out," Uncle Tot says.

"You should sleep over," Skipper says.

"Not that big."

"Eh?" Grandma says. "I remember when . . ."

"What do you remember?" Skipper asks.

"What's that?"

"You were telling us something about the weather."

"Oh, I don't know." Skipper gives up on learning what it was, but then Grandma says, "We drove up to the city once in weather like this. Steve had a fancy car that could drive itself, but he clutched the wheel so his knuckles were white, like he was sure it would quit and drive us straight off the road. I've never been so scared in my life." She smiles yellow teeth, remembering.

"That's awful," says Skipper, who has only ridden in a car a few times in her life. The town is small enough she can get everywhere on her bicycle.

"Why would you go up there?" Uncle Tot asks, because he is, to his bones, a homebody.

"Huh?" Grandma's gaze loses its focus again.

Carmen settles in next to them, and Uncle Tot takes up the carving knife.

"People were hungry, and we thought we could help," says Grandma. "We packed the car full of corn and beans. That's what we had. This was before Tot was born."

"I never heard this story. Was it during the shortage?" Uncle Tot deals out breasts and drumsticks.

But Grandma tunnels inward to somewhere they can't follow.

"Did you find anything at the beach?" Carmen asks. She used to enjoy scavenging down there when they were children. It was something the three sisters would do together. Once, they found a complete child's playhouse, only missing the door and one of the window shutters. They hauled it home and set it up in the yard, where it stayed until one day they came home to find an empty patch of brown grass. Grandma had traded it to the Martins down the street in exchange for half a deer.

It's one of the many things they haven't forgiven Grandma for, though it was true even Skipper had outgrown pretend by that point. They'd graduated to breaking into the collapsing homes on the far side of the harbor in search of treasure: machine-stitched socks decorated with cats in spacesuits, jars of white pills, crystal bottles of perfume, and tubes the size of a pinky finger, half-filled with chalky toothpaste.

Later, when the sisters began working on their boat, their scavenging became more purposeful. They hunted for pieces of wood they could cut for boat furniture or decking, and collected new, unopened cans of paint.

"Did you get mussels?" Carmen prompts.

"Someone took them," Skipper says.

"That's terrible!" Carmen's dutifully performing her outrage, Skipper can tell. "What are you going to do?"

"There's nothing I *can* do." Skipper spears a bean.

"Serving spoon," says Carmen, even though there's no point now, the bean is on Skipper's fork. Then Carmen rattles off all the things Skipper should do tomorrow: report it to the town, ask the harbormaster, offer a reward for information. This is Carmen, with the relentless urge to fix people and things, and it is draining.

The conversation moves on.

"Are you going out the day after tomorrow?" Uncle Tot asks. To the garbage patch, he means. The mile-long stretch of trash scattered across the gray water offshore is left over from a barge collision years ago. Uncle Tot likes to act like Skipper's manager, providing weather reports she already heard and advice she doesn't need on how to fix things. Uncle Tot taught them how to sail, but it's been years since he's been on the water.

Skipper hesitates, because this is her opening to tell them what she's thinking of doing, but she can't bring herself to say the words. To commit.

"Mm," she says instead, chewing her green beans more than necessary.

"By the way, I responded to John." Carmen fishes Grandma's napkin off the floor and slips it back onto the old woman's lap.

Skipper's fork halts halfway to her mouth, corn pudding balanced on its tines. "What did you say?"

"That it was all right to throw out Nora's things, but he needs to talk to the police about her case. They said they can't do anything without more information."

"You didn't," says Skipper, panic rising, thinking of the bumblebee mug. Of course Carmen didn't check with her. Skipper resents the efficient way Carmen moves through the world, as if everything can be sorted into labeled boxes.

"Why not?" Grandma asks, who may or may not be referring to Carmen's response, but either way can never resist drama.

"We discussed this," says Carmen. "We can't afford the shipping for a bunch of junk."

"She's going to want her stuff when she gets back."

"Apparently, she has money. She can buy new things," says Carmen.

"How can you act like everything's normal? We don't even know what's happened to her."

"Don't," says Carmen.

"We're all worried," Uncle Tot says.

Grandma's eyes dart among them. A family squabble is the best birthday present she could have asked for.

"We're doing our best here," Carmen concludes.

But that isn't true. They've stayed in their dry house and watched the rain come down. They've done nothing but write messages and wait and wait and wait for someone to come and tell them what is going on.

Skipper pushes back from the table, propelled by a fear that grips her around the shoulders. She gets up and sets her plate in the basin to soak, and when she comes back to the candlelight of the table, she says it: "I'm going up to the city."

"You can't take the car in this weather," says Grandma.

"We don't have a car," Carmen says. She's unimpressed. "How will you get there?"

Not by truck. It could be two weeks before the next one comes through.

"I'll sail. It's just a few days," she says. As soon as she says it, she knows this is exactly what she must do. "I'll go up there and find her."

She's done overnight trips before to the patch and to the bigger town down the coast to trade for supplies. But never to the city.

"What?" says Carmen. "If this is because you don't want to sell the boat . . ." They've circled the subject since Grandma's medical bills came due last year. The boat is expensive to maintain, its upkeep barely covered by what Skipper makes from skimming garbage. If they sold it and Skipper got a "real job," they could pay for Grandma's care and a new boiler too.

Carmen argues it belongs to all of them, and it's only fair they consider selling it. Fortunately, Nora agrees with Skipper.

"We're keeping it," says Skipper. Even after Skipper thought the discussion was settled, Ollie announced she'd found a buyer. That's when Skipper cornered Ollie and told her if she didn't butt out, Skipper would tell Carmen about her crap generator scam. Blackmail, maybe, but it worked: Ollie's buyer disappeared. "It's not about that."

Mostly not.

"That's a far way to sail by yourself." Uncle Tot's face darkens with worry. He turns to Grandma, as if the old woman still has any say in the house.

Eleven years ago, a few months after they finished the boat, the sisters had been out sailing a few hours from shore. A sudden squall descended, and Skipper almost drowned.

Grandma wanted to burn the boat to ash that night, never mind how many years they worked on it, but Uncle Tot stopped her. She's held a grudge against the boat ever since. But Grandma isn't paying attention anymore. She's organizing the green beans on her plate in neat parallel lines.

"It's not that far," says Skipper. What is she thinking? For all the years she's thought about it, can she really just leave? Her nascent resolve flickers. But no, Nora might be in trouble. And it's a short trip. She knows sailors who do it regularly. "I'll be back in a week." With answers, and, she hopes, Nora.

CHAPTER THREE

Skipper readies the *Bumblebee* for the trip. She swabs flotsam from the storm off the deck and replaces a badly frayed mooring line.

The *Bumblebee* is a single-masted boat with patched sails. The compact cabin sleeps three, though it's been years since her sisters came aboard. The hull is black with a faded yellow stripe all the way around. The solar panels on her deck are scratched, and the wind vane on the stern could use a fresh coat of paint. She's ramshackle, and Skipper loves her all the more for it.

Grandma bought the boat from an old sailor as a project to keep the girls out of trouble, and, more importantly, out of the house. Uncle Tot was charged with supervising the project and reporting on their progress regularly.

Nora and Carmen did odd jobs to pay for parts, leaving Skipper, only five, to earn small amounts of money doing chores around the house after school for Grandma.

Uncle Tot was a halfhearted taskmaster, dozing in a lawn chair on the dock while they worked. That they avoided dismemberment was no thanks to him. "Those who can't do, delegate," he liked to say, and so he bribed his friends to teach them how to hammer, patch, and paint.

To Uncle Tot's bemusement, his nieces stuck with the project even after Grandma herself stopped asking for updates. They patched the hull, replaced the mast, and retrofitted much of the interior with salvaged plywood and abandoned furniture and parts from other boats.

Nora lost enthusiasm first, and Skipper was too young to do it all alone. It was Carmen's persistence that drove them to finish. They finally launched the boat the year before Nora went away, slipping out into the harbor and tacking into the wind until they passed beyond the breakwater into the bay.

Skipper stood tucked up against the mast, the deck thrumming under her feet. For the first time in her life, she felt powerful, the three of them in that boat, pointed toward open ocean.

They built out the *Bumblebee*'s cabin with fantasies of overnight trips. It's small but tidy. Between the cockpit stairs and the bow, there's just enough room for a kitchenette, storage, and a tiny work desk with her radio and quirky navigation equipment; two narrow bunks and a fold-out table where they used to play cards and drink Uncle Tot's homebrew cream soda; a head and space for hanging wet gear; and a bunk at the bow made from a salvaged piece of foam Skipper had cut into a triangle and wedged in.

After cleaning up the boat, she packs jugs of water, beans, rice, walnuts, and a few apples. She fantasizes about a hard wedge of cheese, but it's gotten too expensive.

Grandma cycles between anxiety and fussiness. She senses something is up but keeps forgetting what. Each time Skipper passes through the house, she stops by Grandma's chair in the living room—to comb her hair, trim her nails, fetch her a snack. She frets about leaving her.

"I'm going away for a short trip, Grandma."

The old woman squints at her.

"Uncle Tot will take good care of you." He isn't happy about it, muttering how no one will want to come *here* for Wednesday night poker. He helped Skipper carry several bags of supplies down to the dock so he could talk her out of the trip.

"What if there's another storm? It could be dangerous. And the city is huge. You could look for her for years and never find her."

Skipper appreciates his pessimism, because it ignites her stubbornness, which is the only thing keeping her own doubts at bay.

Now, Skipper stands in the living room, where her shoes have worn tracks in the carpet. She wants to press her lips to the plane of that dry, wrinkled cheek, but Grandma would swat her and snap, "I don't need you to do that." She pats Grandma's hand instead.

"I don't know what you're making a big deal about. I guess you want attention," Grandma says.

"What do you mean?" says Skipper, hurt even though she knows better, because she has never known how to love their grandmother, how to make their grandmother feel loved. When she was a child, she tried to wrap the old woman in tenderness. She read too many fairy tales about the goodness of enduring thorns.

"You'd be happy if I die."

Skipper sighs. "That's not true." She collects Grandma's cold mug of tea.

"Don't steal that."

"I'll make you a fresh one." Skipper shouldn't be fixing tea. She needs to go. Outside, she hears the bang of the hammer: Carmen's up on the roof, fixing new leaks.

Work slows in the winter, and Carmen makes the most of it. She picks up spare shifts at the bar and takes extra courses. With her new nursing degree in hand, she just interviewed for a job at the county hospital, and waiting to hear back has fueled her productivity. Finishing other people's to-dos is Carmen's coping mechanism. Now that she's broken up with Ollie, she'll be a menace.

Skipper wonders again if Ollie told her about Skipper's threat. But it's day two of Carmen's four-week moratorium, so Skipper can't ask.

Skipper goes out on the porch, and Carmen frowns down at her, nails pinched between her lips. Carmen didn't say much when she came over this morning, which is unusual for her, and Skipper can't help but think it's because Skipper is the one taking action for once, and worse, Skipper is doing something that wasn't Carmen's idea.

There's a dead rabbit in the middle of the lawn. Budding horns crown its little head above its eyes. Skipper grimaces. The mutations crop up from time to time, from improper application of Amaranthine, people think. She looks away, because she can't deal with another awful thing right now.

"Have you seen my new sail thread?" Skipper asks her.

"Mm-mm," says Carmen around a mouthful of nails, pretending—Skipper *knows* she is pretending—to be wholly absorbed in her work nailing blue tarp to the roof.

"I bought it last week."

The bang of the hammer is loud enough Carmen might not have heard her. But she has heard her. The banging goes on.

"It wasn't with the rest of the sewing stuff."

Carmen spits the nails into her palm. "You're the one who lives here."

Irritation rises in Skipper, along with the impulse to shake her sister off her perch—not to kill her but to make her listen.

She goes back inside to pack her clothes.

At least Skipper's doing something. Carmen probably doesn't believe Skipper will go through with this. Skipper regularly tumbles down off firm intentions. She hates that about herself.

She breathes raggedly in the middle of her room, bare feet cold on the wooden floor. The room is contained chaos. Clothes litter her bed and floor in accordance with organization known only to Skipper. The scratched bureau displays an army of plastic action figures that once belonged to Uncle Tot scattered across the threadbare runner.

Stained glass hangs in the window: the image of mushrooms blooming at the base of a tree. Nora spent months making it for Carmen. She told her it was a good luck charm, that it would prevent evil spirits from breaking through the glass pane. And while it may have only added shadows to Carmen's bedroom walls, Carmen trusted their older sister, and that made the talisman more effective than anything. Skipper took it after Carmen moved out.

On her bed is a box full of letters from Nora. Lately, Nora prefers physical correspondence, even though letters can take weeks to arrive.

Since the message from John-the-colleague, they'd tried sending a few messages to Nora, but never heard anything besides the auto-response. That's not unusual for Nora, but now it increases their worry.

The last letter is from June, over five months ago:

> *Hi all, All's well. I can't come home this fall as I'd hoped—trapped by work. Afraid I can't send more money either; I'm a little short right now. Carmen, thank you for the gloves even though it's hot enough to fry an egg: You're right, they're a hideous orange, and I love them. Skipper, I hope the mussel project is a great success. I can't wait to see them. Uncle Tot, stop cheating at cards. Grandma, take care. Looking forward to pie when I make it home. Love, Nora*

Skipper rubs her collarbone, anger subsiding. It doesn't make sense. Nora loves her work—why would she leave her job without a word?

Skipper tries not to think of all the awful things that might have happened to her sister up there in the city.

She sits, the old bed frame creaking under her, and feels, suddenly, like it's for the last time, which is silly. She'll be gone for a week at most.

A slash of sunlight inches across the floor, and the sky out the window burns a robin's-egg blue. The weather conditions are perfect for sailing: bright and moderately windy. Downstairs, Grandma mutters to herself about pickles. Skipper wonders if this whole idea is a mistake.

Grandma criticized her for not finishing any of the things she sets out to do: school, the electrician apprenticeship, projects around the house. She's lost the few friends she ever made through uneventful unwinding, even though they live in the same town. She doesn't bake, because she used to abandon her concoctions on the counter, sometimes all ready to go into the oven before a strange malaise seized her and off she drifted, unmoored from any desire to complete her task.

She should have left this morning, less prepared, maybe, but at least she'd have been on her way before her determination leaked out of her.

In despair, she goes to the kitchen and assembles sandwiches. Bread, pickles, lettuce, mustard, leftover chicken. A dab of cranberry relish for her grandma. Cheese for Carmen, to make up for her uncharitable thoughts. No cheese for herself, because she doesn't deserve any.

"What are you doing?" Carmen asks. She holds the dead rabbit.

"Shouldn't you be wearing gloves?"

"Don't stress about it," says Carmen.

"I was going to deal with it," Skipper says, meaning the rabbit. Her temper flickers again as she slides the sandwich over to her sister. This is good. She can fight with Carmen, because it's Carmen's fault, somehow, that Skipper hasn't left yet.

"Thanks." Carmen sets a spool of stiff white thread on the table, speared by a brand-new needle, and goes out back to toss the rabbit corpse into the woods.

"Where did you find it?" Skipper asks when she returns.

Carmen scrubs her hands in the sink. "Shed."

"I looked there."

Carmen takes a bite from the sandwich. She watches Skipper as she chews. "When are you leaving?"

There it is. Skipper flushes. "I don't know. Tomorrow?"

"Okay," her sister says, wiping a dot of mustard from the corner of her mouth. "I'll come with you."

"Why?" Skipper's heart twists. This trip was her idea, and she doesn't want Carmen to come, not when Carmen wants to sell the boat. "You get seasick."

"Everyone will feel much better knowing you're not alone."

Exaggeration as usual. There is no "everyone," just Uncle Tot and Carmen at this point.

"Don't you have to work?"

"A week won't break the bank. I'll let the bar know. Hopefully I'm quitting soon, right?" That's the plan, if she gets the nursing job.

Skipper opens her mouth, and Carmen says, "I don't want to fight about this," which is an infuriating thing to say. But then Carmen says, “I’d rather not be around while Ollie moves out,” and Skipper softens. They were together a long time. Carmen must be devastated.

And also, if Carmen comes, there’s less chance for Ollie to tell her about what Skipper did.

“Do you have a list of what you’ve packed?”

“No.”

Carmen takes a yellowed pad and pen from a drawer next to the fridge and makes Skipper recite her provisions. Already, Skipper has lost control.

“Tomorrow, then. The morning forecast looks good.” Skipper hefts the sandwich she fixed for Grandma.

“Tomorrow,” echoes Carmen.

Together, they study a faded map tacked to the wall, the edges crinkled and torn, the creases hairy with deterioration. The trip seems straightforward enough, but then, maps never show the whole truth, just what a place could be without people or time.

CHAPTER FOUR

The sun is only a promise on the horizon when they shove off. The air over the town smells of smoke from a distant wildfire, but the wind is good. They escape the harbor and breathe salt air.

Skipper considered sneaking out early without Carmen, but Carmen was sitting on the front porch when Skipper woke up, feet propped on a duffel, drinking tea from one of Grandma's chipped white mugs.

It's weird having another person on the boat. The *Bumblebee* has been Skipper's hermitage for years.

At the same time, Carmen's presence is familiar. It reminds Skipper of learning to sail with Uncle Tot on his small boat, ducking under the boom as they tacked upwind.

Carmen earns some curious looks from other sailors, and word gets around the sisters are heading up to the city.

Their radio crackles with well-wishes, which Carmen cheerfully responds to with excessive personal details about Nora and John-the-colleague, PhD, Grandma's nightly bed routine, and the funny

I AM NOT A DUCK shirt Skipper is wearing—all broadcast to the whole harbor, until Skipper confiscates the radio.

"You're such a grump," says Carmen.

"You're such an exhibitionist," Skipper replies.

Carmen laughs and leans back, soaking in the morning sun around the edges of her thin gray T-shirt. She complains about the sour mildew scent from the spare life jacket.

Skipper ignores her and steers closer to the wind. Past the breakwater, they peel away from the other boats, and Skipper finally relaxes.

"Tacking," says Skipper, pushing the tiller toward the sail.

Carmen jumps to trim as the boom swings over. They cut across the wind and settle into a new angle close to the coast, where the waves are bigger than the harbor, but not unruly.

Carmen settles on the higher, windward side of Skipper and tips her head back to blink at the blue sky. A wooden bench runs around the rim of the cockpit, big enough to seat six. Skipper needs to replace some of its slats; some of the wood is loose, and they have to watch for splinters. This is one of the many things Skipper fixates on with Carmen onboard.

Skipper focuses her gaze on the water. She likes to imagine an ocean full of infinite triangles: Each time they tack or jibe, they begin again at the apex of a new one.

"What if we get all the way up there, and Nora's completely fine, just ditched work or something," says Carmen.

Skipper hopes Carmen is right. But while Nora might be neglectful, that doesn't explain the bounced paycheck.

Skipper studies the clouds for signs of unexpected weather. No rain on the schedule, but that's not a guarantee. These are an ambling parade of fluffy sheep. The skies should hold until evening. So long as they stay close to the coast, they should be able to pick up weather schedules and forecasts over the radio.

Only one boat owner in town is rich enough to afford the fancy equipment that can receive data anywhere via satellite. The technology once was more common, when materials, production, and electricity were cheap. Sailors make do, though. They have made do for millennia.

A sliver of yellow-gold winks on the horizon, and then the sun washes over the surface of the water. Skipper's eyes tear from the growing brightness, and she slides on a pair of sunglasses. Carmen's sunglasses are newer; Skipper will need to make her a strap so Carmen doesn't lose them to the water. She feels unexpectedly buoyant despite the circumstances.

"Did you talk to anyone about the mussels?" Carmen asks, spoiling Skipper's mood.

"I didn't have time." Skipper keeps the coast parallel to their port side. The sound of clanging filters across the water from a distant buoy.

"They would probably have made you sick, anyway," Carmen says.

"It would have been fine," says Skipper. "We consume more Amaranthine in the food we buy." Carmen spends too much time on land to understand the scope of the ocean. There's a reason Skipper opted for saltwater mussels. The river is notoriously dirty, especially after rain. No one wants to eat crimson-dyed fish with two tails.

"That's different." It's an old argument. Carmen defends Renewal. Skipper repeats Nora's arguments about the weakness of depending on a cycle of chemicals and engineered crops. Carmen points out Skipper is just recycling Nora's arguments, and anyway, Nora also works for Renewal, so what's her genius alternative? Without modern agricultural technology, they would starve. And Skipper will have nothing to say to that.

Past the ruins of a lighthouse, Skipper cuts closer to the coast.

"What are you doing?" Carmen asks.

"Shortcut." With the high tide, they can save four hours this way instead of going all the way around the sunken spit of land. But also, she wants to demonstrate a mastery of the boat she didn't have as a child. She straightens out their course.

Ahead, waves wash up against a row of neat gray-shingled peaks: the roofs of submerged houses. There was a beach town here once, maybe forty years ago. Grandma remembers it: a place with a few good restaurants and a movie theater. Ten thousand people.

Then the sea came, year by year, eating away the coast. Half the houses crumbled down, others washed out to deeper water, but some stand where they were built, haunting the shallows with their A-frames and plastic siding. Rusted satellite dishes perch above the surface, open-mouthed to the morning sun.

"We'll run aground," says Carmen. They came here a few times when they were younger—everyone did, because they were explicitly warned not to. Too much unknown beneath the water, and if their hull scraped the wrong thing, they might sink before help came.

Two kids they had known had died out here, and a third had gotten a bad infection when he cut himself diving into a rusted car beneath the water. All that for an inoperable gun tucked under the front passenger seat. When he returned to school, he was thin and shaky, the stub of his arm wrapped in white bandages.

"We're good," says Skipper.

Carmen is not just a rule follower, she enforces rules for others. In another time, she might have been a politician. After the incident with the two kids, she stopped coming, and she forbade Skipper from coming here too. This was after Nora had moved away, so Carmen was the boss.

"I'll tell Grandma," she had said, which was a rare and serious enough threat that Skipper had obeyed.

But years passed, and later, as an adult, Skipper returned, unable to resist the mystery of so many people's lives hidden beneath the water.

A ragged yellow rope lies submerged across the main street. Skipper aims for a gap where she knows the line hangs particularly deep in the water.

"We're going to catch," says Carmen, meaning the keel beneath their boat.

"We're *fine*," says Skipper, though she isn't 100 percent sure. "Drop the sails."

Carmen hesitates before following her direction. She goes up to the mast and pulls the mainsail down, flaking it into tidy folds as she goes. The boat slows, and Skipper starts the motor, hoping there's enough battery to get them through. The electric motor is fickle, and the battery is ancient.

She should replace them, but the battery's thirdhand, and it took a year to save the money for it, so she can't admit it is a disappointment.

In the before times, when fuel was abundant and global supply chains robust, you could order whatever you needed. Now, it can take a year to get something that requires materials from far away. That and the expense encourage people to repair and reuse.

Skipper catches her lip between her teeth and adjusts the tiller.

The *Bumblebee* passes over the line without a hitch, and then they make their way up the two-lane main road into the heart of town.

They pass the tall spire of a church. The clock face has been licked clean by waves so only the hands remain, frozen at three thirty—in the afternoon or morning, Skipper wonders.

She imagines a sudden ending: a line of cars moving out of town, piled high with people's belongings, the torrents of rain making the roads slick. Or maybe it had been a slow reckoning. The ocean taking streets one by one over the years, and the final residents hanging on until even they had to admit there was nothing left to save.

"You come out here a lot?" asks Carmen.

"I'm careful," says Skipper.

"I didn't mean that. I was only— God, don't be so defensive. I'm just curious."

Skipper navigates around a spot where she knows from a previous, harrowing experience a pickup truck sits under the water, a piano strapped to its bed. "There's a bunch of scrap out here. Sometimes it's easier than going out to the patch. Like you don't have to deal with Frank trying to dictate where you work or listen to Amy's bad music."

She waits for Carmen to revive the discussion about selling the boat and braces for the inevitable fight.

Or Carmen could comment about how Skipper needs to learn how to get along with other people, and that it is better to have friends than not. If Carmen doesn't get back together with Ollie, she will find someone else.

Carmen has lots of friends. She's not warm so much as magnetic. A person is either born with that quality or they aren't. And Skipper wasn't.

Carmen admires the abandoned town, not unlike their own. "It's spooky but kind of peaceful." The houses create a calm in the middle of the water. "I would have liked to be a lawyer. Like a prosecutor. Maybe commute to the city and live in a house on the weekends—that one." She points at one of the taller houses, yellow paint nearly all peeled off, a colorful array of stuffed animals lined up in the third-story window. "Married, four kids, a dog, and two cats. The neighbors come over for barbecue once or twice a month."

Skipper does this too. In her mind, she's been a programmer, an architect, or an office worker for some nameless company. In her fantasy, she wears a crisp white blouse and sits at a desk with a computer, and her fingers make a *clackety-clack* sound at the keyboard.

They're always trying to scratch the veneer off the past, from books and the few movies they watch in town and what older people like their grandmother can remember. They use the sketches of history to try to see themselves in that warped mirror of time.

There's a park at the far edge of town with woods behind it. The underwater forest is a tangle of rotten wood and muck. But one of its hills has become an island, and on the flat top of it is an old gazebo. Around the gazebo, the ground is carpeted with tall grasses, purple and gold, and spindly young pine trees shaped like lollipops. Black turtles slide into the water as they approach, and a squirrel scrambles up a roof. Near the top of the hill, a deer lifts its head to watch them pass. A crimson lump protrudes from its forehead like a unicorn.

Skipper flinches, wondering if it hurts. The deer doesn't show any sign.

Carmen smiles. "Nora would love this."

Skipper nods, throat tight. "We'll have to show it to her."

They leave the ghost town to continue its slow disintegration below the water, and Skipper marvels at how much of life is like that: unwitnessed by any but the person living it. How things can disappear overnight without anyone noticing.

CHAPTER FIVE

This is the farthest I've ever been from home." Carmen stares at the shore, as if trying to memorize the way back.

In the distance, marsh and wooded estuaries cover the sandy coast. Wild ponies graze near the beach.

They turn to deeper water to avoid the brackish saltmarsh. It's midmorning, and they make good time. The wind is perfect: enough that the boat heels, but not so much to raise stomach-turning swells.

Skipper worried all last night about the weather for Carmen's sake. She doesn't want her sister's first time back on the water to be misery. Skipper hopes along the way Carmen will remember her love for the *Bumblebee* and understand why they can't sell her, no matter the price Ollie could have gotten them.

The day goes on without mishap: The wind stays steady, and they don't kill each other, so on the sibling scale, that is a win.

As the light fades, they drop anchor in a shallow inlet of an island. "This is the farthest *I've* ever been," says Skipper.

She boils them a pot of beans on the stove next to the cabin stairs. She's embarrassed she can't offer more.

As Skipper cooks, Carmen rifles through all the cabinets and storage areas, reorganizing the food, water, and gear.

"Don't move that," Skipper says, as Carmen removes tools from under one of the bunks.

"This place is a mess."

Skipper flushes. "I have a system." She turns up the radio to listen to the weather report: Rain scheduled to the south of them, but the way north should be sunny tomorrow. "Did you move the stock?"

"No. See? This is my point."

Skipper opens the pantry and finds a glass jar of money wrapped in a canvas bag wedged behind the plastic canisters of flour and sugar. She frowns at it.

"Oh, that," says Carmen. "I brought some money in case we need it."

Skipper is stunned by how casually Carmen says this. It's more than Skipper's managed to save in years. She flushes, knowing how much Carmen and Nora earn, and how pitiful her own takings are as a garbage patch skimmer. And when Carmen gets her nursing job, she will earn even more. Deep down, Skipper gets why Carmen judges her.

She oversalts the beans, but her sister doesn't say anything.

They sit across each other at a square table, the boat rocking gently. Skipper is conscious of every patch of grime on the boat. When did she last clean the cabin? Months ago.

"What's that smell?"

"Oh!" Skipper snatches up the offending, mildewing ball of socks and stuffs them in her sack of dirty clothes.

"Ugh," says Carmen, and her laughter stings.

"It was so late the last time I came home, I forgot." She's defensive again, which is unnecessary. She knows it is.

"I bet," says Carmen, in her patronizing tone. "It's amazing the toilet doesn't smell worse."

The toilet in the head is a lidded bucket filled with pine shavings that Skipper empties into the sea. She's got the hang of carrying it through a moving boat, but it's an annoying process, and she doesn't empty it as frequently as she should.

Skipper shovels beans into her mouth, trying not to count how often Carmen reaches for her glass of water to quench the saltiness. She wants to retreat to her bunk with a book and listen to the coyotes yipping in the distance. She wants to be alone.

Carmen sets down her spoon. She hasn't finished her beans. She cocks her head, listening to the boat creak, unable to see past the darkened windows, and when something thumps against the hull, she jumps. Probably driftwood. Hopefully not an alligator.

"Do you remember that time Grandma made us hike all over in the middle of the night?" Carmen asks.

It was a year after their mother died. It must have been winter. The night was unusually cold. Carmen had been crying, because she was convinced she'd heard something outside, and Grandma came in and said eight and a half was too old to be afraid of the dark. Skipper didn't know what frightened Carmen so much, but Skipper was too loyal to ask.

Grandma made Carmen get dressed in her frayed, hand-me-down army jacket and boots, so Skipper and Nora got up too. Even at five, Skipper knew the sister code: You stick together. She'd slipped her hand inside Carmen's mitten. They went out into the night, boots crunching loudly on twigs and dead leaves.

They walked a circuit of the house, right up against the trees in the woods. Carmen sniffled. Nora took her other hand.

"See, there's nothing here," said Grandma, gesturing at the window. The yellow of Skipper's stuffed duck was visible, pressed against the pane. Carmen sobbed, and Grandma growled in a way that made Skipper flinch.

Grandma turned and went into the woods, forcing them to follow. Skipper's and Carmen's palms slid against each other, slick with sweat. The quiet in the woods had a different quality to it: thicker, laced with whispers. They were surrounded by skeletal arms draped in shadow. Carmen froze, unable to move, and Nora threw an arm around her shoulder. "Just one step and another," she whispered. "Look at your boots."

Grandma was too far ahead, and she had the only flashlight. In a minute they'd be lost. "There's nothing to be afraid of!" they heard her say, even though they'd found enough carcasses to know death was real out here. Two years before, the toddler down the street was attacked by a pack of wild dogs with scarlet eyes and feline claws.

"Come on," said Nora.

The musty scent of rotting things filled their noses. They began to walk again, and then to run, until they had caught up. They had no idea where they were. The night transformed familiar trees into strangers. It seemed they walked for hours, and their fingers were stiff with cold. At last, they broke over a hill, and there was the main part of town, and the ocean, sparkling with starlight. They followed Grandma into the unlit streets, past candles wavering in the windows, past the closed-up shops by the water.

A group of men lingered outside the bar. They laughed loudly.

And Grandma hesitated.

"Can we go home now, please?" asked Nora.

But they'd been spotted.

The men's words were indistinct, smoky, but there was a threat beneath them, and she realized Grandma was right after all. Nature wasn't dangerous. People were. Later, remembering Grandma's nervousness, Skipper would wonder what the old woman went through years ago when things collapsed.

Carmen laughs, as if to dispel the memory. Tucked in their boat listening to the night, Skipper thinks of Nora in the city, heading home alone from work late, maybe. How vulnerable she might be. Her stomach tightens.

"Why were you so scared of the dark?" she asks Carmen.

Carmen stares at the porthole. "I was a kid. That's all."

The boat creaks and thunks, and Carmen stills. "Is something on the boat?"

"No. Want me to check?" Skipper stands.

"Don't," says Carmen. "I'm sure it's nothing." But Skipper can tell she's nervous.

Skipper pulls out her logbook and records the last segment of their day: the weather, the wind, how far they've come. The activity calms her. This record is the trace she leaves in this world—for what future, she doesn't know, but she likes to think of someone reading her numbers. She writes: *I don't think Carmen liked the beans.*

"Did Nora ever tell you what she was working on?" Carmen holds one of Nora's letters between her fingers. Skipper took them in case they contain any useful information. She stashed the box in a drawer beneath her own bunk, but Carmen's gone and helped herself as usual.

"Testing Renewal plants for how well they do against blight?" Nora had told her a bit, but Skipper hadn't understood it.

It takes Carmen so long to respond as she riffles through Skipper's things that Skipper forgets they are talking. "It was more than that. I asked her a few times, but she was secretive about it." Carmen folds the letter and taps its edge against the table, a thoughtful expression on her face. "She hated her job."

"What are you talking about?"

"She told me."

Confusion, then jealousy jabs Skipper. She never had this impression; Nora never told her this.

Carmen flops onto her bunk, wincing at the thinness of the mattress and the hard board beneath. Skipper offered to share the bigger bed at the bow—the foam is thicker—but Carmen said Skipper talks too much in her sleep. Carmen brought her down pillow from home, which she will regret as soon as it gets wet.

"She thought people had it out for her. You know Nora, paranoid."

"No, she's not," says Skipper.

Carmen rolls her eyes. "You always defend her." She jumps up and, in a burst of energy, begins to scrub the soaking pot. She jerks her head at Nora's last letter. "If she was having money issues, maybe she moved and doesn't want to tell us until she's figured things out. Because she's embarrassed. Maybe she's up there waiting for an intervention."

Interventions are Carmen's specialty. Skipper has been subjected to more than one of them.

Skipper wraps the box of letters in a waterproof bag and puts them away.

Carmen freezes. There's a noise outside: a bobcat screaming in the distance. It sounds almost human, like it's shouting, *Run*.

Carmen slips back into bed holding the kitchen knife, and Skipper pretends not to notice. Her sister stares at the closed wooden hatch, as if expecting something to come in through the cockpit any minute.

Skipper makes a fist and raps on the side of the boat. She knocks twice, pausing longer after the second, then continues. Three long pauses, then long, short, long.

Nora taught them Morse code when Skipper was only seven. As a consequence, Skipper knows it as well as she knows her letters. Few people use Morse anymore, but Nora read about it in a book, and she thought it would be cool to have a secret language. They used to tap messages at the dinner table to each other while Grandma interrogated them about why their grades were poor and whether their teachers were doing an adequate job.

Skipper repeats the sequence. *AOK.* All okay.

She isn't sure Carmen remembers, but then Carmen says, "Skip, I have to tell you something."

There's a seriousness to her voice that makes Skipper tense.

"Don't worry, it's just something you should know." Carmen lifts the hem of her shirt. Below her right breast is a purple stain, the size of a bottle cap, like a splotch of ink. It's the recognizable mark of fungal infection. Untreated, it could continue to spread beneath the skin, until Carmen's organs are overgrown with it.

Skipper recoils.

"I noticed it a few weeks ago. I got the pills that keep it from growing," Carmen says. "They can remove it, but the surgery's expensive. I just—even if I get the clinic job—"

"You will."

"—I may need you to take care of everything else for a while."

"Are you okay?"

"It doesn't hurt."

Skipper feels leaden. "Everything" means maintenance of the house and food, maybe medication. She tries not to panic. She could get a second job, maybe, and double her trips to the patch. It'll be tough, but she could do it, for Carmen. Without selling the *Bumblebee.* She wishes she were sure that'd be enough.

Ordinarily, in a situation like this, she would write to Nora and ask for help. But they don't know where Nora is.

Neither of them sleeps well. She hears Carmen rustling about in the middle of the night, tidying and cleaning.

Skipper dreams she is a bobcat, that she hunts something big. But also that something hunts her. She doesn't know. In the dark, she catches a shadow, and she tastes blood. When she wakes up, she finds she has bitten her tongue.

CHAPTER SIX

The next day brings strong winds from the north, and the first test of Carmen's constitution. They have to sail close-haul upwind for hours. Skipper keeps them both busy swapping out sails and reefing the main as the wind increases.

At first, Carmen stresses about how much the boat heels, but soon she's wholly occupied with vomiting into a spare bucket. This isn't helping the *Bumblebee*'s cause.

Skipper tries not to hover, but she can't stop looking for signs of Carmen's infection, as if it should be obvious now that she knows. But Carmen doesn't act any differently than she normally would—in this case, tense and miserable.

The wind picks up even more, and they both get up on the windward side of the boat. Carmen's feet slip on the hull before she finds her footing, and Skipper makes her put on a safety harness.

And it's like flying: the wind rushing past them as they cut through the water. Skipper lets rip a yell.

Despite her nausea, Carmen laughs and joins her howling, because it's just the two of them in open waves, the coastline a smudge in the distance. Carmen wipes tears, maybe from the wind, but also, maybe she, too, feels swallowed from the inside by a powerful, anonymous spirit.

Skipper and Carmen are not as close in age as Carmen and Nora, who squabbled and competed over things when they were growing up.

Carmen tolerated Skipper, but Nora took care of her. Nora taught her how to read and made sure Skipper brushed her teeth every night.

When Nora moved away, something shifted between Carmen and Skipper. Carmen began enforcing curfews and lecturing her on social behavior.

It was around the same time Grandma started to recede into her fog. Now, Skipper and Carmen are finally starting to meet each other as equals, and the constant pull between the two sisters is not so different from the wind in the sail versus the thrum of the water and the force of the keel beneath it.

They reach their next planned stopover point at the end of the second day. It takes them twice as long to navigate the harbor because the motor won't start. Carmen thinks the cables need replacing, which is the cheapest possibility, but even so, Skipper dreads hunting for spares.

The beach town is well past its glory days. As Skipper pulls the oars, Carmen goes on about what she's heard about this place from friends. They have a restaurant that serves penne alla vodka and even burgers, sometimes, on a fresh roll. Not that Carmen has ever been here or eaten these things herself, but she is confident the food is excellent. By the time they reach shore, this dinner has become a lifelong goal at last to be achieved. Really, even if Nora weren't missing, Carmen might have sailed up here for the meal.

The edges of the boardwalk are soft and weathered, and boards are missing here and there. Seagulls cry, and the air has the fishy scent of a working harbor. The ribs of a Ferris wheel stand like some colossus, its ankles submerged in the swollen tides. There is a roller coaster too, half disassembled. Up and down the streets, unlit glass lights hang on strings.

Carmen loops her arm in Skipper's, walking drunk on legs unused to land. Skipper leans into her, glad for her sister's warmth and the sunbaked pitted concrete against the breeze.

"If you had told me *this* was the city, I would have believed you," Carmen admits. The shore is lined with glass-and-steel towers that could house thousands, though the population has shrunk over the past half a century. At the dock, workers unload crimson-stained crates of Amaranthine as if they are inured to the ghost of prosperity that haunts this place.

They find Carmen's famous restaurant a few blocks up. The waiter invites them to sit at a table outside. He has a violet-silver rash on the side of his face and corner of his eyes. Ama-rash people call it, though no one knows what actually causes it. He's tried to cover it with makeup, but it glints like fish scales. It looks itchy.

They are the only patrons in the place. As they wait to be served, Skipper takes in the shuttered shops and the skinny cats that climb about a container of garbage. The few passersby eye the sisters warily.

Blackened produce is piled in the center of the street, and every time the breeze shifts, they smell it: rotten and sour. A young person bikes up in a pedal wagon and adds carrots and squash, contorted and pimpled with fungus, to the pile. Their hands are stained scarlet up to their wrists.

The menus are dog-eared and irrelevant. The restaurant doesn't have burgers or penne alla vodka. They don't have fresh rolls.

The waiter flushes with embarrassment. "It's the blight," he admits. "We got through most of the season all right but then spots appeared a few weeks ago. Lost most of the autumn harvest. Now everyone's hoarding." He tightens the waistband of his trousers, like he is already hungry.

"It's okay," says Carmen kindly. "What do you recommend?"

Their waiter considers. "We could make you a salad and pickle sandwich."

The "salad" is a slaw drenched in mayonnaise, and the sandwich bread is stale and dry. The sisters eat in silence. It is impossible not to be disappointed by the dissonance between their expectations and reality.

"They must not have bought this year's seeds," says Carmen.

Skipper frowns at Carmen's lack of sympathy. "Maybe they couldn't afford it."

"That's faulty math. It's more expensive in the long run."

"So they deserve it?"

"Don't be ridiculous. It's not about what people deserve. It's just how it is."

What worries Skipper is this town isn't so far from home. Blight here means blight soon down coast, even if they take precautions.

The blight evolves with frightening rapidity. Renewal develops crops that are resistant to it, extreme weather, and the copious amounts of Amaranthine necessary to burn back superweeds and blight alike. Each year, they release the latest generation of seeds with new protections, trying to stay ahead of nature's vengeance.

They're the leader in crop engineering, though recently other companies have entered the market.

Even with agricultural innovations, it's never enough. When they lose the battle, as they always do, all they can do is hunker down and wait out the growing season, relying on government distributions of Renewal heat-to-eat meals to supplement what they've lost.

Bad times are ahead again.

"At least when you have the clinic job, you'll be able to afford to buy stuff before things run out," Skipper says.

"I haven't gotten the clinic job yet. I might not."

"You will," says Skipper, because Carmen always gets what she wants. But also, Carmen needs the job, for the medical coverage if nothing else.

"Maybe." Carmen stirs the puddle of watery mayo on her plate with her fork. The sound raises gooseflesh on Skipper's arms.

A few folks gather in front of the pile of ruined vegetables. It takes time to get a burn going, but soon, the crackle and pop is audible from across the street.

Skipper forces herself to finish her crusts, though it takes several swigs of water to wash them down.

"I'm glad I didn't come all the way here just for this," says Carmen, and then she giggles, and they both giggle, because everything about this trip is so abnormal in the first place, and they shouldn't have expected otherwise.

They find a public spigot near the marina where a listless group of children watch them fill their jugs. Down the dock, Renewal workers are loading crates of Amaranthine into trucks.

Carmen offers a smushed bit of oat bar wrapped in a handkerchief to some of the kids in exchange for help carrying their jugs back, and the kids are up in an instant, shoving and kicking.

"Shit," says Skipper. The bar disappears, the water spills, and by the time they fill the jugs again, the kids are gone too. They carry the water back themselves, quiet in the aftermath.

It reminds Skipper of sitting at the table every night, spooning thin broth in taut silence, because Grandma was tired of their complaining, the pang in her stomach from going to bed unsated.

A bad blight could be the end of a community like this—people will leave if they have to, migrate to other towns or the city. Better that than drown in loans or starve to death.

As they reach their dinghy, a shout and loud crash prompt them to turn back. A broken cable dangles from a crane, and one of the crates splits in two like an egg.

"Hurry," says Skipper, lifting her shirt over her mouth and jumping into the boat. She yanks Carmen after her. A great scarlet plume envelops the workers running for the open warehouse, the truck, the crates, the dock. It all unfolds in slow motion.

They can outrow it, but they are lucky: Wind carries the potent cloud into the town, away from the water.

Carmen's got the oars. They dip and splash in hasty retreat, and Skipper watches as the red dust settles over everything. The town will be cleaning up for weeks.

They're making poor headway.

"Let me row," says Skipper.

"I can do it," Carmen says, which is not true, and Skipper says so. Her technique is all wrong, and she won't accept Skipper's advice.

"Stop!" says Skipper.

Carmen continues to flail.

After several frustrating minutes, Carmen surrenders the oars and retreats to the bow. Water washes back and forth against the nearby rocks, and the floating dock squeaks in time.

Carmen sniffs, and Skipper realizes her sister is crying.

"Hey," says Skipper. "I'm sure the burger wasn't that great anyway."

"You think I care about a burger?" They reach the *Bumblebee*, and Carmen disappears below with the water jugs to sulk, leaving Skipper to hoist the rowboat and tidy the *Bumblebee* for the night.

Carmen reappears with a huge smile across her face. "I got the job." There's a message from the clinic on the ship computer.

Skipper jumps to her feet. "What? That's great! I knew you would. When do you start?"

"I told them three weeks," says Carmen. "So I have a couple of weeks once we get back to prepare."

"I knew it," says Skipper. "Who else were they going to hire?"

"Wow, thanks," says Carmen, but they both laugh. Skipper is overwhelmed with relief. Carmen will be able to pay for the procedure, at least. Everything will be all right.

Above them, the stars emerge in the velvet black. It is one of those rare moments when tomorrow promises them everything: Nora found, and Carmen's job begun. And Skipper? Maybe anything. Why not?

CHAPTER SEVEN

The city occupies the banks of a long river that spills into a broad bay. From the ocean, they pass through a gauntlet of leafy islets, and they spot the dully gleaming towers midafternoon on the next day. Buoys mark a path, but Skipper steers with one eye pinned to her charts, mindful of urban detritus hidden below the gray-green surface.

The city is so much bigger than they imagined, even with a quarter of it submerged and another quarter abandoned. The rivers are spanned by stone and steel bridges, and there are buildings that stretch to the sky. It's like entering the Old World, with all its noise and vibration. No one pays them any mind when they slip into the arms of the artificial cove. The dock appears to cater to pleasure craft and larger boats outfitted to transport luxury goods.

Clouds darken the sky, and they make it to dock before the rain rolls in. It takes them some time to figure out the berth payment system. The harbormaster quotes a dizzying price. Even Carmen's jar of money isn't enough.

"You could sail around while I look for her," Carmen says.

"Definitely not." There's no way Skipper's going to sit out the search after coming all this way.

"Or we could take turns."

Skipper scoffs. Carmen would crash into the first motorboat that crosses her path.

"Can you be constructive?" Carmen says.

"What?"

Carmen shakes her head and leaves Skipper standing next to the boat on the dock to go back to the harbormaster. Whatever she says, he takes pity on them and tells them about a more affordable cove at a distant end of the city.

It drizzles as Skipper steers two hours around the coast, far enough from the downtown that the city skyscrapers could be a mirage in the distance.

They pass dozens of boats of all shapes and sizes. A low roar startles them as a plane forges a white path across the sky. Another fossil from the past: A ticket on one of those is double the cost of the mooring they refused that morning.

The new dock is cheaper, if not cheap, and the sailors are nice enough to explain how to find the address on Nora's letter.

Carmen convinces Skipper that wandering around an unfamiliar place at night is a bad idea, so they hunker down in their cabin with rice and beans. They don't bother with bowls, just take turns dipping their forks in the pot.

It rains again, and water drips from a leak in the ceiling. Another thing Skipper needs to fix. Her eyes smart from blinking into the wind all day, and she's so tired she can hardly lift her utensil. She hopes finding Nora will be easy, now that they've made it here.

They set out early the next morning. It takes them two rickety trains to get back to the part of the city where they started the previous day, then another train uptown. Everything is loud: The city pushes inward, pinching and grasping with its concrete fingers. Skipper hears different conversations happening at once. Even Carmen seems overwhelmed.

It feels like a different century. As they approach the city center, they see people with glitter-painted skin and communication devices on their wrists.

Holographic advertisements peddle face creams that can reverse time. Fruits and vegetables are sold triple-packed in bioplastic, each one perfectly ripe.

Restaurant menus posted in a window advertise salads that cost as much as a day's worth of trash. Skipper's glad they ate breakfast.

They start with the police, even though the messages Carmen previously exchanged with them have made it clear they aren't going to do much. The precinct building looks like it's falling down, and the automated reception tells them they can't talk to a live person unless they have an appointment. Carmen tells them it's an emergency. It directs her to send a message, but they'd have to go back to the boat to do so. Finally, Carmen catches an officer on her way out the door and convinces her to fetch the detective on their case.

"I'll be honest with you," he says. "Unless you can find out more information about where she might have gone, I'm not sure what we can do here."

"If we had more information, we wouldn't be here," Skipper says.

He raises his eyebrows, and she realizes too late how that sounded.

"We appreciate your help," says Carmen. She tries a little longer, but they go in circles. "We'll see what we can find out today."

He may not hear the subtle rebuke, but Skipper does. Carmen expects to find out more in a day than they have in almost two months.

Somewhat discouraged, they go next to Nora's apartment. Unfortunately, the front door is locked, and they can't get in.

Carmen tries pinging Nora from the door controls.

Skipper holds her breath.

No answer.

Carmen tries again.

Nothing.

"Maybe she isn't home," says Carmen, trying other buttons.

"Yeah?" a voice barks through the speaker. The screen is broken, maybe has been for years, but their hostility is audible.

Carmen explains they are looking for Nora.

"Who?"

"Nora Shimizu."

"Don't know 'em," says the voice, and there's a sharp click.

Skipper sits on the top step. "This was a bad idea, wasn't it?" She grates her fingers against the grit of the stoop, as if to test reality. They've come so far for nothing.

"You're going to give up? We're just getting started."

A person in a stunningly purple coat with a duck in black slippers on a leash climbs the step.

Carmen steps forward. "Excuse me."

Within minutes, they've exchanged introductions and chat like old friends. The man has time to satisfy his own curiosity. He lets them in and takes them to Nora's apartment up four flights of stairs. The door is plastered with red stickers warning of impending eviction for late payment of rent.

"Don't worry," says the neighbor. "It takes a few of these before they evict you."

Carmen bangs on the door, but no one answers. The duck shits on Nora's doormat, and they all pretend not to notice, because the man is being helpful. He picks up his duck and takes them to see the building super in an apartment at the bottom of the stairs, and then, hungry for gossip, hangs around to hear the answer.

The super is a soft-featured middle-aged woman in a faded blue bathrobe. She blinks at the crowd on her doorstep but leans forward to pet the neighbor's duck, which nips her.

"She paid two month's rent ahead of time four months ago, and I haven't seen her since," says the super.

Carmen charms access out of the woman (because "you do look like her," the super says; she doesn't say that about Skipper), and the party troops upstairs again.

The apartment is only two rooms. The lights don't work, so everything is illuminated by the thin light trickling through the windows that face a brick wall.

The front room has just enough space for a table pushed up against the window, a couch, and an empty bookcase. The bookcase is empty because the contents are scattered across the floor: creased old paperbacks and textbooks.

Either Nora trashed her own place, or someone else has been here.

Dirt is strewn all over the floor and table, and the houseplants lie in the wreckage of their clay pots, shriveled up and dead.

In the second room, there's a mattress on the floor and a crate for a bed table with a clock on it. The sagging wardrobe is open and empty, save for an ugly green sweater Grandma gave her years ago. Skipper doesn't blame Nora for leaving it.

A pungent smell emanates from the kitchen, and the duck quacks and flaps its wings when they troop in. Everything in the disconnected fridge has gone off.

"I'm not cleaning that," complains the super.

"She'll be back," says Skipper, without conviction. Nothing about the place indicates this, and a heavy weight settles on Skipper's shoulders.

"It's none of my business," says the super, "but you probably know she was having problems."

"What kind of problems?" Carmen asks.

"The money kind," says the super. "She fell behind on rent, then all at once, she paid everything. Must have borrowed a lot of money from the wrong people. They came around and broke the front door looking for her. The landlord wanted to evict her then and there, but I stuck my neck out for her."

Skipper looks at Carmen in bafflement. In her last letter, she mentioned not being able to send more money home, but they hadn't realized something more serious was going on. Nora must have borrowed money for Grandma's hospital bills. Had she gotten in over her head?

Carmen's worried face is a mirror of her own.

They go out onto the sidewalk and blink into the sun. It's the kind of winter that feels like summer. Skipper removes her sweater, then puts it back on.

Carmen puts an arm around her shoulders. “Let’s not jump to conclusions,” she says, but Skipper doesn’t know what to think. Her older sister exists in two states: city and home. If she’s neither place, where could she be? And who is she?

CHAPTER EIGHT

Carmen talks their way into Nora's old workplace, located in a four-story stone building flanked by stone urns of flattened flowers.

Carmen tells the bored security guard they are there to see Dr. John Goode, implying but not saying that they had an appointment, then engages her in conversation about the book the guard is reading, the city, the guard's dog, and the guard's favorite restaurants.

John-the-colleague isn't answering, but the security guard, thus disarmed, says, "If you want to just take a quick look . . ." and gestures for them to go up.

Skipper has contributed nothing, her funk only matched by her irritation with Carmen's befriend-the-stranger routine. It must be exhausting to be Carmen. It is exhausting to be *with* Carmen.

Nora's lab is a large room on the second floor. Carmen catches the door as someone is exiting and walks in like she's wearing more than a temporary security badge. Long rows of plants and blue-white electric lights line the lab, separated by clear dividers. Sprinklers along the ceiling mist water and Amaranthine periodically.

The air smells metallic. Serious-looking people in white jumpsuits, masks, and goggles bustle about tables full of equipment at the far end. The sisters can't hear the murmured conversations above the oppressive, electric hum.

Nora's lab is not what Skipper imagined. It is cold and clinical. It hurts to think of Nora coming here day after day, working herself to the bone.

"Hello!" Carmen calls.

Skipper wilts as curious glances flick in their direction. One of the figures detaches and hurries down the rows.

"No, no, no, no, no," he says. "You can't be in here."

He pushes them from the room with desperate fanning and leads them to a break room down the hall. He removes his mask and proceeds to nibble carrot sticks over a metal sink. He doesn't offer them any.

John-the-colleague, PhD, is a man with a neat beard and pinched expression. He is shocked to see them.

"I can't believe you came here. I told you, we haven't seen her in months. That's why we hired someone new." He glances around the break room as if hoping for a rescue.

"She didn't say anything about where she was going?" Carmen asks.

"It's like I said." He scratches his beard with a single, long finger. "She went up north on that ridiculous field trip. It was supposed to be for a week."

"Field trip?" Carmen says, because John never told them anything about that.

John blanches. "Oh, I wasn't supposed to—Well." He leans forward. "Strictly between us, she convinced the higher-ups to fund a trip up there. I had no interest in going myself. She claimed she discovered something."

"Where?"

He names a town Skipper's only vaguely heard of, way up the coast.

"What did she discover?"

"Nothing, it turned out. Should have stayed here and gotten her work done."

"But what was she looking for?" Skipper cuts in. She wants to shake him.

"Come on, I can't tell you that. It's proprietary." John picks a piece of carrot from his teeth with his pinky nail.

"Of course," Carmen agrees. "You don't have to tell us specifics. I'm sure we wouldn't understand it anyway. We're just trying to find her. A general sense could help narrow things."

John eats another carrot, and Skipper suspects he's buying time to think of a suitable answer. "Blight resistance. I didn't like it. The project was a distraction from her core work. Anyway, once she got up there, she wrote me and said she was taking annual leave. Complained she hadn't gotten to go home or taken vacation in a long time. For the record, I never discouraged her from taking time off. That's why I assumed she was going to stop by for a visit on her way back."

"It's not on the way back," Skipper says. "We live south of here."

"Yeah, well, I didn't know that. I try to stay out of her personal business. I reached out a few times when I didn't hear from her and kept getting those annoying auto-replies. Eventually, we had to hire someone else. We have work to do. I've got too much on my plate as it is." He brushes invisible carrot crumbs into the sink.

"I'm sure you do," says Carmen. "You seem very busy. This seems like a very busy place. I'm sure the work you do is very important."

Carmen's making fun of him, but John puffs up further with each sentence. "Yes, well, I'm sorry."

"What about the mug?" Skipper blurts.

John's eyebrows knit together. "What mug?"

"The bumblebee mug. The one I made for her."

"You mentioned it when you wrote us," Carmen says.

"Oh." He winces. "We got rid of it a few days ago when you originally said we could throw everything out. I didn't think you'd come all the way here, did I?"

Sudden rage catches fire in Skipper's chest. She's not just angry at John, but at Carmen too, for being too quick to take care of things. "But we told you we were coming."

"It was already done. There wasn't anything valuable, I promise!" says John.

"Thanks, anyway," says Carmen, taking Skipper by the elbow. "We'll be back if we have more questions."

"Right."

He ushers them down the stairs and past the security guard who is now pretending she never had anything to do with them.

They cross the street and sit on a bench by a playground so Skipper can take off her shoes and inspect her blisters. The shoes are synthetic blue leather, and they've begun to strangle her toes. Skipper put them on that morning thinking they were more fashionable than the comfortable ones she wears on the boat. She shouldn't have bothered. No one has paid any attention to their clothes.

"Are those my old shoes?" Carmen asks.

"You left them in the closet."

"Because they're uncomfortable."

"I'm realizing that."

"Also, your feet are wider. Why'd you think they'd fit you?"

They are talking about shoes because neither of them knows what to do. The happy noises from the playground assault Skipper's senses. The children are carefree, and she resents them.

Staff file from the lab building, heading for lunch—something beanless, probably. Fresh bread. Giant sandwiches. Pizza. Her stomach growls. It's John's fault, him and his carrots. They split that pot of rice porridge so long ago.

"If she were having trouble with creditors, maybe she decided to stay up north until they forgot about her," Carmen says.

If that's true, Nora shouldn't have given them the money. They could have found another way. But how? Not without selling the boat.

Skipper puts her socks back on. She wants to go back to the *Bumblebee* and curl up into a ball. Everything has been so overwhelming, and it's gotten cold. Her sweater isn't warm enough.

"Excuse me." One of the lab technicians hurries across the street. "Do you know where Reny's is?"

"Sorry," says Carmen. "We're not from around here."

"Reny's," repeats the technician. "My friend Nora and I used to go there. Cheap beer." The technician walks off before they process the words. A slip of paper drifts down, and Skipper jumps to retrieve it before it blows away.

Reny's, it says, and an address.

Reny's is a garish lounge in a downtown neighborhood where the tides lap at the streets in the late afternoon light. The sidewalks are dry, at least. The place is furnished with baby blue couches and throw pillows shaped like clouds, and they serve the kind of swill on tap favored by sailors and students alike. Carmen gets the cheapest beer on the menu; Skipper, water.

They settle into an L-shaped couch. The pillows aren't comfortable. "Maybe we misunderstood," Skipper says. It's been an hour, and she's falling asleep.

"Just wait."

The difference between them is that Carmen thinks of herself as a main character, and Skipper doesn't think of herself in a fictional context at all.

The waiter checks if they want another round, but they don't have the money.

"Hi," says the technician, setting a box down on the table. "Sorry, I had to go home to get this. I rescued it when John threw it out." His name is Marcus, and he is a friend of Nora's. His arms and face are covered in intricate tattoos. A stenciled holographic bee hovers over his left eyelid, and Skipper warms to him. She doesn't ask if it is a coincidence, she just pretends it isn't. Inside the box are Nora's things, including, yes, the mug.

Skipper clutches it, rendered frail by sudden emotion.

"So you know where she is?" says Carmen.

"No, and I'm worried. She has a bad habit of not knowing when to quit something. Obsessed with questions she shouldn't ask."

Skipper's stomach flips over. "What happened? What kind of questions?"

"Those kinds. She went up north hunting miracles. I think she's still up there."

"Nora doesn't quit," Skipper agrees, shooting Carmen a look, which Carmen ignores.

"Can you tell us anything about what she was working on?" Carmen asks. "Everyone's so secretive."

"You can't tell anyone I told you. That's why I wanted to meet here. I could lose my job. It's— "

"Proprietary," finishes Carmen. "We'll be careful."

"She was bored. The work we do is basic, testing plants for resistance to blight before they're released to market. She went to John and pitched him a side project, testing plants with natural immunity. John let her do it for a while, because he didn't think anything would come of it, and she intimidated him."

"But something did?" Carmen prompts.

"Not directly. But she heard about some guy with a type of soybean that's completely immune to blight. Can you imagine? It would be huge. But people make claims all the time. Still, she got the bosses to pay for her to go up there to look for it. Unfortunately, the whole thing was a bust. She should have come home after that, but she didn't. I haven't heard from her since. Who knows what trouble she got into up there. She has a knack for it."

Carmen swirls her glass, so the last trickle of beer slides around in a lazy circle at the bottom. "Do you know about Nora borrowing money from people?"

Marcus's gaze darkens. "It wasn't a loan. She promised some people she'd do something for them. I told her not to, but she needed the money. I offered to lend her some, but she never was good at accepting help."

Skipper shrinks. It's all her fault. If she had agreed to sell the *Bumblebee*, they wouldn't be in this situation.

"Who?" Carmen asks. "What did she promise to do?"

"EarthWorks," he whispers, naming one of the world's biggest worm companies. "They've been trying to expand into the ag market. They wanted her to get them a sample of whatever she found. But then of course she didn't find anything, but she spent their money, so she couldn't return it. You can't tell anyone, understand? She's in serious shit."

"They must be the ones who searched her apartment," Carmen says.

"They did? Fuck those hacks," Marcus says. "Their ag products are terrible. They're desperate to get hold of something decent. I told Nora to stay far away from them."

"Do you think they followed her up there?" Carmen asks.

"They better not," says Marcus darkly. "Shit, I hope she's okay."

"What about Renewal? If they found out, would they . . . ?" Carmen trails off, unable to finish, and Skipper shivers. She needs to get outside, back in the sunlight, away from this nightmare.

"No. They would have fired her, and then maybe sued her."

They subside into thoughts.

"Anyway, here." Marcus taps the half-open box between them. Wedged between a pair of scarlet high-heeled ankle boots is a letter addressed to him. "I responded, but she never wrote me anything else. I don't know if she even got it. She was sure people were reading her messages. She thinks that's how they found out about what she was working on."

"You mean EarthWorks?"

Marcus shrugs. "Probably. Maybe Renewal too, if they had reason to suspect her."

Skipper takes the letter from the box, wishing it was a month and a half ago, when she knew less. The more she learns, the more things there are to worry about.

"Gimme that." Carmen takes it and skims it. "Well, then. I guess this is something."

CHAPTER NINE

Dear M—
This was a dead end. I mean literally dead. There's nothing left. My contact, Prometheus, is gone too. Dead in the fire, possibly, or disappeared. No one knows, but probably for the best, someone told me. Can you imagine? I don't think these people understand what they've lost. I talked to Lucy about it, and she said, "People are okay with how things are. As long as we can eat, isn't that what matters? Life's hard enough."

Am I wrong? They sow their seeds year after year, they harvest their crops. Who am I to question that?

This trip was a waste. I'll stay up here a few more days while I figure out what I should do. Renewal booked me a ticket back by bus, which sure beats a truck. I'll take the ferry back to the mainland tomorrow and catch it there. I'm dreading the "I told you so" look on John's face.

This bleak little town reminds me of home. The view of the harbor and the sound of the bells tolling out in the water. My sisters. Carmen's long rants about mundane vegetables and the who's who and what's what of local politics with a very, very small "p." Little Skipper, who isn't little anymore, with her mysterious long quiet spells, who dies for pudding and is happy to read books together and not talk. My uncle and his conspiracy theories, even my cranky old grandmother telling me to take my feet off the coffee table.

Everyone here is sick with something, fever on and off, and digestive issues I won't get into except to say it's messy from both ends, and I'm sure you get the idea. I haven't caught it yet and will do my best to be unsociable, but it feels inevitable.

Also, it's cold. Why didn't anyone warn me what real winter was like? I've had to borrow a big old sweater from my kind host. It's thick and brown and smells like cookfire. I dream every night of bacon.

I miss the city, and I miss you too, friend. Even more, I am heartsick for the future. Has anyone asked about me? Tell John, if he's good, I'll bring him back a souvenir.

Be well. Stay safe. Will catch up when I get back. Maybe burn this or something.

—NS

They ride on the creaky old train back to the marina with a cardboard box of Nora's things, plus a few items from the apartment.

Skipper's mind keeps drifting inappropriately to pudding. She reviews what they have left in the pantry. Beans, obviously.

"At least we have her things," says Carmen. "That's a win."

"Do you think she got sick?"

"That letter was months ago."

"She never sent anything else," says Skipper. "Why didn't she write to us?"

"She was paranoid." Carmen runs her fingers through her hair. After days of sailing and washing in the ocean or from a bucket, her hair shouldn't look this good, Skipper thinks resentfully. But it is lustrous and full and only a little frizzy.

"I wish we knew for sure."

Out the window, a giant factory passes by with a billboard on the side of it. On it, a hand tosses a plastic cup that tumbles into a mass of worms, and it all transforms into a new, sturdier cup full of gleaming light. EarthWorks, the billboard says. Making the world better. The massive complex takes up several city blocks. Several trucks arrive, full of trash. Maybe one has come from home.

The ruins of the old city fly by under their feet: tall, burnt-out buildings and empty lots. A flock of birds fly up from the roofs and circle the air. Most cities are like this now: baggy around the contours of a diminished population.

"I'm glad we came," says Carmen, at the same time Skipper says, "We should go up there."

Carmen blinks. "How far is that?"

"Less than a week. We've got enough food." Skipper clutches the box of Nora's things.

Carmen shakes her head. "I've got to get back. My new job starts in a few weeks. I need to get my surgery done. And there's Grandma and—" She stops, and Skipper thinks she was about to say "Ollie," before remembering that isn't true anymore. "We should reach out to the town. Find out more before we go all the way up there to a foreign country. Nora's an adult. She doesn't need our permission to go on a weird trip."

Skipper sinks lower in the seat and wraps her arms around herself. The sway of the train isn't so unlike the rocking of a boat. Skipper squints out the window and wishes she were out on the water, the late afternoon rays warming her face. She could sleep, but at that moment, she doesn't like her sister enough to lay her head on her shoulder. "Neither do I."

"No," says Carmen. "This isn't something you can decide. I'm not taking a truck back."

"Then stay here, and I'll pick you up on the way back." She's so sick of Carmen, sick of her practicality, her smug confidence, the way she acts like she always has an answer when she doesn't.

"Be reasonable."

"You act like I'm a kid," says Skipper. "I'm capable of doing things myself. I go out to the patch several times a week, and I help pay for Grandma's medication, and I . . . well, and . . . I do all those things."

She wishes the list didn't sound so short, that the demarcation between being a child and an adult felt sharper and not an illusory movement. "I wish you hadn't come."

Carmen gapes. "You would have gotten all the way here and sailed up and down the river for days because you couldn't find a place to dock, since that would have required talking to people, and then you would have eventually gone home again."

And Skipper can't say anything to that, because the truth is, without Carmen, Skipper might not have come at all, but she's not going to admit that.

They return to the boat in silence. The dock creaks as the water rises and falls, and the waves glitter amber in the sinking sun.

Carmen climbs into the boat first, and that's annoying, because everything Carmen does at this point feels hostile. Skipper doesn't want to spend a night in a cabin with her, but hunger forces her to follow. Carmen stops short.

"What?" says Skipper.

Carmen inches sideways into the room and points. Nora's old letters lie on top of one of Carmen's novels, and in the middle of the floor, glinting in the afternoon light, is a large wet boot print.

"I told you we need to get a lock for the hatch" is the first thing Carmen says.

Skipper checks all the spaces a person could hide, and then, more irrationally, the places a person couldn't.

Carmen adds, "We can't stay here."

For once, Skipper agrees, even though it's getting dark. She's been violated. Someone has been here, on their boat.

At least nothing is missing.

"EarthWorks?" says Skipper.

"Fuckers," says Carmen.

Skipper goes above deck and preps the boat to depart.

"Can you see well enough?" Carmen asks as Skipper steers between the long shadows of the buoys. The motor is inexplicably working again, at least for now. She keeps the sails down and hopes the battery lasts. They shouldn't be leaving this late in the afternoon, but they're both rattled.

Carmen switches on their running lights.

Skipper glances back to see if anyone is following them.

"Boat!" says Carmen. Skipper swerves to starboard, and Carmen is thrown against the far side of the cockpit. Water sprays across the deck, and Skipper tastes salt water on her lips.

Curses filter across the water. They narrowly missed a boat heading in the opposite direction back to shore. Her heart pounds from the near miss.

"Sorry!" Carmen calls back.

"We had right-of-way," mutters Skipper.

She sweats the whole way out, weaving in and out of traffic. At last, they reach the mouth of the harbor.

"So what did we decide?" Carmen asks, carrying a steaming pot up the cabin stair. She knows they haven't discussed anything. In addition to cooking, Carmen scrubbed the cabin floor, as if it was urgent to remove all traces of trespass. Skipper is grateful.

The first star emerges, and Skipper breathes easier. Ahead lies open ocean. To port is the town where Nora is supposed to be; to starboard, their way home.

Carmen checks the messages on the ship computer. There is only one from Uncle Tot, who is offended Grandma doesn't like his chili and is attempting to cook for herself. Skipper worries Uncle Tot will let her. Grandma will light the house on fire.

"I want to know Nora's okay," says Skipper, voice a whisper over the breeze. An ache catches in her throat. "But we can go home first, if that's what you want." She doesn't know what she hopes Carmen will say. She needs Carmen to decide, because despite Skipper's previous words, the ugly pink house on Magnolia Lane tugs at her. Grandma needs her as much as Skipper dreads returning. They're both missing work, and they can't afford it.

It's been only three days since they left home. A few days of routine, and this misadventure will be a strange memory. Except Nora is still missing.

"It's really less than a week away?"

Skipper nods. "We could go up there and back with half a week to spare for your new job."

Carmen fetches the chart and points to a natural cove an hour to the north of them. "There's a spot we could anchor for the night."

"Are you sure?" asks Skipper.

In answer, Carmen goes and hoists the sails.

Skipper turns the *Bumblebee* to port. They head north, away from home.

CHAPTER TEN

The air turns cold and foreboding as they travel north up the coast. Even from a distance, they can see the forest change—late autumn colors fade to bare brown branches interspersed with straight-trunked fir, spruce, and maple. The air has an herbal, piney scent. The color palette of the houses transforms, too, from bright colors to predominantly gray, brown, white, and red.

Borders are invisible out here, and the horizon remains the same unbroken line, but after three days of sailing, Skipper's chart shows they've entered the waters of a new country.

She raises flags they stitched together earlier that day. They haven't seen anyone all morning except a solitary fishing boat.

It's winter in a romantic sense of the word: Snow dusts the pines and rocky coast—something they've only seen a few times down south. Long stretches pass without any sign of civilization.

They stop to report their arrival at a small town. A sign nailed to the dock warns of a stray cat named Quickpaws, who is known around these parts for being a proficient thief.

"Seems excessive," says Carmen.

They worry about Carmen passing her health check, but the inspection is conducted by a glitchy drone, and it's unclear if the authorities care or not about her condition.

The settlement covers a large, long island that was once a peninsula. Where the water has risen between the mainland and the town, parallel highway roads run right into the sea, and rust-colored buoys warn of shallows.

There's a ping on their ship computer: It's an anxious note from Uncle Tot, asking if they made it safely. He's been tracking the weather along their route and has been worrying about the forecasts. Have they found Nora yet? By the way, he is having trouble with Grandma's nocturnal wandering. Does Skipper have any advice?

Play some piano music before bed, Skipper recommends. *It knocks her right out.*

But I hate that stuff, says Uncle Tot.

She knows she should be there to deal with all this, and at the same time, the idea of returning to it feels impossible.

In the distance, a stag comes out and stands looking at the beach, maybe looking at Skipper. Its antlers are too big for its head; it lowers them to rest on a rock. Skipper aches with sudden melancholy.

"How's your thing?" Skipper asks, gesturing at Carmen's chest.

"Fine," Carmen says.

They haven't packed properly for the weather, so they pull on all their clothes: T-shirts, a long-sleeve shirt, a button-down, and rain gear; pajamas stuffed under two pairs of pants. It's hard to move in so many layers, but it beats misery.

Uncle Tot reports he played Grandma something "with maybe too much drums," and she got up to pee three times.

How do you manage? he writes, and Skipper thinks, *I don't know.*

"Have you seen the butter?" Carmen asks as she makes dinner.

"Shit," says Skipper.

All that's left is the wrapper and a greasy trail of paw prints, a rude welcome to this new country.

After two more days, they reach the end of the continent, and for the first time, they sail across truly open waters, untethered. The wind drops for half a day to little more than a breath, and they struggle with the motor again. Skipper smells the acrid scent of Carmen's increasing stress.

They take the engine out and disassemble it on the table. The problem is more than superficial. Salt water has infiltrated the casing. After hours of fruitless fiddling, Carmen tells her they'll need to buy new parts.

The battery is low anyway, because it's been so gloomy and calm. This far north, the day is an hour shorter than back home, and it's much cooler. Skipper monitors the radio anxiously for storms.

The wind picks up again, and they finally arrive by late afternoon on the sixth day. It's a young city, full of construction scaffolding and noise. The harbor is crowded with ships freighting passengers and cargo across northern ocean routes. A massive warship looms over the breakwater, stationed here to patrol. Strands of twinkling lights and lanterns illuminate the boats and water like starlight. After the frustration of the last day, the sight fills them with cheer.

Nora's letter was posted from a town farther inland. It's too far to walk, but they're close. Skipper tries not to think about the trouble Nora might be in, focusing instead on how surprised and happy Nora will be to see them.

They row up to the dock as the sun sets. Carmen tries to direct their approach, until Skipper snaps at her to stop, after which Carmen makes her irritation known by breathing loudly.

The strains of a fiddle reach them from down near the water's edge. It is sad and sweet and full of longing for a time that will never come again. The air smells like kebabs and sweet potatoes charring on a grill, and Skipper knows they will spend whatever the price for a hot meal that isn't from a can.

Across the road near the dock, the glowing windows of a tavern beckon. Without discussion, they go there first, homing to its warmth.

It's strange to settle in a crowded room after so many hours at sea with only each other for company. A few heads, then more, turn at their entrance, and a pause ripples through the room. This bar is for regulars, and the sisters are not.

"What can I get you?" calls the bartender. People continue to watch them, but the burble picks up.

The house special tonight is venison stew with a side of dark beer. Skipper tries not to think of the deer they saw a few days ago. They settle at the last open table in the middle of the room, with everyone watching as if they are on a stage.

"It's your imagination," Carmen says.

"I didn't say anything."

Carmen smirks, because she's taken Skipper drinking enough times to know Skipper hates places like this: bad music, too loud to think, and no one worth talking to. Usually, Carmen ignores her half the night, and then acts disappointed when Skipper didn't have more fun. No, thank you.

Half the people in the bar wear faded crimson-stained Renewal coveralls. They must be workers from the Amaranthine plant up the hill.

"Excuse me." A man sits down and introduces himself: His name is Jackson Barker, and he, like them, isn't from here. He is tall and barrel-chested, dressed in stained denim jeans and a too-small sweater. Carmen clocks the curls in his dark brown hair and the authoritarian angle of his jaw and bites her lip, and Skipper kicks her.

"Please, do sit," says Carmen, in that sarcastic, sassy tone she used to use with Ollie.

Jackson grins a tea-stained smile. His front tooth is chipped in a way that is disarming. Almost.

"Do you mind?" says Skipper. "We're having dinner."

"I see that. Not bad, right?" He spreads his mustache with two fingers that don't quite hide the upturn of his lips.

"Beats beans," says Carmen.

In five minutes, Carmen extracts the bones of his life: born southwest of here in a city full of rusty bridges. He lost his family young. They were murdered, he says, by Renewal, but what he means is two died of cancer, one in a factory accident, and one from a drug overdose, related to a work injury.

Jackson himself worked in an Amaranthine factory for years until he hit the road in search of something better. Ended up at an advocacy organization down in the capital. Didn't last long. Boss ran for office and was assassinated. So he's come here until things cool down. He's got a new job, but he won't say what, he's not ready to, maybe once they get to know each other better. Anyway, he doesn't mind; he likes to travel, meet new people. He is, it sounds, always in search of a battle. He wants justice for all people, and it is impressive the purity of his convictions do not scorch the table.

He sees Renewal as the source of all problems in his life, and he talks freely about how one day he'll exact his revenge, even if he doesn't yet know how.

"See, we forget how Renewal got their start," Jackson says, which is Skipper's cue to ask how, but she isn't interested in a history lecture right now.

"They were a small chemical manufacturing company," Carmen says.

"Ha!" Jackson takes a deep swig of beer, then leans forward. "But *how* did they do it? That's the real story.

"They had this toxic byproduct, and they hired a local waste management contractor to dispose of their waste. But the contractor cut corners and illegally dumped it in a swamp instead of disposing of it properly, and it leached over to adjacent farmland.

"The farmers complained. Their corn was infected by blight already, and they were rightly worried the chemical spill would finish them off, which it did, because that stuff is potent. They sued Renewal for damages, but courts take forever, and in the meantime, they realized a curious thing. The soil may have been contaminated, but the blight didn't come back. So they lost their suit for damages, and overnight Renewal became the most powerful agriculture company in the country."

"The best inventions are always accidental," says Carmen.

Jackson laughs. "My point is, the little guys never matter in history, okay? Except sometimes we forget that we're the little guys. They don't forget. Well, you know what? One day, they're going to know me."

He takes a lot of things personally. Skipper waits for Carmen to defend Renewal or question this bold claim, but her sister only makes noises in her throat like she's fascinated and wants him to go on talking about himself. She assumes Carmen is distracted by his dark eyebrows.

He leans back, fully at ease as they converse, and laughs often. He's an autodidact who talks about Thomas Hobbes and Friedrich Nietzsche and Noam Chomsky as if he is intimately acquainted with the men. He thinks utopia is still attainable if people rise up and band together. That humanity is waiting for a moment of true solidarity, and that's the problem—the waiting when they could be making it for themselves. He seems to believe he is the first person who has ever thought this in all of history.

Carmen flutters her eyelashes and swallows his words like she's never been so impressed. She'll let him bore them with his interminable monologues until they're asleep under the table.

"I think I'm done," says Skipper, when Jackson goes to get another round of beer.

"Okay," says Carmen, but she makes no move to follow as Skipper puts on her coat.

"I'm tired." Her back hurts and her cheeks are windburned. But also, a part of her wishes she were still sailing a straight line of movement.

"So rest for a bit."

"Fine," says Skipper, because she has no good argument about why Carmen should come back with her, except that Carmen just ended a long-term relationship with Ollie and may be emotionally vulnerable. Carmen will tell her she can take care of herself.

Jackson returns with mugs for him and Carmen. "Sorry, I only had two hands."

"I'm leaving anyway," says Skipper.

"It was nice to meet you." He turns back to Carmen.

"Be careful," Skipper tells her sister right in front of him. She gives him a measuring look, so he knows she could pick him out of a lineup if she had to.

"I thought you were the younger sister," laughs Jackson, unfazed.

As Skipper trudges back across to the dock, she worries. Carmen is prone to liking people too much. It isn't a lack of constancy so much as accumulation: She collects her affections like figurines. Her heart is an open drawer. As judgmental as Carmen is in all other aspects of her life, she isn't discerning when it comes to attraction.

But maybe Carmen is allowed a palate cleanser after Ollie.

Aside from her constant scheming about money, Ollie's sense of humor was always at the expense of others, like the time she agreed to watch Grandma for an afternoon when Grandma was recovering from surgery and dressed the old woman up in their mother's "going out" outfits.

Skipper wonders why they finally broke up, but she's been respecting Carmen's moratorium on asking.

The idea drifts into her brain that when they find Nora, this might be a new beginning for all three of them. For the first time, she allows herself to fantasize about never going home. Where would she go? With a boat, well, anywhere.

As she rows her dinghy back to the *Bumblebee*, she passes a sailor sitting on the deck of another boat tied up not so far from Skipper's. The sailor smokes a wooden pipe.

"Aren't you cold, honey?" The sailor's voice rasps as if she's swallowed grit.

"No," Skipper lies.

"You must be from somewhere warm with a coat like that," she cackles. "Come here." Skipper reluctantly rows closer. The sailor fetches something from her cabin and, before Skipper can object, drops it right into her boat with a thump. Skipper opens it. It's a beautiful coat made of reindeer skin.

"I can't take this," says Skipper.

"Sure you can," says the woman, sucking her pipe. "I won't need it soon. I've decided to die somewhere tropical."

Skipper doesn't know what to say. The woman doesn't look old.

"It's yours," says the woman.

Her name is Anika, and she was born far away. She's sailed around the world—to lands full of sun where she cooked on her deck every night with a solar oven and to island nations with stilted cities surrounded by imposing seawalls. Long ocean crossings where Anika played solitaire, learned chords on her guitar, and read the same book ten times, then ripped it up and threw it overboard, then wished she hadn't. She can't decide whether the world is in its last breaths or slowly coming back to itself. Joy can be found in all places.

"Was it dangerous?" Skipper wants to know.

"Sometimes," Anika says. "You haven't asked me if I was lonely. That's what most people ask."

"It doesn't sound lonely."

Skipper rubs her chest. Deep envy has settled there like a pain beneath the bone. What would it take to live a life like that? Did you have to be born with the gumption? She longs to ask her, but Anika will laugh.

In the distance, the fiddler plays on, but now she knows it is only a recording, coming from speakers strung along the edge of the water.

Later, as she settles in her bunk, Skipper wonders if all those times Nora encouraged her to leave home and join her in the city, Nora ever believed Skipper would do it. If she thought Skipper was *capable* of it, or if—as Skipper worries in her moments of deepest insecurity—the invitations were an empty gesture of generosity Nora never expected to have to fulfill.

Now that they're so close to finding her, she hopes that Nora will be impressed at what they've done. She wants to stand before Nora, and for her sister to look at her, really look, and say, *Yes, this is what I've always seen in you. You didn't fail at anything, you just needed more time to become yourself.*

CHAPTER ELEVEN

The next day, they follow Nora's last letter inland.

Skipper wakes to morning sunlight and Carmen shaking her socked foot. Jackson motored her back to the boat in his tender the night before, so she didn't have to radio Skipper for a pickup.

"Come on," says Carmen, alert like she's been up for hours. "Jackson found someone who can take us."

As they row to dock, Skipper sees Anika, sitting on her deck, eating a steaming cup of porridge. Skipper lifts her hand, and Anika waves back.

"Who's that?" Carmen wants to know.

"A friend," Skipper says.

Carmen raises her eyebrows, impressed.

Jackson meets them at the dock, bouncing in a navy blue puffy jacket like this is a game.

Jackson, it turns out, is also a sailor, or at least the owner of a beautiful boat, *Leviathan*, bigger and fancier than theirs. Well, he's living on it. He's vague about the details.

Carmen thinks the story is the boat was built in a northern shipyard, and he was paid to deliver it somewhere to someone. If that is the case, Skipper suspects the recipient will be waiting a long time.

He knows how to sail, though it is a relatively recent skill. He doesn't do it for a living. It is still unclear what he does. He is, Carmen tells Skipper, a revolutionary. He's interested in their situation from an "intellectual point of view." Sure, that's why. Anyway, he wants to help.

"Don't worry, little sis. We'll find her," Jackson tells Skipper.

"She always worries," says Carmen, as if Carmen doesn't. "It's her nature."

Everything's been arranged. For a modest fee, Jackson's friend will let them ride in the back of her delivery truck to the town. All three of them, because Jackson is coming too. He doesn't have anything better to do. Skipper could suggest half a dozen things.

"My good deed for the week," he says, touching Carmen's elbow.

Skipper ignores his offer of assistance and climbs in between stacks of boxes. It smells like wet cardboard.

When the woman shuts them in, Skipper tries not to panic. This is the opposite of sailing. They sit in darkness, jolting every time there's a bump in the road. The driver could be taking them anywhere. The boxes could tumble down and crush her. The truck could stop short and slam Skipper against the back. All the while, Jackson talks. It's like his life requires narration.

"I like to say capitalism is based on the assumption we're lazy. It's insulting. But sometimes it's also true, right?"

"Right," laughs Carmen, who has never been lazy.

A column of boxes slides against Skipper. She braces it with her elbow and covers her neck with the other arm. She might be sick. The drive goes on forever. By the time they arrive, Skipper is amazed her teeth haven't fallen out.

Jackson's friend drops them at a crossroads in the middle of empty fields. The ocean is a sparkle on the horizon.

"The town's that way," she says, pointing at a speck in the distance.

"You're not taking us all the way?" Jackson asks, and Skipper's embarrassed by his irritation, but also understands it, because he brokered this, and now he looks bad if he can't deliver.

"I don't set the route, Jack," the woman says, gesturing at the dash.

Carmen steps in and smooths things over. "It's no problem. Thank you so much." She confirms their pickup when the friend comes back this way in six hours.

The truck drives off, leaving them in a cloud of dust. Jackson curses.

Everything is eerily quiet. The road crumbles underfoot, more pothole than paving. A forest of wind turbines turns slowly in the distance along a ridge. Most of the fields are fallow this time of year, but they pass one full of corn, illuminated by giant lights. Renewal released a breed last year that could produce in winter.

Scrawny cows graze on scrawnier brush. Their coats are covered in knobby lumps. One of them turns and growls at them, a sound a cow doesn't normally make. They all jump.

This cow is small, with a vaguely canine head.

Jackson recovers first. "Gross."

"The meat tastes the same," Carmen says.

"Is that smoke?" Skipper asks, sniffing the air. Down the road, they find a charred field, the wooden house and barn burned to the ground.

They go on, and the houses bunch closer together. The buildings are modest, with weathered wooden siding and patched roofs, spaced for cars few people own anymore.

Dread coils in the pit of Skipper's stomach. The slap of their soles on broken road pierces the hush. There's a clatter, and a tall ginger cat emerges from a garbage can to watch them with narrowed eyes.

The town itself appears normal. There's a hardware store, a café, a church, and a general store, outside of which an old man sits eating a sausage out of a paper wrapper, taking the next huge bite before swallowing the first. Meat juice dribbles down his shirt.

Skipper wonders what he thinks of them: two strangers in salt-stiffened clothes, and a man dressed to chop wood.

"What's the address again?" says Carmen.

Skipper takes out Nora's crinkled letter: *32 Maple Street.*

As they puzzle over how to find it, the sausage person introduces himself cheerfully as Robert Feder. He owns the local store.

Skipper peers through the window and sees the shelves, most of them bare, except for a tin or two.

Robert wipes his chin ineffectually with the sausage wrapping and points out Maple Street.

"It's good to see you," he says. "It's been a while since we've had new faces." He wants to know where they are from, and why they've come, and bless them for visiting—and what is the name of their missing sister, and, hm, he may or may not remember Nora, but he does know the person they want to speak to, Ms. Lucy Walter, who runs the guesthouse, yes, on Maple Street, and have they tried this town's sausages, because they are really all right and—

"We should get going," Skipper says, because it looks like Carmen and Jackson are about to sit down and go on chatting, and she's too cold to stand around accumulating frost on her toes.

"Oh," says Robert.

"Sorry," says Carmen. "We'll see you around."

"We sell ice cream too."

"Mm!" says Jackson.

"That was rude," Carmen chides Skipper after they walk away.

Skipper's face heats. "You don't have to make friends with everyone." She walks on before Carmen can reply.

Maple Street is a cul-de-sac that winds up a hill.

"If something's happened to Nora—" Carmen says.

"Nothing's happened," says Skipper.

"She'll be all right," agrees Jackson, even though no one asked him.

Number 32 is a two-story brick house at the top of the hill. The elevation offers a view all the way to the sea. From here, they can also see the remnants of the fire they saw earlier. The burn extends much farther than it appeared from the street.

There's not much to the town itself, and it doesn't seem like there's ever been much. Squat conifers overrun houses and yards.

Skipper's palms sweat inside her pockets despite the chill. Her optimism fades. She's so afraid of what they might find. Jackson steps forward and knocks.

The door opens.

"Lucy Walters?" asks Carmen.

"Yes," answers the woman who stands before them in stained jeans and an artist's smock. "Are you looking for a place to stay?"

Carmen makes introductions, and Lucy invites them in. "You'll lose some fingers standing out in the cold, and I had the sickies weeks ago, so you won't be catching it from me."

Skipper needs no more encouragement than the heat that beckons inside. She and Carmen sink into the soft beige couch. Jackson takes an armchair.

Skipper's heart drops, because it's obvious Nora isn't here. Where is she?

Lucy's impressed they've come all this way. She's a person who takes in strays. Every town has someone like this. Nora showed up one day on the back of the dry-goods truck. She said she was some kind of plant scientist. She asked a lot of questions about what crops people planted, and if anyone wasn't using Renewal seeds.

"It was harmless," says Lucy. "But I told her to be careful anyway. People get skittish about that kind of talk around here. Don't want Renewal thinking we aren't good customers."

Jackson opens his mouth, but Carmen touches his arm, forestalling another rant. "Sure," she says. "Where is she now?"

"Nora got sick. There was a flu, and she got it worse than some," says Lucy, then stops to cough. "We thought she was going to die."

For the first time, Skipper relaxes a fraction, because the way Lucy says it means Nora *hasn't* died, and Skipper admits to herself she was worried that might be the case.

At first, Nora was feverish and weak, but then she got a skin rash and a terrible cough. She couldn't breathe, and the town sent her and the other sickest people to the hospital down in the city where they are staying. That was four months ago, around when she sent the letter to Marcus. They passed that hospital this morning on their way here.

Skipper's pulse picks up. "So she's all right."

Lucy hacks into a handkerchief, then takes a rattling breath. "Oh yes. As far as I heard, she's doing fine."

The tightness in Skipper's chest loosens even more. Nora is fine. Nora is *fine*.

"But she never came back here?" asks Carmen.

Lucy shrugs. "I'm not offended."

She gives them a suitcase full of clothes Nora left behind, including the brown sweater that smells of cookfire that Nora mentioned in her letter. Jackson insists on carrying the suitcase for them.

Lucy also gives them a bundle of papers in a cloth bag, along with a jar of different seeds. "She came here looking for Mr. Marshall's soybeans, but there was a fire before she got here. Poor thing, she spent days tramping about the woods and the marsh and people's fields hoping to find something left over. Always came back with filthy boots and disappointment all over her face. Never did find anything, except that nasty cold."

Skipper peers into the bag at its contents. The paper is rough-edged from being torn from a notebook, the writing ragged and uneven.

"I'm sure she'll be happy to see you. Tell her hi for me."

As they climb back down the hill, Skipper removes the bundle of papers from the tote bag and lifts it to her nose. Inhales. She gets a faint whiff of woodsmoke and bluebell.

It's been so long since she's last seen her older sister. A year? And what did they talk about? The weather, Skipper's mussel experiment. Nora was so excited about it, even more than Skipper. She talked Skipper through the steps, the necessary materials. They made a plan. Nora couldn't wait to come back and try them. And now Skipper will have to tell her the mussels are gone.

We'll start over, Nora will say, and maybe hearing it will give Skipper the energy to do so.

Skipper unties the string that bundles the papers together. Most of the pages are notes and sketches. There's only one letter. She doesn't want to read it out loud in front of Jackson, but Carmen insists.

She unfolds it. *My Dearest Sizzles* the letter begins. "Sizzles" was Nora's nickname for them, some sort of evolutionary descendant of "sisters."

> *I miss you. I'm so sick. They're taking me to the city hospital. Remember that time with the blueberries?*

To anyone else, this reference would have been meaningless, but Skipper gets it right away. They'd sneaked into Mr. Farrow's orchard to steal fruit. It was during a bad season of blight, when everyone was hungry. But Mr. Farrow had blueberries that escaped every year.

They weren't the only ones to covet Mr. Farrow's blueberries, but they assumed they were smarter. They went right before dawn instead of late at night, through the woods and over the back fence.

And Mr. Farrow came out with a gun and shot them. Maybe he meant it as a warning shot, or maybe he was sick of kids coming around. The bullet went right through Nora's shoulder, and she tripped running and twisted her ankle.

Carmen and Skipper screamed and cried and carried her home between them.

Grandma was mad. She told them they were grounded for a year, with more punishment to be determined later. Then she called the doctor. Then she left and went over to Mr. Farrow's with an axe and broke down Mr. Farrow's door, and Mr. Farrow was so terrified of Grandma that the shot he fired at her went wide.

Grandma ripped Mr. Farrow's gun from him and shot every last bullet into his favorite armchair. She hacked it to pieces with her axe. And according to the neighbors who had piled into the doorway to watch, Grandma said in her scary voice: "Next time, that'll be you."

She shoved her way out the door, axe in one hand and gun in the other. She chucked the gun into the pond. And then she came back home where the doctor was extracting a bullet from Nora's arm, and all three girls were sobbing.

The doctor did a bad job, and Nora was sick and weak for a long time, and even now, none of the women ever eat blueberries.

I wish you were here. Or I was home. I shouldn't have come. Where are you? Come find me please. I'm scared.

I want

There, the letter stops, as if Nora's wants are too great to express in naked ink.

Carmen loops an arm in Skipper's, like a promise that things will be all right. Carmen's worldview is that with hard work comes reward, but this hasn't been Skipper's experience. Even so, she clings to Carmen's belief now.

They reach the main street. They call around the Renewal office, but it's closed, and all they can do is peer in the darkened windows. They cross the street back to the general store, where Robert feeds a red fox bits of jerky.

"No one's around," he tells them, having watched them knock. "The county rep died two weeks ago from the flu."

Carmen insists on buying Robert's sausages for lunch. They are awful—greasy and a touch rancid. Jackson retches and tosses his into a pasture.

But Carmen and Skipper finish them because it would be wasteful not to, given how little money they have left. Only the extreme saltiness makes them bearable. Skipper makes it through taking large bites and chewing quickly without breathing through her nose.

"Sorry," mumbles Carmen.

"It's all right," says Jackson, but he passes on the ice cream.

It's early afternoon as they make their way back to the crossroads. The light is fading, and a deeper cold settles into their bones. The world turns gray in the fading light, and the hollow eyes of the empty houses watch them across the fields. The monstrous cows moo low and melancholy.

"I'll take you to the hospital when we get back," Jackson says.

Skipper regrets her meanness, which has kept her from appreciating his help. She wishes she were a better person. She resolves, when they find Nora, to become that person.

It's late when they get back. The town has red bicycles scattered around town for communal use, and they take three of them over to the hospital. They ride through quiet streets lit by charming lamps, past warm cafés and cheerful window displays.

At the top of the hill, the hospital appears in the gloom, big and concrete. Every window is lit. This is not a half-empty city, but one still growing, fueled by the melting transforming the north.

They talk to one of the nurses. Their name is Chuck, and they awkwardly bump elbows with Jackson, and then with Carmen and Skipper.

Chuck finds Nora's records in the system. "She was in intensive care but she recovered." They frown. "It says she left three and a half months ago, back in August. Didn't even bother to check out."

"What happened?" Carmen wonders.

Skipper sits down in a blue plastic chair worn white in the seat. It's not like she expected Nora was still here, but she's disappointed anyway.

"Does anyone know where she is now?" Carmen asks, squeezing Skipper's shoulder.

How could they know? Nora was just someone who momentarily stopped in their patch of the world. All they have are the pictures of her insides, retained for records.

Skipper listens to the murmur of voices intersecting. She slips inside herself. She doesn't know anymore where they are going or how they came to be here.

Her legs ache from walking all day, and she feels as if her body is a bag of wet sand, slowly leaking. They are losing Nora; the farther they go, the less real she becomes, like trying to catch up with a shadow, slipping ahead over cracks and holes, always just out of reach.

CHAPTER TWELVE

They should go home, but they don't. It's hard to walk away from a question. Nora has evaporated.

Jackson takes Carmen to the local community center, and Carmen returns with bags full of warmer, secondhand clothes. They talk about what they should do next, but the conversation withers.

Once or twice, Skipper catches Carmen examining herself in the toilet mirror. The growth has become more three-dimensional. It resembles the soft ear of a mushroom under her skin.

"What does it feel like?" Skipper asks.

"Nothing," says Carmen, dropping her shirt.

With every passing day, the window narrows to make it back for Carmen's new job.

Skipper fixes things on the *Bumblebee*. Jackson introduces them to a mechanic, who prints them the new parts. The cost of it makes Skipper sweat, but Carmen helps her pay for it from the jar of money without complaint. She's anticipating, Skipper supposes with a pang of jealousy, the money she'll be making soon.

Two days after visiting the hospital, Jackson invites them over to his boat for a simple dinner with some friends. There isn't enough for seconds, but Jackson produces a bottle of moonshine that's enough to make everyone happy. They try to sing songs, but no one can remember the words. Everyone is drunk. The conversation turns to Carmen's job, and how excited she is to be starting something new.

"What about you?" Jackson asks Skipper. "Do you want something different?"

"I couldn't," says Skipper. "Our grandmother needs a lot of help."

"You could if you sold the boat," Carmen says. "It'd make your life a lot easier, but you always like to do things the hard way."

It's embarrassing to have her faults scraped out for these strangers to see. She doesn't need them to know her worries.

"Skipper was always such a martyr," Carmen tells the others, and flashes her confident, older-sister smile.

Skipper's face burns. "Some of us don't have the luxury of being selfish." She intends it to cut, but as soon as she says it, regret floods in. It's too late to unsay the words.

"Seriously?" Carmen says.

Jackson laughs to cut the awkwardness. His friends shift uncomfortably.

Skipper hunches down. "You don't know what it's like. I'm the one who stayed and took care of her."

"And I'm the one who's come with you on this terrible trip."

"Because you think you need to protect me."

"Don't I?"

"No. Not when it mattered. I've always protected myself."

They glare at each other, stony-eyed. The corpse of the evening sprawls out on the table between them. Skipper excuses herself, and no one asks her to stay. She rows back to the *Bumblebee*.

As she climbs up onto the deck, she hears a cascade of crashes—the cans from the pantry. She processes the meaning of the noise at the same time she realizes there's an extra dinghy next to the boat.

Someone is on the *Bumblebee*.

"Hello?" she calls, wondering if she should get the others. She hunts for a makeshift weapon.

A shadow rushes past her, and she gasps. It shoves her hard, and she falls backward, nearly tumbling over the side of the boat into the frigid water. Sharp pain shoots up her arm from banging it against a cleat. She scrambles to her feet as the intruder motors away.

She goes down into the cabin, blood thudding in her ears.

"Hello?" she says, in case there's someone else, but the cabin is empty. She radios Jackson's boat, but their music must be too loud to hear.

The pantry latch she fixed lies on the floor, along with the contents of the pantry. One of the jars is broken, and she squats to pick up shards of glass. Carmen's money sits on the table untouched.

She goes to her bed, lifts the mattress, and relief floods her. Nora's letters and the jar of seeds are safe where Skipper tucked them.

She should fetch Carmen, but she doesn't want to leave the boat unattended.

Up on deck, she spots Anika, clipping her toenails into the water. "Everything okay?" Anika asks.

Skipper tells her about the intruder, and Anika is outraged. "That's rude. How are we supposed to feel safe out here? This city is going downhill. I should've left weeks ago."

Skipper wishes she had the foresight to trip the intruder, or something. She might have had answers rather than more questions.

Carmen appears after midnight, cheeks flushed with merriment. Predictably, the first thing she says is "Now will you get a lock?"

She tells Jackson, who has nothing useful to contribute but is excited. "I bet it was Renewal."

"It was EarthWorks," Carmen says and tells him about the previous incident back in the city.

"Maybe, maybe not. Listen," he says to Skipper. "I was hired by a legal firm to investigate the Renewal factory up here. They are putting together a class-action suit. I found a guy who was willing to talk, and the next day he was floating face down in the harbor. Drowned." Judging from Carmen's face, none of this is news to her.

"Was it an accident?" Skipper asks.

"That's what people said. But come on, we use our brains, okay? And there was another guy whose bicycle brakes failed as he was going down a steep hill on the way to meet with me. Crashed into a building and fractured his skull." Jackson makes an exploding motion next to his head. "You have to be careful."

Skipper's considered and rejected it before, but the idea worms back in again that Nora might be dead.

Carmen hugs her. "The fact they were here has to mean whoever's looking hasn't found her."

"She's hiding," says Jackson. "Shit, she sure stirred things up. I'd love to talk to her."

They each carry a different understanding of who their sister is. They could all be wrong.

In the morning, Carmen writes to the clinic to negotiate a later start date. "Six weeks isn't a completely unreasonable time to wait for a new person, given the time of year."

"You shouldn't wait for the surgery," Skipper says.

"I've got the pills. And we'll be back sooner. I'm being cautious."

Skipper suppresses her misgivings.

Uncle Tot writes. He hopes they're well. He's sent them money to buy a nice meal. They need it more than he realizes, because they burned through half of Carmen's stash of bills already, especially fixing the motor.

Also, Grandma is in the overnight clinic for observation. She's got a chest infection and has been having trouble breathing. She's all right. But it's serious. But they shouldn't worry. But it would be good if they came home soon.

Skipper tries not to think of the expense, and how they will afford it. She can't help feeling Grandma's illness is her fault.

"Uncle Tot is a worrier," says Carmen. "I'll reach out to people and get a real update. Don't feel bad. He got out of taking care of us and her for twenty years. He can manage for a couple of weeks." She says it as if she's ever taken equal responsibility for Grandma.

So they don't depart. Over the next few days, Skipper continues to work on the boat, and Carmen goes off with Jackson. Only when Carmen calls to her from the dock to get her coat and come to town does Skipper realize Carmen has been doing what Skipper should have been: searching for Nora.

She stopped by the police precinct, the firehouse, city hall, and all the local boardinghouses and hotels. She talked to the night staff and the day staff at the hospital. And now, she's finally found someone who knows something.

They meet the woman at a café with hot, weak tea and dusty plastic flowers. Her name is Lili Liang, and she's a retired botanist and avid gardener. Apparently Nora tracked her down, asking about soybeans.

"She told me her name was Mara Craven," Lili says. That's their grandmother's name.

"She had such an interesting way of thinking about things," she says, and Skipper stiffens at the past tense, but Lili goes on. After leaving the hospital, Nora came to her asking about a guy from a neighboring town who had grown non-Renewal soybeans. She wanted to know where he could have gotten them from. "As it happens, I knew him, because he bragged about it at our monthly Botanical Society meetings. Must have gotten himself into trouble with all his talking. He said he got them from a vault of seeds across the ocean that was built to endure the end of civilization."

Skipper takes her bundle of charts from the inside of her coat. She's been carrying it around like some kind of charm. Now she unfolds it across the tippy table of the café.

Lili points out the spot. It's three weeks' sail—nearly three times the distance they've traveled. It's hard to believe people live up there.

"I've heard of that place," says Jackson. "I know a guy who worked on a cargo ship that stopped there a few times. He said the place is more secure than some prisons. I didn't know about seeds."

"Renewal owns the whole settlement, including the vault," says Lili. "It's where they conduct their most sensitive research."

Lili's cup trembles as she raises it to her lips, and Skipper realizes she's nervous. Lili adds in a softer voice: "She wanted to know how she could go there."

They absorb this in stunned silence.

Jackson hoots.

"Did she go?" Carmen asks, at the same time Skipper says, "Could she?"

"I don't know. I told her the only way they'd let you in there is if you worked for Renewal. And she told me that was all right then. She could figure something out, and she'd be back in a couple of weeks with some experimental tomato seeds for me that grow in cold temperatures. But that was months ago."

"A couple of weeks! She'd have to *fly* there," Skipper says.

"She couldn't afford that," Carmen scoffs.

"Not unless Renewal paid," says Lili.

"They wouldn't have let her take seeds," says Jackson. "From what I hear, they throw people in prison there for less. Renewal controls everything."

Skipper chews her bottom lip. Nora has little respect for authority. She picks and chooses the rules she follows. Back home, everyone let her do what she wanted, because she was clearly a "once-in-a-generation mind" and the "town's best hope." But it's easy to imagine the ways she might have run into trouble in a place like they're describing.

"If she went there, then Renewal must have known where she is all along!" Carmen is outraged. She has worked for the company for years; this must feel like a betrayal.

"Of course they did," Jackson laughs.

"But why wouldn't they tell us?"

"Maybe something happened to her. Some accident or shit, and they're protecting their ass."

"That's grim," says Carmen.

"Sorry," says Jackson, realizing how that sounds.

Skipper stares at the island on her chart, as if she might divine the truth of Nora's whereabouts if she looks long enough.

Carmen sighs. "I know you want to go there," she says to Skipper, without accusation.

Skipper does, but even she knows they can't. Sailing across the ocean is very different from sailing up the coast, and if the security is as tough as Jackson describes, they probably wouldn't even be able to land once they got there. They've already come so much farther than they intended. Anyway, Carmen has her new job, and also her infection, which needs to be dealt with. And Skipper needs to get back to Grandma.

They've pretended for a while that they aren't attached to life, but it's time to go home.

"Skipper . . ." says Carmen.

"I know," says Skipper. Accepting reality is not the same thing as giving up.

"We'll find some way to contact her," says Carmen. "We can talk to the company."

"Assuming they cooperate," says Jackson, stroking his beard.

They return to the boat and make plans to leave the next day. Jackson is disappointed by the loss of excitement, and also, wherever things were going with Carmen. Uncle Tot's worry over Nora is overcome by his eagerness to have them home. He's making silly fish hats for a nautical-themed welcome home party.

But when they wake, the harbor is shrouded in heavy fog. While they drink tea in their cabin, waiting for it to dissipate, there's a shout from the water. Someone is outside the boat.

They go up and find a launch drifting near the *Bumblebee*. A person in a navy parka with a Renewal sunburst logo stands at the rail.

"Hello, there. Can I come aboard?"

"Sure," says Carmen, before Skipper can stop her.

The person's name is Sasha. He has a badge and everything. He works in the area, and he wants to introduce himself. "Were you able to find your sister yet? We would like to speak with her. She hasn't responded to our messages."

Skipper glances at Carmen. It's one thing for Renewal to lie when asked; it's another thing for them to expend resources looking for her when they know where she is. Skipper doesn't know what game they're playing, but she doesn't like it.

"Don't take it personally," says Carmen. "She's been ignoring us too."

They cram together in the cockpit, because Skipper blocks the door to their cabin. Carmen tightens the zipper on her jacket. She's likely hoping there's another explanation here, one that doesn't involve Renewal's deception.

Across the way, Jackson comes out on deck and sees them talking. He frowns in concern, then invites himself over. The boat wobbles as he clambers up onto it on all fours like a bear.

"Who are you?" he wants to know.

"Who are you?" Sasha replies, in a friendlier tone than his.

"Why don't we all sit down?" says Carmen, pushing past Skipper into the cabin. Skipper can't object or she'll be the odd one out. She follows, jaw clenched.

Once inside, they discover they have nothing to say. Carmen boils water for more tea.

"Well?" says Jackson. "Are we socializing?" Skipper feels a rare burst of gratitude for him.

"We heard you came up here looking for your sister," says Sasha.

"How did you hear that?" Jackson asks.

Sasha smiles a thank-you to Carmen and accepts the chipped mug. "Local rep reported it."

"Let's clear something up," says Carmen, crossing her arms. Can the man tell her sister is angry? "You know exactly where she is. So what are you doing here?"

Sasha's brow wrinkles. "What are you talking about? We haven't heard from her since she left the hospital. We want to help. We're just as distressed as you that she's missing." He takes a sip. No one else drinks.

"Just as distressed," repeats Carmen.

"Fuck you," says Skipper, who has fewer qualms about losing her temper.

Sasha sets down his cup. He blinks, reevaluating the situation. "I don't understand. Why do you think we know something?"

No one says anything.

At which point, Skipper realizes there are several possibilities: (1) Nora did not go to the vault, and Renewal is telling the truth; (2) Nora did go to the vault, and Renewal is lying about it for some reason; (3) Nora did go to the vault, but Renewal doesn't know she's there.

If it's the third instance, Skipper worries they've given Sasha a clue. But in that case, why would Nora not want her own employer to know?

"Well." Sasha stands up. "Thanks so much for the tea. By the way, I also wanted to convey a warning about a certain competitor. If EarthWorks approaches you, we recommend you don't engage. They're ambitious for market share and unscrupulous. We've heard things. Contact us first."

"Right," says Skipper.

"Okay." Sasha is the only one who smiles.

After Sasha leaves, Jackson slings his coat over a chair as if he's settling in, and the faint smell of cedar emanates from his clothes—residue from the woodburning stove he uses to heat his boat. He roams about, opening cupboards and examining all the corners. "You can't trust him. These megacorporations are all the same. They'll do anything for profit."

Carmen laughs, as if Jackson meant to be funny.

"What's the profit in lying about this?" Skipper asks. The more she thinks about it, the more she's convinced Renewal doesn't know where Nora is. Her earlier relief bleeds away. She wonders if they are making a mistake in going home.

She goes above deck to check the fog. The sea smoke is thinning as the day warms.

Carmen joins her. "We could stay a little longer and make the rounds again. We have a few weeks to get back now."

Skipper gives in, because remaining in this faraway city is easier than going home. But they don't learn anything new, and when they try to talk to Lili again, she's disappeared.

After three more days, Skipper again accepts they've done all they can. She means it this time.

The night before they're due to leave, Skipper's listening to the weather forecast when Carmen shouts for her. They've received a message on the ship computer.

It's from Nora.

CHAPTER THIRTEEN

Dear Siz. Sorry about missing the party for your birthday but lately city life has gotten very full. I'm planning to take a break after this current spate of work is done. My love to Grandma and Uncle Tot. Don't worry, I'm coming home soon. Nora.

They chew it over. It's from an anonymous account, and everything about it seems off.

First, Skipper and Carmen have spring birthdays. Second, that turn of phrase, *my love to Grandma*, is not something any of them would say, not about Grandma. Third, they know she's not in the city.

Maybe it's a typo, and she meant Grandma's birthday. The Grandma thing is odd, but it doesn't mean anything. And it's possible Nora's lying to keep them from worrying.

Surely, though, she's seen the dozens of concerned messages they've sent. The flippancy of the tone is enraging, as if they haven't been chasing her up the coast, wondering if she's dead.

"She was always such a weirdo," Carmen says.

Skipper wonders if it's fake. But no, the letter is addressed in a manner only Nora would use: "Siz," short for "Sizzle."

"At least that settles it," says Carmen. "We can go home in peace. Glad Nora finally got around to sending us a message. I'm sorry, Skip. But I think we have to accept Nora is as selfish as always, and we've wasted the last few weeks. On the bright side, we've had an accidental holiday. I'm sure it was good for both of us, right?"

Skipper squints at the words, trying to divine some deeper meaning. Perhaps Carmen is right. She should be happy they've heard from her.

To Skipper's annoyance, Carmen summons Jackson, who insists on reading the message.

"Anyone could have written this," he says.

"No, it sounds like her," says Carmen.

"Sort of," says Skipper.

They pore over it again, but all they can do is guess.

"Listen," says Jackson, leaning in. "What if you *did* go to the vault? Would it really be a terrible idea?"

"Yes," says Carmen.

"Yes," echoes Skipper, with less conviction. She's stared at the chart a few times, measuring the distance, made a list in her notebook of the kinds of outfitting necessary to make such a journey.

"Why would we go there, especially now that she's confirmed she's fine?"

Jackson shrugs. "A friend of a friend works over there, someone in the movement. What if I try to get in contact with her? It's a terrible place. Shit working conditions, bad pay, et cetera. Your sister could be in trouble."

"But she's not," says Carmen.

"We could take my boat," says Jackson, even though it's not his boat.

Skipper's face must show what she thinks of that idea, because he adds: "Or yours."

"No." Skipper cannot imagine being trapped on a boat with Jackson for weeks. He would smother her with words.

"We could take both boats."

"You're not serious," says Carmen, but Skipper thinks maybe he is, not because of Nora, but because of the adventure of it. The vault has caught his imagination, and he wants an excuse to go there. He lives his life by his changing passions, and this will be a great story to tell people. Skipper envies how simple his life is.

After circling for an hour, Carmen and Jackson head off to eat dinner at the bar. Skipper declines. She wants the alone time. She's tired of sharing her sister with this other person. Carmen may like him, but what's the point? They're leaving.

Skipper works on a tear in the spinnaker, her stitches as uneven as her patience.

The radio buzzes. She has it tuned to an open channel, and it sounds like some kids have gotten hold of a radio and are playing around.

"S-O-S," says one, before dissolving into giggles.

The radio clicks, and an embarrassed adult—one of Jackson's friends, maybe—apologizes.

The light static returns.

A smile flickers across Skipper's face. She wants to tap a message back to them, a simple hello, but she doesn't know if they'd understand. Probably not. She doubts they learned more than that. They didn't grow up with Nora.

Her fingers halt mid-stitch. She drops the spinnaker and goes to the ship computer and rereads Nora's letter. It takes her fifteen furious minutes to figure it out.

When she substitutes one syllable words for a dot and two syllable for a dash, the message Nora has written is in plain sight:

. -- / - .-. .- .--. .--. . -.. / .. -. / - .... . / ...- .- ..- .-.. -

Im trapped in the vault

CHAPTER FOURTEEN

If we do this, we'll need supplies," says Carmen, starting another list in her notebook. If Carmen could itemize the world, she would. But her powers are merely human, so she exerts control in the way available to her: by lining up her words in numbered formation, a vapid army of ink on paper.

They sit once again in the bar. Skipper can't believe they're thinking of going. It's what she desperately wants to do—Nora's message echoes in her brain—but it's hard to imagine they can.

"What about your clinic job?" Surely they can't hold the job for Carmen for months.

"I'll ask them if I can start end of January." She doesn't look at Skipper.

"But what if they say no? It's your dream job. And if you don't get it, you won't be able to pay for the . . . other thing." Grandma's procedure nearly bankrupted them. She thinks of the fungus growing inside Carmen, extending questing tendrils toward her stomach, heart, liver.

"What other thing?" asks Jackson.

Carmen sets down the notebook. "We don't need to talk about it." Like they don't need to talk about her breakup with Ollie.

Except this is important. Carmen needs the procedure.

Nora's message has aligned them both in urgency, so Skipper gets it. But also, they can't risk Carmen's health. Nora wouldn't want her to.

"We could send you back home," says Skipper.

"You're not doing this alone," says Carmen.

Skipper swallows hard. "Worst case, when we get back, I—I'll sell the boat."

Carmen stares at her. "You can't."

"I can." Skipper manages to say it firmly, even though she feels sick. She loves the *Bumblebee*, and the idea of being stuck on land and giving up her dreams terrifies her. The *Bumblebee* is her world. But for her sister, she will give it up.

"Thank you, Skip." Carmen turns away and wipes a tear. "But it won't come to that."

Jackson glances from one to the other, uncertain what's transpired.

"So, how are supplies?" Skipper asks, changing the subject.

"We have about three days more of food," Carmen reports, and the subject is officially closed.

"We'll need a heater," says Skipper, who talked to Anika that morning about equipment. Her pipe-smoking sailor friend gave her a shovel and rubber hammer, along with tips for keeping lines from freezing to the deck and how to install cheap insulation.

"I know a guy," says Jackson.

"I do too," says Skipper, because Anika gave her a recommendation.

Jackson and Carmen look at her.

"What?" says Skipper.

"I'll talk to the legal firm and see if they'll cover some costs. I'm sure I could gather some valuable information for them."

"You're really coming?" Skipper wonders if there will ever be a time in her life when she isn't dragged along in someone else's wake.

Jackson grins. "I talked to my friend's friend over there, and she says things might be going down soon, some kind of action against Renewal. I'm going to help them. My investigation here is going nowhere. What else am I going to do? I've been waiting for a sign for weeks, and maybe this is it. Especially if your sister's willing to talk. Anyway, someone needs to protect you from pirates."

"Pirates?" Carmen asks.

Jackson shrugs. "The navy doesn't go that far north, and Renewal protects themselves. Everyone else is on their own."

"What are you going to do against pirates?" Skipper wants to know. He winks and flexes his bicep.

So it is decided. They both deal with their anxiety in different ways. Carmen reviews their preparations on the hour, even though Skipper's well on top of things, and Skipper walks the harbor's edge, not knowing how long it will be before she can stretch her legs again.

"He's not coming on the *Bumblebee*, though," Skipper tells Carmen.

"Oh, Skip. Okay," laughs Carmen.

Skipper wants to argue more, but she worries about derailing their momentum, as if one false move will erase the distance they've traveled, and she'll wake up in her own bed, dread weighing down her limbs.

Her blood hasn't stopped drumming in her ears since she deciphered Nora's message. Her mind tumbles over nightmare scenarios that could have befallen her sister.

What she doesn't want to admit is she's glad to have a reason not to go home. Perhaps she's like a cow that accidentally discovered the other side of a fence, and if she keeps going, she may find still more beyond.

They spend a week and the last of Carmen's jar of money preparing for the trip. Anika is a great source of advice. It's she who suggests the problem of how to get past security: claim an emergency that necessitates a landing. They'll have to make it convincing.

"And don't mess with ice," she warns. The harbor may be filled with it. Anika guesses Renewal has icebreakers, but it could be challenging for small boats to land.

Jackson's *Leviathan* needs more work than theirs. The bilge is wet and green; something is wrong with his pump. He should replace it, but there aren't any new ones available, so Carmen repairs it with the help of Jackson's mechanic friend.

Skipper wouldn't have blamed Jackson if he changed his mind. She, in fact, expected him to. But if anything, his enthusiasm for the trip—or at least for Carmen—seems to increase as time goes on. The quest consumes him. In some ways, he believes in what they're doing more than they do, that he is some kind of hero who will rescue the damsel and slay a multinational corporation. He procures a gun. This doesn't increase Skipper's desire to have him along.

Carmen, at Skipper's insistence, visits the hospital to get the fungus inside her checked out again. The doctor gives her more pills, but they tell her to schedule the removal soon.

Skipper worries about Grandma's nightly routine and all the things Uncle Tot could forget, but she's made her choice, and it's no longer in her control.

Uncle Tot frets from thirteen hundred miles away. Every reply is desperate to dissuade. He's convinced they're going to die out there in the ocean, and Skipper has to stop reading his messages, because they only feed her own anxiety. Once they are out in the ocean, they won't be able to communicate much. Jackson's boat has the equipment to pull information from the sky, but none of them can afford the subscription cost. They'll rely on Skipper's navigation by radio, charts, and sextant.

They have heard nothing more from Nora, but not once do Skipper or Carmen discuss the possibility of heading home again, even when the clinic replies saying they don't think they can continue to hold the job for Carmen.

At last, a day of perfect weather arrives: The gray dissipates, the sun shines bright, and the wind is brisk.

They embark.

CHAPTER FIFTEEN

I'm burning," Carmen says, and Skipper wonders if Carmen is going to complain all the way to the vault.

The sun shines in rare abundance, and Skipper's charging every device on the ship in order of importance. The ship's batteries are taking forever to charge.

"You don't have to sit up here," she tells Carmen, wanting to defend the *Bumblebee.*

"I get more seasick down below."

Carmen pulls on a hat. She got one from the community box for Skipper too—a pink wool hat with a bill, gratuitous cat ears, and ear flaps. Skipper suspects Carmen picked it out for the comedic value, but Skipper secretly loves it anyway.

Skipper updates their position on her charts, trying to ignore her doubts. They're making good time.

She catches Carmen admiring *Leviathan*'s brand-new spray shield, which keeps Jackson dry and out of the elements. Jackson's not an experienced sailor and doesn't deserve such a nice boat.

One of Jackson's many jobs was crewing on a couple of long-range voyages. He's been far down the coast to half-submerged tropical islands, where mosquitoes are so thick at night you might inhale a hundred if you don't wear netting, but the fish are plentiful enough they flop right into your boat.

"Sounds like paradise," says Carmen.

"Why didn't you stay down there?" Skipper wants to know.

Jackson stretches. "I'm a man on the move."

At least his mediocre skill makes it easier to keep him in sight.

Carmen chatters back and forth with Jackson over the radio, until Skipper reminds her they need to conserve the power. Jackson sails closer to them so they can shout across the water, but Carmen misses half of his words.

"Can't you get closer?" Carmen asks.

"He'll steal our wind."

"There's plenty of wind to go around."

"Which one of us is the sailor?"

Jackson is talking about a man he knew down south who went to great lengths to collect the skeletons of extinct animals.

Skipper doesn't think Carmen has missed much.

"What?" Carmen asks.

"Just come over!" says Jackson. He's repeated himself twice, but each time he got to the punch line, Skipper tacked away.

Skipper looks at Carmen. "Please don't." Panic blooms inside her, and she doesn't know why. After all, she's sailed alone for years.

"I'll just go over for a few hours."

They drop their sails, and Jackson motors up next to them. He gets up against his starboard rail, reaches down, and grabs their port side. The two boats kiss. Carmen clambers over, laughing as Jackson takes her arms. She settles down in his cockpit.

"See you later!" he tells Skipper.

And then it's Skipper and the *Bumblebee*, as it's always been. Laughter filters across the water. Eventually the distance between the boats grows until *Leviathan* is only a speck.

She calculates her position and updates her logbook and plays music from the cabin. She tends to listen to the same songs on repeat, which Carmen hates, so it's been a while since Skipper has listened to anything.

She leans back against the cockpit bench and picks at the threads of her worn-out gloves and tries not to think about what life would be like without this boat. She dreads having to go back to Ollie and ask if that buyer would still be interested. But this is a problem for when they get back.

A few hours becomes half a day.

The swells pick up somewhat, and soon she can't see the other boat at all, and she begins to worry. They don't know Jackson. What if he abducts her? She shouldn't have let Carmen go. But no, there they are. Skipper peers at them through her binoculars.

They're not minding their sails. Carmen has a hand on his knee. She says something, and he laughs.

Skipper drops the binoculars and pushes her gaze to the multifaceted blues and grays of the water. The ocean is her place of quietude and safety. She leans back and exhales, cupped by the great sky and water below, and cuts her invisible triangles.

She and her sisters were close for many years, but their paths diverged when Carmen started high school. The other two lost interest in the *Bumblebee*. Nora buried herself in experiments and books and nurtured ambitious, wild ideas about what she could make of the world; Carmen got an after-school job and made friends with everyone in town.

Skipper, on the other hand, was stuck in a single track between school and home, where Grandma would berate her for folding socks incorrectly, for her table manners, for the way she wore her hair. It was as if Grandma were trying to pinch and prod her into the shape of something inhuman, not the person Grandma was, but the person Grandma imagined herself to be. But Skipper was a rock, not clay. Even when she tried—and how she had tried for so many years to be what anyone else wanted, to be what she herself wanted, to be more than the self she was—she couldn't change.

She used to cry herself to sleep every night. There was a release to biting down and sobbing silently until her pillows were wet with tears. It was like the relief that came with vomiting when she was sick. She'd go to school the next day with swollen, bloodshot eyes.

The other kids thought she was peculiar. Well, maybe she was. There always had to be a few of those kids in any class: the ones who didn't belong in the herd.

It was easier for Carmen and Nora: They were prettier, smarter, more athletic.

Grandma made Carmen pick up and walk Skipper home after school, as if anything could happen in their small town. They were both fearful enough of her to obey, but sometimes Carmen made Skipper trail a few feet behind if she was with her friends. Skipper didn't mind. She would study the way Carmen rolled her hips when she walked, the way she talked to whoever her best friend of the moment was.

These were the only minutes of Skipper's day that were bearable.

"You should look out for her," Nora admonished Carmen once, in front of Skipper. She and Carmen began to fight after Nora left for college. Their friendship evaporated for no reason Skipper understood. "Have you talked to her? The kids at school are terrible."

"I can hear you," Skipper tried to say, but she wasn't part of the conversation.

"I've tried," Carmen said. "The problem is *she* doesn't." She turned to Skipper. "It's not that hard to make people like you. Smile, and say, 'That's so interesting.' Laugh at their jokes. Look them in the eye. People like you if you like them. It's easy."

Skipper braced herself behind the kitchen table. She had tried, she wanted to say. She tried every day of her life. Maybe she just wasn't a likable person.

The wind shifts, and the swells in the water grow even more, and now it's too rough for Carmen to come back over. They agree over the radio Carmen will spend the night. If the waves weren't white-capped hills, Skipper might think they were looking for an excuse.

She doesn't relish having to solo all night in this weather, getting up every four hours to check her position. At least they're in an infrequently trafficked area.

In the early afternoon, Skipper notices a change in the color of the water. She's sailed right into a patch of Amaranthine, and the *Bumblebee* is an island in a sea of crimson. This happens sometimes near home, but she didn't expect it in the middle of the ocean. The slick, oily color extends for miles, its sweet-and-spicy scent filling the air. She gives up wiping pink spray from the deck and waits for it to pass.

A thump against the foredeck makes Skipper jump. A seagull crash-landed onto her boat. Its feathers flutter in the wind as the bird struggles to its feet. It braces itself against the deck and hops toward the bow, away from Skipper to a pocket of calm at the base of the mast.

Skipper goes down below to fetch her headlamp. She fixes dinner in its red light: instant noodles adorned with a few precious vegetables from the cooler they'd stuffed with snow and ice before leaving. It's so much better than beans.

The boat heels sharply, and waves wash across the hull. She tunes the radio to listen for an updated forecast, but they are out of range from land or other boats.

She takes the pot and a fork back up to the cockpit. She has the idea she might eat with the bird. Steam curls up from the broth, and she realizes how cold she's been all day, despite Anika's coat. Across the swells, *Leviathan* rises and falls like a toy boat. Neither Carmen nor Jackson is visible.

Skipper tosses a noodle, and the raggedy bird opens one eye. It waits before rousing itself to inspect the thing. The noodle is gone in a gulp, and the bird looks at her. It wants more.

Warmth blooms inside her.

She tosses it another and glances again at the other boat. Her sister loves animals.

The deck is still empty.

Through her binoculars, she can see one of the lines on *Leviathan* has come loose and drags in the water. Careless. She picks up the radio.

"Carmen!" she shouts, and more reluctantly, "Jackson!"

They don't respond. The boom swings wildly around, and the boat veers sharply. Something must be wrong with his windvane.

The door bangs open, and Jackson staggers out. His shirt is unbuttoned, revealing ample chest hair.

Skipper flushes, first with embarrassment, then with anger, because Jackson has been sloppy, and her sister is on board. Jackson hurries to trim the sail and right the boat. He waves sheepishly at Skipper.

"Do you want some dinner?" he asks over the radio.

"No!" she says. "Thanks!"

He disappears again below deck, and Skipper thinks of Ollie back home.

She had done her best to like Ollie for Carmen's sake, but there was something about her that reminded her of a shark, always circling the next hustle. During the time Carmen had dated her, Ollie'd tried selling hats, artisanal jams, glass sculptures, and mushrooms. Nothing ever stuck.

One afternoon, when Skipper was returning to dock, she saw Ollie buying a generator from a guy. Skipper'd seen that guy around before, peddling salvaged equipment. Everyone knew his stuff was crap.

"I can fix it up," she heard Ollie say. "It just needs to last a few weeks after I sell it. Then it's their problem."

Later, when she saw Ollie strapping the generator into her pedal wagon, Skipper thought of telling Carmen. But what would Carmen say? She'd make excuses. And anyway, it was only the day before Carmen told her Ollie found a buyer for the *Bumblebee*, and they should consider the offer, even though Nora had agreed with Skipper that they shouldn't.

She could try to warn the buyer, but she didn't have proof, just a pile of resentment.

So Skipper confronted Ollie.

Ollie promised she wasn't doing anything wrong; she didn't know for a fact the generator was shit. Even though everyone knew that guy's stuff was junk. Anyway, they all needed the money, didn't they? "Please don't tell Carmen," Ollie begged, and Skipper, because she was furious with Carmen, offered her a deal: Ollie would pretend the buyer she'd found for the *Bumblebee* wasn't interested after all and Skipper didn't tell Carmen. And Ollie agreed.

In retrospect, Skipper hates she did this. But it's done.

Skipper isn't surprised Carmen and Ollie broke up. She's surprised they stayed together so long. And now here is Carmen, already on the rebound.

The seagull perks up. It walks a few feet down the deck, toward Skipper.

"So greedy," says Skipper. She holds out the remnants of the pot, but the bird spooks and takes flight. It dips and rides the wind, and that void expands in Skipper again. As the bird grows smaller and smaller, she wonders if Nora is scared or hurt.

It grows dark, and the stars emerge.

Once, Grandma had to go to a hospital for a few days for surgery when they were little, and Uncle Tot stayed with them. He took them outside in the middle of the night, and they sat in lawn chairs in the street. While they drank warm milk, he uncased his homemade telescope.

When it was Skipper's turn, she squinted, and the lunar surface jumped into sharp relief: its ancient, shadowed craters and gleaming ground. It was the first time she had ever seen another place with her own eyes, and she wished suddenly she could crawl through the tube of the scope and tumble out onto that other land. Nora said she'd asphyxiate immediately because there was no air on the moon.

Now, Skipper looks at the moon and all the stars above, and she can see the shape of infinity. Everything else recedes.

Does Nora exist at all? Perhaps Skipper has always been in the *Bumblebee,* sailing for the horizon, and her memories are simply things she wishes had happened.

CHAPTER SIXTEEN

After a few days of good movement, the wind dies to a whisper, and Skipper wants to scream every time she updates their position. They motor, but Skipper's battery dies quickly, and so they're left to drift on a becalmed sea.

Carmen remains on Jackson's boat. Laughter wafts across the water.

Skipper cleans and mends some clothes. She reads one of Carmen's novels. She naps and wakes up disoriented.

Some of the food begins to spoil: The bread is spotted with mold, the winter greenhouse tomatoes have gone soft, the vegetables wilted. She radios *Leviathan* to let them know, and it's the first time she's talked to anyone in hours.

Carmen, who made the extravagant purchases, takes responsibility. She keeps apologizing. It's not like Skipper stopped her, though, and she could have. They were craving fresh things after eating beans for so long.

The situation isn't dire as long as the trip doesn't take much longer than expected. They won't get far without wind, though. It's midday, and they've hardly moved.

"Let's have a party," says Jackson. "We'll cook everything that's going bad and eat it all."

"Great idea," says Carmen, and Skipper goes along, because what else are they going to do at this point?

So they eat five meals the first day, and four meals the next, and after a lifetime of restraint, the gluttony is overwhelming. Skipper drags herself above deck, stomach aching, hoping the fresh air will keep it all from coming back up. As she lies limp across the cockpit bench, she hears noises from the other boat. It sounds like her sister, moaning with pleasure. Skipper flushes through her entire body, and she waits rigidly for the sound to come again to confirm what she heard. Then she realizes some questions are better left unanswered, and she crawls back down to her bunk, clutching her abdomen and fuming.

Skipper has had exactly three romantic entanglements of any significance: There was Gee, in third grade—a four-month schoolyard fling; then as an adult, there was Robbi, another fisher, who talked almost as much as Jackson; and Zed, who actually thought Skipper might give up sailing to start a family. Carmen told her she was too picky, but Nora sympathized: "This town is so provincial. Don't waste your time."

And yet Carmen finds plenty of options. Skipper considers that enough for both of them.

Skipper turns over and lies on her side. Out the porthole, the moon sinks, white and swollen. The water is awash with stars.

Last year, when Carmen first talked about selling the *Bumblebee*, Nora suggested Skipper do it, take her share of the money and move to the city. "Come live with me for a bit."

For a week, Skipper entertained it, because it would mean, at least, finally escaping.

Skipper never told Carmen. She knows instinctively Carmen would see it as a terrible betrayal, though Carmen never showed any interest in leaving home before this.

In the end, Skipper couldn't do it, and Nora defended her desire to keep the boat. She likes thinking of herself as a person who might one day be someone somewhere else, but maybe it's only a game she plays.

Yet, here she is, in the middle of the ocean, and that's thanks to Carmen, who has come all this way with her like it's nothing. Skipper doesn't appreciate her enough.

She owes Jackson more generosity. He may see them as yet another cause to adopt. He has too high an opinion of his sailing abilities. He definitely talks too much. But he has tried to help, and Carmen likes him. Again Skipper resolves to be nicer.

In the morning, the wind hasn't changed much. The ocean stretches out in all directions, a vast, featureless plain, and their sails hang limp from the masts. In the distance, a column of rain drifts across her path, but it dissipates before she reaches it. She stares for a long time into the dark teal water, trying to gauge the color, and when she blinks, freckles of sunlight dance inside her lids.

A speck of black moves across the horizon—a nuclear-powered naval ship on patrol. Skipper radios the first mate, and he shares an updated forecast: A storm's forming a few days out. He warns them about pirates, but Skipper hopes the fact they don't have anything worth stealing will protect them in this wild, unconquered ocean.

Jackson and Carmen lounge above deck. Carmen hallos and waves at Skipper. They paddle closer.

"We think we should try fishing," Carmen says. "Jackson has some top-rate fishing gear on this boat."

"Sure," says Skipper. She fetches her rod, fishhooks, and tackle. She hunts the pantry for suitable bait. In the garbage bucket, she finds chicken gristle and bones from days ago. The smell makes her gag, but she picks everything out into a cup and rejoins the others.

"How about a competition?" suggests Jackson, hooking a piece of jerky.

Skipper bites back a rebuff, and smiles. "If you want."

Carmen snorts. "As long as you're okay with losing. Shimizu sisters always win."

Maybe for Carmen and Nora that's true: They always excel at anything they attempt. Growing up, their only competition was each other. One summer, Carmen took up embroidery with surprising and sudden enthusiasm. She progressed quickly from handkerchiefs to napkins and tablecloths. Then Nora decided she, too, wanted to embroider. They amassed between them a collection of colored thread. Each one embroidered an intricate piece—Nora, a curtain, and Carmen, a dress. Both were stunning. Opus completed, neither of them ever touched their needles again.

A few years later, Skipper tried it, but maybe it wasn't the same without a sister to compare with. She enjoys adding subtle detailing to her clothing, but she never accomplished anything close to what they had done.

"We'll see," says Jackson. "I'm usually a winner myself."

They cast their lines.

"Would you play some of that music you were playing earlier?" Jackson asks.

Skipper wonders if Carmen put him up to this, but Carmen says, "Oh, that. She's always playing it."

"I liked it," he says. "My mother was a musician. Her father was in a band. I wish I had that guitar. I love to sing, but I won't subject you to it. Like a fork on a plate, my mother used to say."

So Skipper switches on the speaker, and they listen to a song about a woman who wakes up alone, uncertain if she's the only one left on earth.

"It's nice to know someone else has felt the way you do, isn't it?" He blinks at Skipper with sad brown eyes, and she begins to understand what her sister likes about him.

A tug on the line saves her from replying. Carmen wakes from her doze. She springs to her feet and cheers as Skipper reels it in.

The herring on the other end is silver and whole, so long as Skipper ignores the patch of fur and second mouth. Skipper drops it in a bucket of water and sinks her line again.

"I told you Shimizu sisters always win." Carmen grins at Jackson.

"Well, if you're going to root for her, maybe you better go back to your own side," he says. His tone is sharp, and Skipper realizes he takes the competition seriously.

"It's not a big deal," says Carmen, ceasing her victory dance.

"You're sure acting like it is," says Jackson.

Skipper clears her throat. "Go again?"

This time, they don't talk as they wait. The air cools. The faint breeze leaves trails of gooseflesh on Skipper's arms. Carmen pulls her clothes back on. In the distance, the white pillowed clouds blossom into mushrooms.

Skipper catches another herring, and Jackson curses. This one has growths around its gills like cauliflower. The color reminds Skipper of the thing growing over Carmen's ribs, and Skipper throws it back, too squeamish to eat the poor creature.

"It's the fancy rod," says Carmen.

"No, she has the better position," says Jackson.

Skipper offers him some of her trash bait.

He wrinkles his nose and waves her off. "You won't want to eat fish you catch with that."

"It's fine," says Carmen. "We'll clean it."

"I'm not eating it."

Skipper catches a halibut, and Jackson snaps his rod in half and chucks it into the water.

They watch, stunned, as the painted wood recedes slowly behind them, but no one moves to retrieve it.

"I'll come over and help you clean the fish," says Carmen, stepping over the rail.

"I see how it is," says Jackson.

"What?"

"Forget it."

Skipper looks between the two of them.

"Come on," says Carmen.

The sisters go below. They fillet the fish together. It takes a long time, because they don't know how, and one of their kitchen knives is too large and the other too small. By the time they are halfway through, they can't cut for laughing so hard—about what, it doesn't matter.

Skipper's stuffed after so many meals, but Carmen insists on tossing the first fillet in flour and frying it. They haven't done the best job, so they spend a lot of time picking the bones out, which sets them laughing all over again. The fish is shockingly good: The flesh flakes off greasy and moist in their mouths.

They offer Jackson some over the radio, but he says he isn't hungry.

"He's sensitive," says Carmen. "He cares about everything. It's refreshing after Ollie."

Skipper doesn't want to talk about either of them. "I wish Nora were here."

"I guess," says Carmen, eyes flicking away.

"What happened between you? You used to be so close." It's something Skipper has wanted to ask for years. Out here, she can.

"She had too many secrets," Carmen says. "Ollie too. That's what I appreciate about you, Skip. You carry everything in your face."

Skipper turns away, thinking of the plans she had with Nora, the deal with Carmen's ex. What would Carmen say if she knew?

The wind picks up, and Jackson's boat becomes a blue blob on the horizon. Tonight, Skipper will have someone to swap watch with, and she's grateful for that.

They curl up under a blanket in the lee of the cockpit, and Carmen reads aloud from a novel about a woman solving a mystery in a seaside town with plenty of good food. As Skipper drifts off somewhere halfway through the second chapter, she wishes she could stretch this moment, wrapped in the comfort of her sister's company. If only they could go on like this.

CHAPTER SEVENTEEN

The next day, the winds return with a vengeance and a surprise, when they spot something on their radar.

It's a floating platform, one of those old, defunct deep-sea oil rigs, covered in huts. A fleet of boats bobs along a dock built between the stilts. They've found a village in the middle of the ocean.

Skipper hails over the radio but gets no response.

"We should be careful," Jackson calls over the water. "You never know who's out here."

"I see children," says Carmen, looking through Skipper's binoculars.

A lifeboat comes to meet them. Jackson retrieves his gun from the cabin and tucks it under one of *Leviathan*'s fancy seat cushions so he can reach it easily.

"What are you going to do?" Skipper asks.

"It never hurts to be prepared."

Skipper hands the radio to Carmen and luffs their sails.

The welcome party consists of a woman and two teenagers. They're pale with straw-colored hair. They wear long knives stuck in homemade sheaths at their hips, which makes Jackson nervous, but Carmen thinks he's overreacting.

The platformers shout a greeting, and their speech carries the accent of a distant island nation. Carmen finds it charming, but Skipper can barely understand what they're saying.

The platformers decide the three travelers aren't a threat, and their tone shifts. They smile and gesture for them to follow.

"What did they say?" Skipper whispers to Carmen.

"They want us to join them for a meal. They're open to trading us food and water if we need it."

"Watch out for that big gun," Jackson mutters over the radio. The metal barrel points down at them.

"That must be ancient," scoffs Carmen. "Anyway, they have a right to protect themselves."

"You're so naive, hon," says Jackson. "There are only two types of people left in this world: the ones who take or the ones being taken. These guys seem pretty comfortable."

Skipper rubs her neck. It would be simpler to move on, but she's too loyal to Carmen to say it.

"Let's see what they're offering," says Carmen.

"Fine," says Jackson. "But we stick together. I promised I would protect you."

"Of course," says Carmen.

They drop their sails and motor in. The dock is made of plastic jugs and wooden pallets strung together. The boats tied to the dock are even more eclectic than at first glance: yachts and fishing boats and sailboats like theirs. These people have amassed an impressive amount of gasoline, stored in tanks on the dock. They're rich.

Getting up to the platform requires riding in a makeshift elevator, a platform rigged with ropes that hangs from a crane. The woman nods encouragingly for them to climb on. Skipper clutches one of the ropes and positions herself close to the center. The lift jerks up.

At the top, the solidity of the platform is disconcerting after so much time on a boat. The view from the sky is breathtaking, though;

it is funny how the same ocean can look different from a new angle. The sun sets on the horizon in a splatter of yellows and oranges.

The platform has five levels. They've built out the top with houses made from the curved ribs of a yacht, walls of canvas sails and chopped-up decks. The houses ring the outside, arranged around an empty space in the middle like a town square, where the citizens of this scrappy settlement are currently eating dinner.

The woman invites them to join the line for a communal pot of chowder. As they wait, she observes Skipper and Carmen must be sisters, she can tell, and Skipper says, "You think?" and everyone around them agrees. Skipper's wariness melts away.

For so many years, people have told her the ways she is different from Nora and Carmen—in looks, in personality, in achievement. But this woman thinks it is obvious they are sisters.

The platformers ply them with terrible beer. They sit at tables and benches of all different sizes. Like everything else, the furniture has been ripped from boats. Someone plays a violin, another sings. It feels like a celebration, and Skipper is charmed by the happy, celebratory atmosphere, even when she is not clear what they're celebrating. Life, maybe. Food.

Their country experienced terrible famine driven by blight and scarcity of fish. They lived on their country's coast in those days, and their people began to sail farther and farther away in search of food. One day, in a bad storm, some of their sailors found this place. At the time it was still stocked with provisions, dishes long dried in the drying racks. When they made it back home, they decided to move out here.

"What do you eat?" Carmen asks. Like Skipper, she's measured the pink of their cheeks and the plumpness of their bodies.

"Whatever we can catch," the woman says. Skipper is beginning to understand her accent. "Mother Ocean provides." She shows them the body of a giant squid they caught that day draped over a butcher table, its tentacles long and damp from the ocean. They have smoking equipment too, and a makeshift freezer and pantry for whatever they've scavenged. "Sometimes we have to sail for food. Sometimes it comes to us. Our children learn to contribute from a young age. They become adults when they go out into the world and bring in their first catch for the village."

"I guess we're finally grown up, then." Carmen nudges Skipper with a smile.

"You can't find much meat out here," says Jackson, gesturing at the large, empty meat hooks.

"You'd be surprised."

"Bob found some sheep," a kid volunteers. He wears shorts and an old T-shirt, and every other bit of skin is covered in freckles.

"A ship with sheep," the woman clarifies.

"And they gave them to you?" Jackson asks.

Carmen elbows him, but the woman isn't offended. "We manage out here."

The chowder is milky and rich. A sheen of oil glistens on the surface, and Skipper skims it and licks it off her spoon.

Jackson loosens up and helps himself to seconds. He concedes these folks might just be folks. Anyway, who can judge how others live? It's not like he's proud of every chapter of his life.

After dinner, someone produces a white object about the size and shape of an egg. They take turns holding it as if in prayer, murmuring.

"What's that?" Skipper asks, but Jackson recognizes it.

"It's one of those know-it-all devices," he explains. "I haven't seen many of them before. How do you have one?"

The woman grins. "We're scavengers. Do you not have one?"

"No." Jackson sounds angry again. "They're extremely expensive."

The egg is passed to her, and she demonstrates how to use it. "Hold it like this and ask a question. Anything."

Jackson takes it, and quizzes it in quick succession: "What's the population of the world? What's the best way to make money?" And the egg miraculously responds with answers.

After a few minutes, the woman encourages him to pass it to Skipper. For a moment, Skipper thinks he won't let go. His big fingers curl over hers, awkward and intimate. He says, "I wish I had one of these."

The egg is soft and pliant. Skipper tastes lemons and hears the sound of a piano. Something gently massages her scalp.

"What's the weather this week?"

The egg rattles off information: humidity and likelihood of rain. It confirms a storm is on the way, and the updated numbers make her nervous. It will be followed by clear skies for days after. The magic of the device leaves her breathless. She memorizes what she can, to jot in her logbook later.

Carmen asks the egg: "What do you know about the vault?"

"The vault is a tightly controlled community managed by Renewal Corporation. Because of the value of its contents, security is considered of premium importance. Visitation must be authorized in advance and is highly discouraged. Arrivals and departures are heavily screened by local authorities."

"Ah. So you're heading to the vault?" says the woman.

Skipper can tell Carmen wasn't thinking when she asked the question. Up until now, their mission felt secret, though Skipper doesn't see the harm in this case.

"It's dangerous this time of year because of storms and ice," says their host. "And they're not welcoming to strangers." She wrinkles her nose.

Jackson reaches for the egg again. "Come on. You don't mind, do you? I never tried one of these before. It's really something, isn't it?"

They decide to sleep tied up at the dock and get a good night's rest and breakfast tomorrow, the whispers and creaking of the joints of the makeshift structure its own lullaby. The platformers offered to let them stay to ride out the storm here, but Skipper is anxious to get ahead of it. This was their compromise: One night, Carmen argues, won't change anything.

Skipper expects Carmen to sleep over on *Leviathan*, but Carmen slips back in as Skipper is drifting off.

"He snores," she says, which cheers Skipper immensely. Skipper's last thought is the peacefulness of a warm, full belly, and what she'll say to Nora when they find her.

She wakes in the middle of the night to one of the teenagers standing over her, sharp knife drawn. His face is red in the cabin light. In that moment, she learns her body can move even when her brain is frozen.

Whatever we can catch, the woman said. The platformers are pirates.

Skipper scrambles back and gets her pillow between them just in time. The force of the blow comes down. The tip of the blade bites her shoulder, and she finally remembers to scream.

He dives forward, crushing her with his body, and jabs the blade again. She blocks his wrist with her own, and the tip of the blade kisses her thumb and collarbone. Then she scissors and kicks and catches him in the thigh and groin, and he rolls over, wheezing.

She could try to escape out the forward hatch, but that would mean abandoning Carmen. Instead, she throws herself past her attacker, slamming into the head wall, then scrambles through the narrow passage to the common area where Carmen sleeps.

Carmen's not in her bunk. She's a light sleeper, and she must have woken up when they came in and grabbed an oar from the wall. She's fending off a second attacker in the kitchen area near the cabin stairs. The new lock to the hatch lies broken on the floor along with a pair of bolt cutters.

Skipper snatches up the other oar as her own assailant comes after her. Now four of them are wedged together in the dark, compact space.

"We don't have anything valuable," Skipper says, batting away the boy's knife. "We don't have anything."

"You have the meat on your body," says the boy. "That's why Mother Ocean brought you here." He jabs again, and Skipper narrowly blocks him.

Carmen accidentally snaps the pantry door with the back of the oar, and cans and jars rain down on her and her attacker. Carmen's attacker stumbles back, and Skipper hollers for her to grab the kitchen knife from its magnetic strip. Carmen fumbles for it—

A loud bang erupts in Skipper's ear, and she realizes in a daze that Jackson stands at the entranceway, gun drawn. She can't hear on one side beyond a high-pitch ringing, and she smells blood. Where is it coming from? She's spattered and wet, but feels no pain beyond her shoulder. She's okay, but he shot the boy, oh God, he shot him.

There's another bang, and Skipper flinches with her whole body.

Jackson doesn't wait for either of their assailants to collapse. He grabs Carmen's attacker, who is clutching her side, rips the knife from her, and drags her up the narrow stairs.

"Get the kid," he shouts. As he goes, he takes Skipper's emergency jug of biofuel that cost her weeks of work.

And Skipper wishes he hadn't used that word, "kid," because now she has to look at the boy lying on the kitchen floor with half of the back of his skull blown off and the blood seeping out around him in a widening pool. Carmen whimpers, but she and Skipper grab his legs and arms and haul him down the aisle between the bunks and up the stairs.

The boy's necklace catches on a cleat and snaps, and it clatters to the deck.

They hear a splash and a cry—Jackson dropped the woman into the water where she struggles in vain not to drown.

More people run toward them from the lift. It's a good thing it can only fit a few people at a time. The dock is a branching mess, about ten *Bumblebee*s long, and they have maybe thirty seconds before the reinforcements reach them.

"We can talk to them," says Carmen.

"There's no talking," Jackson says. "Let's go."

The sisters roll the boy onto the jury-rigged dock.

They're going to have to jump out and untie the knot from the cleat, but the pirates are almost upon them. Carmen is closer, but she's staring in horror at the boy's body.

Skipper jumps down.

Bang! goes Jackson's gun, and *bang!* again.

Jackson shoots from the deck of *Leviathan*, tied up next to them. People scream and run back toward the elevator.

He keeps shooting.

"Stop!" shouts Skipper. "They're running!" But he reloads when he runs out of bullets and goes on firing.

Skipper doesn't want to be here anymore. She wants to be anywhere else.

She unties both boats, glad her fingers know the knots even when she can't see what she's doing.

A sweet, sulfuric smell fills her nose. Her ears are still ringing, and she can't hear the water splashing against the dock or tell if Jackson hits anyone. She hears Carmen call her name as if from underwater.

Skipper shoves the *Bumblebee* hard and leaps after it, clearing the rail. She shouts for Carmen to get the engine. They motor away, not even waiting to see if Jackson follows.

Carmen clutches the tiller, sobbing, but manages to rev the engine to the max. Smears of blood paint the deck. Some of it, Skipper realizes dizzily, is hers, and the copper scent of it makes her gag.

There's a dull boom, accompanied by a spray of water as something hits the surface near them—the pirates are firing the ancient gun from the top of the platform. Carmen screams and swerves to starboard, dousing Skipper in icy water.

Skipper dives into the cabin and kills their running lights, hoping it's enough for them to blend in. The gun sounds again, but then the firing stops, overcome maybe with age.

The radar shows only two boats following them. The sisters make the most of the head start.

When they're far away, Skipper risks hoisting the sails.

Her shoulder throbs with pain. Salt water stings her wounds, and blood soaks through her T-shirt, accentuating the cold air. She shivers and grits her teeth to keep them from chattering.

The wind increased overnight into something wild. It tosses them about. Skipper hopes the conditions will dissuade a heavy pursuit, because she doesn't think the *Bumblebee* can outrun an entire fleet.

"Oh no," says Carmen.

The makeshift part of the dock they had moored to is on fire. The bright orange-blue flames burn an afterimage in Skipper's eyes, and a column of smoke climbs into the sky, blotting out a wedge of the night. As it breaks apart, Skipper remembers the jug of biofuel Jackson took from her.

Leviathan roars behind them. With her expensive engine, she catches up quickly.

They watch the fire devour the wooden dock, until it reaches the tanks of gasoline stored below the platform. There's a loud boom and bright flash, and then again, and again. The explosions reverberate across the water.

Skipper lifts her binoculars with shaking hands. The fire lights up the night enough to show the platform is unscathed, but many of the boats are on fire, and the dock under the platform disintegrates in slow motion.

On the radar, the boats following them turn back.

They watch in silence as they go, because they are the only ones here to witness what they've done.

CHAPTER EIGHTEEN

They flee through freezing rain. On her first watch, Skipper finds the kid's necklace in the cockpit, snapped in half. She carries it into the cabin, wiping water from her eyes.

"What's that?" Carmen asks.

Skipper can't speak, because now that she's inside she can see it clearly, and her throat closes around the words. She holds it out to Carmen, begging her to take it.

A full set of human molars and incisors are strung together so they clack against each other.

Carmen yelps, and, realizing what she holds, drops it on the table. "Ugh." She rubs her arms and torso as if to scrub away her revulsion.

"Should we toss it overboard?" Skipper asks, finding her voice.

"Let's wait. I want to show Jackson."

Skipper doesn't know why they need to, but as long as Carmen deals with it, she doesn't care.

They take turns above deck. As they swap hot tea for rough weather gear, Skipper longs for the fireplace back home, the warm blankets, and her soft bed. She hopes Uncle Tot remembers to put an extra pair of socks on Grandma's feet at night.

Outside, Jackson's singing carries through the wind. He must have better foul weather gear. Or maybe he's drinking.

When Skipper returns above, he chirps, "Hello!" over the radio, and his cheer is more shocking than the ocean spray.

"How are you in a good mood?" she asks.

"I'm grateful we're alive. Aren't you? Thank God."

Jackson has found the adventure he came for.

Skipper can't stop thinking about the glint of his teeth as he fired his gun. He saved their lives, but the memory curdles her insides.

When Carmen replaces her, Skipper climbs under a blanket until her violent shivers subside. Then she forces herself out of bed to resume scrubbing brain and blood off the floor. She wishes they'd never left home. For the first time, she feels a tendril of resentment toward Nora, who's knocked their normal lives so far off course.

She estimates their position and hopes she is right. The barometer bottoms out, a portent of worse weather to come.

At least they're getting farther away from the pirates. The village has long since disappeared beyond the horizon.

Skipper and Carmen eat dinner together, hip to hip and thigh to thigh under the blanket, passing a pot of beans between them. Skipper thinks she'd eat anything but beans for the rest of her life. She tries not to show her nervousness about the wind howling outside, because Carmen is already scared.

"Do you think this is what Grandma imagined when she gave us this boat?"

"Grandma just wanted us out of the house," says Carmen.

Skipper's gaze drifts back to the hole in the hull near her bunk made by one of Jackson's bullets.

"You have to admit, it's a good thing Jackson came with us," says Carmen, licking her spoon.

The hole looks like a cat if Skipper squints at it. "I can't believe he burned everything."

"We don't know how much was destroyed," says Carmen, as if not knowing protects them from guilt.

They did what they needed to, to get away. Skipper does believe that. And maybe there isn't such a thing as right. Nora would say every living thing wants to live. It's millions of years of success. It's extracting minerals from the earth and pulling flesh from the sea. It's building a house and erecting glass between you and the insects outside. It's making sure you and your family have water and food and a house and electricity before you look to your neighbor. You will fight them if you have to.

It wouldn't be normal to say, *Here is my throat for you to eat.* No animal would submit to death like that, and Skipper wants to live. So does Jackson.

And yet, she hates understanding she will do these things, or watch Jackson do these things. That she is, in the end, like any other creature.

"What's your problem with him now?" Carmen asks.

"He didn't hesitate," says Skipper. "And now he's acting like it was nothing."

"You are unbelievable," Carmen says. She gets up to drop the pot in the sink with a clatter, and Skipper mourns the loss of her sister's body heat. "You never like anyone I date. And don't even *try* to say you liked Ollie."

"I didn't," says Skipper. "But she wouldn't have shot someone cold and been singing the next day. Anyway, you're dating Jackson?"

"I haven't decided, but that's not the point."

"Maybe I don't like them because they aren't good enough for you."

Carmen scrubs the pot, and the *sha-sha-sha-sha-sha* punctuates the thick silence.

"It's been four weeks," says Skipper.

"What?"

"The moratorium. You said we wouldn't talk about Ollie for four weeks. It's been more than a month. So. What happened?"

"That's all it's been? God." Carmen stops scrubbing and stares at the clock on the wall. "It feels like it's been a year."

She rinses the pot and fixes some tea, and Skipper can tell she is stalling. "Well?"

"Does it matter? I was done with her a while ago; I didn't know it."

"She made you miserable," says Skipper, thinking of the times she stopped in and found her sister crying on the sofa.

"Because you're an expert. I loved her," says Carmen. Then she stops. Sets down the pot. "I didn't know you knew. Did everyone know?"

"I don't know."

The ship bucks under them, and Carmen throws back a motion-sickness pill. "You're trying to distract me from the storm, aren't you? Fine. I came home one night, and Ollie was having beers on the front porch with some guy."

"She cheated on you?" Skipper says, outraged, but Carmen holds up a hand.

"It was a business discussion. This man traded in food and other goods. Went around to towns and bought stuff to sell down in the city."

Carmen sits next to Skipper and gestures for her to take off her shirt, and she cleans and rubs ointment into the knife wounds. The sharp scent of alcohol fills the room. Skipper hisses from the pain.

"But they weren't having sex," says Skipper.

"No. They were talking about her business idea."

"The muffins?" Skipper asks.

"No, the mitten lights."

"I didn't get that one."

"I know."

"Wouldn't a headlamp be better?"

"Skip!" says Carmen, capping the pot of ointment with finality. "She stole your mussels."

"What?"

"I'm sorry. She told the guy about them and arranged for him to come and take everything. I told her you were saving them for Nora. That it was a science project or whatever. She said, 'Well, that's ridiculous. Someone in this family has to be financially responsible. Skipper can't just eat them.' So she found a buyer, and she sold them. She was going to buy some equipment for her new business. Anyway, when I found out, it was too late."

Skipper gapes at her sister. "But money wasn't the point."

"I know," says Carmen.

A realization seizes Skipper. "The jar of money. I wondered where you got so much."

Carmen winces. "Yeah, well. We couldn't have gotten this far without it."

"You had no right. You should have stopped her," Skipper says.

"I tried. I told her not to. She didn't listen to me."

"But you could have told *me*. I would have talked to her."

"That wouldn't have stopped her," says Carmen. "I didn't want you to think—I don't know."

"You *don't* know," Skipper says, and then, because she's upset, she finally tells Carmen about the generator scheme, and her corrupt bargain with Ollie. She can see Carmen's anger building by the way she's so calm on the surface.

"I can't believe you," says Carmen, and Skipper isn't sure which part she can't believe. Maybe it's the whole of Skipper, that Carmen realizes now there are things she doesn't know about her. Something bursts inside Skipper, because this is what she's been trying to tell Carmen all along. That she's more than what they think of her, this person she can never fully be when she's on land.

Carmen gets up again and begins to wipe down the kitchen, and Skipper wishes she'd sit for once so they could really talk, so she could understand what Carmen is saying.

"You're right. I never liked her. You brought her to my graduation, which I thought was weird, by the way. I don't know why you did that. And she said my outfit made me look like a duck, and then Grandma agreed with her and lectured me about how I dressed generally, and it was like, every single person in my life was standing there, including you and Uncle Tot, laughing at me. As if we could have afforded to order new clothes. And I remember how I felt. I felt small. On a day that was supposed to be a great moment of my life. If *Nora* had been there, she would have said something."

"No," says Carmen. "She wouldn't have. She didn't even bother to come home for it. I hate when you say things like that. You've always thought Nora is better than us, like she is this special, perfect person. But she isn't, okay? Maybe luckier. That's all."

"She's brilliant," says Skipper.

"So fucking what?" says Carmen. "So are you."

The rain drums against the window, and Skipper wonders what Jackson is doing in his boat by himself.

"I broke up with her," says Carmen. "What else do you want from me?"

"Because she didn't listen to you?"

"No! What are you talking about? Because she was shitty. She was shitty to you. And you lied to me. So I guess we're even."

Skipper tucks her head down. She doesn't want to be even. This far away, in the middle of the ocean, none of this should matter. But it does.

"Nora's okay, isn't she?" Skipper asks.

"Yeah," says Carmen, and Skipper knows this is just the lie she asked for, the thing one sister says to another, but she's grateful.

CHAPTER NINETEEN

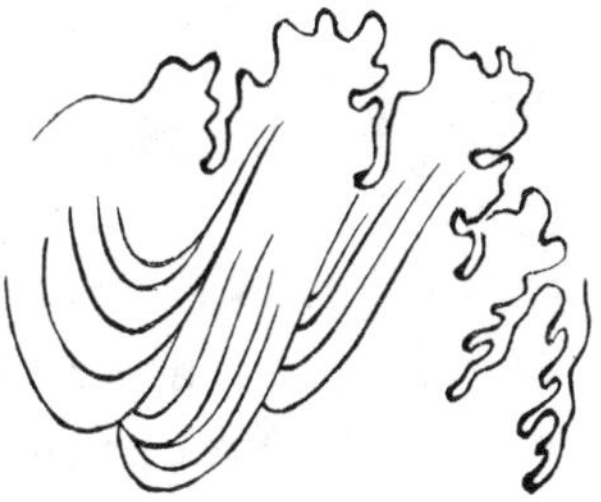

The storm arrives the next night while Skipper catches a nap during Carmen's watch. The boat pitches so much, Skipper narrowly avoids concussing herself against the bulkhead. A loose mug tumbles out of the drying rack and shatters against the floor. Skipper jumps over it, hauling herself above deck to assess conditions.

"You should have woken me up!" Skipper checks Carmen's harness before she scrambles to drop the jib. She is fast, terror and muscle memory fueling the motion of her arms.

In the distance, rain and heavy winds pummel *Leviathan*. Her sails aren't reefed enough, and Jackson is nowhere in sight.

Skipper seizes the radio. "Jackson!" No answer. He must have fallen asleep.

She can't hear anything over the howling wind. *Leviathan* crests an enormous wave and smashes down hard into the trough. The next wave washes over the boat. It broaches, the top of the mast slicing through water and the whole keel momentarily exposed.

Carmen grips the tiller, eyes wide with terror.

Skipper tries the radio again. "*Leviathan.* Come in, *Leviathan.*"

No answer.

"Keep hailing him," she tells Carmen, taking the helm. She hits the next wave at forty-five degrees, and then rides the back side of it to avoid the same violence that's beset *Leviathan*.

Leviathan broaches again, and this time, the main sail tears off. The boom has snapped.

"Jackson!" Carmen screams into the radio.

"I'm in deep shit," Jackson says.

Skipper sucks in a breath. Carmen stands next to her so they can both hear him.

"It's that damn bilge pump," he says. The cockiness in his voice doesn't quite mask his fear. "What a hack job. I should have replaced the entire thing."

Skipper can't feel her face. She's freezing and numb, and each time a wave crashes over them, she gets a mouthful of ocean.

Without its main sail, *Leviathan* turns violently in the water. The shredded jib flaps wildly back and forth across the bow. The distance between the two boats shrinks.

The *Bumblebee* thrums with power. Water washes over the bow of the *Bumblebee* again and again.

Lightning cracks down too close for comfort.

When *Leviathan* rights on the next crest, Jackson appears on deck.

"What are you doing?" Carmen asks, but he must have left his radio below.

He clutches his head, staring at the broken boom and torn sail, maybe remembering *Leviathan* isn't his. Worse, he's not wearing his harness. Or maybe in his supreme confidence, he doesn't think he needs one.

She watches everything in slow motion: the way his feet slide across the slick deck, the rain lashing his bare chest and legs. A swell rears up behind him. A gust of wind pushes the still-hoisted jib, and *Leviathan* rolls again. Skipper can see Jackson clinging to the side. It's a miracle he isn't lost overboard.

Carmen's jaw stretches open, and she screams, but Skipper can't hear the sound.

They're close enough that Skipper has to angle to stay clear of the other boat.

Leviathan hits another enormous swell, and the bigger boat rights itself. Jackson scrambles to his feet. He disappears below deck.

A moment later, they hear him shriek over the radio: "This boat is fucked!"

Carmen grabs Skipper's elbow. Another wave sloshes over them, leaving them both sputtering. Skipper wants to heave to and go below. Boats, properly sailed, are designed to float, and she trusts the *Bumblebee.*

"What's happening?" Skipper radios, surfing down another tall wave. The ocean has become hills, and they lose sight of *Leviathan*. They wait for his reply.

When they see it again, they can tell there's a problem. *Leviathan* sits decidedly lower in the water and lists like a drunken thing.

"I think the hull cracked," says Jackson. "I'm knee-deep in water."

"He's going to sink," Carmen says, gripping Skipper's arm.

A rescue operation would be dangerous. She would be putting them and the *Bumblebee* at risk. If something happens to Carmen or her boat, she will never forgive him. She'll never forgive herself.

"We have to do something," Carmen says. "Skipper? What do we do?"

Skipper makes a decision.

"Prep the dinghy." She maneuvers windward of *Leviathan*, shouting as they come abreast of the bigger boat, but her voice is snatched up by the roaring wind.

"I need to get off. Fuck. *Fuck!*" shouts Jackson.

"We're coming." She moves into position and gestures for Carmen to take the tiller.

"Wait," says Carmen, face full of panic.

"We've got this," Skipper tells her. "Stay clear and play out the line until I'm close enough to grab him."

They deploy the dinghy. Skipper's heart hammers as she jumps into it. Carmen lets out the line attached to the dinghy until Skipper's close. The waves grow even bigger. There's no sign of Jackson on deck, and he's not answering the radio.

"Come on!" she shouts. He doesn't appear. Skipper begins to count.

The next bolt of lightning is closer than the last. The air smells electric.

"Forty-two," she says.

At forty-seven, Jackson reappears, carrying a grab bag.

She has Carmen extend the line. He tosses his bag into the dinghy. It thumps heavy against the boat, and she wonders what the hell he has in it. She has to give him credit for his aim.

The next wave comes and sweeps him off the deck.

Skipper hurls the flotation device into the water where she last saw him. He surfaces and swims hard for the orange-and-white ring. Once he has it, she pulls him to her, grabs him by both arms, and they both struggle, as if his goal is to drag her into the water with him. Then he's in the boat, Carmen reeling them in.

Together they heave him aboard, soaked and blue.

"Get him warm," Skipper orders Carmen.

"Got it."

The two of them stagger below while Skipper takes the tiller, charged with adrenaline.

The storm rages, but they've reached the eye of it. The winds and waves calm somewhat.

Leviathan is nearly gone. Its colored lights glimmer like some hungry ghost beneath the surface of the water. Skipper's headlight illuminates all that's left: the top of the mast and the flag of their diminished nation on top.

And then it is swallowed, and nothing remains.

Once, when they were younger, the three of them were caught out on the water in a sudden squall. The wind picked up, and the bright sky went dark, like someone extinguished the sun. Nora clutched the tiller. A line came loose, and Nora told Carmen to get it. But Carmen froze.

So Skipper climbed up onto the deck, riding the huge waves. Laughing at first, because she was that scared. She couldn't stop laughing. She thought she could do anything. The next moment, a huge curtain of water rushed over her, and she was swept off the top of the boat into the cold ocean.

In seconds, the *Bumblebee* was out of reach. She tried to swim, but the boat kept lurching farther away. Her sisters were screaming. At least Skipper was wearing a life jacket. Her sodden clothes and shoes slowed her strokes.

The boom swung around and hit Nora in the head, and Skipper cried out, but she was helpless to do anything. Nora fell back, stunned.

And Carmen did nothing, just wailed and clung to the cockpit.

It was Nora who saved her, Nora who staggered up and managed to come back around. Skipper swam the gap and hauled herself into the boat. She'll never quite know how, but she did. She helped Nora drop the sails and waited for the storm to pass.

Years later, Skipper thinks about this. And she thinks, *I take care of things. That's what you never give me credit for, when you go on about how I need to act like an adult and stick up for myself with Grandma and move out of that awful house. As if I couldn't do all those things if I wanted to.*

Because the point is, she's been the one doing the hard things all along. She stayed when everyone else left. She was the one who decided to go after Nora. And when she finds her sister, she'll go home and sell her boat like she promised, because she might be stubborn, but she understands the cost of love.

Hours later, she ducks below to catch her breath. The air in the cabin smells of salt and damp, but it's warmer than above. Jackson lies swaddled in a blanket on the third unused bunk. Nora's bunk. Carmen rubs him all over as the tea kettle whistles.

"Well," he says to Skipper. "I guess we're even." She doesn't know what he means. As if this is a competition.

"I'm sorry about your boat," she says.

"Eh." He coughs until watery spit comes up from his lungs. "Wasn't mine anyway. I'll get another."

Carmen pauses her ministrations.

Don't ask, Skipper thinks at her, because some things are better not to discuss when everything in the room is tumbling around.

Carmen catches her gaze and closes her mouth.

"I've been having nightmares of drowning," he says. "Of being in the middle of the ocean without a boat. And then tonight I woke up, and the ship was making these awful noises and tossing me around, and I thought, well, Jackson, this is it. The nightmare has come to life to drag you to the bottom of the sea. I thought I was going to die tonight. Do you believe in visions?"

"No," says Carmen, and Jackson snorts.

"I don't think you have a romantic bone in your body," he tells her, pulling her down until she squirms. He is thrilled to be alive.

The observation amuses Skipper. But it is true, Carmen is practical to a fault. Except for her taste in romantic partners.

Jackson's presence is like a weight in his corner of the cabin. It isn't the physical space, but the heavy quality of his energy. He sucks half the cabin's air into his lungs every time he takes a breath. The narrow space is hotter and stuffier than before.

The sisters aren't used to men in their house.

Well. Despite her worries, he is on the boat now, and they will have to manage it.

CHAPTER TWENTY

The storm eases before dawn, leaving them to pick up the pieces. Skipper takes a sighting with her sextant. In her head, she imagines all the possible triangles they may have traversed in the night.

"Well?" Carmen asks, as Skipper labors over calculations.

"I don't think it's as bad as I thought." They're about two weeks from the vault or a third of the way.

The *Bumblebee* has gotten through the storm fairly well. If not for Jackson's presence, the recent nightmare might not have happened. Poor *Leviathan*. She deserved a better captain.

Jackson remains below, dead asleep. He must be exhausted from sailing single-handed and the ordeal of the previous night. He doesn't stir as they eat watery porridge and dried fruit.

They inspect the boat in the soft rain and clean up the aftermath together, as they did all those years ago when they fixed up the boat in the first place.

Carmen takes stock of their inventory. They may have enough

food and water if they're careful. The *Bumblebee* is stocked with enough for two, but with three onboard, it'll be a stretch. Skipper regrets not filling her tanks when it was raining, and she knows she'll regret it more if they run out.

When the clouds clear and the sun emerges, the blue sky feels enormous. Skipper sets about charging everything. She hasn't slept since the previous evening, and when Carmen relieves her, she crawls into her bunk and passes out immediately.

She wakes up shivering, the sun already setting. Jackson continues to sleep, curled up in his too-small bunk. Carmen was right. He *does* snore. It's not that he doesn't have a right to sleep, but he takes up so much space.

Skipper takes back the helm, and Carmen announces she'll make an early dinner, because Jackson is awake and hungry. She brings Skipper a cup of instant noodles, and it's the best thing Skipper has ever eaten, because it's not beans.

Jackson appears above deck a couple of hours later, carrying a thermos of tea to share, and Skipper's shirt. To her surprise, he mended it where the knife slashed her.

"You even got the blood out," she says.

"Years of experience." He laughs at Skipper's face. "Not like that. Working in an Amaranthine factory. Now, those stains will haunt you. My stain remover is a family recipe." He tosses Skipper the shirt.

He sits next to Carmen in the cockpit and throws an arm around her.

"You almost died saving your stain remover?" Carmen giggles.

"Well, and this." Jackson rifles around in his grab bag and comes up with a round, white object.

"What's that?" Carmen asks, but they know. Skipper's skin tingles in recognition when he squeezes it—it's the pirate's device.

"You stole it," Skipper says with growing horror.

"It wasn't theirs to begin with," says Jackson, continuing to fiddle with it.

"That's why they attacked us."

"Don't be silly. They hadn't realized it was gone yet."

But now Skipper isn't sure. She was happier thinking they were unprovoked.

He grabs the boy's necklace of human teeth from his pocket and shakes it at her, and Skipper is even more outraged he kept it, as if it's his trophy. "This is why they attacked us."

She doesn't want to look at it. Her insides churn in disgust.

"Put that away," Carmen says. "Please."

"Okay, but it's true." He turns back to the egg. "Anyway, this thing is amazing. We can send messages. It can tell us exactly where we are, so you don't have to do all your complicated calculations. I bet it can even help find your sister." His lack of remorse is shocking. It doesn't escape Skipper that he's waited until now to share it with them.

"But—" Skipper reddens, too upset to articulate what she wants to say.

"You shouldn't have done that," says Carmen, frowning.

"Oh, relax you two." Jackson laughs. "What are they going to do, call the police?"

"That's not the point."

He finally absorbs the mood. "You're so uptight. You can't survive if you follow every rule. Well, wake up. The system is rigged. Renewal and the government and everyone else are out for their own survival. And I refuse to let anyone tell me how to live. If you want something, go for it." His lips curl back in an expression that might have been intended as a smile, but it's more a snarl. He slams his palm against the deck by Carmen's head. "Or sink."

The sisters flinch.

"The country that makes these is rich while we struggle with famine and power failure. It should be us. Our country used to be the wealthiest in the world. We invented this technology. We deserve it."

He disappears into the cabin, leaving Skipper and Carmen in his wake.

"What an asshole," says Skipper at last.

Carmen says nothing for once, just presses her lips together and stares at the water.

The air in the cabin sours. Whenever one of them goes down there, they have to step around Jackson's long legs hanging off the edge of his bunk or stand next to him while he eats their food at their table. He really does remind her of a bear, the way he opens his jaws wide to take his monstrous bites, the size of his hands as they cup the egg.

She was already aware of his size. Most of the time, he seems as easygoing as he was when they first met him, but there's a tense energy winding tighter and tighter underneath the surface.

There's no escape on a boat in the ocean. She dreads his gaze, the way it pins her to whatever corner she folds herself into while she reheats beans or boils rice.

They're all cranky from lack of food and sleep.

What Carmen doesn't point out, but Skipper thinks she should, is Jackson eats and drinks a lot more than they do. It's cold, but he sits in the cabin perspiring like it's summer, and she resents every drop of sweat, because it means he'll drink even more water.

Skipper hopes for rain like she never has before. She obsesses over her barometer and tries to divine weather in the clouds, which remain an ambling herd of sheep in the sky.

They debate detouring to a country to the southeast of them for provisions, but it would add at least a week and take them back in the direction of the pirates.

Jackson rubs his beard. "I guess three is a problem."

"I'm sure we'd have other problems if you weren't here," Carmen says generously.

"Yeah, actually, you'd be dinner if I weren't here." He laughs.

The egg consumes a huge amount of energy. There's a reason no one uses these devices back home. A couple of times, Jackson bleeds their ship batteries dry, leaving them without electricity to cook. They knock around the cabin in their headlamps.

"You have to limit your use," Carmen tells him on the third day.

"Fine," he says, but he doesn't. He does share weather forecasts, at least. He also claims he's in communication with the friend of a friend who works in the vault. "This thing they're plotting, it's going to be big." He makes it sound like all they are waiting for is his arrival. He claims he asked them about Nora, that they've promised to help them, but they have no information about how she is. Skipper thinks he's lying, but she doesn't know if it's about their sister or everything. She takes the scraps of information he parcels out and pretends to be grateful.

When she was young, she believed it was possible for people to reach a point of knowing everything, that there was a golden peak ahead for human enlightenment. Not that the perfect future would happen in her lifetime, but that's what people like Nora were working toward.

But it's a lie. People built a cliff and ran right off it. Like weather, for example. For all the meddling and engineering, the weather person can't promise clear skies tomorrow with 100 percent certainty. These days, Skipper believes they only know less as time goes on.

They split the day into four-hour shifts and take turns. Except Carmen wants Skipper to keep her company, and she seems to think Skipper wants the same. Or maybe Carmen is tiring of Jackson.

He talks and talks. The infinite flow of his speech is remarkable. He is the sort of person who thinks thoughts are unfinished unless expressed out loud. He must be, Skipper concludes, one of the loneliest people she has ever met. He doesn't think anyone can understand him, so he tries to explain himself from every angle.

"My sister was so annoying," Jackson tells them, as he gnaws at the core of their last apple. Skipper can't help but watch him, mouth yearning for the juice of it. "She made sure I never got away with anything. I couldn't shoplift a piece of candy without her telling Dad. Older sisters are the worst. I bet Nora was like that, eh?"

She focuses on adjusting the sails. "She wasn't."

Carmen props her shoes on the tiller.

"Don't do that," says Skipper.

Carmen laughs. "Nora loved her secrets. When we were growing up, she would go hide in the woods with a book for the whole day. It took us a year to figure out she was going to this abandoned container she'd made into a secret fort."

They followed her one day. It was Carmen's idea, but she was afraid of getting lost. Too many creatures that could eat you, she warned

Skipper, like mutant coyotes or giant flesh-eating bog turtles. Those things existed, but it was the mosquitoes that were deadly, according to Nora, because they carried diseases that could eat a person up on the inside.

"She decorated it like a house," Carmen explains to Jackson. "I cried for a day, because I thought she was going to abandon us with Grandma. Which, eventually, she did."

Skipper frowns at the dissonance between her version of Nora and Carmen's. "I don't blame her. Nora protected us from our grandmother when we were growing up. Like, one time, Grandma was upset because I hadn't done my homework, so she told me I couldn't leave the kitchen table until I finished my math worksheet. Except I didn't know how to do it. I sat there until I peed my pants. After Grandma went to sleep, I was still sitting there, until Nora came and made me go to bed."

"I tried to help you with the worksheet," says Carmen. "But it was like you wanted to prove something. You were always so stubborn."

"I was scared," says Skipper.

"No, you were mad," says Carmen. "And I was the one who made you hot milk and washed your clothes."

"The next morning, Nora told Grandma to leave me alone, and they had a big fight."

"Which made things worse. She almost kicked Nora out of the house, favorite grandchild or not," says Carmen. "The best way to deal with Grandma is to apologize or ignore her, but the two of you had too much pride."

"Absolutely," says Jackson, which is his way of changing the subject so he can talk about himself.

The temperature drops sharply, but Jackson's used all the electricity again, so they're forced to eat cold, leftover rice porridge. Ice forms on the deck, and Skipper spends half her watch knocking it off with a rubber hammer. She once again appreciates Anika's help with their preparations.

Jackson is an hour late taking over his shift, and when Skipper goes down to the cabin to thaw, it's freezing, and she can't even boil water for tea.

Carmen huddles in Skipper's bed trying to keep warm, and Skipper wonders if she slept there to avoid sleeping across from Jackson.

Skipper considers the lump her sister makes under the blankets, then goes and cuts the electricity to most of the cabin outlets so Jackson can't charge the egg.

Later, when he finds out, he flies into a rage, storming out of the cabin to the cockpit where the sisters sit on the bench. He hurls obscenities in Skipper's face. She smells liquor on his breath; he must have had some in his bag. She's impressed and appalled by all the things he managed to bring with him when he abandoned ship.

"You don't fucking trust me after I fucking saved your life?" he says.

"We saved *your* life!" says Skipper.

"I should have let them eat you," he says.

Carmen steps between them and puts a hand on his chest. "Calm down, babe."

He bats her away. "Don't manage me. Bitch." Carmen and Skipper back up a step as he looms.

Then he exhales, and it's like a string cut. He collapses on the cockpit bench. "I'm sorry. That was out of line. It's being stuck in this little boat. I need space. I'm claustrophobic."

"It's okay," says Carmen, even though it isn't.

"This is a nightmare," Skipper hisses to her after he goes back into the cabin.

"We're two thirds of the way. It's the long sea voyage. It's hard on everyone," says Carmen, squeezing Skipper's shoulder, as if everything is fine, like this is normal behavior. "We just need to get there." This is so Carmen, always trying to avoid conflict.

Skipper sighs and thinks about using Jackson's egg to check on Uncle Tot, but she's not about to ask Jackson now. A twinge of guilt tightens her throat, but she finds the farther they get, the less she feels it, as if she's been shedding her responsibilities scale by scale.

Jackson bangs up the cabin stairs. "There's something on the radar!" He snatches the binoculars from Carmen. "I think it's land!"

That can't be. There's nothing on the map.

Skipper takes the binoculars.

It isn't land, but it is something almost as familiar to Skipper. It's a gigantic patch of trash floating in the water, ten times bigger than the one back home, and Skipper's heart expands like she could float.

CHAPTER TWENTY-ONE

Plastic sludge appears on the surface of the water, a vanguard of the patch. Then solitary bits of trash. A plastic bottle, a shoe, a ring of six Os that signifies nothing. A bounty for the worm factories.

Skipper gets out a fine net and scoops one-handed, letting the water drip out so all that's left is slime.

She imagines all the animals that ever roamed the earth, the age of dinosaurs, the age of the mammoth. And the ground full of bones slowly turning to black oil. And then the age when everything was made of plastic, because it was cheap and plentiful. And now this, a smear across the water, the residue of greatness.

"How much is that worth?" Jackson asks, eyes gleaming as she shakes the contents into a mesh-bottomed bucket.

Skipper doesn't have to think about it. "A pound of this could buy a sandwich."

Jackson rocks back on his heels, disappointed. "That's a lot of work for not a lot of money."

Skipper ignores him. She scans for the treasure, and she finds it a while later, a shifting island of solid debris floating in the soup.

"What is all this?" marvels Carmen.

It is the detritus of everything that has ever been loved and bought and consumed by people. It is twenty-five cent bouncy balls, the lid that comes on cups of coffee bought harried in a rush from a café, cheap earphones that broke almost immediately for no reason, cat toys, dog toys, sex toys, fidget toys, baby toys, water bottles, suitcase wheels, an infinite number of pens running out of ink at the moment its user needed to write, telephones with curly cords, flip phones, smartphones and the oversized boxes they came in, clocks that never got someone somewhere when they needed to be there, microwaves, hangers, rubber duckies, packaging from favorite snacks, jewelry bought by teenagers with the first money they earned themselves, slime, food containers, picture frames, trophies painted gold to look like metal, magnets, key chains, just one shoe, battered license plates from first cars, high heels that ended up being too painful to wear but looked fabulous once, little bottles of shampoo from one-night stays in hotels, pill organizers, ukuleles bought on a whim, spoons, forks, knives, chopsticks, bridal shower souvenirs, yoga mats, takeout containers, flat-screen televisions, rubber bands and rubber-band balls, cleaning wipes, retainers lost and found and lost again, gas station sunglasses, straws, hair ties, makeup containers, suitcases bought for special vacations, blenders, juicers, cassette tapes, floppy disks, CDs, records, music players, charging cords, the wrong adapters, plastic plants that could survive neglect, the spirals of spiral notebooks optimistically purchased but only half-filled, the other shoe, beer cans, liters of soda left over from an impromptu office pizza party, and an army of plastic eggs no longer containing a surprise.

It is the last two hundred years of human history come to rest in the great gyre compressed into one, singular, cacophonous moment.

Her net has a long hook at the end of the pole. Skipper flips it around and pokes about. She catches the end of a knot of fishing net and pushes it away from the boat as they pass. If their rudder catches, that will be a major headache. She should, in fact, stay on the edges, but it's hard to resist.

She fills her stores with sludge and wayward, half-degraded objects.

Carmen takes a turn dragging the water with the net, until she cuts herself retrieving a broken window frame.

"Damn," she says, as blood seeps out. There's so much of it, and it reminds Skipper of the kid Jackson shot. She feels dizzy.

"Get the med kit and a clean cloth," Carmen says, hopping back to the cockpit and lowering herself onto the bench.

"Where is it?" asks Jackson.

All the rags are dirty, so Skipper grabs one of Nora's old T-shirts and hopes it's clean. She fetches the hard metal case from its bracket on the wall in the bathroom while Jackson anxiously bumps around. She opens it and fumbles through the contents.

"I need the antibiotic ointment," says Carmen, grimacing and pressing the T-shirt against her foot. A crimson stain seeps across it. "Not that, no, not that either. God, this is why you need to organize things."

Finally, Skipper finds the right tube.

"This is five years past expiration," says Carmen, and Skipper is amazed at her sister's capacity for condescension even when her face is taut with pain.

She washes Carmen's foot with salt water, but Carmen insists on applying the ointment herself.

The skin patch is so old, it doesn't stick, so they have to go with a bandage instead, clipped with a stray clothespin Skipper scrounges from the hold. All the while, Carmen lectures her on a long list of items she should have included in the kit, only one tenth of which is relevant to the situation. Skipper's worry dissolves into annoyance, and she figures the cut can't be that bad.

Night falls, and Skipper slows the boat to a crawl, worried about hitting something as they slide through the mass.

Carmen and Jackson sleep below, curled up together in one of the bunks, Jackson's arm looped loosely across Carmen's collarbone. So Skipper is alone when the other boat drifts out of the gloom.

It resembles the *Bumblebee* so much she searches for the name on the side of the bow, but it is shrouded by an old fishing net. She half expects to see herself standing on the other side looking back.

It's humbling: the feeling that everything about her life that she considered unique has in fact happened before and might happen again to someone else, who will also think themselves the only one to feel those things.

Then she notices a dark stain. The entire boat, she realizes, is rotten. The miracle is that it floats.

She reaches out with a pole and touches it once, to make sure it's real, and there's a groan. Slowly, the boat collapses and sags into itself like it is being swallowed, its mast tipping over. The boat has been held together who knows how long, among the lost things, and now, found, it sinks beneath the water.

Carmen is sluggish when she takes her watch. Skipper tells her to go back to sleep, but Carmen insists. They've reached the blurred edges of the great patch, so there's less risk of hitting something.

When Skipper wakes again, Jackson's on watch. Carmen tosses in her bunk, feverish. Her wounded foot is hot and weeps with foul-smelling pus.

"You should have told me," Skipper tells Jackson.

"I thought she should sleep," he says.

"That's not your decision to make. I'm the captain."

He laughs, like she's joking. "Relax. It's a cut." He doesn't see how sick she is; he doesn't know Carmen. Skipper blames herself for not catching it.

She and Jackson take turns tending to her on top of splitting watch between them.

Whatever invaded Carmen's body is vicious and fast. She sleeps long hours and mumbles from her dreams. She's angry. She scolds Grandma for depriving them. She shouts that dogs have eaten their mother. She tells Ollie she's a monster. She asks Nora why she can't come with her. She cries over and over for everyone to please climb out of her brain and let her rest.

The malignant fungus under Carmen's skin seems to pulse like something bloody and mammalian, and Skipper's dismayed at how much it's grown, even with the pills. It's the size of her hand.

She dumps the entire contents of the first aid kit on the table, pawing through it for anything that might help. She forces her sister to swallow various pills marked *fever* and *infection*, but like the ointment, they expired years ago. She dabs cold seawater across Carmen's face and arms and tells her everything will be all right.

If Nora were here—

But she isn't.

Skipper wonders if, in bringing her sister on this journey, she has killed her.

In the morning, though, Carmen improves. She sits up and drinks soup. She apologizes for the trouble, and Skipper's so relieved and happy she's even grateful when Jackson eats the last of the beans.

CHAPTER TWENTY-TWO

Four days out from land, they run out of food. Skipper decides to fish, which has its intended effect: Jackson disappears below, and the sisters have the cockpit to themselves again. Later, Skipper goes to use the head and finds him eating the last three packs of noodles, straight from the cooking pot.

"Whatever you catch will be way better," says Carmen, when Skipper complains.

It takes hours, but Skipper catches a sea creature that refuses to die for fifteen minutes, even after Carmen batters it over the head with a pot and carves off its face with a hacksaw. It's half as long as Skipper is tall and has bulbous eyes the size of her fists. Its fins have digits like cat's paws, or—when Carmen spreads them—like little fingers.

They take it down to the kitchenette for butchering. Jackson agrees to help with the carving, but despite his bragging, it turns out he is no better at cleaning a fish than they are.

"Not so easy, is it?" Carmen teases.

Jackson stabs the knife into the wooden table, and blood and guts trickle down. "Do it yourself then."

He shoves past Skipper to the stairs.

"Are you taking over watch?" Skipper calls after him.

"Fine."

The flesh inside it is crimson like tuna. It's so full of bones and cartilage, after they remove all of the inedible bits, they are left with a mound of hacked-up meat that is just enough for a couple of meals. Its stone heart inexplicably continues to beat even after it's plucked out and separated from the rest of the body.

Jackson returns when the meal's ready, and they eat until their stomachs hurt. Later, they have horrible indigestion and hallucinations and regret eating the fish at all.

On watch, Skipper imagines the constellations are animals that speak to her. They congratulate her for finally leaving the pink house.

"If we're being honest," says a sheep, "we never thought you'd do it. You wouldn't have, if we hadn't stolen your sister. You're welcome."

"I just want to find her," Skipper says.

"And then what?" asks a bobcat.

"Go home," says Skipper, even though she can't bear the idea of it.

"Liar," hisses the bobcat.

"Traitor," booms the man in the moon.

"What?" asks Skipper, unsure whom she has betrayed, but her heart gallops faster than the *Bumblebee* could fly, because she suspects they are right.

"What's going on?" Jackson asks, poking his head out the hatch. His teeth grow too long for his face.

"Ahhhh!" he recoils, covering his eyes. "Don't hurt me."

"It's the fish," Skipper says, but she relishes whatever he saw in her, even if it's false.

He retreats, and the icy air makes frost of the fever sweat on her skin. She vomits overboard several times, but she keeps their course true. Skipper is an excellent sailor.

They run out of water the next day, three days away from the vault. Carmen is surprised, because she's been measuring their use. Skipper, who has seen Jackson stealing gulps in the pantry, is not surprised. At least the thirst distracts them from their hunger.

They seriously discuss drinking their pee. Or piss, as Jackson calls it, but that sounds even less appealing somehow. Jackson offers to be the first.

"Urine's sterile, right?" Skipper asks Carmen.

"It definitely won't hydrate you," Carmen says. "Even if you could distill it, you might as well drink salt water."

Skipper tries rigging a desalinator in their kitchen with the pot, a bowl, seawater, and ice chips from their deck, but the result is a dead battery and a few sips of water for an hour of labor. She sweat more making it than she consumes in the end.

"What about me?" asks Jackson, after she drinks it, and she can't tell if he is joking.

"All right." Her words sound foreign—a combination of the fact that she hasn't spoken much aloud in the last day, and because her tongue is awkward and swollen. "I'll drink your pee."

Jackson frowns. "Drink your own pee."

He gets a mug and pisses in it, right then and there.

The smell of it makes Skipper gag.

"Never mind," she says, and goes back above to find a miracle: It's snowing.

They capture what they can in every container they have, fill the kitchen and bathroom tanks and sinks.

They make tea with it, drink it too quickly, feel sick, drink more.

It is the sweet celebration of not dying, at least in the immediate term.

Another day passes, and they're so far north now the sun sets after only a couple of hours. Jackson's presence becomes increasingly oppressive.

He wants to dictate how things should be on the ship, even though it's their boat. He asks Carmen to clean the cabin. It's getting messy, and he says it is her mess, which is only true because she has been doing all of the cooking. He insists Skipper take longer shifts at the helm after they spot icebergs in the water. "I have terrible night vision. I don't think it's safe for me to be on watch. I can't see a thing. You're the best sailor, and you have the best eyesight. We can bring you hot drinks."

She doesn't have the strength to argue. The cold has drained her of any energy to resist, and also, she agrees. She doesn't trust him to keep them from crashing, or Carmen for that matter. She trusts herself. They are close enough to the vault that she can power through, stealing naps here and there, keeping an eye stuck on the radar.

The weather worsens suddenly, and Skipper's breath steams in the garnet shaft of her headlamp. Her brain conjures shapes in the dim water, mythical animals and deserted islands.

Her fingers and ears go numb with the cold. She huddles in the reindeer coat and every piece of clothing she has.

It snows again, and Skipper walks carefully up and down the deck with a shovel, scraping what accumulates into a pot. Carmen comes up periodically and warms Skipper's face with her hands: Skipper's nose, then her ears, then her cheeks. They stand, face to face.

"Are you okay?" Skipper whispers.

"Are you okay?" Carmen replies.

And neither of them answers the question.

Carmen leans in and sets her soft, warm cheek against Skipper's icy one. Then she adjusts Skipper's scarf around her face. "Two more days, right?"

"If the wind holds," says Skipper.

"It will. And then we'll find Nora." But the confidence leaches from Carmen's voice.

Around dinnertime, Carmen and Jackson argue. Their voices rise from below. Carmen's voice breaks in anger, and something crashes to the ground.

Skipper's throat constricts. She gives the water a quick scan, and then ducks down into the cabin. Blissful warmth enfolds her, and she could stand there luxuriating in it, all the fine vessels in her extremities expanding, pulsing blissfully with blood.

A deep scarlet shadow of borscht leaks across the white floor. The pot lies tipped over.

The stove is on. The red ring of heat emanates from the cells beneath the surface.

"Stop ordering us around like you're some petty king. This isn't your boat!" says Carmen, whose eloquence always increases with anger.

"After everything I've done for you, you should be grateful!" Jackson says. "I didn't have to come!"

"You're unbelievable," says Carmen. "Just because you had a hard childhood doesn't give you a right to be an asshole. You've been treating us like shit, and we don't deserve that."

If there is one thing Carmen is good at, it is making someone feel small. She's done it to Skipper countless times. It is maybe not the right tactic when dealing with this man.

But Carmen keeps going: "Your hero complex has gone to your head. You're emotionally stunted. You're a *child*. You know that? *A child*."

Skipper hears the crack before she registers the motion of his hand.

Carmen clutches her cheek.

Jackson wheels away. "Why aren't you on deck?"

But Skipper can't move. Her feet are frozen to the floor.

He growls and shoves past her, banging the hatch closed behind him.

Skipper goes to her sister and hugs her, and Carmen begins to cry.

"I'm sorry," says Carmen. "I shouldn't have provoked him."

"It's him," says Skipper. "Shh."

"I shouldn't have invited him along."

Well *that* is true, but it doesn't seem like the moment to affirm it.

"And I spilled the soup. I made it for you with these sad beets you must have squirreled away with the tools."

Skipper goes and gets a rag and mops up all the red liquid. The smell of it makes her mouth water, and her stomach tightens in hunger.

Carmen watches her helplessly. "I just washed that floor. All morning, on my knees."

"Then we should be fine to eat these," says Skipper, dropping the chunks of beet back into the pot. To her relief, Carmen laughs. They add more water and salt, and cover it again with a lid.

"Not my best work," says Carmen, when they sit down to eat the watery result.

"Thirst-quenching," says Skipper, thinking she should go back above, but the relative warmth of the cabin makes her sluggish. She could fall asleep in it.

Jackson appears in the doorway. Skipper braces herself. Carmen's grip tightens around her spoon. They wait for him to complain they are eating without him, to criticize them for missing a spot on the floor. But Jackson's expression is remorseful. "Hey. I'm so sorry. I don't know what came over me. Please forgive me, Carmen. I just want to say I respect you, and I know my behavior has been unacceptable. It's just—what you said—it made me lose my temper. It's the dark. The lack of sunlight is getting to me. I'm turning into someone else out here."

"I get it," says Carmen. "Want some soup?"

His nose wrinkles. "Are you eating off the floor?"

"Yes," says Carmen.

"No, thank you. I have jerky." He fetches some from his bag, then holds the egg out to Carmen. "Here. If you want to use it."

It's a generous gesture from Jackson. He figured out how to reconnect the electricity, but without the sun, their only means of charging their batteries is the small wind turbine on the stern and a silly antique pedal charger Nora installed in the cabin years ago.

It might be helpful to try the egg again to see if there's any more sign of Nora or if Jackson's contacts have guidance about getting past security. Carmen doesn't take it. Her gaze is fixed on her soup. "It's okay. Thank you."

He works his mouth, like he wants to say something else. Then he takes the device and goes back above.

When they go to relieve Jackson an hour later, he's in high spirits. He's been drinking again, but not a lot, just enough to keep warm. His face is pink from the cold air.

They expect him to head back into the cabin, but he lingers, wanting to make peace.

He is happy to talk about anything—dramas, books, people he's met, and things he's done. It is hard not to soften. Nice, funny Jackson returns. He tells good stories, even if Skipper suspects half are fiction.

Skipper tunes her radio. It bursts into sound, crackly at first, then clear: the strains of a violin, and then a flute and a cello. They listen, rapt, passing around Jackson's whiskey.

When the song ends, it leaves behind an emptiness in the air.

"Where're you picking that up from?" asks Jackson, voice husky.

"Must be a boat nearby," she says, scanning the horizon for lights.

The radio crackles again. "If you're listening, that's the latest composition by Pablo Soler." The announcer explains the music was played by the national orchestra of a country to the south across the sea.

"I've always wanted to go there," says Jackson. "The people there are so rich, no one ever goes hungry."

"No wonder they can make music like that," says Carmen.

The next piece begins.

"Wow," says Carmen. A phosphorescence flowers in the water.

"Jellyfish?" Skipper guesses. But it isn't jellyfish, it is a pod of whales: huge and black and white-green, glowing impossibly beneath the water. They don't seem to notice their unnatural phosphorescence. At least they are alive. One of them blows a column of water into the air, and then another throws itself up and slams down, so close to the *Bumblebee* that the boat rocks.

Then above, the sky ripples with wisps of color. It goes on for minutes, and they are surrounded by so much beauty, they don't know where to gaze.

They sit in the frigid air together listening to the music. After, they mourn the departure of the whales and the lights, and all the moments of pure wonder like this that only come once in a life and can never be fully remembered.

In the distance, red lights blink out at them close to the horizon: A giant cargo ship—an endangered species itself—moves slowly across the water like history, leaving in its wake the turmoil of consequence.

CHAPTER TWENTY-THREE

"Look," says Carmen, pointing at the cockpit bench next to Skipper. The egg sits, inert. Jackson must have forgotten it. Carmen picks it up and turns it over.

"Be careful," says Skipper. *Don't break it*, she means. But also, *Don't let Jackson see you.*

Carmen scoots over next to Skipper. "Hello."

"Hello," says the egg. "What would you like to know?"

Carmen flicks a gaze to Skipper, an invitation or a dare, Skipper isn't sure. Then, she quickly sets the egg down. Jackson comes up the stairs.

Skipper's palms prickle with sweat.

He catches sight of the egg next to Carmen, and his face darkens.

Brace, Skipper thinks. They can weather this too.

"What are you doing?" he says.

Carmen hands it to him with remarkable cool. "You left it."

Jackson scowls and snatches it.

"We were going over the plan again for landing." If the conditions hold, they should arrive tomorrow.

"Yeah, I've been thinking we should go somewhere else instead," says Jackson. "My contact says we shouldn't come. The unionization efforts are on hold. Half of the organizers have been rounded up. Two died trying to escape, or that's the story they're being told. If we try to land, we'll be imprisoned without proper documentation, especially if Renewal suspects we're there to cause trouble."

"Are you serious?" says Skipper. Has he forgotten the point of this trip was to find Nora? "We're so close."

Jackson looms over them. "You don't even know for a fact your sister is in the vault. All you have is a bizarre message."

Skipper wonders if this is what he's been thinking all along—if he believes this to be a wild, fruitless chase fated to end without answers.

"What will you do if you can't find her? Keep on sailing forever?"

And Skipper thinks, well, maybe. She could do that. She likes the idea, just her and Carmen in the *Bumblebee*, after they dump Jackson and his endless palaver on the vault dock.

"Where would you go instead?" Carmen asks Jackson.

He wants to go south down the coast of the eastern continent. He's been inspired by the music they heard from the cargo ship. "Or if you want to take down Renewal"—but they don't—"we should go to their headquarters." Skipper is surprised to learn Renewal is not, in fact, based in their country. Its headquarters are somewhere else, with more generous tax policies and even weaker regulation.

They should have known he would do this. He changes his mind all the time. Just like he walked away from his last two jobs without a real plan.

Jackson veers off onto a tangent again about how terrible Renewal is, and how they need to be punished.

"When you finish taking down the big bad," Carmen says, "what will you do about the blight? How will you eat?"

"I'm not worried," he says. "People are ingenious. We always find a way."

"That's not how it works. And anyway, maybe Renewal *is* people's ingenuity."

"Ingenuity that relies on the exploitation of cheap labor."

"I've worked for them for five years," says Carmen, "and I'm happy to have the job."

"Even now?"

Skipper cringes, thinking of how Carmen wanted to be a nurse, and now they've probably blown her chance.

"It's a job. It's better than nothing."

Skipper agrees with Jackson, but there's no way she'll say that out loud, so instead she adds: "Nora worked for them too. She wasn't some corporate robot."

"You don't even know your sister," he sneers.

Both Skipper and Carmen bristle.

"What's that supposed to mean?" asks Carmen.

"Yes, I do," says Skipper.

"You've come all this way," says Jackson, "but you don't know why she might have come here. You don't know what she was working on. You don't know her friends, you don't know her life. You may have been close when you were kids, but people change."

He doesn't know what he's talking about. His own sister is dead. His whole family is dead.

"It doesn't matter. She needs us."

"Does she?"

"Stop it," says Carmen so sharply Skipper braces for his temper, but Jackson is not in that kind of mood. He laughs.

"I thought you were sick of being stuck on a boat," says Skipper.

"I can last longer for the right destination."

"It's too far," says Skipper. "We don't have enough food or water to get there." She wonders if Jackson is nervous about the upcoming dangers of the harbor. Their long discussions of how to navigate the ice in winter have burrowed in his mind. He's been having nightmares again of drowning.

"It's fine. We can last another week if you catch us fish. Harvest ice from an iceberg. I already used the egg to plot a new course down along the far coast."

"We're operating on partial battery with almost no sunlight," Skipper tries to explain. "And we'll be going against the current."

"I'm not going to the vault," says Jackson. "I'm not. We'll get ourselves killed." He is, Skipper realizes, a special kind of coward.

"Bullshit," says Carmen. "The time to make that decision was three weeks ago." She stands up. Her head doesn't reach his shoulder, and she tips her head back to face him. Her voice shakes. "You promised to help us."

"And I'm helping you not make a bad decision."

Blood pounds in Skipper's ears. She should be watching the water, but she's looking at him instead. "He was lying the entire time," she tells Carmen. "There never was any contact, and now he's afraid we'll find out."

He laughs again, but there's an edge this time to it. "What?"

"Is she right?" Carmen asks.

"This is stupid," he says, and steps toward them. "You're not thinking straight."

Skipper bends over the tiller, trying to block him with her body, but he pushes her aside like she might as well not exist.

He sets the egg on the bench and turns the boat, and they tack away from their course.

"You can't sail all the way by yourself," says Carmen. "Be reasonable." Then, maybe because she saw she couldn't displace him from the tiller, she tries to take the egg.

The *thunk* of her sister's body cuts through the rising wind.

Skipper reaches out and slams the hatch door to startle him. Her vision wavers from fatigue, and, possibly, bad fish. Because what she sees is not a man, but a large white bear, with a long snout and massive frame. He charges past her into the cabin and smashes about the pantry. He swipes at the bedding with long claws. He roars.

Carmen pulls herself to her feet. Blood runs from her arm. They watch as the bear ransacks their cabin.

Skipper is fully awake now, fear thudding through her.

"This trip was a stupid idea," shouts the bear. "Your sister is a grown woman. She's responsible for herself and whatever mistakes got her into this situation. Anyway, how do you know she didn't come all this way to get away from you? And if she *is* in trouble, what are you going to do? You're helpless. You can't do anything."

The bear comes back on deck holding the chart in his teeth. He occupies half the cockpit on all four paws. Carmen and Skipper retreat up onto the windward side of the boat, against the rail.

"I saved your life. You owe me."

"You're a bear!" Skipper tries to say, but her words are lost to the wind.

The bear drops the chart to the cockpit floor. "You'll never find her," he growls. "She's probably dead."

The bear leans down with his massive paws and rips the chart in half.

And Skipper can't take it anymore. It's too hard. She's spent too many hours of her life trying to contort herself to other people's needs.

"No!" Skipper throws herself at him. The air gives reluctantly between them, as if it is honey. Then he catches her and hugs her around the shoulders, laughing because she is that insignificant to him.

Her face is crushed against fur, and she smells alcohol and the musk of unwashed body.

She tries to grab the chart, but the bear flings her aside. Her skull connects against wood with a crack, and her vision blurs. Nausea hits, then pain. She staggers to her feet.

A gust rolls the boat hard to port. Carmen hangs on to the rail, her head framed by night sky. She shouts for the bear to stop.

The bear stands up on his two hind paws and shreds the chart into strips. The wind takes the pieces. The bear dangles the last scrap of the chart, maybe still enough for them to find their way. "This is for your own good."

Skipper dives at it again, and this time she stomps hard on his paw. Digs her fingernails deep into his fur. She, too, can be an animal.

They fight, bobcat and bear.

Then he lifts her up and tosses her, so she tumbles down the leeward side, close to the water and the boom of the sail. She hastily clips her harness onto the safety cable.

"You fucking animal," he says, following her, great paws shaking the deck as he advances. The boat heels even further, unbalanced by his weight on the lower side, but he isn't paying attention.

The bear catches her around the neck with his paws, and then she can't breathe, all she sees is his face, inches from hers, his large nose and black gums, and sharp teeth, grinning at her with a terrifying appetite. The bear opens his mouth, and she thinks, *Here it comes, the bear's teeth on my face, tearing flesh. Chewing with his horrible manners.*

She chokes, unable to fight anymore, vision darkening.

Distantly, Carmen shouts, "Prepare to jibe."

Skipper tries to unravel what it means, and then the boom rushes back over the rail, fast, propelled by the wind, and smacks the top of the bear's head.

The bear tumbles back against the rail at the same time they crest a swell, and Skipper wonders muzzily when the waves became mountains.

They're tossed in the air, and the thought occurs to Skipper, before gravity yanks her, that only one of them wears a harness.

Then the boat slams down into the trough, bow angled right into the next wave, and a great sheet of water rolls over the deck. It catches the bear in its maw. Nothing is hungrier than the ocean.

The bear rolls right over the rail with a grunt of surprise.

The boat flattens out, and Carmen helps Skipper back into the cockpit.

When they look back, the bear is a glint of white in the water.

"I'll fucking kill you, you bitch!" says the bear, even as he shrinks.

"We have to go back," says Skipper, words forced out between numb lips.

But they don't. They watch the bear reduce and reduce until there is very little left of him.

When they finally return, it is impossible to find where he was, though they sweep the dark with their headlamps for hours.

The bear, of course, was not a bear, because there are no such things as bears anymore, only men. But it is easier to think of something wild and uncontrollable. Something with blubber and the ability to swim for miles through cold frigid water to an iceberg that it could ride safely until the next mass extinction.

CHAPTER TWENTY-FOUR

Skipper wakes with a start, uncertain why horror grips her. Then she remembers, and she breaks out in a sweat despite the cold that invades the cabin. She looks at herself in the mirror nailed over the toilet. How is she so unchanged?

"What did you do?" she asks.

Her skull feels like it's being stabbed with a fork.

They keep a bucket of seawater by the sink, and she splashes some of it on her face. The cold hits her like a slap, so she does it again.

Then, not knowing what else to do, she brews a thermos of tea and takes it above to her sister.

Carmen sits in the cockpit, holding the egg. She managed to charge it a little, thanks to the gusts moving against them. She hugs Skipper, as if they've done nothing to be ashamed of, and offers her the egg. "He was right. This is much easier to navigate with."

Skipper takes it, and she sees, projected against the deck of the cockpit from a hole in the egg, a bird's-eye view of the ocean, and a red dot moving slowly toward land. She forgets everything and admires the gadget.

This far north, she can no longer trust her compass. It's a good thing they have the egg.

Carmen fetches the first aid kit and examines the lump on the back of Skipper's head. Then she shines a light in each of her eyes. Skipper gags from the pain.

"Fucker," says Carmen. Her lack of repentance shocks Skipper, when she herself has been swallowing a wail all morning.

"What we did—" Skipper begins.

Carmen offers Skipper two red pills for the pain. "Don't. We had to." She holds Skipper's gaze until Skipper looks away.

"We won't tell anyone, do you understand?" says Carmen. "Not even Nora."

Skipper nods.

"Listen to me. No one will miss him, and no one will care. Anyway, it was me. I did it, because he was going to kill you, and I'm supposed to protect you. I haven't done a good job of it in the past."

Skipper has thought this many times, but hearing Carmen admit it makes her want to contradict her. "Sometimes you tried."

"You don't get points for trying. I never know the right thing to do in the moment. Not like you or Nora. I thought, so this is who I am: useless. And I've had to live with that version of myself."

The flint in Carmen's tone frightens Skipper. "That's not true."

She doesn't know this side of Carmen, but when it comes to her sisters, her love isn't conditional on the knowing. It is the invisible tie between them, and all the things they once understood about each other. Her memories are soaked with their presence. She has left pieces of herself in each of them as they have done to her.

"Maybe not completely," concedes Carmen. "But it's my fault he was here. You didn't want him to come, and you were right. And I made my choice. For the first time, I did something when it mattered."

Ice floes bob in the water all around them. Her sister touches her knee, demanding her attention. A convection of unidentifiable emotions rises inside Skipper.

"There are two people in this world who matter to me: you and Nora. I would do it again."

Skipper exhales, a broken, shuddering noise. She felt, growing up, she had to share her sister with the crowd of friends around her. Carmen loved people. She spent her free evenings out, over on other people's porches, or down at the bar with friends. This is the first time Carmen has expressed anything akin to exclusivity. Skipper's longed for this moment, and now here Carmen is, presenting it to her without ceremony, as if it is something Skipper should have known, should have taken for granted all this time. Skipper is bitter. But also, the new knowledge fills her with lightness, like if she isn't careful, she might lift right off the boat.

"Okay" is what Skipper manages to say.

"You asked what happened between me and Nora," says Carmen.

Skipper leans forward, afraid to disturb the moment.

"After I graduated from high school, I wanted to join her in the city, get a job up there, go to college like she did. I studied for the test. I applied and everything."

"What happened?" Skipper is bewildered. She never realized Carmen considered leaving.

"She told me not to come." Carmen's voice is sharp. "She said I would hate the life, that I would be better off at home. As if she knew what was best for me. And she said, anyway, I needed to take care of you."

Skipper can't speak. It's a wonder she can breathe. She regrets asking.

"It didn't matter in the end, because I didn't get in. I guess I wasn't as smart as Nora. I followed her advice and got my degree remotely instead. And then I started dating Ollie, and that was that."

The water is full of ice now. They drop their remaining sails and motor forward, trying to steer clear through the maze of it.

"There," says Carmen.

Because in the distance, there's a strip of gray on the horizon: land. The sun remains below the horizon, and the world is bathed in an ethereal purple glow. A white bird wheels above them in the sky. It alights on their deck, and the two sisters hold still until it flies off again.

Skipper scans the land with her binoculars. In the pale light, she spots the vague angle of black roofs and red siding. It is too far to see people, but she imagines she feels the vibration of human activity even this far out. They have finally made it. Now all that remains is the difficult navigation of the harbor and convincing the authorities to let them land.

CHAPTER TWENTY-FIVE

They ease into the harbor, only a hazardous hour from their goal. The path is littered with floating chunks of ice and wisps of fog, but the wind and waves remain steady.

The ice groans and knocks around them, and every once in a while, one of the thinner sheets breaks in two with a loud crack.

Through sea smoke, toy houses appear in miniature, illuminated by the stars. Smoke rises from chimneys, and Skipper imagines the warmth of a cozy sitting room, hot cider settling in her belly. She anticipates the first long sleep she'll have under a thick quilt.

They make contact over the radio, and the official that responds to them is brisk and all business. "You don't have authorization to land."

"We're in trouble: We've run out of food and water and are experiencing engine issues due to a shitty battery." All these things are conveniently close to the truth. "We need a temporary exception. Sorry."

She and Carmen wait, trying not to count the seconds that pass in static.

"The harbor is dangerous this time of year. We don't recommend trying to land unless you're in a very sturdy boat," warns the official.

"I don't think we have a choice," says Skipper, surveying the *Bumblebee*. Their boat has always been a workhorse, but these are different conditions. "She's the best we've got."

"All right, then. Good luck."

Carmen pumps her fist.

The egg chirps a battery warning, and Skipper hesitates. She could charge it, but the engine takes priority. If they run out of electricity, they'll be dead in the water.

She squints at the projection, trying to memorize the shallows and obstructions. Then she turns the egg off to save the battery.

Carmen fetches them a fresh thermos of hot water since they're out of tea. They wrap their faces with their scarves, but the wind cuts against the soft flesh of their eyelids, and Skipper's eyes tear.

"It's damn cold," says Carmen, always one to state the obvious. She scoots in next to Skipper and wraps an arm around her shoulders. A strait of warmth spreads slowly between their bodies.

Now they are close enough to see doors and windows if they squint. Skipper tries to suppress her rising hope. They have come so far. Her excitement overshadows any nervousness.

The fog increases, and snow falls, fast and thick. The flakes stick to their eyelashes and the fabric of their clothes. It forms piles beneath their feet in the cockpit, and damp creeps into her tripled-up socks. In minutes, they suddenly have no visibility.

Skipper tries to check the egg, but it won't turn on.

"Damn," she says. An understatement. Her gut lurches with the next forward rev of the boat.

"Let me try," says Carmen, as if Skipper can't be trusted to competently turn on a high-tech device.

"All yours," says Skipper, but her voice betrays her irritation.

"Maybe your hands are cold," says Carmen. No surprise, it doesn't wake. Carmen continues to fiddle with it for a few fruitless minutes, both of them becoming increasingly frustrated.

Skipper slows the boat even more. Carmen gets up on the bow to spot the way. The ice hems in around them. Every gap between the ice sheets beckons like a false path. A few times, they realize they've gone the wrong way.

The remnants of light die as they push on, Skipper gripping the tiller.

She doesn't know how far they are from shore when their motor dies. Maybe fifty feet, maybe a mile. It's too quiet to hear, so neither of them notices right away. When Skipper finally checks, because the lack of movement at this point can't be an illusion, her heart drops. How long have they been drifting, the wind pushing them back out to sea?

She goes to fetch her emergency jug of precious biofuel, before she remembers Jackson took it.

"What are we going to do?" Carmen asks. It could take days to recharge the battery without sunlight.

Skipper unslings one of her long-handled garbage nets. She stands on the side of the boat and leans out, groping until she finally catches a floe with the hook at the end of it. Then she pulls.

Carmen fetches an oar and they proceed by inches, painstakingly, paddling and poling along until their shoulders are stiff and aching.

All around them, the ice closes in. Hot panic flares through Skipper, and she poles faster.

They must be close to shore—they've been doing this for hours.

"Watch out!" shouts Carmen, too late. The next wave lifts them up as Skipper shoves them forward, and when the wave descends, there's an awful crunch of hull splintering against jagged rock revealed only by the brief recession of water.

Skipper tries to push them off when the next wave comes, but they land even more squarely on the rocks.

She radios the shore again. "Mayday." She describes the situation to the voice on the other end.

"Hang on," comes the reply.

Carmen runs below to check the cabin. She returns to report on the gravity of the damage: a splintered hole the size of a pie. Water fills the bilge too fast for the pump to drain. It infiltrates the cabin.

Skipper tries the emergency pump, but it's no match for the cold seawater flooding in. Each wave drives them farther into the rocks.

"What's your location?" the official says.

But they don't know where they are.

The *Bumblebee* is going to sink. Skipper sees it with sudden, horrible clarity. She goes for the flares. It takes her a few times to pull the trigger, because her hands are shaking.

The voice on the other end reports they can't see the flare, because of the fog.

The *Bumblebee*'s half submerged, and the rock may be the only thing keeping them above water.

While Skipper wrestles with the dinghy, Carmen fetches their grab bag and Jackson's, hastily stuffed with a few precious items.

They climb into the dinghy, and Skipper takes up the oars.

"We're in the tender," Carmen reports over the radio.

Skipper gets one last glimpse of their beloved *Bumblebee*. She tries to memorize the black hull and yellow racing stripe. How she loved their boat. If only she had sold it. At least she wouldn't have to lose it like this.

Carmen pats her. "Come on."

Skipper begins to row.

Every time cold water splashes over the side, it steals her breath.

The fog is so thick, she can't feel the outlines of herself.

"Wait," says Carmen, because she can't find the egg. She must have dropped it on the boat. It's too late to go back for it, and it was dead anyway. "I can remember which way to go," Carmen says, and Skipper will have to trust her.

They row forever. Stroke after stroke. Carmen directs her, and she obeys.

The ice thickens, and they come to a standstill. Skipper realizes they are stuck. Several minutes pass while Carmen continues to try to coordinate their rescue with the official on the other end of the radio.

Skipper thinks, *I did it. I got us all the way here. And now we are going to die.*

As she huddles in her coat, her lungs aching with cold, memories come to her in fragments: Climbing a tree with her sisters to eat sandwiches in its branches, voices rising in a chorus as they plot an epic journey that might carry them far from Grandma's dictatorship. Uncle Tot teaching them how to swim in the creek. A wispy memory of Nora braiding her hair. The taste of stolen blueberry. The airy summer morning they launched the *Bumblebee* into the water for the first time with all their neighbors lined up to see if it would float.

Carmen reaches up and tests the ice with a gloved hand. "I think we're going to have to walk."

She clambers up, bags and all, and Skipper follows. They proceed gingerly. The ice creaks as they walk. It's uneven and surprisingly hilly, and Skipper slips several times on the hard surface.

The wind picks up, whipping around them in a vortex of ice and snow. The suddenness of it steals Skipper's breath.

Carmen moves faster, and the distance between them grows. Skipper falls again, and a part of her thinks, *What if I let her keep going? I could rest, here on the ice, for the rest of my life. Would it be so bad to give up?*

She never loved anything as much as the *Bumblebee.*

Her sister's dark shape fades into the snow and fog.

Then Carmen's voice comes back to her: "Skipper!"

It's amazing how Carmen has the strength to shout even now. Her sister's fear seizes Skipper's limbs, and she starts moving again. She feels warm, maybe on fire. Every nerve in her body cries out.

She catches up to her waiting sister and sags against her, Carmen's arm looped around her waist.

"Just a little farther," Carmen says.

"Are you sure?"

"Yes," Carmen says, who's always sure.

So Skipper obeys, propelled by the lifelong habit of doing whatever her older sister tells her to do. Even though she is certain Carmen is wrong. As they walk, Skipper clings to one thought: She has lost her boat, and now she will never have to go home.

PART 2

CARMEN

CHAPTER TWENTY-SIX

Carmen despises the dark, the way it cloaks everything in uncertainty. She knows, rationally, she is too old to be afraid of imaginary things. She's lived through thousands of nights without being dragged outside to have her intestines devoured by monsters.

On the other hand, the world is full of real things that can steal her breath and leave her undone on the floor. That's the thing their grandmother never understood all those years she tried to cure Carmen of her childish tendencies: It wasn't just fear that immobilized her, it was the anxiety of not knowing, and also, of being alone.

In daylight, Carmen can control things. Then night falls, and she lies awake in bed, her mind disassembling the world with its long fingers and laying out the pieces.

The problem with sleep is it offers no solace in doing. Back home, Carmen would get up before the sun and clean the house from top to bottom. Ollie always loved that about her. Or maybe Ollie just loved a clean house.

This time of year, close to the top of the world, Vault City lives in darkness. The sun went down in early November and won't rise again until the end of January. From the window of the clinic where Carmen and Skipper recuperate, they can see the houses that fit snug together, without space for home gardens or individual farms. In the distance, long glass greenhouses at the edge of the settlement glow with artificial light twenty-four hours a day.

Vault City isn't much of a city. It's a company town, and all its tidy corners exude order and purpose. It scratches an itch in Carmen. She always yearns for life to be more organized than it is.

Carmen and Skipper lie side by side in hospital beds, under observation and hooked up to IVs. Carmen lost fifteen pounds on the voyage over. After the *Bumblebee*, the clean white sheets and mattresses are soft beneath their spines.

The clinic staff are friendly, and their interest is like heat from a stove. Carmen hasn't had other people to talk to in weeks.

They want to know why two women would venture this far in a small sailboat so obviously ill-equipped for the conditions. It's unfathomably stupid. But also romantic. There is no end to their appetite for facts that are wholly irrelevant to their medical care, and Carmen enjoys feeding them tidbits. Beside her, Skipper whispers at her to stop; they tussle about it, and then Carmen wins and goes on talking to them.

"Did you not know about the ice?"

"Did you think you would die?"

"Why didn't you wait until spring?"

Their accents are a mix of familiar and unfamiliar. Despite her previous objection, Skipper keeps asking Carmen to repeat what was said, which amuses Carmen. The consequence is everyone addresses themselves to Carmen rather than Skipper.

One of the senior nurses, Piotr, tells her they were lucky. The harbor team likes to drink—well, a lot of people do, not that Piotr judges, but clearly he judges—and half the time, they are too inebriated to save anyone.

Piotr is a tall man with a crooked nose and a plump mole on his upper lip that sits like a period at the end of everything he says. It may make him seem more serious than he is. Carmen hasn't figured out if he has a sense of humor. She likes his sincerity, though, and his compulsion to be helpful. She feels he is someone who always tells the truth.

He is the one who warns them as he fusses with the heater in their room: "Security is going to question you. My unsolicited advice: Keep your answers short and consistent. Don't have too many opinions about things. If you're worried, say you don't know." He presses the sheet next to Carmen's hand, and she notices he is missing two fingertips.

He notices her noticing.

"Unsolicited advice: Don't be cheap about gloves," he says, removing his hand. "And get that thing removed soon." He gestures at her torso, and Carmen imagines the subcutaneous growth flares at his attention. Despite the pills, it has unfurled tendrils up and down her right side from her belly button to her collarbone. She imagines it nibbling her organs. It doesn't hurt, though. She agrees about the removal, and Piotr gives her more pills with an increased dosage.

A pair of security officers comes an hour later and stands by Carmen's feet: One asks questions, the other frowns and sighs sympathetically. The questions are a sterner version of the medical team's. More importantly, they know who they are, which is to say Nora's sister, so there's no point in the elaborate story they concocted.

The lead officer asks about Nora, and what the sisters know about her. "Did she talk to you? Did she tell you anything about her work? What did she tell you? Why would you come here if you haven't heard from her in months? Are you telling the truth? Are you really telling the truth?"

They're just doing their job. At least they aren't mean about it.

"Why did you think Nora was here?"

"We heard she came this way," Carmen says, knowing how thin it sounds, but they agreed they wouldn't tell them about Nora's message.

"What are these?" they ask, holding out Nora's jar of seeds.

Carmen coughs. She had wasted a precious minute stuffing the jar into their grab bag before the boat sank. Now she was glad she'd missed Nora's letters. "Some, uh, seeds from home," she says.

They confiscate it, and Carmen shoots Skipper a warning look not to protest. It isn't worth it.

The questions go on, and the sky darkens from smoky blue to black. Carmen tries not to fall asleep even though she's only been awake a few hours. She needs to rally. She asks her own questions: Where is Nora? What happened to her?

The security people tell them nothing. They can't confirm she is here or was ever here, and anyway, it is above their pay grade or something. They don't know anything. Or they know and won't say. So, it is an unsatisfying conversation all around, except Carmen convinces them she and Skipper are useless and well enough to be released.

~

A Renewal representative in a yellow jumpsuit named Andi takes them to the worker quarters. The worker quarters are long barrack-style buildings, the spaces separated only by flimsy dividers to create a semblance of rooms. Carmen and Skipper have been assigned one of the spaces.

Their room is cold and basic. Two cots sit under a dim tube of electric light that illuminates the entire row of "private" rooms.

Andi's the Deputy Director for Worker Management. Her buoyant attitude is a contrast to Piotr's grimness. It seems out of place in the spartan room. Andi smiles like she's trying to make the best of the situation for everyone's sake. This is something Carmen both resents and understands.

Skipper hugs the coveralls they were given, and Carmen's heart squeezes.

"How do we turn off the light to sleep?" Carmen asks Andi.

"You can't," Andi says apologetically, because the light is always on. Everyone lives like this. She gestures at the dingy eye masks on top of the thin pillows. "These help."

"We appreciate you letting us stay here," Carmen says.

"Not at all," says Andi. "Unless you can afford a plane ticket, the next boat won't come for two months."

Two months—they'll be stuck here much longer than Carmen anticipated.

Carmen thinks about the job offer at home, past stale, and feels unexpectedly relieved. She wanted for so long to be a nurse, but what she really wanted was to be indispensable. If she were honest—and she generally isn't about this—she's been afraid she will be terrible at it, and she can't stand being mediocre. That's why she got the machine maintenance job with Renewal in the first place; it was something she always knew she was good at, because she understood machines better than Nora, even if it didn't bring her joy. It paid okay and was the responsible thing to do, so she did it because she had to do something. She thought Skipper would too.

Except Skipper didn't. She sailed around in that boat making barely enough to eat, and it upsets Carmen as much as she struggles against the feeling. Because Carmen was the sucker who crammed herself into an okay job, so they wouldn't have to worry about how to pay the bills.

She wouldn't have gotten the nursing degree if not for spite—toward Skipper and Nora, who were fine with her living a mediocre life. That isn't fair, she knows. She did it to herself. In a way, this trip has been an excuse to avoid finding out whether she is a failure or not.

"You should buy tickets soon. They're not cheap." Of course they aren't. Carmen thinks of her dwindling bank account. "Until then, you've been granted temporary authorization to stay."

That means they have two months to find out what happened to Nora, which shouldn't be hard in a town as small and well-organized as this.

"Thank you," Carmen says, since Skipper is not going to help her keep the conversation going. Skipper never does.

Andi breaks into a real smile. Most people, Carmen can tell, are brusque with Andi, but Andi is trying to be helpful.

"In the meantime, we'll get you set up with jobs," says Andi. "Everyone works here. I'll match you with something suitable." She makes it sound like a wonderful opportunity, but it's mandatory.

Carmen sneaks a glance at Skipper, scowling at graffiti scratched into the room divider. They need the money, but working will rob them of time to search for Nora.

"Do you have any skills?" Andi asks, scratching her nose. There's a false brightness to her pleasantness, like she's worried they don't.

"Carmen's a nurse," Skipper volunteers, and it's the first thing Skipper has said all morning. Carmen doesn't know what to say. She wishes Skipper had kept her mouth shut. Carmen wouldn't have made such an absurd claim herself. She's never done the job. It will be obvious. Carmen's cheeks flush with anticipatory shame, but then it occurs to her Skipper has done them a favor. As a nurse Carmen may have access to people and places she wouldn't otherwise.

"That's great," says Andi. "We're short-staffed in that department. And you?"

Skipper's lip protrudes in her stubborn expression. "I sail," she says, after a long pause.

Andi's smile falters. "It's winter. Not a lot of sailing right now. How about mining?"

Skipper's face shows her panic.

"Isn't there something above ground she could do?" Carmen asks.

"Hm. Worm factory?"

Skipper nods. She must realize she has little choice. They're stranded in the middle of the arctic.

"One more thing," says Andi, handing over a tablet. Her nose twitches with embarrassment. "We'll need you to sign these." They're a promise not to disclose anything they see or learn while here to the outside world, and new financial accounts opened in their name. The tally is in the negative including the cost of accommodation, medical care, clothes, and the weekly meal plan. Everything in Vault City has a price, and they're already paying.

CHAPTER TWENTY-SEVEN

After Andi leaves, Skipper drops into one of the cots and pulls the blanket over her head. She's been like this since they were rescued—wretched and monosyllabic.

Carmen pushes her cot up against Skipper's and sits down next to the lump Skipper makes under the blanket. The mattress is so thin she can feel the bars through the padding, and the blankets are inadequate and smell inexplicably like onions. A draft slides between the wall dividers and under the floor.

"Hey." Carmen pokes her sister. "You okay?" What a silly question.

"Mmph," says Skipper, which is better than her pretending to sleep.

Skipper has this tendency to disappear somewhere inside herself. She admitted to Carmen once that she often feels depressed, and Carmen worries she's spiraling. Not that Skipper doesn't have good reason, with the loss of the *Bumblebee* and what happened with Jackson. "What happened" is quite a euphemism.

Carmen tries not to think about it. Logically, she knows she should feel the same as Skipper, full of remorse. And she does feel horrible when she thinks about it, like she's coated herself with oil on the inside. But she doesn't have the luxury to wallow. Only one of them can fall apart right now, and she's older, so it can't be her.

For all her life, that's how it's been. Nora ignored reality, sequestered herself from bad things, and focused on what she wanted. And Skipper was too sensitive, delicate, at the mercy of their grandmother. She was apt to crumple when things got hard. It was up to Carmen to take care of her.

When Skipper decided to go after Nora, Carmen did the only thing she could do: She went along. But now Carmen is unable to help her—Skipper hurts in a way she can't touch.

She sighs and pats Skipper's foot once. She unlocks the locker in the corner and adds their bags.

When they'd left the ship, she took Jackson's bag, because it was out on his bunk. She thought she'd emptied it before she'd added her things (a photo of the three of them; a sewing kit; and the bumblebee mug—why had she bothered with that?), but now Carmen discovers a few items at the bottom of the bag: a sock full of money, a tin of his homemade stain remover, boxers covered in ducks wearing tuxedos, and that awful necklace of human teeth. Their own bag is just necessities: first aid kit, a radio, flares, their identification, and Skipper's fishing gear. They already consumed the emergency food and water.

Time to figure things out for both of them. It is probably easier without Skipper in tow, hollow-eyed and drifting.

Carmen changes into the blue coveralls and parka, grateful for their warmth. The hallway between the rooms fills with noise as a crowd enters. Carmen has never been shy about introducing herself to people. "Excuse me, what time is it?"

"Eighteen hundred," someone tells her, but doesn't stop to chat further.

They are all in a rush somewhere, so Carmen leaves Skipper and follows along with them to the building next door, which turns out to be the worker cafeteria, a loud, brightly lit area filled with long tables and benches and several hundred people eating dinner. She sees more than a few people with an infection like hers: blue-purple fungus curling along their necks and hands. The growth against her ribs throbs.

Experimentally, Carmen gets in line, grabs a tray, and helps herself to food. She's hungry. At the end of the line, a worker scans the black-and-white code embroidered over her breast pocket, recording the meal for payment.

She eats along with everyone else: cornbread, peas, potatoes, and a hunk of something unidentifiable and gamey drenched in gravy that reminds her of the pirates who would have eaten them. She pushes the meat—if it is meat—around her plate, unable to finish it.

She scans the crowd but doesn't see Nora. No one talks to her. Her questions are answered with "yeah" or "nope." They should be more interested in her, an obvious stranger, but to the contrary, everyone avoids her. She begins to feel insubstantial, all edges and no inside, as if the wind outside could blow right through her.

She wraps the cornbread inside the cuff of her long sleeve and trails after everyone else back to the barracks. As she passes from one building to another, she sees a second stream of folks heading out into the dark. From the conversations she overhears, it sounds like they are going to work a night shift.

Skipper accepts the cornbread but doesn't say thank you.

A rebuke rises to Carmen's lips, an urge to provoke a reaction. She swallows it, and the words stick in her throat.

There's an unlit area between the barracks and the communal showers, and since Carmen missed the rush, she must pass through the tunnel of shadows on her way to and from brushing her teeth with the yellow-and-navy company toothbrush. Every muscle in her body tenses in the seconds it takes to cross the snow.

Skipper asked her before why she was scared of the dark, but she didn't tell her why, and now is not the time to dwell on the reason. The problem with Skipper's question is the past-tense wording of it; Carmen is still afraid. Ollie used to make fun of this, and sometimes wielded it to frighten her as a joke, like turning all the lights off while Carmen was downstairs studying in the living room, or smacking the kitchen window from the outside while Carmen washed the dishes.

A hand snakes out of the shadows and catches Carmen's sleeve, and she freezes, because that is unfortunately what she does when faced with danger. It would be better if she were a runner or a screamer, but she's a mouse; she isn't proud of that.

"Where's Jackson?" the voice asks.

Carmen's eyes adjust, and she sees the person is the same medium height as her, with pointy features, long, beautiful eyelashes, and close-cropped hair. Not worth the terror coursing through Carmen. She exhales to try to slow her heart.

"Are *you* Jackson?"

And Carmen remembers Jackson didn't know anyone here personally, he was just connected to them through a friend.

"No," Carmen says. "His boat sank during a storm." She hopes that's enough, because she lies badly.

Jackson's contact digests this. "I'm Emilie. Come meet my husband."

She takes Carmen to a room ten rows and three aisles from theirs, where her husband, Jan, plays a soft, mournful tune on a harmonica. Jan is tall and thin, with sandy hair and a gentle demeanor.

By contrast, Emilie is angry about a lot of things. Eight years have honed her hatred for Renewal. They originally came for the money: The worm factory here pays better than the ones at home, and there's always the possibility of the next bonus, which Renewal issues periodically at unannounced times and in unexpected amounts, to keep workers on their toes.

Emilie isn't the revolutionary Jackson described, but that's probably because Jackson didn't really know people, he just dressed them up in his assumptions.

"This is a terrible time to be here," Emilie says. "You shouldn't have come. I warned your friend, Jackson."

Carmen glances away. "We had to."

They've never heard of Nora, not even from Jackson.

"I don't know if we can help you," Emilie says. "It's easier than you'd think to lose people here."

Carmen knows Emilie's trying to manage her expectations, but Carmen's been worrying for so long, her expectations are already well managed.

"Be careful, yeah?" adds Jan, with more sympathy.

"So how is the strike?" Carmen asks, because they've been nice to her.

"Over," Emilie says. "The people's hearts have shriveled up. They're rabbits."

They find Carmen extra blankets. Emilie has an attractive efficiency about her, but it's Jan's quiet calm that comforts Carmen.

Emilie and Jan both have the same shift as Skipper.

"We'll keep an eye out for her," Jan promises.

Emilie frowns at him, but says, "We'll make sure she doesn't stick her fingers in the compactor."

At that point, a cat shimmies out from between the boxes of personal belongings crammed under the cots. She's black with green eyes, and she comes over to assess whether Carmen's foot is interesting or not.

Carmen bends to scratch her ears, and Jan tells her the cat's name is Luna. Carmen agrees she's a beautiful cat. She's plump and her coat is glossy, like they brush her daily.

Emilie takes a piece of dried fish from her pocket and offers it to Luna, who chews it daintily.

Then Luna darts from the room as if suddenly remembering an appointment. Carmen knows she shouldn't trust them, but she likes their cat.

Carmen trades Jackson's duck underwear to send a few messages home from someone else's device. She asks Marcus if he's heard anything from Nora. She asks Uncle Tot for money. She hates it. She's worked so hard not to rely on anyone; she's happier when people rely on her.

She goes back to their miserable room and watches Skipper sleep with her mouth open and her cold fingers curled over the edge of the blanket. She puts the extra blanket over her and the motion of it invites a flood of feeling: love, for her sister; the weariness of responsibility; and dread. Not for the first time, she thinks how much simpler her life would be if she didn't have sisters, and she hates herself for thinking it.

Once, when Carmen was younger, they followed Nora out into the woods. She wanted to see what her sister did when she disappeared, and why she wasn't allowed to come along. And they saw it—Nora's secret house. Skipper went home, but Carmen watched Nora for hours, angry and confused, as Nora read her books and sang to herself and swept the house as if she were living in a fairy tale. Carmen didn't understand why Nora would want to do these things without her.

Her feet fell asleep, and a couple of bees buzzed around her, but she remembered Grandma had told her they only stung if she moved, so she kept very still and very quiet. After Nora went back to the house, Carmen thought about wrecking Nora's sanctuary. Then she heard a deeper hum she hadn't noticed before. She looked up and saw it: A giant beehive had been hanging over her head the whole time.

She ran all the way home screaming, and for a long time she attributed the bees to some magical power Nora had to bend the world around her. Carmen knows better now, but even so, it's hard for her to worry about Nora. Because she believes her older sister will always triumph in the end. It's natural law.

Skipper opens her eyes. "Where have you been?"

"Out," says Carmen.

"I woke up, and you weren't here."

A stray meanness climbs Carmen's throat. She tamps down on it. "I didn't want to wake you." She goes to the locker and takes her medication, resisting the urge to run her fingertips over the growth under her shirt, test the warm boundaries of it.

She wouldn't have actually let Skipper sell the boat to pay for her procedure, though she was moved by the offer. She would have let her sell it because it was the responsible thing to do. She needed Skipper to be able to stand on her own feet so Carmen could focus on taking care of herself. Now the boat is gone, though, and everything is still on Carmen's shoulders. She wonders if she can take a third job.

"Did you find Nora?"

"I'm pretty sure I would have led with that if I had," says Carmen, lips quirking.

Skipper tucks her head down so half her face is hidden by the blanket, and Carmen's frustration flares again. The past weeks, Skipper surprised her with her competence and fearlessness. But now, as Skipper retreats into her old self, Carmen does too.

"I need you to snap out of this," she says. "You can't sit here waiting for me to solve things for you. We're not going to find Nora by doing nothing. I'm not yelling at you—" Though she is, in fact, yelling. "I'm tired of you being so passive. That's not how the world works, okay? I'm sorry you lost your boat—"

"Our boat," says Skipper, voice cracking.

"But what did you think was going to happen when we came here?"

Skipper complains Carmen talks too much, and at this point, Carmen wishes she could stop herself from talking. This always happens: She hears her own voice with horror, wills herself to stop, and yet her lips continue to expel words that cannot be retrieved.

Skipper, to her credit, takes the verbal beating without a change in her facial expression, which makes Carmen feel worse. It's the same way Skipper endured Grandma's tirades for years.

"I thought we'd have found her by now," whispers Skipper.

Skipper's unvarnished despair extinguishes Carmen's anger. She hugs her younger sister.

She wants to promise her it will be all right, that there aren't a thousand things that could have happened—could still be happening to Nora. But this is a place without sun, and bad things happen in the dark.

CHAPTER TWENTY-EIGHT

The summer Nora moved to the city, Carmen went and stayed with their father. She wrote him to propose it, without expectation and against Nora's advice. He'd been inconsistently around for as long as Carmen could remember, but he was nice when he was.

She was fond of his mustache, which never changed. It was dark brown and even, like a broom over his top lip. It lifted slightly when he smiled, framing white, square teeth. She struggled to picture the rest of him when he wasn't around, which was embarrassing. Surely, there was more to him as a person, but whenever people asked her what he was like, her mind went blank and all she could think about was his mustache.

Skipper was twelve and old enough to be left alone, Carmen figured, and if Nora was going to have an adventure, Carmen wanted one too.

To her surprise, he wrote her back: *Yes, come. I'd love to have you. We can get to know each other better.*

She barely knew her father, but she liked the idea of him. When she was younger, she felt sorry for Skipper, because Skipper didn't have her own. Nora said she envied Skipper, because she couldn't be disappointed.

It's true he sent birthday presents months late, and they were always the wrong thing. He didn't read books. His life was too simple for Nora, and Nora was embarrassed of him, so for a long time, Carmen pretended the same.

But actually, she didn't mind his faults. The only person she expected things from was herself.

Their father lived and still lives a few hours inland in a log cabin in the woods. He was medium height and stocky, with a large nose, and, of course, the mustache, which was just as she remembered. He liked animals and kept a salt lick out in the yard. Deer and rabbits and chipmunks would come, and he would photograph them. A menagerie of beautiful black-and-white pictures crowded his walls.

"All creatures like salt," he told Carmen.

"Is it good for them?" Carmen asked.

"Sure," he said. "They wouldn't eat it otherwise."

At the time, Carmen thought this was a deep perspective about the world, and she treasured the idea, that nature could regulate itself like that. It was only years later that she found it reductive. It didn't consider the salt lick was humanmade, purchased from a store, so there was nothing natural about it, a lump of minerals fastened to the top of a wooden post.

Occasionally, her father would shoot the animals and carve the meat up in his freezer for winter. He didn't eat a lot of vegetables, and most of his shirt sleeves were stained here and there with specks of old blood.

Carmen hated the woods back home, but she didn't mind these. It smelled like honeysuckle, and the animals that came around seemed healthy, with their glossy coats and bright eyes. At night, she could hear the stream burbling, mixed with her father's snores, and she could ignore the way the dark curled in around the cabin walls.

"You can sleep on the couch," he told her when she arrived, because he didn't have a bed. What he meant was, he would sleep in a sleeping bag on the floor, because he loved her.

He spent most of his time at the shop, or on the road hauling back large, broken vehicles across terrible roads.

She liked everything about his life: going out to answer a call for help, mostly automated signals from unmanned vehicles but sometimes from people; lifting the hood and diagnosing whatever lay beneath; pressing Start on the giant, battered, wheezy machine in the corner of his shop that printed new parts; the satisfaction of fixing something, even if it inevitably broke again.

Like Carmen, he had friends everywhere. They came over and drank on the porch, or they invited them out to the local bar. Everyone liked him, and he liked them. She felt the love around him and knew Nora wouldn't understand it, and that made her feel superior to Nora.

For three months, Carmen worked by his side, until her shirts were stained black with grease, and the machine that printed spare parts reverberated in her ears even when she slept. She made herself useful, cooking for him, fitting herself into the corners of his life without being a bother.

In fact, she had come to stay with him with a secret purpose: to convince him of the merits of taking her and Skipper in permanently. Grandma's behavior had become notably erratic. Nora thought she might be at the onset of forgetting herself. In any case, living with her had become more unpleasant than usual.

So Carmen talked about Skipper at every opportunity. She mentioned how diligently Skipper had worked on the *Bumblebee*, how little Skipper complained about anything, how quiet Skipper was, and how a few times Carmen had come into the living room and not noticed her sitting on the couch reading a book for a good fifteen minutes.

At first, Carmen worried about Skipper. She wrote letters home checking in on how she was, but Skipper's replies were infrequent and short. Skipper was okay (she'd said) so no need to worry. As the weeks went on, Carmen's worry about Skipper began to leak away. She felt the relief of being out from Grandma's constant criticism. She thought, maybe this is what childhood should have been like.

At the end of the summer, her father delivered her back to the pink house.

Skipper sat on the porch mending a pile of clothes. Her fingers were blistered, and she kept having to get up and rinse the blood off her fingertips. Was she always so scrawny?

"Grandma missed your cooking," she told Carmen. "So did I." And Carmen wanted to cry, because the weight came back with a thud as she looked at Skipper's uneven stitches, and the angle of her collarbones. Carmen thought about all the things that might have happened while she was gone. She was angry Skipper hadn't told her how things were, and angry with herself for pretending this wasn't so predictable.

Her father offered Skipper a candy bar, and Skipper's grin broke Carmen's heart. She should have invited Skipper to come along with her this summer rather than worry Skipper's presence would undermine her mission.

"Carmen told me the boat sails great," he said, and Skipper needed no further encouragement. She told him all about the *Bumblebee* and what new improvements they were working on. She gave Carmen credit for everything, even though Carmen hadn't touched the boat in months. Carmen regretted not spending the summer with her sister, who was talking like she hadn't talked to anyone in weeks. Carmen missed the simplicity of working on the boat. Or maybe she felt guilty she didn't regret her time away more.

"I think I know how to fix the engine now," Carmen told Skipper, and Skipper cheered.

"I wish you could live here," Skipper told Carmen's father. "Will you stay for dinner?"

"You didn't make it sound very good," her father laughed. "I have to get going."

The feeling, long ignored, came back to Carmen: Her father didn't want to be here. He didn't want to be with them. Suddenly her shoulder blades began to itch, as if she'd been bitten.

"Are you okay?" he asked, as Carmen contorted herself to scratch a spot she couldn't reach. Carmen's back stung as her nails tore a track through her skin.

"I think I've got an ant inside my shirt."

"What?" he laughed, but she didn't explain further.

Skipper went inside to wake Grandma up from her nap, and he said, "She's so funny, isn't she?"

The itch spread, because he didn't mean it as a compliment, and all the good feeling of the summer washed away.

She had planned to take him aside after arriving, perhaps after dinner before he headed off. As she'd envisioned it, they would have a sentimental chat, and she and Skipper would take him down to the dock to show him the *Bumblebee.* They'd stop by the dockside restaurant and her father would treat them to dinner. But now she saw it would never work. He wasn't up for any kind of responsibility. Carmen was easy because she could take care of herself, and even so, he was glad to be returning her. She could see the way he smiled under his mustache. And he definitely didn't want Skipper; he thought she was weird.

"Well," Grandma said, coming out onto the porch half-asleep. "Here you are."

She said it the same way Nora did, each word dripping with judgment.

"Thanks for a great summer," Carmen said to him.

"We'll do it again," he said, though she knew from the way he avoided her gaze when he said it that they never would.

"If you'd told me you were coming today, we could have gone to the store," said Grandma.

"Sorry," Carmen said for both of them. Why couldn't they all act like normal people? She was the only grownup in the family.

"I don't need anything," her father said.

"Not right now, anyway." Grandma eyed Skipper's pile of old clothes. "You're still working on that?"

"I'm going to finish it," said Skipper, taking up her needle. It was bent like a comma, as if Skipper had tried to force it through too much cloth.

He laughed and shook his head. "Stay in touch, then," he told Carmen.

She was so angry, she didn't know what to say. *Nora was right*, she thought. *Dammit.*

The air cooled as they stood there, the last embers of summer turning gray.

He didn't say goodbye to anyone else, just walked back to the truck and climbed inside.

Grandma went in to decant some soup from the basement.

The trees menaced the house with their shadows.

"You came back," Skipper said, picking at splinters sticking up out of the porch, her words so small Carmen almost missed them.

"Of course I did," said Carmen, and she wondered wearily as she joined Skipper on the step if the only thing they'd been born for was to sit here, watching the sun sink down.

CHAPTER TWENTY-NINE

The next day, before breakfast, Emilie takes Carmen and Skipper outside and points out the imposing vault facility gates. "Your sister's probably in there."

Carmen stiffens. Nora's message from weeks ago said: *Im trapped in the vault*. Nora must be inside.

The walls are thick, as if built for a medieval siege. She wonders what it would take to blow it up. She's thinking again of Jackson and his fantasies, and she shouldn't be.

They want to check immediately, but entry and exit into the vault requires a badge, so they can't walk in there. Bored guards stand by the gates. The three women watch for several minutes, getting colder and colder, and in that time, no one passes in or out. Ice crystals prickle in Carmen's nostrils.

"How do we get in there?" Carmen asks Emilie.

"Anything's possible if you have money."

Unfortunately, the money they have is worthless. By design, Emilie explains: In Vault City, the only money with value is Renewal points—one more way the company retains control over workers.

So they need Renewal points.

Back in their room, Carmen digs through everything they have. It's not much. While Skipper dozes, she goes back to Emilie and Jan.

"Hi, hi," says Jan, looking up from his egg. A lot of people here have a cheap version of them, but the data flow in and out of the town is monitored. The company can't afford to have people leaking their secrets. Carmen imagines how Jackson would react. She has to stop thinking about him.

"And how's your sister doing?"

Carmen shrugs, because there's nothing good to say. "Is there a place around here that changes money? And maybe buys things? Like a pawn shop."

Emilie sits up and puts down a battered paperback of *A Forester's Guide to Poisonous Mushrooms*, which she picked up at a recent swap. "Yes, we know someone. Do you need to go now?"

"If you give me directions, I can find them myself," says Carmen, not wanting to be a bother.

"No problem," says Emilie. "I'm bored anyway. Let's go."

Jan goes where Emilie goes, so Carmen walks along between them. There are mangy dogs everywhere, chewing on bones and snuffling in the dirty snow. Some of them are normal-looking, and some show signs of gene-tinkering: scarlet coats, green cat eyes, and stubby thumbs on their paws. In the deepest parts of winter, Emilie tells her, people race dog sleds across the tundra. The winner gets a large sum of money to send home. It is something to do, anyway.

Their buyer is a few buildings over. The city is laid out in a massive half circle with the vault facility in the middle, and long streets radiating out from that lined with dormitories, municipal services, factories, and shops, all ending at the waterfront. From above, even the town resembles the Renewal logo. This is the height of tackiness, but Emilie flashes Carmen a sharp look when she says so.

"You need to be careful what you say," she warns her in a hushed whisper that makes Carmen's pulse accelerate. "I got into trouble once with security. Detained for a night, no reason. Then, oops, mistake, you can go. It was not a mistake, okay? It was because I was criticizing Renewal to the wrong person."

"It was a joke," Carmen says, wishing she'd said nothing, not because of Emilie's warning, but because Emilie hadn't laughed. Carmen's not used to her jokes not landing.

"It was a funny joke," Jan says.

"But not funny enough to be worth it," Emilie says.

Their boots crunch on packed snow as they walk, breath steaming in plumes. Carmen appreciates the Renewal parka that covers her knees.

They turn left past the vault, down the next couple of streets. As they pass the facility, she glances furtively at the two security personnel at the entrance. They hold larger guns than she's ever seen before, and her shoulders tighten. This isn't the kind of place she could sneak into even if she were the sneaking kind of person. Which she isn't.

"Why do they even need that much security?" she asks. "We're in a remote place. Everyone here works for the company."

"The treasures of the vault are priceless," says Emilie. "Seeds that could be used to revive every kind of plant in the world that has gone extinct."

"Preservation. It's important work," says Jan.

Emilie rolls her eyes. "Yes, they are saving it for the end of the world."

Carmen opens her mouth to ask why they don't open the vault now.

But Emilie shakes her head a fraction, as if reading her thoughts. "Not here."

The buyer operates out of a noodle shop. He's a sprightly old man with wispy gray hair and a soft, wrinkled face.

The noodles are overcooked and overpriced. Carmen pretends otherwise, because there's no benefit in being rude. She turns on the charm. Skipper thinks it's fake when she does this, but it isn't an act. People want to be liked, and Carmen likes people. Like with

Jackson—she had liked Jackson. She isn't happy he's dead. But every night when she dreams of him, she kills him again.

She hands over Jackson's money, and the noodle shop owner offers a pitiful exchange rate.

"It's the best I can do," he says, and she thinks he's sincere, but it doesn't stop her disappointment.

She shows him their emergency kit: the radio, medical kit, and flares. She hesitates, then also shows him the necklace made of teeth. She doesn't know why Jackson held on to it. To her surprise, the buyer brightens. "These are in excellent condition. I know a guy who could make dentures out of these."

Carmen suppresses a wave of disgust. "How much?"

"Two thousand," says the buyer. A badge on the black market, Emilie explained, costs at least six thousand.

Emilie snorts. "We have better things to do. Come on, my friend."

"Three thousand," says the buyer. "That's a lot."

"Three thousand five hundred," says Emilie.

"No."

Emilie tugs Carmen's elbow. "Come on."

"Three thousand two hundred," says the buyer. "I swear I can do no more."

Carmen starts to name another price, but the buyer repeats: "I can't."

Carmen gives him the necklace. She negotiates a couple hundred points for everything else.

"Do I want to know where you got those?" Emilie asks as they walk away.

"I don't think so," says Jan.

"Mother Ocean," says Carmen.

Emilie squints sideways at her, like she is reevaluating her usefulness, and Carmen tries not to warm to it.

She has no idea how they'll get the rest of the money. Carmen will figure it out one way or another. She always does.

When Carmen gets back, there's a reply from Uncle Tot: *I'm so glad you're all right. I've been worried sick because I didn't hear from you. I'm doing okay. I was going to have my friends over for poker, but your grandma melted all my poker chips in the casserole dish, I assume in revenge for my chili. I* like *my chili. I'm sorry I can't send more money. Is this enough?*

What he sent won't buy them new gloves.

Marcus, Nora's friend back in the city, has also replied. *Thanks for your message. Please don't write again.*

Vault City is a great machine, extracting and recycling the fragments of apocalypse, and Carmen and Skipper are pulled into its rhythm of work and meals.

Few people are born here. Most residents arrive with work and sleeping places assigned. The business of Vault City is Renewal's business, and in case anyone forgets they own the place, the rising sun logo is visible everywhere: on the crates of food delivered by boat, on the workers' helmets and the vans shuttling into the tundra toward the mines, on the clothing people wear, on the building doors, the signs, and the blankets.

Carmen and Skipper ask everyone they meet about Nora, but no one seems to have heard of her. How can a human being disappear in a town of a few thousand people?

There's a registrar with the records of everyone in town. It's open on Mondays and Wednesdays. The first Monday, four days after their arrival, Carmen and Skipper walk down together.

It's midmorning and everyone else is working or sleeping, but they both are slated to start night shifts, so this is the best time to do it.

Carmen wishes Jan and Emilie could have come, not that they offered to. It would have been reassuring to have them here, explaining how to handle things.

"It's that way," says Skipper, pointing out a white municipal building opposite the vault compound.

Carmen is surprised Skipper paid attention when Emilie gave the directions. The building is gracefully designed, its curved façade an echo of the ocean waves in the distance beyond. Outside it is a clear case filled with ice sample cores. They are labeled in a fine print that tells a fraction of the history of Earth. It's the sort of public exhibit no one, Carmen included, ever stops to study, but the image of it sticks with Carmen: the way eight hundred thousand years can be summarized so succinctly, and how so little of it belonged to humans.

The doors at the base are small in comparison, made of some composite that mimics wood. They are heavy to open, but no one appears to offer assistance. Inside, the lobby is empty, save a bored security guard near the door, and a receptionist at the far end. The guard checks them for weapons, and then they have to walk all the way across the white tile floor. Carmen's footfalls are obscenely loud, and Skipper's left boot sounds like one of Uncle Tot's dog toys. The squeak, once noticed, is impossible to tune out. A snort escapes from Carmen, and then they both giggle uncontrollably.

The security guard coughs but doesn't ask them what's so funny.

Their laughter subsides when they reach the other end. A chill settles around Carmen's shoulders. There's a faint smell like artificial mint.

The receptionist informs them it costs ten Renewal points for each search, then gestures to the monitor on the left. Automated. The fact that the machine has limited hours when it could operate twenty-four hours or simply be accessed from an egg makes the situation even more pointless than Carmen imagined. They search in the system for *Nora Shimizu* and then *Nora S* and *Mara* and *Craven*, Grandma's last name, and *Nanda*, their father's last name, and any other name they can think of.

No records found, the machine tells them.

"Are all visitors and residents included in here?" Carmen asks the receptionist and receives a tart "obviously" in return.

Carmen sighs too loudly.

"Time's up," says the receptionist, tapping the clock on the desk.

They've spent two hundred and thirty Renewal points for nothing, and Carmen thinks about all the questions she's ever asked for free without appreciating the cost of the answers.

CHAPTER THIRTY

Carmen arrives for her first night shift at the clinic with sweating palms. What will happen when people discover she's a fraud?

From the outside, the clinic resembles the other buildings. It's three stories, with an elevator, and employs a full staff of twelve around the clock—not enough to cover their needs, in other words, so everyone is happy to see Carmen.

She recognizes Piotr, their dour nurse from before. He doesn't smile when he greets her, but he pats her shoulder once in a perfunctory but familiar way she finds reassuring.

"You'll keep up," he tells her, and she swallows the apology she carries in her mouth. She's got to pretend she's someone else. The real Carmen would never sneak into a Renewal settlement on false pretenses or sell human teeth on the black market. She wouldn't leave a man to drown either.

Piotr nods. He's pale and wan in the electric light, like he's been drained of all his blood and might fall over. Despite this, he talks too fast, and Carmen gives up taking notes and just tries to remember it all. Bathroom, there. Work shift check-in, there. Assignments, here. Equipment, there. Do you know how to use this machine? No? We'll teach you. This? No? We'll teach you. How about that? Jesus, where were you trained?

Carmen's face heats as she starts to explain, but he doesn't actually care. He hands her a pair of white coveralls to change in to. "We've been thin on the ground, since—" He stops and looks at Carmen. "Be careful who you hang out with. We've lost staff before. This is not a place to have political opinions, okay?"

"No problem," Carmen says. All she wants to do is find Nora.

"I can't protect you if you make trouble," Piotr says, brows knitting in a scowl, but then he softens. "Try to avoid trouble, okay?"

"No problem."

And then the work begins, and it's fast-paced and wretched as Piotr warned, and Carmen needs even more guidance than she feared, but Piotr repeats whatever needs repeating without losing his temper, and it's so much better than repairing battered old machines and breathing dirt and Amaranthine dust that Carmen forgets her nervousness. She almost forgets why she came here in the first place.

Skipper, to her credit, doesn't complain when she comes back covered in grime from her first factory shift. She spends extra time in the shower, until a line forms.

"You'll never get it off," Emilie tells her, rubbing her fingers together. "The plastic. It coats your skin like an invisible glove."

She's been at the factory with Emilie and Jan, and Carmen feels a flash of jealousy, even though she has no desire for that kind of work.

Skipper sits on her cot, dragging her nails along her arm, leaving red tracks.

"Stop it," Carmen says out of habit, even though Skipper won't listen.

"Why are you talking funny?"

"What do you mean?"

"Like that. You talk like them." Because Carmen has already begun to absorb the cadence and accent of people here. That's what Carmen does. She blends in.

"How was it?"

"Fine." Skipper hangs the jumpsuit on a hook. The front of it is wet, like Skipper tried to clean it. She hasn't done a good job. It's spattered with something dark.

Carmen tosses Jackson's stain remover to her, trying to forget its origin.

Later, Emilie takes Carmen aside in the bathroom. "Hans could have died today, right next to your sister. There was something in the machine, and it exploded. Sharp pieces everywhere. Hans took it in the face and neck. Lots of blood." Emilie's eyes smolder with anger, and she violates the advice she gave Carmen. "Fuck this shit."

Carmen's stomach roils. She'd seen the man brought into the clinic earlier, but the story was somehow garbled in the telling—that he was from the mines, not the factory, that he had slipped and fallen.

"This place needs to be burned down," says Emilie.

Luna appears. She rubs against Carmen's legs, purring, and her contentment is the purest thing in this place. Carmen squats to scratch her between the ears.

"Why don't you leave?" Carmen asks.

"We stayed too long," Emilie tells her. "The bed, the food, the clothes—they charge you for it. It's so expensive. We've saved almost nothing. It's not in their interest for any of us to leave, and they've decided this is cheaper than paying us to stay."

"What do you mean?"

Emilie looks meaningfully at the vents, at the clock on the wall, at any corner of the room that might credibly hold a camera. "You learn things here."

"Like what?"

"Better for you not to know," she breathes in a lowered voice that forces Carmen to lean close enough to see each hair of her eyelashes and smell the sweet chemical scent that permeates her clothes.

Emilie straightens and washes her hands. "Anyway, what would we go home to? We don't have anything to do back there. At least here we eat. No, we must change things instead." She gives Carmen a long, measuring once-over. Then she comes to a decision. She gestures for Carmen to grab her parka and follow. They walk around the town, in and out of the soft penumbras of lights.

"What did Jackson tell you about us?"

Carmen concentrates on keeping a straight face when Emilie says his name, and because of this, she takes too long to answer. Jackson told her many things, but the truth is, she wasn't paying attention. Skipper wasn't wrong; he did talk a lot. If he told them anything specific about Emilie and Jan's plans, she can't remember.

"Hm," says Emilie, and Carmen worries Emilie's concluded from the awkward silence Carmen can't be trusted. "Have you ever wanted to change the world?"

Carmen thinks of Nora, and her experiments, her never-ending pursuit of knowledge, her ambition for *better*. She thinks of her own, passionless life in comparison.

"Not really."

Emilie purses her lips. "Because you have always felt powerless. But you're not. Look at what you've done."

Despite herself, Carmen thrills at Emilie's words.

"What I'm going to tell you, you cannot repeat, do you agree? Recently, someone repeated something to the wrong person, and they arrested a lot of people. They would have gotten us too, but Jan paid them to leave us alone. I'm taking a risk with you, because we need help. What do you think? If you help us, we'll help you."

Carmen's guess had been that the "movement" wasn't more organized than a loose collection of grumbling people, but now she believes there is more to it.

They pass a kennel, and some of the dogs run over, teeth sharp and gleaming in the moonlight. The wind shifts and they bark; she imagines they smell the fresh soap on her skin.

"What are you offering?" Carmen likes Emilie. She wants to be friends with her. She likes Jan too, but Emilie seems like the kind of person who can get things done.

"We have people inside," Emilie says, gesturing at the vault gate that looms over the square. They've been walking circles of the plaza. "We can find your sister."

Carmen feels a thread of optimism. "How?"

"Don't worry about it. We're working on it."

"You didn't tell me!" says Carmen. She rubs her hands together and resolves to take Piotr's advice about getting better gloves.

"We weren't friends yet, were we?" says Emilie. "Don't be mad. I didn't know I could trust you."

A voice in Carmen whispers, *How do you know you can trust me?* But she quashes it, because she's always seen herself as the kind of person people invest their secrets in. Even Skipper.

"Can you help us get her out?" Carmen asks.

"That's a very serious ask," Emilie says. "It would be dangerous for everyone involved." She pivots and turns back to the barracks. "You haven't asked me what we need you to do."

This is a transaction. They will only help her if she cooperates. Emilie slides an arm through hers.

"What do you want?"

Emilie whispers the names of several drugs available in the clinic. If Carmen steals them for her, Emilie will get her information about Nora, maybe even a message to her.

Carmen tries to suppress her anxiety. It isn't fair to expect Emilie to do more for her for nothing. They've just met, and as Emilie says, what they're asking is a big thing. But the idea of stealing something from the clinic fills her with dread. It doesn't feel right, and she can't imagine how she will do it, given how she goes limp as soon as the adrenaline hits her.

Be someone else here, she tells herself, and wills her body to absorb this as truth. *Be ruthless.* It's not working.

"You can make friends anywhere," Skipper mutters when Carmen climbs into the cot next to her to sleep through the day.

"You could too," Carmen says. "It's not that hard." Again, annoyance bubbles up. She picks again, because she wants to fight, the catharsis of flinging barbs against a person who will forgive her. Petty sibling squabbles are built on a foundation of trust—trust that their relationship is strong enough to continue unaffected by the argument of the day. She never had that with Ollie. That's probably why it didn't work out. Carmen would fold when things got too tense.

Skipper thinks of Carmen as a strong person, but Carmen only pushes so far. Just enough to defend herself, never enough to break free. It was like that with Grandma, Ollie, Jackson. She wishes she were braver.

Carmen first met Ollie when Ollie was working for Renewal as a seasonal farmworker, and Carmen was called to fix one of the spraying machines. Ollie kept coming by to make sure Carmen had enough water. She offered Carmen half of her sandwich. Ollie was direct and confident in her attention. They started dating.

Carmen moved in as soon as she could, mostly because she couldn't take living with Grandma anymore. Not that moving out freed her of any responsibilities—she cooked for them and cleaned the house. Ollie complained about this, and at the time, Carmen thought Ollie was being protective. She liked that too, so much that even later, as Ollie's barbs began to accumulate—her criticisms about Carmen's family, the way Carmen supported them financially without appreciation, and the frivolousness of studying for a nursing degree when she had a decent job—Carmen told herself it didn't matter, because Ollie took care of her in a way no one else did. After their awful fights, Ollie would apologize. She loved Carmen too deeply, she said. She wouldn't be disappointed if she didn't think so much of Carmen. And Carmen accepted that too.

Skipper turns over, and Carmen sees her face. She's holding something.

"What's that?" Carmen asks.

Reluctantly, Skipper unfurls her fingers. In her palm is a necklace with a bumblebee. It's a match to the one around Skipper's neck. Carmen has one too, but she left it at home—for safekeeping, she said, but she never wore it. She found the necklace a bit cheap, the kind of trinket a teenager would wear. This one must be Nora's.

"Someone salvaged it at the factory a couple of weeks ago. I bought it off them."

With money they can't afford to spend, but Carmen doesn't ask how much. Whatever it cost was worth it. It's the first tangible proof their sister is here.

But how did something so precious end up in the garbage? Carmen feels a foreboding and an urgency to get inside the vault.

She takes the necklace. The metal retains the warmth of Skipper's hands. She raises it by the chain to the pale lamplight above. One of its wings is missing, and the stripes on its belly have mostly worn away, but the shape is familiar. She swallows.

"I stopped by the vault after work," Skipper admits.

This is a surprise. In Carmen's experience, Skipper rarely engages anyone in conversation if someone else—usually Carmen—can do it for her.

"I tried talking to the security guards there. Assholes. They just kept saying no, I couldn't go in without proper credentials and no, they couldn't confirm if Nora was inside and no, they couldn't pass a message to her for me if she was."

Carmen tries to pass the necklace back, but Skipper stops her. "You're less likely to lose it."

So Carmen slips it on around her neck. She brushes her collarbone and finds a raised bump. She goes to the mirror in the bathroom and pulls down the edge of her T-shirt. Purple threads curl around the base of her neck, and there's a second nodule on the inside of her right breast.

She sucks in a breath. All the more reason to hurry. They have fifty-five days until the next boat arrives. Before then, they still have to get into the vault, find Nora, and earn the money they need to leave. It should be plenty of time, but, of course, it isn't.

CHAPTER THIRTY-ONE

It's too easy to burn through the days in this place while Carmen tries to figure out how to get into the vault.

She works each night at the clinic, then comes home and has breakfast with Skipper and whispers in the dim light of their miserable room. Sometimes, their shifts don't align, and she has to make do with word of her sister through Jan or Emilie. Jan, at least, is generous with information, unless Emilie is in a bad mood.

At work, she's grateful for Piotr, who keeps her afloat. He never returns her smiles, but he saves his patience for her. He repeats instructions she can't remember and explains things beyond the bare necessity, so she can understand the science behind why medications work and how machines function. He reminds her somewhat of Nora, the way he examines everything with quiet tenderness.

In her way, she gathers bits of his life, not just the facts but the soft flesh of it: his partner who works in the mines, drilling deep under the thawing permafrost. They fell in love years ago but only got together recently. He embroiders curtains to hang on his wall in the barracks, so he can believe a window lies behind it. He is planning a special breakfast to greet the sun with when it returns and keeps a countdown in the staff lobby. He is a person who collects small joys inside him.

Skipper doesn't understand why Carmen invests in fleeting friendships, why she's always falling in love. But Carmen thinks, *Isn't this the best thing about me?*

Once they leave here, they will never see these people again. But Carmen craves the warmth of other people, as if there's something unlit inside her that can't burn without their fuel. Perhaps it's growing up in the middle of two sisters, and never being alone. Or perhaps it's that she doesn't know how to love herself without context.

"How did you bear it?"

It's the first full sentence Skipper's spoken in days.

They lie on their creaky cots. Carmen's been having trouble sleeping—a symptom, maybe, of the growth inside her. She stares at the wall for hours or roams the hallways of the worker quarters.

Before Skipper spoke, Carmen was thinking about stealing the drugs from the clinic. Emilie is growing impatient. She's friendly when they run into each other in the dormitory, but their conversations always bend back around to her request. "We are running out of time," Emilie says but won't explain what her broader plan is against Renewal. She has shared nothing more about Nora; if she knows anything, she won't say.

Even the thought of stealing makes Carmen sweat. She's never done anything like it in her life. She wonders if she's desperate enough. Piotr mentioned another nurse was caught stealing pills. They were imprisoned for a year. He told her the story as if he were sharing gossip, but Carmen couldn't help feeling he knew, somehow, what Emilie has asked of her, what Carmen is contemplating. Carmen can't afford to be caught.

"What do you mean?" Carmen asks, because she realizes she's missed what Skipper was talking about.

"Going every day to the same place, doing exactly what people tell you to do hour after hour. I don't know how you did it."

When Skipper graduated from high school, Carmen assumed Skipper would join her in working for Renewal. She put a word in for her with her boss's boss, and it was all worked out. She bought her a Renewal hat, a new (used) pair of jeans, pills to counter Amaranthine exposure, and sunscreen for long days in the fields. It was her graduation present. She set it all on the kitchen table at the house for Skipper to find. The next day, Skipper left the box on Carmen's porch.

"But I got it for you," Carmen explained.

"I can't," Skipper said.

That was deflating and then infuriating. Skipper didn't want any part of Carmen's world. She wanted to sail the *Bumblebee* like she was a kid, and pretend it was some kind of living. She didn't make enough to get by, which meant Carmen had to support her and Grandma, usually in ways Skipper wouldn't realize, because Skipper was always so sensitive about it. Carmen paid the utilities a few times, because Skipper forgot. She took Grandma to the doctor and paid for that too. All the while, Carmen collected her resentments like pennies in a jar, because Skipper thought she was too good for the kind of work Carmen did.

When she first got together with Ollie, she loved how practical Ollie was. Ollie worshiped at the church of rationality, and she believed wholeheartedly in selfishness. When Carmen was with her, it felt like freedom, at least at first. Carmen began to entertain the idea it was okay to live for herself. When Ollie found a buyer for the boat, Carmen thought, finally, someone agrees Skipper's life could be so much better if she weren't trapped in a cycle of endless maintenance, trying to keep that boat afloat. And when Ollie sold Skipper's mussels, there was a part of Carmen that thought, *Well, Skipper doesn't want the money anyway.*

Now Skipper turns over, eyes drooping, lips bleeding and chapped, and Carmen realizes Skipper was right. Skipper wouldn't have lasted a month in the fields.

"Why do people have to work?"

Skipper isn't naive, she's asking a deeper question. She is asking why human civilization is constructed this way. This is not a question

Carmen can even attempt to answer when she's spent and trying to figure out how to steal from her job, which she actually likes.

Carmen answers her original question: "You just do it. And each day, you tell yourself stories about the future you're making, and the day when you can do something else. I liked knowing I was taking care of myself." *And you and Grandma*, she thinks, but she doesn't want to make Skipper feel bad.

Carmen spends a few points to check her messages again. She considers writing to Ollie for help, but the thought sours her stomach.

Instead, she asks her father for money, even though she'd rather not, because she hasn't asked him for anything since that summer she was fifteen. He responds with alarm: She never told him Nora was missing, and now he wants to know more than Carmen can explain when Renewal might be reading her messages.

Please, can you send money? she says, and each back-and-forth costs a little more. She regrets reaching out, but then he surprises her by sending more money than Uncle Tot did, though it's not even close to what they need. He says he'll work on getting more, but she doubts he can, and he promises he's alerting authorities, which she didn't ask him to do given she already tried that in the beginning.

She should have had Skipper deal with him, because as an adult, Skipper weirdly has a better relationship, probably because she doesn't have anything to hold against him.

The thing about Carmen is she thinks about things too much. She thinks about the fact that drugs in this place are limited, and that stealing might mean a patient won't have enough. She thinks about the fact that Emilie could be using her to steal drugs she can sell on the black market. She thinks about how disappointed Piotr will be if he finds out what Carmen has done.

She doesn't have a choice. They haven't been able to make any progress finding Nora, and now that Skipper knows Emilie can help, she asks Carmen every day about it, until Carmen snaps at her to stop.

"Emilie says we need it by tomorrow, otherwise we can't help you," Jan says, all in a rush, like he doesn't like the way the words taste. They stand in the dining room in front of a pile of the hard bread rolls that accompany every meal.

"It's impossible," Carmen says. "I need more time."

"I'm sorry, Carmen." He takes a roll and pretends to examine it.

She can see specks of mold on the edge of it, and wonders if she should point them out.

He drops the roll on his tray. "We do want to help." He leaves her standing by the rolls, worrying about how quickly time is leaking away.

The clinic building is shaped like a square, with an inner courtyard on the upper floors covered with a pitched steel-and-glass roof. The specialist rooms are on the ground floor beneath the courtyard, and the patient rooms are arranged all around the outside. Medication is stored in a walk-in closet in the northwest corner, next to the examination rooms. The door is locked, and only the pharmacists and senior staff have a key fob. They pass the fob around, because the place is so short-staffed, it would be difficult to get through the work without broader access, but there's been enough previous incidents of theft that they've been taking precautions.

To get to the closet, Carmen must pass the benches where people sit, the staff room, and the open doors of patient rooms. The hallway is always busy, staff moving about from room to room. There are cameras, also, in the hall, but that's a problem Carmen will need to deal with another time.

All shift, Carmen finds reasons to walk past the door, trying not to look at it. She's amazed she hasn't been caught, even though she hasn't done anything. Around midnight, as she wheels an examination machine from one room to another, she realizes the corridor is relatively empty. The few other staff are walking away, the closet door behind them.

She stops and stands staring at the door for several long moments. Maybe someone has left it unlocked. It's possible. The day before, she heard the pharmacist getting scolded for such negligence.

Move, she tells herself, trying to even her breath. *You can't stand your entire life in front of a door.*

With liquid limbs she reaches for the knob. A century passes before her fingers close on cold metal. It's locked.

"Carmen." It's Piotr, who is everywhere. "What are you doing?"

Carmen jumps. "Sorry, I was looking for the closet for this machine. Everything all right?" She asks this last question to disarm, to turn the focus of the conversation back on him.

He frowns at her, the mole on his lip twitching. "It's over there," he says, pointing across the hall.

"I'm sorry," says Carmen, again. "I promise I'll do better." She doesn't know which would be worse, that he believes she's so incompetent she hasn't figured out her way around after almost two weeks on the job, or that he knows she is up to something.

"They should label things better." He watches her store the machine. After he walks away, she has to come back and retrieve it to take to the intended patient room.

The white door of the pharmaceutical closet throbs out of the corner of her vision. She's hopeless. She'll never manage to pull it off.

But in the end, Carmen's anxiety is unnecessary. Around three in the morning, she hears a commotion down the hall of the lobby. A figure streaks past her, screaming. Several staff restrain him, and she glimpses a constellation of fungi bursting from his jaw, the same as what's been growing inside her. But that's not what's causing this pain.

Scarlet veins bulge from his neck and face. He's suffering from acute Amaranthine poisoning. He must have drunk a liter of it. Maybe he thought he could cure himself. It's a horrible way to die. He screams again and takes off in unfathomable pain, smashing windows and slamming doors. He knocks over all the boxes lined up on the shelf. He stampedes through staff not fast enough to get out of the way.

Chaos reigns.

Piotr shouts for someone to get a sedative, but no one is paying attention to him.

When this all starts, Carmen is immobilized as always by shock. Then she remembers: *You aren't Carmen. Not here.*

Piotr turns to her and thrusts the key fob at her. He describes what they need.

Carmen stares at the key.

"It's going to be all right," he says. "There is tomorrow, okay?"

She feels the words distantly. Tomorrow, when she's found her sister, and they are gone from this awful place.

A beat longer, and she realizes no one is paying any attention to her, and Piotr has delivered her exactly what she needs. She runs to the pharmacy, clutching Piotr's key fob. The door opens immediately, and she finds the sedative right where she remembers it. Then, before she can think about it more, she stuffs the rest of the box and the other items Emilie asked for in her pockets.

Piotr calls for her.

She returns and hands him a loaded syringe, heart thudding. She can't believe she did it. Surely, he can see the sheen of sweat on her face and read the guilt in the twitch of her nose. But obviously, Piotr has more important things to worry about, like subduing a patient rampaging through the clinic.

Carmen spends the rest of the shift pressed back against the wall, waiting for someone to notice the slight bulge in her pockets. But no one does. As she leaves, Piotr thanks her for acting swiftly.

CHAPTER THIRTY-TWO

You did well,” says Emilie, taking the roll of socks Carmen used to hide the stolen medication. “I was starting to doubt you.”

A storm hammers the roof. Emilie and Jan have been here long enough they’ve managed to trade for a room with a window, and they can see as the wind drags a bench along the street, banging it against buildings and signs. They can hear its methodical progress.

“What about Nora?” Skipper asks impatiently.

Emilie goes to check the door, as if someone might be listening.

“We confirmed she’s inside,” says Emilie.

Carmen sucks in a breath.

“Is she all right?” Skipper asks, slipping her hand into Carmen’s.

“She’s fine,” says Carmen, squeezing back, even though she doesn’t know.

“Yes,” says Emilie. “She’s well. I have a message for you from her.”

“Emilie,” says Jan, frowning.

“It’s necessary,” Emilie tells him.

Carmen and Skipper knock shoulders as they lean forward to see what Emilie is unfolding: It's a sheet of crumpled paper with Nora's prim cursive. As far as Carmen can tell, it's just notes about some experiment she's conducting, but her pulse quickens. "What does it mean?"

Skipper reaches for it, but Emilie puts it back in her pocket. "You can't be found with this. But your sister says to tell you, 'I'm in danger. Please get me out.'"

The words sit between them until the window rattles. Outside, there's a streak of white as the stray bench flies up and bangs against the edge of an adjacent roof, where it sticks legs-down in corrugated metal. The howl of the wind muffles the sound.

"We will," says Skipper. "You'll help us, won't you?"

"We want to," says Jan. The couple share a silent conversation.

"What do you need us to do?" Carmen asks.

Emilie recites a list of things they need. It's a lot: chemical compounds and plastic tubes. Empty bottles and cloth. As she goes on, Carmen shivers. They mean to blow up the mines. It's a response to the previous roundup of workers who were peacefully organizing. But also, they've come to believe there's no way to profitably extract minerals from the ground without oppressing workers and damaging the land. Their goal is to force the company to shut down those operations once and for all.

Carmen doesn't know why this bothers her so much. After all, she killed a man. She should be able to do anything. She's not so naive to believe Renewal is some benevolent entity deserving of her loyalty. But many people, including her, depend on them for jobs and food. What right do they have to get in the way of that? And this kind of sabotage isn't without risk. The mines are operated twenty-four-seven. Innocent people could die, people like Piotr's partner, who just got reassigned to the night shift to align with Piotr. She pictures giant clouds of ash unfolding across miles of white snow. She doesn't like this. But what if it's the only way to get Nora out?

"We're going to need time," Carmen tells her.

"For what?" Emilie's brow creases in concern. "I thought you were with us."

"It's a serious ask," says Carmen, echoing Emilie's earlier words.

"We're serious people."

"Carmen," Skipper says, and Carmen thinks of Skipper looking up at her from the porch when Carmen came home that summer, like she wasn't sure they still knew each other.

Carmen considers Emilie's proposal all shift. They're running out of time, and they're no closer to getting into the vault. What if they can't get Nora out before the boat comes? What if the boat comes, and they don't have money for the tickets?

Jan promises they'll be careful, that no one will get hurt—that's what the sedatives are for. They could have asked for something toxic. But there's always a gap between intention and reality.

Carmen hasn't changed as much as she thought she had.

"I can't do it," she tells Emilie.

"Then that's that."

"I'm sorry—" begins Carmen.

"I need to converse with myself right now," Emilie tells her.

So Carmen walks away. After that Emilie stops talking to Carmen altogether, which hurts more than Carmen admits.

Carmen takes the long way back from her shifts at the clinic so she can glance through the vault gate. She tries to befriend the guards, but they keep changing who's on post.

She forces herself to ask Ollie for money.

Ollie sends back a brief reply: *Fuck you.*

Carmen's cheeks burn when she reads that, and she thinks, fair enough, maybe she could have explained the situation better. She's used to being persuasive. She wonders if her illness is affecting her. She hasn't slept much, and she's begun to have painful stomach cramps if she misses a meal.

She's eating a rancid stew in the cafeteria when someone she doesn't know sits down next to her. They wear their parka hood pulled up over their hair and a mask over their face like they've just come in from the cold. "I heard you wanted to make extra money."

Carmen puts down her spoon, because she's no longer hungry. The stew is so salty it's inedible.

"Keep eating. We're having a chat."

Reluctantly, Carmen picks up the spoon again and stirs the oily mess.

"A friend asked me to ask you if you'd be interested in a job."

"Okay?" But she's listening. She's out of ideas after all.

"They want something from the vault. They will pay you for it."

Her mouth, despite the amount of grease that was in the stew, feels dry. She's desperate for water. "What's in the vault?"

"Power. Information."

If she were holding a fork instead of a spoon, she might have stabbed them for being so goddamn mysterious. She's sick of everyone skulking around. She starts to clear her plate.

"Soybeans. Not the latest generation, but some other breed not headed for market that's even more resistant to blight," they add hastily.

"You have the wrong sister. I can't even get into the vault."

"You seem resourceful."

"Who's asking?"

They pull off their glove and flip over their hand to show her their palm, where there's a logo drawn in lipstick, and she snorts a laugh because the gesture is so ridiculous. It's meant to be a planet with a W behind it. EarthWorks.

Carmen stares at her dinner companion.

As if reading the question in her eyes, they add: "Your sister promised them. They're done waiting."

It amazes Carmen how Nora must be this special that two companies are fighting over her. It reminds her how Nora won all the awards at school. Sometimes Carmen was embarrassed to be Nora's sister, because she could never measure up.

". . . but they're willing to give you a bonus." The person names an amount that could not only resolve their current predicament but set the family up for comfort for the rest of their life. "Think about it," they say, and then leave.

Carmen considers this alternative, which is also dangerous and most certainly illegal, but maybe less likely to hurt people. She never shoplifted potatoes from the general store the way Nora did. She was the one who scolded Skipper for breaking into abandoned houses.

The worst thing she ever did was try to steal blueberries from Mr. Farrow's orchard, but that was Nora's idea and look what happened to Nora: shot in the arm and almost bled to death.

But they do need money, and after several weeks so far north, she's less certain which way is up. Which is to say, she thinks about it. She reconsiders Emilie's proposal too.

Just as she's decided to go talk to Emilie again, they receive a message from Uncle Tot. He's gotten a message from Nora: *Don't worry. I'm okay. Please be careful.*

She and Skipper debate what this could mean. If it's encoded, they don't know how. But if Nora's okay, why doesn't she come out and tell them herself? Was she forced to send this message? Or is Nora warning them not to do anything risky? Maybe she's being a martyr.

The message, which should have been reassuring, confuses them more, which is so typical of Nora.

The next day, as Carmen leaves work, two security officers approach her. They both have beards, one short and the other long. They tell her they want to talk, and not to be afraid, which is bullshit, because she's terrified, especially after the stories Emilie has told her about the conditions of imprisonment here: the urine-stained walls and frozen food.

Her fungus throbs as they take her to a windowless room. She wonders if they know about EarthWorks or about Emilie, and which carries greater punishment. Maybe they know everything, or maybe they think they do, and what they think is even worse than anything she's done.

"Let's talk about your sister," Long Beard says, and for the first time in a while she doesn't know which sister they mean. "Rosa's been making friends with the wrong people."

"Skipper doesn't have friends," Carmen laughs. If it were Nora, well, that's another thing, but not Skipper.

"Do you know Emilie Larsson?"

"Not well," Carmen says, happy to be able to add: "We haven't talked recently."

"We've heard Emilie asked about acquiring certain materials that could be used to construct an explosive, and your sister has been helping her. We have a recording of your sister stealing wire from the worm factory." The news hits Carmen like a blow, and she's ashamed to admit the part that hurts the most is Emilie must have decided Skipper is more useful than she is. Carmen's also upset Skipper has been doing whatever it is without her, and Carmen blames herself, because she was the one who was supposed to do it.

"There's no way," Carmen tells them. "You don't know Skipper."

They aren't convinced. "This is your chance to come clean first. We've already brought her in for questioning. The thing is, your sister is new here. People make mistakes. The person we're most interested in is Emilie. I don't think your sister deserves to take the fall for her, do you?"

Carmen cringes, thinking of Skipper alone in a cramped, cold cell. She worries Skipper will say the wrong things and get herself into more trouble. She doesn't know how she could rescue Skipper on top of Nora.

"Fine," she says, hating herself for this. "You're right. It was Emilie." She tells herself Emilie knew the risks, and it's the only way Carmen knows how to protect her sister. The security staff go away happy, and Carmen walks out into the biting air full of nausea. She's beginning to hate this other person she's become, but she needs her.

When she gets back to the dormitory, Luna waits on her cot, staring out of the dimness with judgment, as if she knows Carmen's betrayal.

"Don't look at me like that."

Luna turns and stalks off, and Carmen feels even worse.

Emilie's sudden absence in the worker quarters isn't so different from Jackson's on the *Bumblebee*. Carmen thinks of the empty expanse of ocean, the way the water closed over his head as if he'd never existed.

Jan is distraught. He sits alone in the dining room, staring into his soup, and Carmen steals bits of chicken for Luna to make sure she doesn't starve. Carmen can't tell if Jan suspects her, but she reminds herself she can't afford to worry about it, since they weren't going to help them anyway.

When Skipper's released, Carmen tells her what she did. She means it as a warning. "You have to be more careful. We didn't come here to get involved in other people's problems."

Skipper gapes at her. "How could you?" She's never been angry like this, not with Carmen. "She was going to help us free Nora. Now we're fucked."

"I have another way," Carmen promises, or begs, depending on one's point of view.

Skipper can't believe Carmen would betray someone who had helped them, who was a friend, even if it was to save Skipper.

"Stop it," says Carmen. "You always want me to fix things. Well, I'm working on it. You should have trusted me. Instead, you had to go make a mess. I'm sick of cleaning up after you."

Skipper turns away. "I can do what I want," she mumbles, but she won't. Carmen won't let her. As soon as there's an opportunity to get into the vault, Carmen will take it.

Piotr praises Carmen for having a level head. She never asked his opinion, and she doesn't know if he knows, and if so how, or if he's referring again to the way she fetched the sedative when he asked, but she resolves to keep her head down more around him.

So without Skipper, she has no one. For the first time Carmen is alone, and she attempts to ease into the feeling. It's not so bad, right? She's too busy to be lonely. She finishes her meals in five minutes and brushes her teeth staring at herself in the dinged-up bathroom mirror.

A cluster of purple-blue mushrooms bud through her skin above her right kidney. It's revolting, but it doesn't hurt too much, and when she runs her thumb over their velvet caps, she feels a pleasurable tingle in her spine.

A day goes by like this, then two, then three. Each evening, she goes to the clinic and spends the night administering drugs and learns how to operate machines far more advanced than anything back home. It's a bit exciting, though she shouldn't think of it that way. It isn't hard for her to fall into a new rhythm here. It is harder to forget she shouldn't. She's always wanted to please people.

The longer she stays, the more color leaches from her. She struggles to retain her curiosity, for without curiosity, she will never get out.

A glow returns to the horizon. At last, the long winter polar night ends and the sun returns, cloaking the land in dawn for a whole hour.

Everyone celebrates. Piotr brings her a sliver of bacon, wrapped in a napkin in his pocket, and it's the best thing she's tasted in months.

But she's no closer to getting into the vault. Then, two weeks before the boat is due to arrive, she gets her opportunity.

CHAPTER THIRTY-THREE

A patient is brought to the clinic with a rash, fever, and terrible stomach pains. He wears the gray uniform of a vault facility worker. The three guards that carried him in on a stretcher instruct everyone to garb themselves in baggy protective jumpsuits that leave just enough room for a mask.

Carmen's anxiety spikes as she zips up the thin suit to her chin and straps on the face shield. Change is coming, whether or not she's ready.

She should be grateful—she wasn't getting anywhere. She's been too comfortable with how things are. But inside, her internal coach goes into overdrive. *You will be okay. If there's an opening, you will take it. You aren't worthless. Pretend everything is normal, and everything will continue to be normal, and* you *will be normal.*

She's lying to herself, and it's not going well. She's adjusted to this place, and she's proved herself to her colleagues—to a point. She's gotten better at working under pressure in a way she never has before. But it's a paper-thin premise, never tested by crisis.

"Whatever it is, it's contagious," they warn. "Three people have it already."

Illness isn't unexpected in a harsh environment like this where everyone lives packed together in communal housing. People worry about the risk of melting permafrost and the microscopic things that might awake.

The doctor on duty tells her to take the patient's vitals. Carmen can see fear in the slight widening of the doctor's eyes, which doesn't help Carmen's nerves. Her mental monologue collapses into a string of curses.

"Don't make me look bad," Piotr tells her as he passes by.

How does he know this is exactly what she needs to hear?

The patient retches and clutches his abdomen but lifts his arm for Carmen's needle. She exhales and leans over to take a blood sample.

The patient, with spittle on his lips, wheezes a name: "Aurora?"

Carmen flinches. That's their mother's name. She doesn't want to think about that name. It reminds her too much of the dark and the bad things people pretend never happened, the reason she has nightmares several times a week even twenty years later.

Maybe it's a coincidence. The man must be confused. But his bloodshot eyes burn her.

"It's Carmen."

"Oh." The man isn't insistent. "I'm sorry, you look like her. I'm not making sense."

"Who?" Carmen straightens. Aurora. It *must* be. "Nora? Do you know her? Where are they keeping her?" She's had such hope since Emilie confirmed Nora was inside the vault, but now she realizes that hope was flimsy. She's never stopped worrying.

"Not Nora, Aurora. No. No," says the man. "I wish she'd never told me."

"Told you what?"

He moans softly: "It hurts."

The doctors return, fear cloaked in their importance, and they tell Carmen to back up, to stop bothering the patient. They trundle the man away, and the last she sees of him is his bare foot sticking out from under the sheet, blistered and oozing pus.

Carmen searches for the patient during her break but can't find him anywhere. Twenty-four hours later she hears the man is dead.

Carmen walks about the clinic in a daze. She volunteers for a double shift. She couldn't have slept anyway. As scared as she is, she knows she's where she needs to be.

Three years ago, a respiratory virus burned through their town. The neighbor boy caught it. He was only six. Carmen was friends with his parents. She'd babysat for the boy when he was a baby. When he got sick, she went to visit him. She'd gotten the virus early and was one of the lucky ones; it had been a mild case. She sat with him because his parents had to work, and so she was alone with him when he stopped breathing.

She didn't know what to do. The clinic was overstretched, the emergency services too. She tried chest compressions and mouth-to-mouth, but in the end, it was of no avail. The worst part was, his parents didn't blame her, at least not to her face. They thanked her for staying with him through it all, for doing her best. She went home and cried herself to sleep. A few weeks later, she filled out the application for nursing school.

This isn't her opportunity for redemption. She doesn't believe in that. But she wants to contribute, and also, if she's patient, her opening to get into the vault will come.

She could go down to the registrar and check for Aurora, but they're in full emergency mode, so she can't leave. If Nora's here under false identification, that would explain how Renewal didn't know she was here. It means she probably isn't a prisoner, just unable to leave for the same reason as everyone else: lack of money.

More patients arrive. One recovers, another dies.

At last, she has her chance.

The doctors line them all up in the front reception and explain the company wants to send a group into the facility to treat the sick and organize a quarantine. Staff will not be able to leave until it's over. They're asking for volunteers.

Carmen forces herself to raise her hand. This could be her only opportunity to get beyond the gate. She'll deal with getting out before the boat leaves, once she finds Nora.

They aren't allowed to return to the dormitory to gather anything. It's probably for the best she doesn't even get a chance to say goodbye to Skipper. Her sister hasn't spoken to her since their fight over Emilie. Who knows what Skipper would say?

Carmen wishes she could see her anyway, so she could tell her to hang on. Carmen blames Grandma for Skipper's tendency to give up, for making Skipper believe she can't do things; she blames Nora, too, for infantilizing her.

If Skipper doesn't stay alert, there are so many things that could happen to her, alone and unprotected.

But also, maybe Carmen's the one who needs reassurance. She's about to walk into a life-threatening situation where other people's lives might depend on her, all while trying to find and rescue her sister without being caught.

Keep moving, she tells herself. *Keep moving keep moving keep moving. Keep your protective gear on. Don't take any unnecessary risks.*

Carmen pulls on her Renewal parka, even though she's sweating through her coveralls.

Except for that summer she spent with her father, she's never gone so long without seeing Skipper's face, and it's possible she's taken Skipper's presence for granted. Carmen's fear increases. She has a premonition she will never see her again.

As she steps into a biohazard suit, she feels more vulnerable than she's ever felt in her life.

Then she chastises herself for being so dramatic and goes and joins the line of others filing out the door.

They walk in a huddle. Earlier brave chatter fades into grim silence as the weight of their task settles upon them. The tall heavy doors of the vault yawn open, and Carmen enters.

CHAPTER THIRTY-FOUR

Everything seems quieter on the inside. No chatter, no music. The hush is unsettling, as if no one is alive.

The walls stretch around them in a half circle. Worker dormitories loom to the left and right in brutalist concrete, three stories tall. Glass-domed gardens occupy the grounds between them, decorated with statues made of dark stone.

And straight ahead is the vault itself, a narrow wedge up against a large hill.

"It's so small," Carmen says, in confusion.

"Because most of it is underground," Piotr whispers. "Unsolicited advice—"

"I know," says Carmen, dropping her gaze. *Don't seem curious.*

They follow the guards to Residence 1, where they unload medical equipment from a dolly and set up tables in the vestibule along with privacy curtains and folding chairs.

The residents line up, spaced six feet apart. Everyone wears masks with the practiced air of people for whom each emergency may as well be a drill for the next. No one talks much, which increases the sense of unreality.

Her task is to test their blood using a special machine preloaded with a hundred needles. It's simple. She tells people to step up and stick their hands inside up to the elbows, and then it plumps and massages their arm until it finds a vein and jabs.

It's the assignment she wanted: She made sure when duties were distributed to step forward and catch Piotr's eye. Now she has a good position from which she can examine each face, looking for her sister, or short of that, the flicker of recognition of someone who mistakes her for Nora.

She hated their similarities growing up. It was a small enough town no one would ever forget they were sisters, but people constantly confused the two of them. "Hey, Nora," they'd say at the store, expecting her to turn around. Nora got credit for Carmen's best ideas. When Carmen was thirteen, she designed and built a windmill from old parts, and years later, people still talk about how smart Nora was, how impressive it was she did that so young, that it's thanks to her the community center has heat in the winter. Even though Nora spent that summer hiding in the forest by herself doing who knows what.

There's a honking beep. Carmen switches out a fresh box of needles, and the line of patients resumes.

According to Piotr, there have been four previous outbreaks in the last ten years, though three of those times happened outside the vault, where people are more densely packed, living in cheaper conditions and eating worse food.

Faces pass, one after another, more tired than frightened. None of them are Nora, and no one seems to recognize Carmen either. She tugs her mask down an inch under her face shield so the shape of her nose and cheeks are more apparent. She starts to accompany each prick with a whisper: "Excuse me, do you know Aurora?"

Her mother's name sticks to her tongue like peanut butter. She doesn't want to be saying it out loud, certainly not over and over. It brings to mind Grandma calling for Mama, frightened she might have done something to herself or them in a period when she was high out of her mind. Carmen forces herself to keep going.

Each time she gets a quick head shake, or a "Sorry, no."

Despair seeps in.

The line finishes, and they move on to the next building, and the next.

"What are you saying?" asks one of the guards who overhears her murmuring. "Hey, you."

"She's all right," Piotr says. "No problem, friend."

"She's been saying something to the residents," says the guard.

"Sorry. I didn't know there was a rule." Carmen stands next to the patient chair, afraid to do anything that will draw suspicion. She smiles to show she is harmless and friendly and absolutely not up to anything, but the mask covers her mouth.

"It's just talking," Piotr says. "We like to be friendly." When the guard turns away, though, Piotr glares at Carmen in warning.

After that, Carmen must return to studying faces, hoping in vain the next person to sit in the chair will be her sister.

Finally, as they work through the fourth building, someone recognizes her. Carmen sees it in the way his body stiffens.

She nearly knocks over the blood test machine. Her hands feel like ice. "Do you know—"

"Yes," he says, eyes wide above the line of his mask.

"Nora? I mean, Aurora? Where is she?"

"Not here." He glances at the guard. His ID badge says *Maintenance Engineer.*

"Everything okay?" asks Piotr, coming over.

Carmen takes the man's blood, because what else can she do, and she waits for the results as if it is the most important test she'll do all day.

"Everything's good," she forces herself to say. "Your glucose levels are elevated. You might want to cut back on the sweets." It is amazing how calm she sounds, because inside she screams: *But where is Nora?*

"Next," says the doctor.

The man hurries off in the direction of the vault entrance.

She needs to get in there.

After they finish with the residences, they are taken to a squat building in the back with narrow windows. It's the Vault City Detention Center.

"Do we have to go in there?" someone asks.

Piotr elbows him.

"I don't mind," says Carmen, because Nora could be inside.

"Carmen and I will handle it," says Piotr, throwing Carmen a grateful nod. "The rest of you go set up a quarantine ward in Residence 3."

The detention center is a long, two-story building with narrow windows and cheap siding. It's not exactly a fortress, but then, it doesn't have to be. Where would fugitives escape to, assuming they could even get past the vault gate?

Carmen drags the blood test machine down the hall, the wheels squeaking loudly across the floor. The plumbing is broken, and it smells like shit. She gags.

The guards sit downstairs playing cards, taking turns swigging from a bottle. They make no move to get up. One of them removes an electronic key from the desk drawer and tosses it to Carmen.

"You're not coming with us?" Carmen asks.

"Yell if you need anything."

Piotr snorts.

They start upstairs, but when they get up there, they realize they left the box of needles with the other medical staff.

"Shit," Piotr says. "I'll run and get it."

After a minute, Carmen abandons the cart and moves down the hall. Each cell has a window with bars. People look up as she passes. No Nora.

She's coming back on the other side when she sees a familiar shape. It's Emilie, lying on a narrow bunk. Carmen is surprised at how relieved she is to see her. At least Emilie's alive.

"Good, it's you," says Emilie. "Now I can tell you to go fuck yourself." They must have told her who betrayed her.

"So tell me," Carmen says.

"Go fuck yourself."

Carmen turns to walk away, but Emilie speaks again: "You know,

I lied about your sister. We never talked to her at all. We weren't able to find her. I think she died."

Carmen stares at her, wobbly, like she might faint. "I don't believe you." She wonders if there's a rule that every time she takes a step forward something even worse must happen.

Is this why she hasn't found Nora? But no, that maintenance engineer recognized her. She must be here. Carmen needs to talk to him.

"Oh well. It doesn't matter. We've both done things, haven't we? You don't tell me, but I know. You show up without Jackson, because something happened, I guess. Am I right?"

Sweat breaks out on Carmen's skin. Her coveralls turn damp with it.

"Don't worry. You don't need to tell me. What were we thinking? That we could make a difference? We didn't have a chance, did we? We're no one important in history after all."

Piotr will be back soon. Carmen should return to the cart.

"I know why you did it," says Emilie. "I'd do the same for Jan." Emilie glances away, and that's even worse, because Carmen didn't expect her to understand.

"I'm sorry," says Carmen, and she means it.

"Don't be. That's insulting. You know what your problem is? You want the world to love you. Talk about ambition."

Her words strip Carmen naked. She's never met someone who can read people as well as she can. Carmen's eyes prickle with tears, and she focuses on the goosebumps rising on her skin. It's so cold.

"Are you going to get me out of here?"

"I can't," Carmen says.

"Then like I said, go fuck yourself."

Piotr finds Carmen bent over, clutching the sides of the machine.

"You don't look good," he says. "Are you sick?"

"I—I'm starving," Carmen gasps, head spinning.

He frowns, then gestures for her to unzip her parka and drop the top of her coveralls right there in the empty hall. The purple fungus blooms across her skin, flowering between her ribs and abdomen.

"Jesus," he says. "You didn't tell me it got this bad." He roots in his pockets and comes up with a small stale piece of bread for her to gnaw on.

She tears at it with her teeth, as if she hasn't eaten in weeks. The crust cuts her mouth, but she can't stop. "Thank you."

"We'll go quickly," he says. "Then rest this afternoon. We'll get you more pills."

When they pass Emilie again, Carmen worries Emile will mention their exchange, but the other woman says nothing, except: "Good luck."

They return to Residence 3. The dormitories in the vault compound have proper walls dividing the rooms, unlike the workers' quarters outside the gate. They've moved all the sickest patients here.

On her way back from eating her fill in the resident cafeteria, Carmen happens to glance inside one of the patient rooms.

Three patients lie next to one another, one on a bed, the other two on army cots. They're covered in pustules. Blood bubbles from one of their lips.

A patient turns over and retches gobs of mucus and blood on the floor, and Carmen hurries to wipe it with a cloth.

She congratulates herself, because she might be lacking in terrifying situations, but she has never been squeamish.

"I told you to rest," says Piotr, sticking his head in the door. He disappears, but she can hear him calling for someone else to come change the patients into robes so they can launder everything.

This gives Carmen an idea. She takes the stack of clean robes and changes the patients, then moves to the next room. Each patient has an ID tag stored in the front of their coveralls, like her. Finally, she gets to a patient with the same tag, hardhat, and uniform as the mechanic she saw earlier. The uniform is only a little stained. It's going over her clothes, she tells herself, and she can spritz it with some antiseptic.

She feels hot and cold all over. She is going to get caught. She could get fired from her fake temporary job.

She ducks into the closet and changes into the patient's clothes.

With the surgical mask, hardhat, and ID, it's possible she could pass as one of the vault workers.

Heart pounding in her ears, she walks out, thankful for once for the long night that hides her face. She reaches the vault entrance, and the doors swing open in response to her badge. A single corridor stretches down into the earth. She thinks how she has spent her entire life afraid of being consumed.

CHAPTER THIRTY-FIVE

The vault is dark, because that's Carmen's luck. Is Renewal that cheap that they won't pay to properly illuminate this place? But electricity must cost a fortune, because during the polar night, the settlement relies primarily on wind and wormpower.

There are bulbs affixed to the walls, creating successive pools of light and shadow. The darkness has a smell: metallic and wet. Carmen imagines she can feel it accumulating on her skin like fine dust. If she stays too long, she will sink under the weight of it.

There's a skittering sound from farther down the corridor. She hopes she imagined it.

She worried she wouldn't know where to go once she was inside, but there's only one way.

Her steps make a freakishly loud clang on the metal grating that lines the floor. Worse, once she starts walking, she can't hear anything else. She doesn't want to know what might be lurking.

So far, she hasn't seen anyone. With the compound on lockdown, only a few people are working. She hopes people in here mind their own business as much as they do outside the vault.

She stops and looks back, but the door she came through is just a rectangle of shadow. In the sudden stillness, footsteps approach from deeper in the vault.

She adjusts her mask and forces herself to put one foot after another, slowing in the shadows between the lights, so when the people pass, she's partially obscured.

The pair in matching coveralls must be able to hear her pounding pulse, but they walk by, talking loudly about a third person they hate who forgot to put the petri dishes back and ruined several weeks of work.

One glances at Carmen, and Carmen sort of nods and jerks her shoulder like she's too busy to say hello. They frown, or at least, she thinks they do, because their faces are shadowed, but they don't stop.

Neither does she.

"Hey!"

She turns slowly around. "Ungh," she grunts, which she hopes passes for acknowledgment.

"How long is it going to take to fix the lights down there?" they call.

"Not sure." She's afraid saying anything more will give her away. She holds her breath, but they must accept this response, because they don't turn around again.

"Those guys are such Neanderthals," one mutters loud enough for her to hear.

"Jerk," Carmen doesn't say, because it doesn't matter what they think.

They disappear up the passage, leaving Carmen alone under the mountain, her terror so acute, she can taste it bitter on her tongue. The only thing that keeps her moving forward is the thought Nora could be at the other end. She has searched everywhere else. Nora has to be here.

She won't be able to face Skipper if she doesn't do this.

The air grows colder as she goes.

She comes to a stop. The lights beyond are completely out. Perhaps this is a sign she should go back, but now she's here, she wonders if it's safer to hide, deep in this burrow. She's trapped herself.

She hears a grinding noise from the other end, some kind of supplemental cooling system.

Between her and the sound is a tunnel of complete darkness.

Fuck. Fuck Nora, fuck this.

She doesn't have a headlamp or light. Every cell in her body protests.

She steps forward. Did something brush her arm? Are there rats here? Bats? Bats wouldn't be the worst thing.

It smells like rust.

Darkness enfolds her.

The tree branches would brush the window of her childhood bedroom like someone knocking to come in. One time, she screamed, and Grandma came into her room and made her get out of bed. Thank goodness Skipper and Nora insisted on coming too. They all went into the woods in their pajamas, mud squishing beneath their worn-out sneakers, the sickly sweet smell of decay filling their noses, and the trees hiding creatures that wanted to eat them.

Even the squirrels were mutated, with wings and long teeth and an appetite for anything, including the fingers and ears of children. Or so Uncle Tot had told her. He was lying; he laughed when he said it. But it could be true.

Grandma told her not to be such a coward. She installed traps and sensors all around the property so she would know if someone came. She did so many years ago, before Carmen was born, when everything was collapsing. That was one thing Carmen appreciated about Grandma, even when she was mean. At least she could protect them.

No, that's not the worst thing she remembers, though.

What does she remember?

Carmen never told Skipper. She promised Grandma she wouldn't, and Nora refused to talk about it.

She puts her hands out and touches dank wall. Tries to gain strength from the solidity of it. This is now. This is real.

But it comes back to her anyway, because of course she remembers.

Her mother, going out into the forest in a fraying white bra and shorts. It was summer, and the heat was making everyone do weird things. The mosquitoes would eat her alive.

The moon was full above the trees. She could see the way Mama was walking, like she was dancing. She knew better than to tell Grandma. Mama was like that sometimes. Carmen didn't want her to get in trouble.

She disappeared into the forest, and Carmen kept watching. After a couple of hours, Carmen started to worry, so she went to Nora's room. "Nora," she whispered.

Her older sister kept sleeping.

She tried to shake her arm.

"Leave me alone," Nora said. "You're so annoying."

So Carmen went down the stairs and slipped out the back with the heavy flashlight, even though she was little. She wasn't scared of the dark yet.

She was a few feet into the woods when she heard a pack of wild dogs howling. Far away, she told herself, but she'd better find Mama soon.

She knew where Mama liked to sit sometimes, on the rock by the pond. She let Carmen join her when she was in a good mood, as long as Carmen was quiet. Just her, and that's what made it special. Skipper was too fidgety, and Nora had too many questions. Sometimes Carmen thought Mama liked her best.

The pond wasn't far. Carmen saw her through the trees, lying pale under the moonlight.

"Mama," she called.

Carmen came out of the edge of the woods to the water, and she saw her. There was blood. There was blood all over her stomach and her legs. She stared at it before she understood what she was seeing, and then she screamed.

Hands clamped around her shoulders, dragging her back.

"Stop that!" It was Grandma.

Carmen couldn't stop.

Grandma slapped Carmen hard across the face a couple of times, and then Carmen stopped and began crying instead, but crying silently, which was acceptable. Grandma told her to wait under a tall tree, and then she went to the pond by herself.

In her confused five-year-old mind, Carmen thought maybe Grandma had killed her. Should Carmen try to run? But where? She stood there, unable to decide.

Something rustled in the woods. She turned her head, and a pack of dogs emerged, their muzzles covered in blood.

Carmen willed herself to melt into the trees. Their eyes were liquid gold, their coats patterned with stripes, as if someone had cut up a zebra for them to wear. Their horrible, pointy-toothed mouths opened in laughter.

"Shoo!" bellowed Grandma, reappearing. She grabbed a fallen branch and smacked a tree. The branch broke with a *crack!* The dogs bolted.

Something snakes out of nowhere and wraps around Carmen's leg in the dark. She shakes her leg and shakes it again, trips and falls on her face.

She lies there until she realizes the thing around her ankle is not moving. She reaches down and unhooks it. It's a tangle of extension cord.

She frees herself and crawls forward, and when she lifts her head, she sees the dim glow of a single light: Up ahead are three doors, encased in thick frost.

The first one's locked, as is the second one. "Dammit," she hisses, just as the third one opens and light pours out. It's so bright. A silhouette stands in the doorway, wearing a toolbelt.

"I'm working on it." He realizes Carmen is not who he thought she was at the same time Carmen realizes it's the maintenance engineer who recognized her before.

She rushes forward, before he can close the door, and seizes his collar. "Where is Nora?"

He steps back in surprise, and the door swings shut behind her.

"I didn't do anything, I swear," he says. His age is hard to tell. His hair is gray and thinning, but his face is unlined. His eyes are bloodshot, and he has a tic in one eyelid.

She lets go and looks around, as if Nora might be hiding.

The room is filled with shelves and shelves of black plastic bins, with neat labels and flags of nations, including some that don't exist anymore. There are so many bins.

"Did anyone see you come this way?"

Carmen tells him about the pair of workers she passed, but he dismisses that. "We're beneath them. I doubt they noticed you. I killed the lights temporarily. After I saw you, I suspected you might try to come in here. So. Which sister are you?" he wants to know. "Never mind, it doesn't matter. Unfortunately, if you're looking for Aurora, you're too late."

Carmen loses feeling in her legs. Too late. So Nora is dead, and Carmen will have to be the one to tell Skipper.

Did Renewal kill her for something she knew? Or did they find out about her deal with EarthWorks? She doesn't know what to do or say. The truth is too big to wrap her arms around.

She sinks to her knees.

"She escaped," the man clarifies. "I'll tell you what happened."

CHAPTER THIRTY-SIX

He gestures for Carmen to follow him into the darkened stacks. He carries a ladder.

She's so stunned Nora isn't here, she doesn't question the direction, even though they are heading deeper into the shadows.

The message Uncle Tot passed along must have been real, just too late to prevent them from going on a wild chase.

The man takes a left, then a right. She digs her hands deeper in her parka against the chill seeping up from the concrete floor.

"They've got a billion seeds in here," he says. "Millions of different kinds. Amazing, isn't it?"

Carmen imagines Nora, opening these neatly labeled containers and running her fingers over the packets of seeds. She understands why Nora risked everything to come here. Nora would have sold her soul for it.

"Aurora arrived almost six months ago," the engineer says. "She was recovering from a bad illness, which made her slower than some of her teammates, so she would work late to try to make up for it. That's how we met."

The man is gruff, and Carmen can't imagine Nora becoming friends with him.

"One evening, she was agitated. It took her time to calm down. I had to give her a bit of my vodka, which I save for special occasions. She confessed to me her name wasn't Aurora. She didn't say what her real name was. She came to find a kind of bean in here that was completely resistant to blight, and she found it. She couldn't believe Renewal was sitting on it all."

Carmen thinks of Nora, so certain that people want the truth. And she thinks of Jackson, and his rants about profit and exploitation, which she didn't completely tune out after all. And she understands why Renewal didn't want a soybean like Nora's going to market. Their top product is Amaranthine. It's not in their interest to sell crops that don't need it. In fact, they would go to great lengths to ensure none of these seeds ever felt the warmth of sun.

It's both obvious and terrible, and the more she dwells on it, the angrier she gets at her own naivete.

"Aurora, you see, couldn't let it go. And she'd discovered something else, but she wouldn't tell me what it was. She told a colleague, in confidence, and they warned her to forget it, that she shouldn't tell anyone anything. She told me now that she knew the truth, they'd never let her leave, even if she finished her two-year contract. Your sister was very smart. Smarter than I gave her credit for. Much smarter than the other losers here. She knew she needed to escape."

He stops in front of a shelf and unfolds the ladder. He climbs a few steps and opens one of the bins marked *39–4829*. It's small, the length of Carmen's arm and half as deep. He opens the lid, and a musty scent fills the air.

"When she asked me for help, at first, I tried to discourage her. It's a dangerous thing, and no one's paying attention to how they run this place. She insisted, though. So I made her a deal. She did me a favor, and I helped her."

It must have been some favor. Carmen wonders what it was.

"She planned everything. Three times a week, trash and compost get removed in large containers. There's a security system, but as a maintenance engineer, I have access. I looped the security feed, and Aurora climbed in. I can't imagine the smell. She hid in one of the warehouses for a week, and then when a boat came, she talked her way onto it. I guess she paid them a lot of money. This was more than three months ago."

"Where did she go?" Carmen doesn't know what to feel: anger at Nora, maybe, because Nora didn't need them in the end, but Carmen always knew that. Carmen didn't do this for her. She did this for Skipper. Anger on Skipper's behalf, then. That feels more right. The flame of it flickers inside her.

"South," he says, and he names the city where Jackson wanted to go, with the beautiful symphonies, warm sun, and plentiful food. Most boats run through that port eventually. That country has gotten rich off what remains of global trade. "She made it, though. She recently sent a message to someone in town who was able to pass it on to me."

Carmen thinks again of Uncle Tot's message, and how they assumed it must be encoded. She can't believe they misunderstood what Nora was saying. It meant they had misunderstood Nora not just then but all along, and that upset her more than anything, because she and Skipper had thought they knew what Nora needed. Carmen has the desperate desire to know whose fault it is, but it's an empty impulse, because they're already here.

"When I saw you today, I almost had a heart attack. I thought maybe it was all a terrible lie, and she never left at all. But no, you are not the same. I figured you could take this."

The engineer roots around in the box under the foil pouches. He produces a package and offers it to Carmen.

"What is it?" She can tell whatever it is, it's important, and she's reluctant to take it.

"What she discovered. I don't know exactly what," he says, but Carmen can guess. It's the soybeans—the unaltered breed that is blight-proof.

"She hid these here. She meant to take them with her, but something went wrong, and she never had time to come back for them. She had to leave right away. Anyway, you can have them. Bring them to her."

Carmen takes the package. The first thing she pulls out is a card. She opens it, and a birthday cake pops up made of cut paper layers. The inside bears the banal scribbles of coworkers, and it's addressed to Aurora. It rattles, and she's disappointed by the lack of clever messaging inside, maybe a pair of maracas and *shake it like you're 27*, with the joke being Nora's twenty-eight. When Carmen holds the card up to the faint light, she glimpses round shapes between the sheets of paper and cardboard.

The second item is a paper-wrapped bit of chewed-up gum, still squishy. It smells like stale spearmint. She wrinkles her nose. She isn't sure if it's trash or not.

The last thing is a case of five syringes filled with golden liquid. She tilts them this way and that, wondering what they could be.

The objects seem too small to be so important. She can't believe after all this Nora failed at what she set out to do.

"All right?" says the engineer.

"No," says Carmen. It's not all right. How can he expect Carmen to do what her sister couldn't? The rage inside her swells. She didn't come here for this. She didn't kill a man for a cause. She didn't sail across oceans to help the world. She got on a boat, even though she hates sailing and it makes her seasick, to save her sisters. And now it's clear neither of them care.

She's not cut out for this. She's not the one who sneaks around.

She takes the piece of chewing gum and slips it into her shoe, under the arch of her foot. She slides the card and case of syringes into her sleeve. She wishes she were braver, but that has never been her thing.

"Good girl," says the engineer, with the wisp of a smile.

"Can you show me where she worked?"

The engineer hesitates but relents at Carmen's expression. He takes her back out, up the passageway to a door she missed on the way in. They exit into a concrete-and-steel building not too far from Residence 3. It's only late afternoon, but the lab is empty, thanks to the lockdown.

Nora's workspace isn't too different from the lab back in the city. She imagines Nora sitting here, hour after hour, through the long nights, building her fantastical future in secret.

Nora's desk is clean, except for a notebook. Everyone else, Carmen notices, has fancy, high-tech setups, but Nora was always old-fashioned, raised to be frugal with electricity. Carmen riffles through the notebook and sees the place where Emilie's mole must have torn the page of notes. She should leave it, but now she has it, she can't. She sticks it in her pocket.

"Good luck," he says.

"Thank you," Carmen says, because none of this is his fault.

They came all this way to rescue Nora, and Nora, it seems, has rescued herself. And now Carmen and Skipper are the ones who are trapped.

CHAPTER THIRTY-SEVEN

"Where were you?" Piotr hisses, catching Carmen's elbow when she returns.

"I went for a walk," says Carmen, heart still racing.

He narrows his eyes. "You know what, I don't want to know. People were asking for you. I told them I made you rest." He produces a plate, now cold, from dinner. "Change out of that thing before you eat this."

Carmen realizes belatedly he means the stolen maintenance uniform. She hurries to follow his instructions.

He isn't satisfied until she sits down with the plate. Her stomach is digesting itself. She ate a sizable lunch, and already she's starving. She's never been this hungry in her life.

"Why are you so good to me?" she asks Piotr.

"It's nothing personal," Piotr scowls.

As she shovels a second helping of stew into her mouth, she's aware of Nora's things tucked against her body. The guards check for contraband at the compound entrance. She tries to think how she'll smuggle them out. No matter what, she can't leave them here.

Now that her shock has worn off, her anger has not abated. Crossing the compound earlier, she had the urge to run to the walls and pull them down brick by brick.

Not only are Nora's seeds real, but there must be other miracles, too, locked in this remote mountain. Back home, people struggle to eat, and Renewal keeps them fed, yes, just enough to work. She doesn't want to live like this anymore. She doesn't want anyone to.

For all she chides Skipper for being complacent, Carmen could have gone on living her life if Nora hadn't gone missing. The boredom would have built up like silt, and one day she would have turned over in her bed and understood she wasn't happy or in love the way she secretly wanted to be, exuberant, but she would have been fine. Fine is what she aspired to. Fine is what makes people complicit.

Down the hall, Piotr coughs, and Carmen looks up in alarm.

"Are you all right?" she asks her friend.

"Stop bothering me," he calls back.

She takes out Nora's notebook and flips through it. It feels a bit like spying, this window into her sister's brain: the plants she loves, both their fragility and their ability to flower in terrible conditions, the way a tree can sometimes sprout from a ruined trunk.

Nora jotted a note:

> *Need to test heirloom soybean for resistance to various weather conditions. Will need some adjustment, but simulations indicate it will perform comparably well.*

Nora isn't a purist. She seems excited about engineering stronger, healthier plants. *Next gen tomato will be gamechanger*, she writes. On another page: *We make it here!*

Food or hope? Or her precious soybeans?

Carmen tucks everything away inside of her parka until she can figure out what to do. For now, she owes it to Piotr to work.

The next morning, Piotr wakes with a fever. He lies in his cot and empties his stomach into a plastic green pail with a rusty handle, and Carmen does everything to comfort him. She spoons broth between his lips and holds his hand. The doctors tell her to stop lingering over her friend. There are more important people to attend to.

"He needs medication for the fever," says Carmen.

"We don't have enough," she's told. "The orders are to prioritize based on operational imperative." She's given a tablet with a numbered list of names. She wants to slam it against the doorframe.

Piotr understands, but he can't speak because of the pain, and Carmen can only watch. She hates this place, and the people who run it.

Other staff succumb, and soon it feels like everyone's fallen except for Carmen. She struggles to pick up responsibilities as they're abandoned, not knowing why she's been spared. Maybe the thing growing inside her is boosting her immune system even as it slowly kills her.

By her fourth day inside, she doesn't know how she's still going. She stops by to see Piotr, who lies listless on his cot. He's soiled himself, and no one's changed his sheets, so Carmen does it.

"I want . . . to see my love," Piotr whispers.

Carmen already tried to get permission for a visit, and they said no. She promises she'll try again.

"You . . . eat," Piotr says, pushing his tray of food toward her.

"You first," Carmen says, even though her stomach practically leaps out of her throat at the sight of the potato and leek soup. She can't stop eating.

"Here." She lifts the spoon to his mouth and begins to weep, because she's exhausted, and yet she couldn't sleep even if she tried. Also, she's hungry, and she's been hungry all her life.

"No," Piotr says, lifting his hand so she can't give him anymore.

She puts down the spoon and goes out into the compound. The sun is rising, and she lets it soak into her skin. The cold air cuts through her fog. The worst of winter is over, people say, but one of the nurses left a water bottle outside, and it burst.

She counts and realizes the boat is due to arrive in a week, but she's trapped in here. She should get a message to Skipper, tell her to spend the money they have and go. There's no reason for them both to stay here. They don't have enough money for two tickets anyway.

As she goes along the path that circles the inside of the wall, she sees a familiar black shape. "Luna?"

The fluffy shadow meows.

"How did you get in here?"

She pets her, but the cat runs away, fickle beast. She follows, and she sees Luna disappear under a bush. When she squats, she sees Luna's black butt, squeezing through a hole in the wall. Carmen realizes what she's looking at.

"I love you," she calls.

She returns a few hours later, after the sun has set again, and squats in the dirt. "Luna!" she calls, as if hunting for her, and pushes the package of Nora's things into the hole.

When she goes back inside, Piotr is dead. They've already carted his body off to the incinerator.

As she stares at the empty cot, Emilie's words come back to her: "Fuck this shit," Carmen says, and she doesn't care if anyone hears her.

By the time Carmen is released from quarantine, the sickness is past its peak. Carmen's clothes have a sour odor, and her hair needs brushing. Her colleagues congratulate her for surviving. There's an air of grim celebration that reminds her of a new growing season after the blight when everyone tries their best to feel optimistic.

On her way back to the workers' residence, she retrieves the package from the hole in the wall.

It's been more than two weeks since she went into the vault. The long-awaited boat has arrived, but they're waiting for quarantine to be lifted. It's been sitting in the harbor for a week. They've finally been cleared to unload and will be leaving soon, but Carmen is out of plans.

She barely recognizes the dimly lit room with two cots. She falls into the closer one and shuts her eyes, willing herself to sleep at least an hour.

"Carmen," says Skipper from the doorway, in a voice so hopeful and sorry, it makes Carmen's heart squeeze, because all this time she thought Skipper was angry with her.

"Hi," says Carmen.

Skipper hugs her until Carmen gasps from the pressure of the fungal growth against her organs.

They don't apologize to each other. It's enough to be together again. They leave what they last said in the past.

"Did you find Nora?" Skipper asks.

Maybe because she's a coward, Carmen hesitates. "What do you think?" she says, after too long a pause.

Skipper's face falls, and Carmen regrets it. She didn't mean to be cruel.

"She was here. But she escaped—before we even got here." She summarizes for Skipper all she learned in the vault. As she talks, she can see Skipper's face closing up. She waits for Skipper to process the truth. "I'm sorry."

"But Jan's in touch with Nora," says Skipper. "He's been working on getting her out of the vault."

"Oh, Skip," Carmen says. "They lied to us."

Her sister shivers for an instant with ugly feeling. Then she rises to her feet and leaves the room.

Skipper returns with prawn sandwiches. They're half frozen, but better than anything Carmen's eaten in the cafeteria.

"Where did you get this?" Carmen asks.

"Friends."

Carmen blinks. "I hope you're not doing anything that'll get you in trouble."

"I told you to stop worrying about me." Skipper flops down next to her. She smells like the camp soap: flowers and rosemary, maybe a bit too much rosemary. It recalls their grandmother's way of making roast chicken.

Skipper, to her credit, has recovered from her shock faster than Carmen expected. Now she shares what she's been up to.

It turns out while Carmen was inside, Skipper figured out how to get them both on the boat.

"Did Dad send more money?" Carmen asks.

"Not enough." Skipper purchased a ticket for Carmen and secured a contract to work for her own passage. The boat was attacked by pirates and is shorthanded.

What's more, it turns out the boat is heading where Nora's gone—there's only one company that delivers all the way up here. Nora must have gone the same route.

So everything is worked out. They just need exit permits. "We can go down to the registrar tomorrow," Skipper says.

Carmen is impressed. "You've changed," she accuses her sister.

"I had to," says Skipper. "I'm glad to have you back."

She snuggles against Carmen, tucking her head into the curve of Carmen's neck, but somehow Skipper's head is too large, her skull too bony, and it isn't comfortable. After a while, Skipper gets up to shower and talk to friends, and Carmen is not part of any of it.

Securing approval for exit permits to leave Vault City turns out to be more difficult than anticipated. They go down to the registrar to apply, and the administrator makes them wait for three hours in the lobby, Skipper pacing up and down to keep warm. Finally, they're told to come back the next day.

"We're closing," the administrator says. "We'll open again tomorrow."

"What have you been doing all this time?" Skipper asks.

The administrator whips her gaze at her. "Excuse me?"

"Come on," Carmen says to Skipper. "We'll come back."

"No," says Skipper. "This doesn't make sense. When we got here, they didn't even want us to land. Our boat leaves in two days. We have *tickets.*"

"We'll come back," Carmen repeats, because she can see the administrator's fury growing, and the last thing she wants is for the woman to make a quick decision and reject their request.

They trudge back to the dormitory.

The next day, the office is closed. It's a holiday.

"What are we going to do?" Skipper says.

Carmen doesn't know. They make a loop of the town, trying to come up with something. "I'll talk to Andi," Carmen decides.

She gets Andi's residence from the noodle shop owner. The Work Management Director lives in the nicer apartments for executives and senior employees near the waterfront. The wind rolling off the icy harbor reminds Carmen painfully of their arrival months ago.

She buzzes the door.

"Hello?" asks Andi, in confusion.

"Hi!" says Carmen, injecting all her warmth and friendliness into the single syllable.

"You can't be here," says Andi, once she comes down. They stand inside the entranceway, sheltered but unwarmed by the glass and concrete.

"Sorry. It's an emergency." She explains about the exit permits.

"Oh," says Andi, in a way that sets off alarms. "With the outbreak, I don't think they'll be able to authorize you to leave."

"What do you mean?"

"You're a healthcare worker." Andi wrings her hands, in physical distress from having to be the one to give the bad news. "I'm really sorry. On the bright side, I think we could get you a good short-term contract with better pay and benefits, et cetera."

"We have to leave," says Carmen, trying to conceal her panic. "The next boat after this isn't for months."

"I know . . ." Andi makes a face. "It's a tough situation."

Carmen tries to think. "Is there a fee or something we can pay for an exception, maybe?"

Andi crosses her arms. "You've got to think of it from our perspective, Carmen. People are sick. People have *died*. We need to prioritize lives."

"I'm not even a real nurse," Carmen blurts. "I mean, I was trained to be one, but I'd never done it."

Andi gives her a calculating look, perhaps weighing how much trouble she will be in if people think she didn't vet Carmen properly. "Well, you're one now. Your colleagues speak highly of you. They say you're learning quickly. We need all the help we can get."

"Come on, Andi. We're not prisoners, are we?" Carmen smiles at Andi to show there aren't any hard feelings. "There wasn't anything in my contract about emergency situations, so it'd be a breach of contract to deny us exit, which I'm sure is not the intention."

The other woman hunches her shoulders. She shrinks a few inches in her pajama bottoms. "This isn't my call."

"What about Skipper? No issue for her, right?"

"I'm not sure," says Andi. "None of this is up to me. I'm trying to give you an honest answer."

"Is this because of Nora?" Carmen asks, dread sprouting.

"No," Andi says, but Carmen doesn't believe her. It's like Emilie warned. Renewal never intended to let them leave.

Carmen stops by the cafeteria for dinner, and the contact from Earth-Works sidles up to her outside. "Did you get it?"

Carmen tries to read the voice, but it's hard. A masculine voice, maybe, but she's not sure. A lock of black hair escapes the hood behind the goggles. Could Carmen recognize this person in light?

She checks to see if anyone is watching. The bald landscape leaves them exposed.

If she gives them Nora's seeds, EarthWorks could get them out of this place. She's certain of that. The old, practical Carmen might have even entertained it. But she can't give them Nora's seeds after everything they've all gone through.

A mail delivery person walks by with a cart of packages and a husky with a bushy white foxtail. Carmen turns back toward the warmth and light of the cafeteria. It's easier for her to lie if she's facing away. A group comes out and the scent of apple pie wafts behind them, and despite herself, her mouth waters.

"I tried," she says, "but I didn't get the chance."

"Your sister is in danger, you know," the contact says. "They're going to find her. It's not so easy to hide in this world."

"You knew all along she wasn't here, and you let us believe she was. So, fuck you." Carmen walks away, leaving the contact standing in the cold.

To hell with all of them. One way or another, they're leaving, authorization be damned. It's easier said, maybe, but later that night, she is vindicated.

CHAPTER THIRTY-EIGHT

Carmen wakes to a *whomp* as the electricity goes out. She goes into the hall, and the light of the moon shines through the narrow window at the end. Unease crawls up her spine.

She doesn't see Skipper anywhere, but people poke their heads out from their rooms, asking the same question: "What's going on?"

Her skin prickles in anticipation. Is this Jan and his people's doing?

She goes back in, throws on warm clothes, and stuffs everything from the locker in Jackson's backpack: Nora's birthday card, the sewing kit, the syringes, the used chewing gum, the silly bumblebee mug, and their dirty clothes.

That's it. They don't own anything else.

Outside, she hears shouting. Luna bolts into the room.

"Stay here," she tells the cat, but since she's a cat, she ignores the command.

She hears shouting. The window in the hallway glows faintly red, and outside the source is apparent: The worm factory is ablaze. Luna follows her, winding between her legs.

Several people run by, euphoric. "Burn it down!" they shout.

"Skipper!" Carmen doesn't see her sister anywhere. Down by the harbor, their ship looms over the dock. It must be a hybrid, because its deck is covered in wind turbines and retractable solar panels right up to the exhaust stack. It's big enough that it could hold a hundred *Bumblebees*.

To her relief, Skipper emerges from the haze. Her face is filthy, and when she grins, it reminds Carmen of the way Uncle Tot's skinny mutt used to bare its teeth when it rained. "There you are," says Skipper. "We have to go."

"What's going on?"

"The settlement is under attack."

Carmen tries and fails to parse this simple sentence, because it's missing crucial information—who and how and why, for example.

In the distance she hears gunfire and screams. She doesn't know what to do with Luna, who clearly doesn't want to be done with. She picks her up, but the cat wriggles out of her arms and runs off.

"People are taking advantage," Skipper adds. "The place is chaos. I was just at the boat, though. They'll honor our passage if we can get down there in ten minutes."

Skipper tugs her arm, and Carmen goes along as if she is dreaming.

The quiet of long winter has splintered into pieces, and Vault City devours itself tail first. They pass a crowd dragging a security guard around on the hard ground. They see things they don't want to: security guards shooting people as they try to run away, others sobbing and trying to hide.

The sisters take shelter in a doorway. It smells awful, like chemicals and charred meat mixed together. Carmen presses the sleeve of her parka over her mouth and nose and tries not to breathe.

The gates of the vault are shut, and a crowd of people bang on the outside begging to be let in.

Carmen turns her head and sees the glint of knives and makeshift weapons. With a shock, she recognizes them: It's the pirates from the offshore platform. So they survived the fire after all.

She has the wild thought they've come for the stolen egg. But no, the egg is at the bottom of the harbor with the *Bumblebee*. Perhaps they heard over the radio the settlement was weakened by outbreak, a jewel waiting to be plucked. Or they were desperate, after the destruction of half their fleet. Either way, for the pirates, this northern icy town is the land of plenty.

The gates of the vault crack open, and security forces hustle workers inside. The people need no urging. It's a stampede.

They shoot at the pirates, who scatter.

Skipper and Carmen huddle closer in the doorway, trying to figure out what to do. Carmen's breath burns.

Flush with success, the security guards leave their cover of the vault and chase after the retreating pirates, and for the first time since they got here, the gates stand open and unprotected.

Carmen spots Jan, edging toward the opening. He wears half the armor from a security guard.

"Wait," she says to Skipper.

"What are you doing?" says Skipper. "We have to go."

"I'll be quick," Carmen promises, darting across the plaza to Jan. "Jan!"

"What?" he says, eyes white with fear.

"She's in cell 213," Carmen tells him. "They keep the master key in the right-hand drawer of the security desk."

"Thank you."

He pulls a bottle from his backpack. A bit of cloth sticks out of its mouth, and it reeks of something sweet and sharp.

"Let me," Carmen says, and she takes it, a wild feeling seizing her. He lights it for her, cupping his hand until the blue flame alights. "Fuck Renewal."

Jan clinks a second bottle to hers in a toast.

Carmen turns and hurls the flaming bottle at the empty guard booth inside the gates. There's a bright flash as the chemicals spatter and the fire catches. They'll be able to fix it. She knows that. But it could be months before they can get replacement parts to lock the gates. And in that time, who knows? In any case, it makes her feel better.

The rapid *rat-tat-tat* of a gun rattles the night. The gate yawns wide open, and one of the glass domes shatters.

Carmen's shock wears off, and her heart races.

Skipper grabs Carmen's arm, and they run toward the harbor. Each moment, Carmen expects the sting of a bullet in her back, for someone to shout for them to stop.

They're swept into a crowd moving down toward the water. She hangs on to Skipper's arm, so they won't get separated. Someone screams in her ear so loud it hurts.

She stumbles, and Skipper pulls her up.

The crowd advances without them.

A horn screeches.

That's the only warning before a snowmobile weaves out of nowhere, nearly slamming into them.

They leap back, falling to the hard ground.

"Don't move," says a security guard to the left of her. She hears the click of a gun.

"Wait!" Carmen raises her hands.

The snowmobile comes roaring back. One of the pirates is driving it. They've probably never been on a snowmobile before; maybe they wanted to try it. It nearly clips them again. Instead, it slams into the security guard, then into a building wall.

They can't stay here. Carmen gets up, mind bright-white and clean. She pulls Skipper to her feet. "Come on."

The docks are eerily calm, save for two pirates who run past them, carrying backpacks stuffed with loot. One carries a chicken, squawking in anger. They take off across the ice and disappear into the fog.

The security guards supervising the unloading of the ship almost shoot them. "You can't come in here!"

"No, it's good. We're with them," Carmen says, waving at the crew. She has to trust Skipper settled everything. "We have documents."

Their grandmother once observed Carmen was like her: She knows how to move people with her words. Ollie called it charisma. Grandma called it manipulation. Whatever it is, when it's on, it lights her body. Also, the chaos works in their favor. Now is not the time to scrutinize documents.

"Fine. Hurry up."

They clamber over the barrier, and someone takes their temperature and administers a rapid blood test. Nothing is mentioned about exit permits.

"This is nothing," one of the crew members tells them cheerfully. "We docked once at a port in the middle of a civil war. It could be worse. I bet everything will all be cleared up by tomorrow."

Beyond them, a crane operator maneuvers a container off the boat and deposits it with a few others. Containers are stacked all over the place, like they were dropped wherever.

"That's the last one," one of the crew reports.

"We'll have to check the list," one of the Renewal folks begins to say.

"The delivery is complete. Authorize the transaction."

"Calm down. Everything is under control," says the security guard.

What a joke. Either way, Carmen's not sticking around. They leave them arguing and head toward the ship. Carmen should be shocked Skipper managed all this, but after everything that's happened, she's too numb.

They stagger up the gangway onto the deck of the enormous boat. A short while later, the captain tells everyone to take their places.

A helicopter circles overhead.

As the ship's bow cuts through sheets of ice, Carmen and Skipper stand at the rail watching the town burn. At the center of it all, they can see, through the open gates, the narrow, blank face of the vault. Already, it looks insignificant, an effect that only increases the farther away they get.

"Where is it, do you think?" Skipper asks her, searching the water for the *Bumblebee*.

"There," says Carmen, picking a spot as good as any. She tucks her arm in Skipper's.

INTERLUDE

CHAPTER THIRTY-NINE

They reach the coast of the country where Nora is supposed to be—Sisterland, Carmen and Skipper call it, with optimism. It's hot and green, and as the ship travels south, they see white sand filled with sunbathers. Rising sea erased most beaches like this years ago; these people must still have resources to transform their world.

As their ship enters the harbor, they're amazed to realize it's small compared to some of the other ships berthed there.

The sisters make their way through busy docks that smell like old fish. Vehicles cram the streets. They almost get hit by a few because they don't look the right way.

They climb a two-story seawall. The top boasts a view down wide boulevards, teeming with life. This city is much, much bigger and newer than the one back home.

Everywhere, people go: walking, bicycling, driving, hoverboarding. A plane crosses the sky close enough it looks like it could scrape the buildings. The two of them stare as it descends.

The buildings here aren't the dull glass-and-steel bones of their country. They gleam white and green, swathed in ivy, moss, and trees. The whole city breathes.

Holographic signs and dulcet voices whisper in their ears, and people walk about with bright-colored lenses.

"Excuse me," Carmen says to one. The person turns around with a vague expression, trying to focus on Carmen through orange goggles. Like everyone here, this person's in a rush, body poised to keep going.

"You want to go that way," they say, pointing out a street, which leads to a plaza with an information booth.

All around, people eat food that smells like spices and salt and fat, and their mouths water. Carmen's appetite is insatiable because of the fungus, but they need to save their money. Skipper worries about Carmen, and Carmen does her best to keep Skipper from worrying, because Carmen's infection is progressing faster than she had hoped.

The fountain in the middle of the plaza is larger than Grandma's garden. People wade among the exuberant jets.

The info booth is staffed by polite, humanoid robots, and the sisters ask them questions until their shirts stick to their body with sweat and they start to burn.

From the robots, they learn there are cheap places to stay not so far from here, and that "cheap" means they can stay for a week if they're careful about their money. If they want to find someone, they can search by name.

No one by the name Nora Shimizu lives in this city, though there are sixty-four Noras, none of them likely. They check any other names Nora might use as an alias. Then the robot informs them they've reached their limit of searches for the day.

Their hostel is cool and dirty and crowded, and full of sailors and migrants like the sisters, newly arrived in the city. Everyone sleeps twenty to a room in rickety bunkbeds, but after the last few months, the sisters are used to communal living. In the kitchen, a cheerful young day laborer generously gives them an extra pack of instant rice pilaf when he hears they're newly arrived, and they eat dinner standing up, elbow-to-elbow with six other people and try not to feel overwhelmed already.

It's very, very hard not to feel overwhelmed.

Despair rises up in Skipper's throat and threatens to choke her, but she swallows it down.

Carmen tries to reassure her, even though she feels the same: "We've only been here a few hours. We'll find her."

The robot told them thirteen million people live in this city.

They wash the sweat from their faces, go out, and sweat again. A sea breeze would help, but the seawall blocks it. It's supposed to be mild in April, people tell them, but a layer of hot air sits above the street, shimmering with heat.

The sisters walk the streets, not because they think they will find Nora this way, but because they think it would help to get to know this city, as if it will divulge her location to them only if they are properly acquainted.

There are half a dozen commercial districts, and each one vibrates with energy. Shops and restaurants are stacked two stories high. They go into a few to escape the sun. Products, tantalizing and new, fill the shelves. The city also has electricity in abundance, a combination of sun, wind, tides, and a nuclear power plant that people don't like to talk about.

They meet people in shops and cafés. Most speak a different language, but their lenses and earrings translate the sisters' funny words.

"Join me for coffee," one says, and the sisters sit down.

They've only tasted coffee a few times. Like many things, it's difficult to get back home. But these people have a different source, and they drink coffee happily with abandon.

The hot drink is thick and bitter, and Skipper gags, and slides it discreetly to Carmen, who drinks the rest of it. Carmen doesn't mind the way it curls her tongue. It tastes like solid ground. She could get used to it.

They're invited to eat something, so they order the cheapest thing on the menu: a salad made of fresh vegetables with a dash of oil and vinegar and crusty bread baked this morning. It's so unlike the cold, dark winter they left behind; they wouldn't mind being this hot for the rest of their lives.

This country doesn't suffer from as much blight, because these people have everything. It makes Carmen angry and jealous all over again that other people can live like this, and she realizes again Jackson was a little right.

The people they meet offer ideas for how to find a missing person: electronic message boards for missed connections, news media, public posts. These are all good ideas in theory, but none of them work.

The sisters have walked through a fraction of the city, and none feel like a place Nora would be, as if they should be able to detect her presence from the music leaking from a bedroom window, the shops of a neighborhood, or by overhearing a loud conversation on a street corner.

A few times, they get the feeling they're being followed, but in a city this crowded, it's easy to get lost. It makes sense Nora would come here to disappear.

Even so, they can't imagine their sister living in this shiny, modern place. They don't understand how *they* are here. They need to figure out who their sister might have become. The idea is so overwhelming they give up and retreat back to their accommodations, where someone has stolen their spare clothes.

Tomorrow, they tell themselves, they will try again.

The next morning, they sit in the plaza and watch a delivery person feed the plump pigeons that cluster around the fountain. They are mesmerized by the activity. The delivery person breaks off bits from a loaf of bread and rolls them into round balls before tossing them one at a time. The birds descend en masse to fight over these bread marbles.

Carmen tries not to envy the birds their stale crumbs when she's faint with hunger. She's lost too much weight, and her clothes hang off her like bags.

"I love Nora," says Carmen, "but she had a look sometimes when I was talking, like she could see through me. Like she thought I was frivolous. She never said so, but that's how I felt.

"There was one time—she was sitting in Grandma's armchair, and I was so afraid about what might happen if Grandma came home early and saw her in it, her feet on the coffee table. I begged her to move, but she kept on reading that book, Dostoevsky, or some brick like that. She told me not to worry, but I was so stressed, I sat there and cried. And she told me, 'You can't live your life like this, a slave to other people's feelings.' I was nine. I had no idea what she was talking about, but it made an impression on me because she said it in such a crushing tone, and I went on repeating it to myself for years until I understood what she meant.

"I don't agree, though. People's feelings matter, and it's okay to care. All I'm trying to say is, I found it hard to connect with her. I think I'm afraid of seeing her again. I don't know if she'll be the way I remember."

Skipper nods thoughtfully, and Carmen loves her, the way she listens to what Carmen says, as if it's something worthwhile.

"Maybe not," says Skipper. "But it doesn't matter, does it?"

"No. But it makes it even harder to find her."

The birds finish the bread. The delivery person goes back to the truck, and the birds disperse. Skipper wishes she could call them back just to watch them lift off the concrete one more time.

They check all the hostels, parks, and botanical gardens. They walk through libraries and museums full of beautiful things.

They try to forget how big the city is, and how unlikely it is they might find her. Each night, they return defeated. They wash their clothes in the bathroom sink and wear them damp until they dry. The clothes mildew, and whenever they move, they can smell a faint, sour odor.

They return to the original plaza in the evenings, where musicians play guitar and violin. The competing melodies form a canopy of sound that floats above the pavement. Someone comes along and asks them for money but stops when they see the red rash on Carmen's neck and the dark purple caps that protrude from her collar, and realize the sisters are more desperate than they are.

They try not to think of that—their desperation—but they probably glow green and toxic with it anyway.

"Do you remember the old container in the woods?" Skipper says. "Why did Nora love it so much?"

"It was so filthy," says Carmen, but she remembers it in the middle of the woods, like a time capsule half sunk in the ferns and mud, and that word stamped on the side. What was it?

Carmen tries to remember.

"What kind of job would she get if she weren't working for Renewal anymore?" Skipper wonders. "I bet somewhere she could do research, even if it were entry-level."

Skipper's right, Nora cares more about learning than anything. She spent the summer before college cramming as if she hadn't already been accepted. She was so excited, she couldn't wait, and once she got there, she didn't write home for months.

Skipper slaps the table to squash a mosquito, like she's punctuating this idea. It could be true. A wisp of optimism swirls inside her.

"ATCO Limited," says Carmen suddenly, getting to her feet.

"What?"

"The name on that old container." She beelines for the information kiosk. "Is there anyone in this city with the last name Atco?"

The robot considers. "There is an Aster Atco who works as a lab assistant." It's a bioengineering laboratory associated with one of the biggest universities in the city.

The sisters grab each other, too excited to speak.

The next day, they take the train all the way across the city. It's full of people who have no clue how far the sisters have journeyed in the last few months. They can't know how, on the other side of the ocean, spring flowers push up through the soil, and Uncle Tot wheels their grandmother into the garden for her morning shot of whiskey. Skipper imagines, though, the other passengers can see the secrets they carry, seeping out wet through paper packaging.

The university buildings reflect an older aesthetic, all stone and ivy, and fronted with lush, expensive gardens. The air smells like flowers and citrus trees that aren't native but suited to what the local climate has become.

Skipper studies everyone, like a dog sniffing for a scent. Carmen tries to manage her expectations, because they've been wrong so many times before.

The campus sprawls a mile wide and serves thirty thousand students. Even if Nora's here, they could miss her in the scale of it.

Carmen coughs into her elbow, and when she lifts her face, her sleeve is stained with purple-black spores. Carmen wipes her mouth.

They walk up the main stone path on feet bruised and swollen from days of canvassing the city and try not to feel intimidated by the grandness and history. They have been so many places in the last few days. They don't know what they will do if they don't find Nora before they run out of money.

They have to stop several times to ask for directions before they find the laboratory at the edge of campus. They worry someone will ask them what they are doing here, but no one does.

They find the building and climb the stairs to the third floor. The ceilings are tall, the hallways dimly lit. It smells like damp soil.

"Which one is it?" Skipper asks.

"There," says Carmen, finding the right door.

They push it open, blinking against the bright sunlight streaming in through tall windows. And then they find her, bending over a tray of seedlings—their sister, Nora.

PART 3

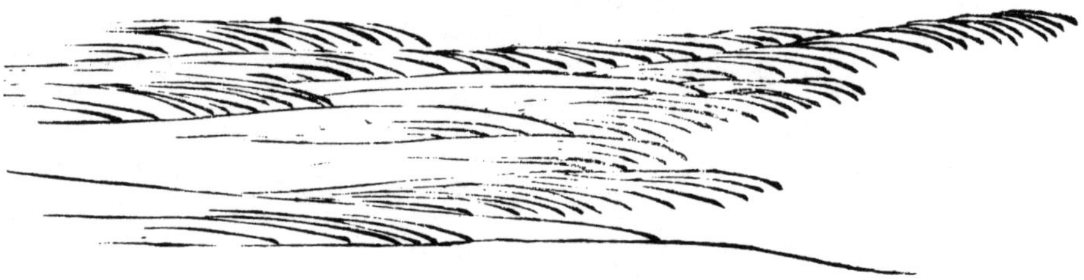

NORA

CHAPTER FORTY

When Carmen was born, their mother was convinced Nora wanted to kill her little sister. According to Mama, Nora tried to smother Carmen several times with stuffed animals. Mama believed this was not a poor attempt at love but maliciousness.

While Mama was working in the garden, Nora tipped over the baby carriage, so Carmen went tumbling out onto the grass, crying in terror and raising up her broken pinky finger.

For weeks, Mama insisted Nora never be left alone with Carmen. They had moved into Grandma's house for the pregnancy and never left, and Grandma watched the drama with skepticism.

One day, when Mama was taking a nap, Grandma sat the children down in the yard and let Nora touch the baby. She hadn't been allowed to since the first night Carmen was born.

Nora put her palms on Carmen's cheeks and pet her fine eyelashes. Her sister smelled like old milk, and her nails were smaller than buttercup petals. Nora grabbed Carmen's chubby calves and squeezed. She rubbed Carmen's skin with grass until Carmen smelled green. In this way, Nora claimed possession. This blob of a human named Carmen watched her all the while, as fascinated with Nora as Carmen was with her. Then Nora pinched Carmen hard, and Carmen wailed.

That must have spent the animus in Nora's system, because after that, they were inseparable until they were teenagers, when Carmen lost her interest in science and told Nora to stop talking about her little experiments so much, because Nora was boring everyone.

Skipper was too young for either of them to play with.

Nora doesn't know what made her think of this.

Nora sees her sisters. They stand in the doorway of her laboratory, dirty and miserable.

Her brain can't process they are here. For a panicked moment, she wonders if this is some kind of trick by Renewal to flush her out. She's been getting anonymous threats for weeks. But it *is* them, and she doesn't care.

She abandons her experiment.

Skipper looks smaller than she remembered, her pale skin flushed with too much sun.

Carmen is thin and bony. Her hair, which Nora always envied, lacks its normal luster and volume. Nora used to hate how effortless it was for Carmen to shine, her unblemished skin, the fullness of her lips and angle of her jaw. Growing up with Carmen was the constant feeling of being ugly and awkward, second-best. Carmen's still beautiful, but the lines of her face aren't quite the same that Nora remembers—a trick of memory or age.

The human body loses hundreds of billions of cells a day and constantly regenerates. Nora believes consciousness, too, exists in moments. So a person isn't one person, but an infinite series of different people existing along a continuum. Or if one believes in multiple universes, multiple continuums. And yet, Nora knows her sisters deep in her body, even if their molecules have changed since she last saw them.

Bright hydrogen lightness fills her. All the happy chemicals flood her animal brain, the feeling of belonging to people.

"You're here," she says in wonder.

Carmen bursts into tears, and that's when Nora sees it—the midnight tendrils creeping along Carmen's neck that Nora almost mistook for a tattoo.

Nora sucks in a breath. "Carmen."

They fall upon Nora, hugging her close, and all Nora can think is she should get them out of the lab, before someone sees them. It's a good thing it's early.

She summons a car, then cancels it, and summons a different car for good measure. These precautions have become habit.

Back at the apartment, she watches them survey the rooms in painful anticipation. She's missed being known by people who remember what it took for her to become herself. She's spent so much of the past year trying to be invisible.

They take it in: the plants Nora bought a few weeks ago flourishing on the windowsill; the soft, colorful clothes she will lend them because they don't have anything else to wear; the tart she baked yesterday—she offers them a slice. She wants them to read her life and say, "She's doing okay."

Her position is so precarious, but there is something lovely about it too, like an azalea sprouting in the crevice of a rock.

See, that is the comfortable couch we found at the side of the road one day; someone was throwing it out. I had to ask friends to help carry it home on foot because it wouldn't have fit on the train. It took hours and three rounds of icy drinks.

And these are the pots and pans given to me by neighbors when I moved in. They're copper. A bit old and heavy, but aren't they pretty?

Would you like some almonds maybe, or chocolate even? See, I have chocolate. I bet you haven't had chocolate in years. How about lunch? I made curry last night, you'll like it.

Why don't you take a shower? You can change into this dress after, it will look better on you, Carmen, than it looks on me. You know it's true. I should give it to you, in fact. Come on, take it.

The more she talks, the more alien she feels. She can't stop the flow of words tumbling out.

Nora fixes tea and sips it nervously while they drift around the room and against each other, touching this and that without intent. Brownian motion. The afternoon trickles away. The scent of tart reheating in the oven filters through the living room. In the distance children's voices shriek and laugh as they come home from school.

"How are you here?" Nora asks.

"We thought— " says Skipper and stops, flustered.

Carmen takes over, as she always does, explaining their worry when they didn't hear from her and their subsequent journey from home, and as she relates all it's taken them to be here, Nora's dismay grows. She hasn't touched her messages since she left the city for fear of being tracked. How could she imagine they'd find the letters she never sent? And when she wrote her coded message—which she's proud they were able to figure out—all she thought was they might tell her friend Marcus or the authorities. She never imagined they would come themselves all this way. How could she? Neither of them ever so much as came to visit her in the city. The force of their love baffles her. It's overwhelming to think they've done all this, without her asking.

Carmen removes several items from her bag: a wad of gum, seeds, and the blight variant samples in syringes.

Nora's heart leaps. "You did it."

"I did," says Carmen. "Though I don't know what."

They talk at the same time, choking on their emotions, and the reality of the moment feels impossible, as if it exists and does not exist at the same time. The tension is unbearable. Skipper gets up, goes into the bedroom, and shuts the door, and Carmen and Nora are left, facing each other out of habit, half a tart between them.

"How long have you had this?" Nora asks, reaching out to brush the fungus growing from Carmen's neck. It's so far progressed.

"A few months," says Carmen jerking away. "I'm on medication."

"I'll make you an appointment. You shouldn't wait. It looks like you've lost a lot of weight," says Nora.

"What was I supposed to do? I didn't have the money for an operation."

"Don't worry," says Nora, "it's free here," and she's startled by the anger and hurt in Carmen's eyes, as if Carmen doesn't want her help. Carmen always needed to do things herself, even if it was harder.

"Please," Nora says. "Let me."

"Fine," says Carmen, reaching for the rest of the tart.

This morning, Nora had gone to work feeling so low. She's struggled with anxiety since she was a child, but her experiences the past half year amplified everything. At work, she argued with her friend and boss, Rafael Aguirre, who was a professor of ecology at the university.

It was an argument about methodology, which could have been resolved if she told him what she'd learned in the vault. She couldn't tell him, and it made her irritable, but sharing the information would endanger both of them.

What was the point of knowing a thing if no one else knew it? Was holding it in her mind enough? She never knew an idea could cause her physical pain. She's been having terrible headaches since she arrived. On and on, her mind cycles around. She can't decide what to do, and so she does nothing, and her headaches persist, as if her skull is too small to contain the contents of her mind.

The bedroom door opens again, and Skipper says, "You left this." She delivers it like an accusation. She holds out a chipped mug covered in a child's idea of bumblebees, copied from a book. The handle must have broken off; it's stuck inside, where it rattles around.

Nora takes it and kisses it, moved by this thing she left behind. The day has been full of the unexpected. "I'm so sorry," she repeats.

"I can't believe you," says Skipper, sitting down again.

"We thought you were in trouble," Carmen adds.

"I was. I am."

"Everything we did—" says Skipper, burying her face in her hands.

"Oh, Skip." Nora tries to hug her, but Skipper shakes her off.

"I don't even know you."

Nora understands, because sometimes she doesn't know herself. But she never meant to drag them into all this. They've been through much more than they've alluded to.

"At least she has the evidence now," Carmen says. "You can do something with it, can't you?"

Nora shrinks inwardly. Maybe. Can she? It's not that simple.

"We've pieced together what happened," Carmen says. "But it would be good to hear it from you."

"Yes," says Skipper. "You owe us that much."

Nora searches for the beginning. Was it when she was five and sat in a field near the ocean and watched flowers unfurl and smelled the grass and salt air?

It feels like she's hidden herself for years. She's been afraid for so long her body barely recognizes the warmth of their presence. She massages the back of her neck, but the sharp pain remains.

"You were looking for plants that were blight resistant," Carmen prompts.

"Yes," says Nora. This is where she begins.

CHAPTER FORTY-ONE

There was bad blight the year before Skipper was born. Mama and Grandma took her and Carmen into the woods.

It was morning, and the trees were bathed in soft sunlight, but after a few hours, they were all hungry and cranky with each other. They'd been eating thin soup and government ready-to-eat meals for weeks.

Carmen kicked over the basket of mushrooms their mother spent hours collecting. Grandma said she would spank her, and Mama told Carmen to quit acting like a child, even though she was, in fact, a child.

Grandma and Mama began to argue, and Nora took Carmen's hand, gestured for her to be quiet. They backed up a few steps, and no one said anything. A few more steps, and then a few more. Then Carmen resisted. She slipped out of Nora's grasp and ran back to the adults, so Nora left her and walked away.

She kept going until she got to a place in the forest where a large container sat, rusting in a clearing. Because she was starving, she imagined it contained stacks of all her favorite foods: cans of pumpkin and pickled beets and powdered milk and vanilla pudding. It was empty, though.

Her stomach growled, and her eyes fell on an oak tree, branches heavy with acorns. She gathered them up, thinking of bread and porridge. She filled the long skirt of her shirt.

"What are you doing?" Mama stood behind her, alarm ringing in her voice, and Nora jumped. Carmen had told on her.

Mama strode forward and hit Nora's shirt so the hard nuts scattered across the ground. "Didn't you see?" She pointed at one, pimpled with knobby growth. She crushed it with her boot until it cracked. The insides were filled with black fluff.

Nora couldn't understand it. The question was planted in her child's mind: Why hadn't the blight killed the trees like everything else?

It would take her years to find the answer.

"So you left me to be spanked?" Carmen says, annoyed.

"You wouldn't come," Nora says. "Anyway, that wasn't the point of the story."

"What was the point?" Skipper asks.

"I'm getting to it."

Nora went to college because she wanted to know why things were the way they were. But once there, she felt oppressed by homesickness. She tried to ignore it; she should have been happy.

She worked hard and cultivated a handful of friends. If Carmen had been there, she would have reigned over the campus, but Nora didn't have time for that.

Her performance was uneven. She got in trouble with her teachers for arguing too much because she disagreed with what they taught. She wanted more evidence. One of her microbiology professors demanded she be removed from his class.

She met Marcus when she was brought before the university disciplinary committee. The university used a system where students were judged by their peers. A student advocate was appointed to defend her—Marcus. He volunteered to represent her because he volunteered to represent everyone.

He was short, with thick, black hair, and a scar from a childhood surgery that bisected his upper lip. His eyesight was poor, and it forced his face into a perpetual squint. He had an air of someone who was smarter than everyone he met. Nora liked this immediately, even though she was pretty sure she could match him. He was in his third year, but had recently switched to bioengineering and was making up core coursework he should have taken at the beginning.

The charge was that Nora had threatened the professor with a stick. It wasn't a big stick, only the length of Nora's arm. She'd cut it off a blight-infested tree on a hike that weekend. She didn't shake it, but she did point it at him. "But what you're saying doesn't explain why this hasn't died," she told him. "Look!" It was the question she'd carried with her all these years.

Marcus, as it happened, had been there, albeit across the room, on his knees hunting for a candy he'd dropped when packing up after class. So he didn't see what transpired, but he heard the professor shriek, "Get away from me!"

"Why *do* you think the tree hasn't died?" Marcus asked Nora, as they waited to speak with the committee.

"Maybe it's developed a resistance," Nora said. "Nature finds a way."

Years ago, after their mother died, Nora would trace her mother's footsteps into the woods. The forest worked so quickly. A week later, any trace of Mama—the blood, a few hairs on a branch—were gone.

Maybe that's why Carmen cowered from the darkened woods as if the trees might eat her. Grandma had taken them into the forest one night to show her there was nothing to fear. As they walked through the deep velvet night, Nora understood the lesson. Her eyes adjusted to the dark, and she heard the song of things industriously alive. She breathed in the rich, loamy scent of the woods and willed herself to dissolve.

"I had good reason to be afraid of those woods," says Carmen, "seeing as Mama was killed by a pack of wild dogs."

"What?" says Skipper. "What are you talking about?"

"I saw it."

"No, you didn't. That's not how she died," Nora says. "She killed herself."

The two sisters turn to her in shock.

"You really didn't know?" Nora takes in their faces.

"How could we, if you never told us? Grandma never talked about it." Skipper is even angrier than before.

"Why would Mama do that?" Carmen asks, tugging at the edge of her shirt where the fungus protrudes from her neck.

"She didn't see the point," Nora says. But Mama was wrong. There was a point to being a part of all of it. To be alive just to be alive, and when you died, your matter nourished other creatures. You didn't need to do anything for this to be true. Nature made it so.

"This is—" Carmen begins, but then stops. "We're coming back to this. Keep going."

Marcus did an excellent job defending her. The students on the committee were afraid of Marcus. The more quietly he spoke, the more they worried he was judging them. Which he was.

Afterward, Marcus told her he'd see her around. They began eating together in the dining hall, discussing their ideas, sharing how they thought. They had a lot in common.

Like her, Marcus had grown up in a small community. His town was a commune split by a schism. Half the town hated the other. His mother was in one faction, his father the other. Marcus avoided the dispute by hiding in the swamp, where he got to know the plants, animals, and insects that had survived the changing world. He fell in love.

Marcus wasn't interested in sex. He was interested in the microbiology of soil.

When Nora reached a point where she couldn't face continuing and took a year off, Marcus let her stay with him. They slept every night head to foot in his narrow bed, wrapped in the sweet funk of his room.

Nora, not knowing what else to do, got a job at a worm factory. It was brutal work. She hated it even more than school, but sometimes there was pleasure in the repetition of it, the way it quieted her mind and made her muscles ache. Still, it propelled her back to school the next year, because there was no way she could do that for the rest of her life.

"Told you," said Marcus, who had told her nothing.

"Why didn't you come home?" Skipper asks.

"I couldn't face my own disappointment," says Nora.

Carmen raises her eyebrows at Skipper, like, *See?*

After graduation, Marcus helped her get a job at the Renewal lab where he worked. Her job was simple: testing soybeans before they went to market. She spent twelve hours each day brutalizing sprouts with heat, rain, Amaranthine, and blight. Each newly upgraded Renewal breed represented a year of prior testing grown under accelerated conditions.

"Our plants are superheroes," John, her boss, liked to say.

They printed the seeds with a bioprinter and dosed them with concentrated cocktails of ZoomGrow, and it was remarkable to see the plants spring up overnight.

The work was stultifying. Anyone could have done it. After a few weeks, Nora went to John and asked if she could work on a side project, on her own time. He didn't like confrontation, so he said he'd think about it. She kept asking him, and finally he took it to his supervisor so someone else could say no. To his surprise, the answer was sure, as long as Nora signed something stipulating her research belonged to Renewal. Marcus warned her not to.

"They'll profit from your work, and you'll get nothing," he tried to tell her.

But Nora didn't care about money. She just wanted to learn, to answer systematically the questions that grew inside her.

She experimented with reducing the use of Amaranthine. In theory, the breeds were designed to survive, and Amaranthine was the cleanup crew, but no one wanted to under apply it.

Everyone knew but didn't like to talk about the side effects of Amaranthine. The county ordered copious amounts of rain in spraying season to wash it away quickly, but it would mix with the water. People accepted Amaranthine because the alternative was famine. The world had become so altered, it was impossible to disentangle it from the complicated processes now in place to keep the great green machine going.

But Nora thought, with the cockiness of youth, maybe they could start to undo the damage.

After a couple of generations, she got the Amaranthine levels down, and the plants continued to survive. Not 100 percent, but enough the results were promising. It got her thinking about how quickly blight evolved, and how they had to race as fast as they could to stay ahead of it. Each year, it felt like they were closer to losing. Was there no way to win the race once and for all?

No, no that's impossible, people said. *There's no such thing as a perfect solution.*

Nora didn't agree. She thought of what it would mean to her family if they could be free of the vise blight had over them.

She continued to chip away at the problem. She read whatever she could on the subject and logged long hours on forums where people shared data. But this was a mountain many people had climbed before her, and people far more experienced than she had failed to summit it.

The first time EarthWorks approached her, she didn't consider their offer. She didn't care about corporate warfare. She only cared about the work. But then, when her sisters wrote asking for money, she thought, why not—

"You shouldn't have done that," says Carmen, from the kitchen, where she roots about for something else to eat.

"What would you have done?" Nora thinks of Skipper's tearful letter, about how Carmen wanted to sell the boat. She understood Carmen's point, but also, she knew they shouldn't do it. Surely Skipper's dreams were worth more than the sum they could have gotten for it.

Nora goes and shows her where the fruit and nuts are.

"Anyway," says Nora, "EarthWorks turned out to be the least of my problems."

She couldn't crack it. One day, when she was particularly frustrated, Marcus took her elbow and dragged her out into the sunshine.

"Where are we going?" Nora wanted to know.

"That's not the point," Marcus told her. "It's called a walk."

They circled the nearby blocks. Marcus talked, and Nora was filled with affection. He knew the worst parts of her, and yet he was her friend. It was humbling.

They stopped by a playground and watched the kids play tag. They both became invested. In minutes, most of the children stood, frozen. Only the expert tagger and a nimble girl with pigtails remained. She twisted and turned like a ballerina. The boy cornered her, and she clambered up the slide. Instead of following, the boy waited until she was halfway up. Then he ran around to the other side and grabbed her hand as she pulled herself up over the top.

"Tag!"

"Maybe we need to go back to the beginning." Nora said.

"What do you mean?" laughed Marcus. "Back to when plants didn't have any resistance to blight?"

Nora thought of Mr. Farrow's blueberries, which had survived the blight each year. She'd led her sisters right onto Mr. Farrow's land so she could steal a cutting to figure out their resilience. In retrospect, without proper training and equipment, it's unlikely she'd have learned anything, but he'd shot her before she could cut the bush. She'd nearly gotten her sisters killed. She should have learned then to be more careful, but the only thing she learned was to go alone the next time.

A few days before this walk with Marcus, Skipper had written with glee to tell her Mr. Farrow had gotten hit by the town for cultivating unlicensed crops. It turned out his blueberries were some kind of heirloom varietal he'd hidden on his property the whole time.

She thought of the blight-infested trees in the forest, sick but surviving. She thought of Mr. Farrow's blueberries.

Renewal had altered soybeans so that they were basically a different plant, and blight had evolved with these changes. What if heirloom varietals were now less vulnerable to blight than the new breeds?

The problem was, she couldn't find any unaltered soybeans. The blight had devastated soybean crops, back before there was any defense. It was difficult to get any now that weren't a Renewal breed.

She asked around on forums, and finally, someone passed on a tidbit. A guy up north who called himself Prometheus claimed he had pre-Renewal soybeans.

Nora was excited. She messaged Prometheus, asking if she could have some seeds. Maybe, he said. He didn't trust her. He wanted to meet first.

To John's annoyance, she went to the higher-ups again and pitched them on funding field work. John was sure they wouldn't, but his bosses were enthusiastic.

"You're a bright young person," one told her. "When you get back, let's talk about your career here, and what you do next."

It also solved her EarthWorks problem. They had been getting more and more impatient for her to deliver them something. Now she finally could.

"I don't like this," Marcus told her.

"It's just a short trip."

"You never think about the consequences."

"I *only* think about consequences."

"Maybe I should come with you."

At the time, Nora thought he was being overprotective. He was like that sometimes, and she attributed it to the fact he was older, and how they had met. Nora told him he was worrying too much.

"You're so wrapped up in your problems sometimes," he told her. "You don't remember there are people around you who could help."

"I don't want to bother people," she said, but that wasn't it. Since she'd come to the city, even when life was hard, she'd relished being responsible for no one. Some nights she was so lonely, she cried while eating cereal for dinner, but then she would wake up in the morning and skip class and go to a museum instead, because she wanted to. She was free to think out loud to herself. She owned each day and the hours were hers to spend. She didn't see what Marcus added to the equation.

They parted on a sour note. Of course, Marcus turned out to be right. That probably was some consolation.

CHAPTER FORTY-TWO

Why would Renewal fund your trip if they didn't want you to find the seeds?" Carmen interrupts.

"They *did* want me to find them. Prometheus stole them from the vault, and I led them right to him. I was a neat solution. If I had found anything leftover, I'm sure they'd never have let me use them."

"How'd you figure that out?" Skipper says.

"I'm not oblivious," says Nora.

Carmen scoffs, and Nora says, "Not completely."

She arrived in a town full of mud and soot. Prometheus's field had been burned to the ground, and Prometheus himself was dead or had run away. The villagers couldn't agree. Either way, he was gone, the charred beams of his house collapsing in a smoking field.

No one tried to claim it was an accident. They'd done it themselves.

"It would have contaminated our fields," they told Nora. "We could have lost our crops. We could have been fined."

She didn't believe it. Someone must have "planted the seed" so to speak, ha-ha. Where else would they have gotten the gasoline?

EarthWorks, Nora thought at the time, and she blamed herself.

She spent the next week scouring for any traces of the miracle plant. As she squelched about, she saw weeds everywhere. It reminded her of Mama's brief attempts at gardening. Mama didn't want to use Amaranthine, even though the government had deemed it suitable for household use. She would roll the dice with blight.

Nora and Carmen spent endless hours weeding. It was an enormous garden, or at least it was enormous in Nora's memory.

Despite their efforts, spiny plants sprouted overnight, devouring nutrients from the soil. They plucked and yanked until their fingers bled. They could never eradicate everything. Weeds escaped them and grew to enormous heights, and Nora, who had been reading about natural selection, wondered if perhaps it was the right of such aggressive, supernatural organisms to own the earth, if they should surrender the rhubarb and arugula to it.

After their mother died, Grandma purchased a bucket of Amaranthine and sprayed the whole plot. They never had trouble with weeds after that.

The town of the miracle soybean had the same recognizable scent. Its people were not skeptics; they used Amaranthine generously.

Nora gathered local soybeans to test, but she knew already they were worthless.

By the time she got sick, she was angry and frustrated. Throughout her childhood, she'd been told she had promise, that she would do something great with her life. She pretended it didn't matter, but that was bullshit; she soaked up praise with every pore in her body.

Was it really knowledge she wanted, or the regard people had for her knowledge? She didn't want to know. She was ashamed. She resolved to henceforth pursue her questions with purity and selflessness.

She couldn't breathe. The illness was getting into her lungs. She was hot with fever. It was only a matter of time until Renewal found out about her deal with EarthWorks, and then she'd be fired.

She yearned for childhood: the endearing shape of Skipper's round, pale bottom as Nora changed Skipper's diapers; the way Carmen doodled mythical creatures as Nora tried to explain a homework problem to her; the repetition of coming home and opening the refrigerator and taking down the cutting board to chop something—every meal she made for her family that began with the drawing of the kitchen knife. She ached sometimes for the rhythm of that life, the comfort she drew from its confines until one day she couldn't anymore.

And she missed her friends, especially Marcus. She wished she'd let him come, even if he insisted on playing chess until two in the morning. But then he'd be sick too, his career as endangered as hers.

She began a letter home but was too weak to finish it.

The woman she was staying with insisted she go to the hospital. They transported her on a horse-drawn cart to a helicopter, and Nora thought, *My God, is this supposed to be progress?*

In the hospital, a Renewal agent paid her a visit. He didn't care Nora hadn't found anything. He thanked her for her diligence and informed her she'd be sent home in a week. Except Nora didn't want to go. Her health was improving, and she had a new question: *Where had Prometheus gotten his seeds?*

If she could figure out where—

"Don't worry about that," the rep told her, but Nora persisted. When they refused to fund further investigation, she wrote to John and requested leave.

The next night, Nora woke to the sound of a cart squeaking in the hall. She heard the knob turn on her door, and she froze.

Someone was entering her room. She kept her eyes shut, peering through the blur of her eyelashes.

A figure loomed over her, syringe glinting in the moonlight. When they reached for her, she rolled out of bed. The figure lunged, and she toppled the IV stand onto their head. Then she yanked the IV from her arm and ran. Her lungs burned from lingering phlegm. She could find a nurse, but she didn't know whom she could trust.

She ducked into another room.

The room's occupant gawked, and Nora raised a finger to her lips, pleading for the old woman not to press the call button.

Outside the door, she heard footsteps. A cough crept up her throat, and she clapped a hand over her mouth to keep it in.

As she slipped out of the hospital and checked into a hostel under a fake name, she put it together: the burned field, the missing man, the miracle soybean, and now, her own attempted murder.

Well, shit, she thought. She had gotten herself entangled in something bigger than she realized.

"So they tried to kill you, and you decided the best thing to do was go to the vault?" Carmen asks in exasperation.

"I thought I was being clever," Nora says, flushing. "I could find my answers, and they'd never look for me there."

Skipper shakes her head. "You're incredible." It's not a compliment.

Nora takes up the wad of chewing gum Carmen gave her and begins to work it with her fingertips as she resumes her story.

She talked to people. Most of them, like the guy in the ancient plaid shirt with the beard who fancied himself a revolutionary and wanted her to come back to his boat, were unhelpful.

She found her answer, though—the vault—and things became clearer still. Armed with a false identity, facial injections, and a résumé that was only a somewhat inflated version of the real thing, she convinced Renewal to hire her. In the interview, she pretended she was someone cheerful and friendly like Carmen. They liked her at once. It helped that not a lot of people were applying to work at the absolute ends of the earth.

She had signed a two-year contract. As she landed on the icy airstrip in Vault City, the sky rippled with the aurora borealis—a trick of the earth's magnetic field, and she thought, how appropriate. Because isn't that why she was there? Drawn as she always had been in search of an answer to a question.

She was assigned a room in a dormitory to herself, with a narrow bed, a desk with a lamp, and a set of drawers. Everyone wore the same Renewal parkas and coveralls, and it was cold enough she did too.

Walking around in those gray clothes, she felt as if she were fading into the tundra.

Her team lead, an excitable man with a salt-and-pepper beard, gave her a tour of the vault the first day. It was an old facility and in terrible condition. The concrete walls were crumbling, and the electricity was often out. But when she saw the hundreds of thousands of bins containing over a million different varietals, she began to cry.

"It's something, isn't it?" her new boss said.

She wandered into the stacks, opened a bin at random, and ran a finger over the foil packets inside. Then she opened another and recoiled at the smell of mold. There were gaps where other packets should have been.

"Spoilage," he explained. A significant number of samples had rotted due to negligence. The previous owners of the vault hadn't accounted for how warm it would get, and when they realized what was happening, they didn't have the money to install a better temperature regulation system. Centuries of preservation were undone in a season. So many old species could never be restored.

They sold it and the town to Renewal. Renewal had done a better job maintaining the facility and seeds since then, at least. It helped to have limitless resources. They considered the endeavor a charitable effort, both from a moral and tax perspective. They saw themselves as the guardians of the future of nature but also its gatekeepers.

It took her only a few days to find her precious heirloom soybeans.

One night, after everyone else had left, she loaded up the vault index and searched for soybeans. There were so many more kinds than she even knew.

Numbers in hand, she descended the dark hall, expecting any minute for someone to stop her. She was prepared to give some story about tracking down a particular wild rice for her current project. But no one came. They had no reason to suspect her.

She found the right shelf and pulled down the bin. There were dozens of different kinds of soybeans. She plucked out several possibilities and carried them back to the lab on a tray.

When she ran the initial simulation tests on the computer, she thought she must have made a mistake. She ran practical tests under accelerated conditions, and she still didn't believe it. Were her blight spores bad?

No, the proof was there: The soybeans were not just resistant to modern blight but immune to it.

But this was nothing compared to what she discovered next.

Nora at this point pauses to gulp some tea. She pitches her voice low, throat tight with fear. She is safe, but also, she will never be safe.

"What was it?" Carmen asks.

Nora hesitates. "I'm trying to decide if I should tell you."

"You should," says Skipper.

Carmen puts a hand on Skipper's arm. "We want to know."

"It'll put you in danger."

"We've already been through the worst," says Skipper. "At least we'll know why."

Nora doesn't argue, because she wants to tell them. She's been alone in knowing for too long, and her sisters are the only people she trusts.

Out the window, the street is full of people heading home. Nora loves the end-of-day scurry, when people have a unified reason to run around.

The gum is soft and pliable. She peels and scrapes stringy pieces of gum away and sticks them on the plate.

"Well?" says Carmen.

Someone plays music outside, and the notes filter in, muffled through the windowpane. Nora closes the curtains. What she's going to tell them, she hasn't told anyone.

The vault smelled permanently of funk, and the temperature control system was loud, but she got used to both.

Her team was responsible for a new, upgraded design of one of Renewal's bestselling varietals of rice. They tinkered with the plants and conducted lab tests similar to the ones Nora had conducted in the city, using blight collected from around the world. There was a freezer full of fresh samples, and a cheerful blond on staff, Blaise, was responsible for sequencing them as they came in, managing the stock, and printing what they needed for the tests.

One day, Blaise fell ill, and the team lead asked Nora to print additional samples. It was a simple task: Go in there, select the right samples, and press Start. Later, Nora would wonder if the illness was contrived, and they were testing her, or if Blaise wanted her to know. Or maybe Blaise had gotten sloppy after too many years in the vault. The vault had a way of dulling people's desire to know things. Nora was new, though, and she was more than curious.

The blight samples and printer occupied a sealed, refrigerated room. The machine sat in one corner among the neatly labeled shelves. Nora had to step into a zip-up suit before entering the chamber. The printer squirted the samples into vials, which were carried out in a case.

Nora sat down in front of the system and entered the code she'd been given. She ordered the samples, and then, while she waited, she began to sift through the machine records.

She noticed the printing history was still in the machine, and she scanned the entries.

What she saw gave her a funny feeling. Most samples were labeled with the year the variant had been discovered and the location. These were marked the previous day, Vault City. That couldn't be right.

Her hands tingled with sweat. Was anyone watching her? But she had to know.

On instinct, she reprinted those samples and removed them with the others she'd printed.

The more she studied them, the more she was convinced they were new, and they had originated in the vault.

All that remains of the gum is a tiny chip. She cleans it gently with her pinky nail.

"What are you saying?" says Skipper, horror growing on her face.

"Let her finish," says Carmen.

"People have never understood how the blight evolves so quickly, or how it affects so many different crops. We're dependent on Renewal, because not only do they produce Amaranthine, but they're the one company that successfully stays one step ahead of the blight with their regularly updated crop designs."

"They're the best in the business," agrees Carmen. "No one comes close."

Nora holds out the chip. "That's because Renewal doesn't just design blight-resistant crops. It manufactures the blight. And this is the proof."

CHAPTER FORTY-THREE

They didn't invent it, but they've been tinkering with it for years." Nora nods to the syringes containing spores. "What you've smuggled out are different versions of it, and this chip contains data that shows when each was developed."

As she talked, Nora thought Skipper would understand, but she can tell Skipper is upset. Would Skipper have preferred to find Nora weak and frightened, so Skipper could save her? Nora is not what Skipper thought—a victim—and worse, that means Skipper is not who she thought she was either.

Carmen's angry too, but that's nothing new. She and Nora don't agree on many things. But Carmen's also her old, practical, unsentimental self. She kept Skipper safe, she found Nora's samples and Nora herself. She did what she set out to do.

They sit, knees touching on the couch, and yet they feel far apart. It is, in many ways, a familiar feeling. The few times Nora came home from college, it had already begun, this separation, as if since she'd left home, she's been accelerating away from them, like Skipper's expanding triangles: three points connected but getting ever further apart.

Nora pours them more tea they haven't asked for, and Carmen examines the chip as if she could absorb its secrets just by looking at it.

"We make it here," Carmen says.

"What?"

"That's what you wrote." Carmen points at Nora's notebook from the vault. "I thought you meant the soybeans."

"Right," says Nora.

"So now that you have the data, you can tell people."

"You can change things," Skipper says, leaning forward.

Nora braces herself.

"Nora?" says Carmen.

"It's not that easy," she says. "I tried posting anonymously when I came here, but people dismissed it as a conspiracy theory. It sunk to the bottom of the digital muck. People don't want to listen. And there are other things to weigh."

"Like what?" says Carmen, her voice deceptively calm. She always sees the world as one thing or the other.

"Like is it worth the price?"

"Were you always such a coward?" Skipper asks.

Nora gapes at her. Does Skipper think Nora's thinking of herself? "If it were just me, that's one thing! But it's not just me. It's all of us. Think of what you went through, of what else they could do."

And then she is saved, because the door bangs open, and a fourteen-year-old girl bursts into the room: Hilda is home.

"Who are you?" Skipper asks.

"Who are you?" Hilda replies. She is small for her age, with pale skin that burns immediately in the sun and freckles everywhere. Recently, she dyed her hair bright purple. It's garish, but she loves it. To Hilda, everything in the world feels important, every day potentially life-changing. But also, she has been through enough in the last year that that's not an inaccurate view of the world.

The sisters gape at Hilda, and Nora realizes she has forgotten to explain: She has a child now. Nora never thought she wanted to be a parent after taking care of her sisters. But with Hilda, it's been different. Nora's proud of how well she's adjusted to the role. She enjoys it.

"She was born in Vault City," Nora tries to explain. "I couldn't leave her there."

Skipper sets down her cup of tea with a clatter. Carmen frowns.

"You're pretty," Hilda tells Carmen, flopping into the armchair.

"So are you," says Carmen, out of habit. They scrutinize each other, trying to find their footing.

Hilda pouts at the empty tart plate. "You finished it?"

"Hilda, these are my sisters," Nora says.

With a shriek, Hilda knocks the plate off the table with her knee and breaks into a smile. "Oh, I know you. I love you already!" She throws her arms around Skipper, who takes it like she doesn't know what a hug is.

"I'm confused," Carmen says. "You went into the vault to find seeds and came out with a child instead?"

"Excuse me. I begged her to let me come," Hilda says. "My father arranged it."

"Your father?" Carmen repeats.

"The maintenance engineer who helped me escape." Nora fixes her gaze on Hilda. "Don't you have homework to do?"

"I see," Hilda says. "You want to talk about me without me being here."

"It's not that. School's important."

Carmen and Skipper exchange looks, and Nora imagines they are thinking, *Is this our sister?* Nora, who had breezed through school without effort or attention and encouraged them to do the same.

"Whatever. Since you ate everything, can I get a pastry?"

Nora transmits money with a wave, and Hilda snatches up her bag. "I'll be back." She leaves the apartment with a clatter, but her presence leaves a new brightness, as if she charged the air molecules just by being here.

Nora fixes yet another round of tea. Her sisters view her with a mix of shock and disappointment, and she tries to explain: "Hilda was one of the few children who'd grown up in Vault City. She had the run of the place in a way few people did.

"I became friends with her father. She'd come to visit him sometimes, to bring him dinner. And, well, you met her. She has a spirit that couldn't be extinguished by the bleakness of that place. She told me her dream was to be a professional dancer. What an absurd dream in a place like Vault City. There was nowhere to do it. She'd taught herself by watching clips.

"When I approached my friend for help escaping, Hilda overheard our conversation. Eavesdropping. She convinced her father this was her chance. He was torn about the risk. But ultimately, he wanted her to have a good life. His help was conditional on my taking her with me. I agreed.

"The night we escaped, someone saw her sneaking around. It triggered a sweep, and there was no way for me to retrieve my things from the vault. All we could do was climb into the garbage and hope the smell dissuaded anyone from checking too closely. I don't regret my choice, though. It wasn't a choice. Wasn't her freedom worth more than my work? I told myself I could start over. I knew what I knew. It would be easier."

Nora doesn't understand their disbelief.

"I was scared. I thought I would never get out of that place. I couldn't know you were coming. And then, after I escaped, I tried to tell you I was okay. I sent a message."

She's about to go on when the door bangs open again. It's Hilda, frazzled and panting from running up the stairs, clutching a sticky pastry.

"There's a man." She goes to the window and peers through the curtain. "I ran when I saw him following me. I don't think he saw which building I went into."

Across the street, a man eats a gelato with slow, deliberate licks. He could be a tourist, judging by his crumpled button-down and sneakers, but when his gaze skims over the apartment building, all the hairs on Nora's neck stand up.

"Are you sure?" Already, Nora is making a list: clothes that must be packed, temporary accommodations found. A cold sweat washes over her.

"Maybe I was wrong," says Hilda. "You know my eyes aren't the best, and anyway, I have an overactive imagination on account of having an artist's soul, don't I?"

Hilda's babbling. Her "artist's soul" has nothing to do with it. She doesn't want to move again.

Carmen and Skipper watch in bewilderment, and an old sensation creeps over Nora, like she's going to be eaten from her toes and fingers. She can't be responsible for so many people.

"He's gone." Carmen peeks through the curtains at the window.

"Please," says Hilda.

Carmen coughs wetly into her sleeve, darkening the inky stain on the inside of her elbow.

Nora decides to believe Hilda, because she can't face moving again either. They'll just have to be vigilant.

She turns to assembling dinner. While Hilda washes up, she asks her sisters not to mention what she's shared about Renewal.

"It's safer for her not to know." It would be safer if none of them did. She already regrets telling her sisters.

"But what are you going to *do*?" Carmen asks.

"I don't know. I need to think."

Nora used to think knowledge was the only thing that mattered, that life was asking a question and going in search of an answer. In the vault, she'd found answers to her questions, and it got her nothing. Truth was worth only as much as it was known, and not just known, but believed.

After she discovered the data in the vault, Nora tried to tell a colleague, a smart, kind biologist she thought would share her outrage. First, he was dismissive: "Maybe you misread it." Then when she showed him the records, he became afraid: "Why would you tell me this? What do you think will happen if they realize you know? Please don't tell anyone you told me." The colleague stopped talking to her, and for days, Nora was petrified he would report her.

"So protecting yourself is more important than helping people?" Skipper asks.

"No!" Nora says, stunned by the venom in Skipper's voice.

"People need to know," says Carmen.

"Know what?" Hilda asks, returning, and Nora holds her breath, willing her sisters to say nothing.

"How good the food is here," Carmen says, stealing a tomato from the cutting board.

"Oh, it is, isn't it!" says Hilda, launching into a list of fruits they *must* try.

Carmen flicks a final glance at Nora, though, letting her know she's on notice. Skipper ignores her.

They talk about other things. It's easier with Hilda here, who asks questions like a stranger, questions Nora wishes she could ask. Nora learns things about her sisters, like Carmen's long relationship with Ollie and their breakup. A terrible boyfriend, whom neither woman wants to discuss at all. That Carmen has learned to navigate by the sky, and that Skipper is still a terrible cook.

"No one ever taught me. It's hard to cook well when options are so limited," says Skipper, eyes narrowed at the table set with pickles, chickpeas, bread, fruit, yogurt, cheeses, and salads mixed with fresh herbs. A breaded roasted eggplant with tomato sauce. It's the kind of meal Hilda and Nora enjoy: a simple celebration of plenty.

It represents to Nora the fragile life they've built. When they arrived, Nora got a job washing dishes at a restaurant. It was hard to get by.

Nora lives in a state of constant worry. They changed hostels many times until she felt safe enough to get an apartment and a job. She knows Renewal and EarthWorks are looking for her. She hopes they haven't already found her.

Then, one day, as she was walking home after a long shift, she saw an advertisement for a free science lecture series. One of the speakers was Professor Rafael Aguirre, and he was giving a lecture on fungi. All week, she couldn't get his face out of her mind. There was nothing in a face. So many things were the projection of the beholder. And yet, there was something about his earnest expression that made her think he might understand.

She dragged Hilda with her to the lecture, just to listen. That's what she intended, anyway. But then she couldn't help herself and began asking questions. He seemed to enjoy the back-and-forth. After,

Hilda insisted they meet him. She ran right down to the side of the stage, forcing Nora to follow.

They struck up a conversation.

Hilda thought Nora and Rafael were flirting, but what they were doing was the academic equivalent of sniffing each other's tails.

Rafael was surprised to learn where she was working.

"She used to be a scientist," Hilda told him. Later, Nora gave her a stern lecture about the importance of keeping a low profile, but it was done.

That might have been the end of it, but he had given her his contact information. "I'm hiring a lab assistant. You should apply."

The salary was better than what she was making, and it came with benefits. She had to consider it, for Hilda's sake. That was a lie. She wanted to, of course. She took the position.

Rafael's family were farmworkers. They had grown up under a repressive regime in another country and escaped here after his father died. Rafael Aguirre isn't the name he was born with.

In the late hours, they share these kinds of facts with each other. They have something between them that is evolving into trust, but Nora has never told him anything about Renewal. She didn't have proof, and the truth is too wild to believe.

He caught her once, conducting an experiment without his approval, and he was upset, because he felt she didn't believe he would support her work. It wasn't that, though. She didn't think he would be able to help her, and therefore it wasn't worth the risk. She had begun to doubt she would ever find her way back to the answers she'd found in the vault. She apologized and promised she would tell him next time.

She remembers with a pang Marcus complaining she didn't know how to ask for help, but thinking of asking Rafael makes her so nervous, she has to set down her fork and cough.

The conversation, she realizes, has gotten away from her.

She studies her sisters' weary faces. It's been such a long time since she has been loved, and now here they are, and it's like they occupy a different plane of existence. She oscillates between frustration and sympathy. She wants to take care of them, give them a bath, and tuck them into bed, as if they were children again.

"Where's the *Bumblebee*?" Hilda asks.

"At the bottom of the ocean," says Skipper.

"No!" Hilda puts a hand on Skipper's. "I'm very sorry."

The pang of regret hits Nora harder than she expected. "I loved that boat."

Skipper prickles. "Not the way I did."

"I know," says Nora, not wanting to argue, but she wonders what it means that the *Bumblebee* is lost, all the years of their childhood, sanding and painting and nailing. The petty frustrations and things they learned along the way. The fights they had, the first night they slept in it together.

Do her sisters remember when they talked about running away, that night Grandma burned Nora's favorite book when Nora came back drunk and smelling like cigarettes? But they never did, and Nora went away to college instead.

Hilda passes Skipper a plate of succulent peaches drizzled with balsamic vinegar, and Carmen helps herself to more eggplant. The living room fills with the sound of forks scraping against cheap ceramic plates. They eat their meal as if it is the last thing they will ever eat.

CHAPTER FORTY-FOUR

Psst. Nora." Hilda crouches next to where Nora lies, tangled in the blankets on the floor. Nora insisted her sisters take the bed. She claimed the floor was better for her back, that she'd contemplated sleeping there before because of that.

Hilda sleeps in the living room so she can have privacy in the evenings. Now, her eyes are frightened. It's the middle of the night.

Nora's first thought is that the man Hilda saw has returned. Did she miss a pounding at the door?

"Your sister's in the bathroom. I think she fainted."

Nora gets up, remnants of sleep evaporating from her brain. She leaves Skipper sleeping in bed.

Carmen slumps in the shower, water spraying everywhere. The floor is covered in puddles. Carmen's head is bent at an awkward angle, and Nora can see now: Her naked body is carpeted with wild growth.

She curses herself for not pressing Carmen on the details the previous night, curses Carmen for not telling her how bad it was. She crouches down and shakes her by the shoulders, heedless of the water raining down.

"Carmen!"

Her sister doesn't respond, though Nora's relieved to see the slight expansion of her chest as Carmen breathes.

"Is she okay?" Hilda asks.

"Tell Skipper we're going to the hospital," Nora says, and Hilda, thankfully, does as she's told. She returns with a dry change of clothes, and Nora's grateful Hilda's had the kind of childhood that taught her to be resourceful in a crisis.

They go to the hospital in a car, Skipper crying quietly on the other side of Carmen. Hilda insisted on coming too, because she doesn't trust them not to panic without her. It's true, Nora's panicking.

The doctors admit her immediately.

"Why didn't she have this removed right away?" they're asked.

"We didn't have the money," Skipper says, then adds to Nora: "I should have sold the boat." Her face contorts in grief, and Nora wants to reach inside her and take it all.

"It's not your fault. It's mine."

"I didn't say you weren't responsible too," Skipper says, and Nora takes her words like a slap. All these years, Skipper's love was something as dependable as the sun. Nora's not used to fighting with Skipper. She's accustomed to, if she's honest, Skipper's unquestioning devotion. Now their covenant is broken. Skipper no longer trusts her; she doesn't take everything Nora says on faith. It shakes Nora to have lost that.

"Don't fight!" Hilda says, and Nora blushes, suddenly aware the doctors are waiting.

"At this stage, the procedure isn't without risk, but there's a 70 percent chance of success if we operate now."

The prognosis sobers them both. "Do it," Nora says, and Skipper nods.

Carmen's wheeled away, and they're left to wait anxiously in a cheerless, windowless sitting area. Hospitals here often have long waits for ordinary procedures, but because of the seriousness of her condition, Carmen's scheduled for surgery right away.

The nurses test them all for the infection just in case, but fortunately, none of them has it. "Does she garden? She could have contracted it there," they say. "We recommend treating the soil with Amaranthine."

"Okay," says Nora, thinking of the fields Carmen was so often exposed to in her work, already drenched in scarlet.

They wait, nerves jangling. When Nora can't take the stress any longer, she tells the others she'll get breakfast, even though the sun hasn't yet risen. She circles the building until she can breathe again, then messages Rafael to let him know she's taking a sick day.

Seven out of ten. That's more than two-thirds.

As she's buying coffee and breakfast rolls at a bakery, the door jingles. She glances behind her, and her blood pressure spikes. It's Hilda's gelato man.

She stares too long, and he smiles at her and nods.

"Excuse me," says the shopkeeper, who is waiting for her to pay.

Nora holds out her thumb, but it's trembling so much, she misses the scanner. She feels the shadow of the man looming behind her. Should she run?

"You all right?" the shopkeeper asks.

Nora glances involuntarily back again, and this time she's less sure. Did Hilda's man have a beard? Blond hair? Maybe she's wrong. She doesn't think she's wrong.

"Fine." She scoops up everything and runs from the store. Only when she's a couple of blocks away does she risk looking back. The man stands outside the bakery, dictating a message into an egg. He doesn't glance her way. Or she doesn't think he does. She isn't sure.

She turns the corner and huddles in a doorway, scrubbing her face. Whatever she does could make things worse. And Carmen could die today. How could Nora endanger her further? If something happens to them or Hilda . . . Better if she does nothing, even if they hate her for it.

She takes the long way back to make sure he doesn't follow.

Rafael messages with a long list of home remedies. He accuses their student workers of spreading germs; they party too much and are walking petri dishes. He doesn't mean it. It's meant to cheer her up, and it does, a tiny bit.

In the lobby, Skipper dozes in one of the chairs. She always could sleep anywhere.

"I'm sorry," Nora says to Hilda, feeling like she's been apologizing for hours; it hasn't alleviated the pressure in her chest at all. "This is scary, isn't it?"

Hilda bites into her roll. "It's no big deal. I had it as a baby already. Papa too. That's why I hate mushrooms. I hope now you understand."

"I didn't know." She wonders how Hilda could have contracted it in those clean facilities, the glass domes sealed like spaceships.

"Why should you? Papa was convinced the company gave it to us." Hilda reaches for Nora's cup of coffee.

Nora stares. "What do you mean?"

"Because it makes you hungry and super productive." Hilda swallows some coffee, makes a face, and hands it back. "No, this is disgusting. It was silly. He thought they contaminated our vegetables, like we ate it with our food. People used to make fun of him."

Later, Nora returns home alone, ostensibly to pick up more clothes for her sister. She's bundled an indignant Hilda off to school while Skipper stays at the hospital with Carmen, who's recovering from surgery.

She finds what she's hunting for in the drain: a ruffled purple-black thallus. Carmen must have shed it in the shower.

"Aster," Rafael says, unaware of the jolt it gives Nora to hear her false name. "What are you doing here? Aren't you sick?"

Nora had hoped he'd be out for lunch, but he's not, because he forgets to eat when he's busy.

"I wanted to check something," she says.

"Don't worry about work," he says, frowning. "Go home."

She has the unexpected urge to tell him everything, but there's too much to say, and it wouldn't be right to burden this man who has been nothing but supportive. Marcus's complaint echoes in her ears, that she's ungenerous with her problems. But why would anyone want the extra burden?

It takes a few minutes to sequence the thing from the drain, and a few minutes more to find a match in the data from the chip Carmen smuggled out of the vault.

It's not proof, but it's enough to convince Nora that Hilda's father's suspicions were more than paranoia. She *knows* it, not scientifically, but in her gut: Renewal's behind this too.

"So what are you doing?" Rafael asks.

Nora feigns a coughing fit. "I'll explain tomorrow," she lies. "I have to go."

Her brain is a riot the whole way back to the hospital: rage, despair. It's a wonder she doesn't combust.

This is not the world I want, she should have said to Skipper.

She wants the people she loves to be safe and comfortable. She wants to protect them, but she doesn't know how. She'll never know enough.

Every choice she's ever made has been wrong.

In the waiting room, someone's holding a baby. She gets a whiff of diaper ointment, and for a brief moment, she's six again, holding Skipper in her arms for the first time. She feels the warmth of her soft, bald head against her cheek, absorbs her milky scent.

And Nora knows the answer, because she has carried this question too long. She has to try.

"Your sister's doing well," she's told, and sure enough, she finds Skipper and Carmen together. Carmen's weak but awake, listening to Skipper ramble about oceans. Skipper stops, and they focus on Nora, expectant.

"Okay," Nora says. "I'm going to do something about it."

CHAPTER FORTY-FIVE

The night Mama died, Nora sat on the porch, baby Skipper in her arms, Carmen clinging to Nora's elbow, while Grandma went to get the doctor. Carmen kept making a choking noise, as if a scream were stuck in her throat.

"It's going to be all right," she told Carmen, because she thought that was the wise thing to say.

Carmen hiccuped, and a tear rolled down her cheek.

Nora's eyes burned, but she was too shocked to cry. She thought of Mama's body, somewhere in the woods. She couldn't tell Grandma that it was her fault. What would Grandma say?

"It was a mistake," she told Carmen.

In her arms, Skipper began to cry, and Nora jiggled her. "Poor baby."

Skipper cried harder, and a whimper stole out of Nora's mouth. She didn't have anything to feed her sister, and she wondered if this was what Mama meant when she said she couldn't face the world, this helplessness.

Desperate, she shoved a knuckle into Skipper's mouth and begged her, "Eat this," and miraculously, Skipper began to suck.

In the morning, Nora drags herself to the lab. She'd sat at the kitchen table most of the night, her mind too full of problems to sleep: Carmen's health; whether they'd been found and needed to move right away; how she would take care of her sisters on her meager salary; and how she might use what her sisters had brought her. She's exhausted from her vigil, but for the first time in weeks, the dull ache in her skull is gone.

"Better?" Rafael asks.

"I need coffee."

Rafael points to the pot, where he's already brewed a spare cup.

"So what happened yesterday? You said you would explain," he says, and Nora curses his excellent memory.

"Oh." She fusses with a case of vials.

"Those are washed. What's going on?"

"I—" Nora begins, intending to say she is fine. But she is not fine. The worry will crush her. She's tried so hard to take care of her own problems. And yet, her sisters came all this way, because they thought she needed help, and did that mean she'd failed them?

"Do you need another day off?" he asks, even though Nora's behind on her work. His gentle, unquestioning sympathy touches something in her, because it's so undeserved.

She thinks about Marcus and how, in her lowest moment, she regretted not asking him for help. If only he were here now, he could tell her what to do, and she could pretend to be annoyed about it.

"Aster," Rafael says, looking at her with that ruminating expression, as if he can see everything inside her. He hands her the coffee she hasn't poured, and she breaks.

"It's Nora," she whispers.

"What?"

"My real name."

"All right." He sits next to her, as if he has been waiting since they met for this conversation.

And so she tells him everything: about her sisters, the things Carmen smuggled out of the vault, and the truth of the blight.

She's shocked him, but he hasn't accused her of paranoia or jumping to conclusions. He wants to see the data, but he believes her, and that steadies her more than she thought it would.

"Can I trust you?" she asks, even though it's too late.

They sit between tables, heads bent close so they can speak without being overheard, even though no one is around.

"My father died of lung cancer. I can't prove it, but I'm sure it was the Amaranthine. Prolonged and unsafe exposure in the fields. If he had taken the recommended safety precautions, maybe he'd have been fine, but we didn't have the money for a respirator. You can guess the story. We might have gotten survivor benefits, but my mother got into political trouble with the government, and we left the country instead."

"I didn't know," Nora says.

"That's why I do this research. We all have stories like this. I want to help you."

"I didn't think you would believe me," she admits, thinking of her colleague back in the vault. "I didn't think anyone would."

"Well. People will accept significant evil, if it doesn't feel personal. They forget negligence can sometimes be as fatal as intention."

Nora thinks of Carmen's sickness and how long Carmen endured that thing growing inside her.

"What can we do?"

He takes the tiny chip and holds it next to his computer. "We prove it. We'll conduct a series of rigorous trials to demonstrate the properties of your soybeans. We'll publish the results once we have unimpeachable data. As for the blight, we can stage simulations of its likely evolutionary rate and analyze for telltale markers of tinkering."

Everything he's describing will take time, which Carmen and Skipper will hate. And in the meantime, they'll have to worry about Renewal catching up with them.

"Are you sure you want to be involved? They tried to kill me, and that was before I even knew about their involvement in the blight."

He skims through the vault data, and she can see the gleam of a scientist's ambition in his eyes. "This is going to be huge. It would be my privilege to be a part of it."

They bring Carmen home to recover. At Carmen's request, Nora sets aside some of the seeds to grow at home. She doesn't know where. Maybe a makeshift nursery in the bedroom, if she ever has the time.

As Nora anticipated, Carmen and Skipper are anxious for results. They're all itchy about Renewal figuring out where they are.

"Just tell people," Carmen says. "Once people know the truth, they'll do something."

"It's going to take more than me waving a packet of seeds in the air," Nora says. "Trust me, I'm working on it. I'm doing my best." She's in the middle of cooking dinner for them, after doing everyone's laundry, after coming home from a long day of work.

"I didn't say you weren't."

"But this will work, right?" Skipper wants to know.

"Yes," says Nora, but deep down, she's even more worried than they are. She doesn't know how she can hold it all together, even with Rafael's help.

It's a tight fit in a one-bedroom apartment. Four people crammed in means no privacy, and it's hard on all of them, especially Hilda. When Nora was a teenager, her refuge in the woods gave her space to think and kept her from lashing out at her sisters when they didn't deserve it. She was so angry about everything in those days.

"How long will they be staying?" Hilda wants to know, which means the fun of the sleepover has worn off.

Nora wants to know too, but with a different hope. She'd like them to stay forever, though maybe not in the same apartment.

Carmen talks of returning home after Nora and Rafael publish their results, and Nora realizes Carmen expects her to go with them. She's surprised. And then surprised that she's surprised. From Carmen's perspective, that was the point in finding Nora.

"I can't go back," Nora says. "Even after, it wouldn't be safe." Here,

Renewal's influence is weaker than back home. And even if it were safe, it's not what she wants. She's been here only a short time, but she's already fallen in love with this city and its long, white days. She doesn't want to leave, maybe not ever.

Skipper, at least, isn't interested in going with Carmen. Skipper longed to leave home for so long, and Nora cheers inside that Skipper has broken free.

Despite the ongoing tension, it's a luxury having her sisters close. Nora didn't realize how much she missed them. Even their arguments are wrapped in the velvet trappings of nostalgia.

But on top of everything else, she's worried about money. She moved some funds to a secure account before she took the Vault City job, and she has her salary, but they're burning through money at an alarming rate, even without indulgences. In a few months, there won't be anything left for rent, much less food.

"Do you think you could get jobs?" It's taken days for her to force herself to ask, because she wishes she didn't need to. "When you've recovered."

Carmen pauses, in the middle of her stretches. "How much longer do you think it's going to take? Weeks? Months?"

Nora cringes. "I'm not sure. I told you, these things take time."

Carmen resumes her exercise. "Yeah, okay. It's better than sitting around here, waiting."

"I can get a job too," Hilda pipes up from the living room, where she's been eavesdropping.

"No, you can't," they all say at the same time.

"It's just an idea. Like a bakery, making cookies."

"You know they wouldn't let you eat them," Nora says.

"Not all of them."

"Do your homework." Nora shuts the bedroom door.

"We don't want to be a burden," Skipper says.

"You're not!" Nora says, frustration washing over her. "I wasn't saying that."

"What Skipper means is, we can figure it out," says Carmen. "You don't have to take care of us."

Doesn't she?

Carmen sees her face. "Give us more credit. We came here to help you. So let us help."

True to her word, as soon as she's able to, Carmen makes the rounds at all the major hospitals. She's disappointed to learn she's unemployable as a nurse. She doesn't have the proper academic credentials, and she can't exactly disclose her prior work experience. They tell her she would need to go to school for two years to qualify.

So Carmen, being Carmen, goes back the next week and tries again. She returns with a job cleaning toilets instead.

Nora is embarrassed to realize she never appreciated how reliable Carmen is. She knew it in a theoretical way, but she never witnessed it for herself. Carmen makes everyone dinner before she leaves for her night shift and returns in the early hours to share breakfast before Hilda goes to school, and Nora leaves for work.

Neither of them is sure what Skipper is up to. She disappears for long stretches of time and comes back with dust in her hair, cheeks red with sun, and cracked lips from not drinking enough water.

"Same old Skipper," Carmen says, when Nora mentions it. "Like when she—"

"Stole Uncle Tot's gasoline and took the boat out without anyone knowing?"

"I've never seen him so mad."

"Because Grandma yelled at *him*."

They both laugh.

They assumed she's just been wandering, so Nora's surprised when Skipper asks for help opening a bank account.

"You have money?"

Apparently, one of her long walks took her down to a shipyard where people build and repair boats. She's been walking there every day, though it takes two hours.

They don't pay her much, but Skipper doesn't mind. Every day, she looks out at the ocean and smells the wind blowing in from distant places. She's content, or content enough for now, and she's started to forgive Nora. Nora's glad. This way, maybe, Skipper will stay.

Two weeks after they move in, Carmen insists on sending a message to Uncle Tot, despite the risk. "He has a right to know we're okay."

His reply comes back almost instantly:

> *Thank God you're all right. I hope you're happy to know I am officially balding (not visibly, in the back), and it's your fault for scaring me. I even took your grandma to church last Sunday and had to endure Wendy Morton's side-eye when Grandma started cackling in the middle of the sermon. Don't worry about us, though, your grandma and I have come to an accord: I said I'll stop with the chili if she'll stop telling me it's a shame I got Dad's nose. Will report back. Please keep me posted on how you are. There's no need to give an old man needless stress.*

"See?" says Carmen, and Nora regrets resisting.

A couple of weeks after that, Nora sees Hilda's gelato man, again, smoking outside the building.

She halts, but it's too late to retreat.

Their gazes lock, and a shiver runs down her spine.

Then he waves the smoke away and offers her a sheepish smile. "Terrible habit, I know. At least I don't do it inside." He gestures at the building next to theirs.

Nora swallows a nervous laugh. He's harmless, she tells herself. He lives next door.

It's been weeks since she's had any sign of Renewal. Even the anonymous threats have stopped. She needs to relax. The important thing is the work.

~

One evening, Nora is working late in the lab when Rafael comes by to let her know he's leaving. She promises she's right behind him.

"Don't stay too late," he tells her. "It isn't healthy." He smiles, because they both know she won't listen, and she sits back down to work.

She means to leave earlier, because there isn't any food in the house except Skipper's leftovers, and no one wants to eat those. But one thing leads to another, and by the time Nora walks out of the building, it's nine o'clock.

She curses, realizing the time. She's been selfish again. Carmen told her earlier that week, "You should try to be at home one night this week, for Hilda's sake." Nora promised she would, but she hasn't.

She's so wrapped in her misery she doesn't process the van, or the men leaning against it.

They move before she realizes what's happening, bracketing her and grabbing her arms.

She struggles, but their grip is iron. She makes herself heavy and tries to sit, but they are strong enough to simply drag her along.

She screams, and it occurs to her that she's never screamed before, and maybe she isn't doing it correctly.

One of the men punches her face, and pain shoots through her jaw. She tastes blood. He stuffs a gloved hand across her mouth.

They're almost to the van. She doesn't know what will happen to her once they put her inside. She doesn't want to know. She thrashes her head and gets off one more yelp.

"Hey!" She recognizes the voice: It's a woman who works down the hall even later than she does. "What are you doing?"

"Stop!" says a second person.

Despite her terror, Nora appreciates that graduate students sleep as little as walruses. She thrashes and kicks again.

She manages to get an arm free and punch one right in the groin. He exhales in pain and his grip loosens enough for her to free that side.

"Shit," says one of her kidnappers.

Because a small crowd is forming. Clearly, they didn't account for how nocturnal a campus can be. They drop her on the ground and throw themselves into the open van, wheels screaming on the pavement as they speed off.

"Are you all right?" someone asks, grabbing her arm.

Nora clutches herself. Her teeth chatter, and her face is already stiff and swelling. She wants to say she's okay, she'll go home, maybe stop on the way to buy groceries. But all she can do is sit there.

"I'll call Professor Aguirre," she hears someone say, and she's so relieved that before she processes why, she begins to cry, because there is someone after all to call, and she doesn't need to do everything herself.

When Rafael drops her off at home after giving a statement to the police, it's three in the morning.

"I understand if you don't want to keep going," Nora says. She doesn't know how she'll do it without him or his lab.

"Are you kidding?" he says, slapping the side of the car. "We're going to nail those fuckers to the wall."

"Thank you." It's inadequate, but she doesn't know what else to say.

Carmen and Skipper are both beside themselves. Hilda snores softly on the couch.

"I'm sorry," Nora says, because an irrational part of her expects them to be angry with her for not being home on time, for not getting in touch earlier. It's an absurd thought. They throw their arms around her, as if they need to reassure themselves she's here.

"I thought we'd have to sail to the vault all over again," jokes Carmen.

"I'm sorry," Nora says again. "What if they come here? Should we move?"

"They know where you work." Carmen frowns. "And you can't quit. Until you and Rafael are ready, we'll just be more careful."

"If they threaten Hilda— " Nora begins.

"What?" says Hilda, waking up. "Are we having cake?"

"Shh," says Nora, going to lay a hand on her head.

"We'll deal with them," Skipper says, fiercely.

But Nora can't shake her fear. Renewal knows where they are. They're running out of time.

CHAPTER FORTY-SIX

The incident puts them all on edge. The university is spooked. They increase their security, installing cameras throughout the campus. Unfortunately, the leadership has also begun asking questions. They want to know what Rafael is working on that might have attracted such attention.

"Are you going to tell them?" Nora asks, stirring the creamer in her coffee too vigorously.

"Don't be silly. We agreed, not until we're ready."

"I'm not sure we can wait," Nora says. Rafael's thoroughness is beginning to grate on her nerves.

"We have to do this right."

"I don't think you know what it's like."

"Don't I?" he asks, raising his eyebrows, and Nora flushes, remembering too late Rafael of all people knows.

Renewal reaches out to Rafael, offering him a fantastically large grant. It's not spelled out in their conditions, but the implication is clear: They would need to drop their current research. Rafael turns the grant down, but Renewal is persistent, increasing the terms, offering to buy him a private car, to pay for two luxurious vacations a year. Fortunately, Rafael shudders at the idea of a spa. Nora doesn't think he's ever relaxed in his life.

"Are you serious? You can't throw all that money away!" Nora hears the university president shouting from all the way down the hall. She's never come here before.

Nora tiptoes closer to the office door to eavesdrop. The department chair tries to smooth things over, followed by Rafael's stiff baritone: "My integrity is not for sale."

"What about your obligations to the university? We pay your salary."

But Rafael declines again.

Someone files a complaint against him: an anonymous allegation about ethics and improper experiments. More complaints follow. There's nothing to prove, but each investigation takes up time they can't afford, and he's on notice with the university. They want an excuse to push him out.

She can see it wearing on him in the bend of his shoulders and the lines on his face.

"Are you going to be all right?" she asks. "Your career—"

"Don't worry about me," he snaps, irritable she's asking again and about the whole situation.

But later that evening, he calls Nora as she's cleaning the dishes with Skipper. He took a taxi home after a dinner date, and it dropped him in front of a large warehouse.

"I'm all right," he says, but his voice shakes.

"Where are you?" she asks, massaging her chest.

He's somewhere in an industrial part of town. There's no one around.

"I'm okay. I'll catch the train." The closest station is half a mile away. He starts to jog. She can hear him breathing loudly, his feet slapping on pavement.

"We should call the police," Carmen says, from the living room.

"And tell them what?" he says, when Nora repeats this. "They'll say it was a malfunction. It's okay. Those assholes just wanted to send me a warning. I shouldn't have let them spook me." He's still running. "But God, the thought crossed my mind this might be it. Can you imagine?"

"At least you're wearing your orthopedic shoes," Nora jokes, trying to distract him.

"What's wrong with my shoes? They're very comfortable."

"Exactly," says Nora. "Great for running away from things. Was it a good first date at least?"

"Not nearly as exciting as this."

Even after Rafael confirms he's safely home, Nora stands at the door of the living room, watching Hilda do her homework. Her nerves are absolutely frayed, and her head aches again with the unrelenting pressure.

The situation is untenable. How long before something happens?

"We can't wait any longer," Carmen whispers.

"We're not ready," Nora says.

"Is there no other way?" Skipper asks.

It's not the first time Nora has asked herself this. Working with Rafael was supposed to be easier, but she's just added to the list of people she has to worry about.

Out the window, she hears a loud grinding noise. The smell of garbage filters up, and Nora goes to close the window. She glances at the familiar planet logo on the truck: EarthWorks.

An idea forms: an easier, safer way to resolve everything. There's a reason they approached her before: They are one of the few entities with the resources and motivation to withstand Renewal's pressure. They've demonstrated their eagerness to obtain blight-proof soybeans.

Sure, her last deal with them didn't go well. Some might even say she cheated them. But all the more reason, hopefully, they'll be receptive to an opportunity for closure. And while they're new to agricultural products, they're one of the industry leaders in recycled plastics. They have deep pockets. The more she thinks about it, the more she's convinced it's the smart thing to do, for all of their sakes.

She reaches out to them that night.

Rafael is furious when she tells him. She's never seen him so upset.

"You didn't ask me," he says.

Nora doesn't know what to say. She thought he'd be relieved.

"I'm not even sure this is legal."

"This way, you can say you didn't know," Nora says.

He rounds on her, shaking his finger. "We knew there would be pressure. I *told* you I could deal with it. Did you not believe me? I promised I would help you."

"I know. But there's no reason to kill ourselves. As long as the truth gets out, does it matter how?" Nora wants to shake him, to dispel this fantasy he has that everything will be okay if they follow the rules.

"It absolutely matters. We were going to publish results, not cut deals like some kind of mafia. This is my lab. Or maybe you've forgotten it's my reputation on the line." It's the first time Rafael's raised his voice in all this time, and Nora feels even guiltier for everything she's put him through.

From their first fateful meeting, their relationship has always been friendship more than professional. Her first day at work, they talked for five hours about mycelial network dynamics. They've spent countless coffee-fueled afternoons messing around with the bioprinters together. He seeks her input on everything and respects her ideas; it's what she loves about working in the lab. With a stab, she wonders if she's cost herself the very thing she wanted to protect.

Her face heats with shame. She took him for granted. But she's also certain she's right. "Why do you think I'm doing this?"

He exhales heavily. "If you're doing this for my sake, don't."

She looks at him, at the dark circles under his eyes, the stains and wrinkles in his normally crisp shirts. If they continue on like this, he might be fired.

Maybe one day, Hilda won't come home from school.

There could be an explosion as Carmen takes the monorail to work.

Skipper might be found, accidentally drowned.

They all know too much. Nora's eyes sting, and she worries if they continue to argue, she'll burst into tears of frustration. She refuses to lose it in front of him. Rafael would be absolutely traumatized.

"I'm doing this for all of us. It was a fallacy thinking we could take Renewal on directly. This is the only way." Nora slips her samples into an empty candy bag. From the outside, it could be anything. "You can publish the results. It'll make a splash regardless. For your career, I mean."

"If you think that's why I did this, you don't know me." She worries he'll have no hair the way he tugs at it.

"I— That's not what I meant."

She waits for her friend to threaten her, to tell her she's fired for going against him. Instead, he gives her such a sad look of betrayal, she almost relents.

"I'll call the police if I don't hear from you in two hours," he says and turns away.

It's vacation week for students, and the hush of the campus and dark evening sky remind her inauspiciously of Vault City as she boards the train. She doesn't want to remember that place, the endless dark and the way the quiet muffled her thoughts. She focuses on how alive the city is with voices and colors and the smell of spicy things cooking.

The hotel where she's arranged to meet is modern and luxurious. EarthWorks probably picked it on purpose, to throw her off-kilter. There are too many corners, not enough exits if she needs to run. They could drag her to a room upstairs without anyone noticing. She should have insisted on a different place. Her adrenaline spikes.

Rafael is probably pacing at the lab, her sisters at home watching the door for her return. She was so confident last night, but she realizes now she has no idea what she's gotten herself into. She's an amateur.

Carmen had hated the plan as much as Rafael.

"They trashed your apartment—" said Carmen.

"—and broke into our boat—" added Skipper.

"They're no better than Renewal, just smaller."

"Carmen's been dating revolutionaries," explained Skipper.

Nora's doubt crests, and she's about to turn and walk away, but it's too late. The EarthWorks representative has spotted her.

To say EarthWorks was excited when Nora reached out is an understatement. She doesn't trust them, but she knows what they want. The agent is a petite woman in a loose-fitting blouse with sunflowers. She sits at a table in the back, drinking a glass of something blue.

"It's good to see you, Nora. We'd hoped to hear from you sooner," the woman says, as if they've met before. Nora doesn't bother remembering the woman's name, because she doubts it's real, and she's just one of their many minions, anyway.

"I got waylaid."

"You're here now." The woman gestures for the waiter. "What can I get you?"

"Water, please." She waits for the waiter to walk away. "I have terms."

Nora's first condition is that they ensure their safety.

"We'll provide security," the woman says, nodding vigorously.

"And you'll make sure people know about the blight?" Nora assumes EarthWorks has a better shot of getting the media to write about the story than she does. It's also safer coming from EarthWorks; at least if Renewal retaliates, it won't involve dumping Nora's body in a worm bin.

"Absolutely. It's heinous what they've done. People need to know about it." She sounds sincere, but it doesn't matter what this woman thinks, it only matters if EarthWorks is willing to act on the information.

Carmen also insisted they ask for more money. It's bold, but Carmen says it's only fair, since the task ended up being so much more than originally discussed. Nora asked for too little the first time, Carmen argued. EarthWorks can afford it and, anyway, they need Nora's discovery. Carmen, as usual, is right.

"Assuming you have the samples this time, that won't be a problem." She smiles at Nora to show there are only a few hard feelings.

"Okay then." Nora wipes her palms on her pants. "Half now, and half once you test these. But if you deviate from our agreement, it's off. I'm sure I can find another buyer."

"Not necessary."

It only takes a few minutes. A bell chimes in Nora's ear: payment delivered. She slides the false bag of candy across the table, and the EarthWorks woman pockets it. "We'll be in touch again once we've verified these."

"Don't take too long." Nora finishes her water. She can't believe things are in motion, that there's an end in sight to this nightmare.

"Don't worry." The woman gestures to the bartender for another drink. "I've been told to reiterate the job offer. But I'm pretty sure I know your answer."

"Thanks, anyway," Nora says, because Grandma raised them to be polite.

As she walks away, she wonders if this is it, if she's finally freed herself, or if she will always be trapped in the metal jaws of her own curiosity.

CHAPTER FORTY-SEVEN

The deal with EarthWorks was supposed to bring them relief, but it doesn't. It throws them instead into a limbo, waiting for an update from the company.

With the first payment from EarthWorks, Carmen and Skipper could have quit their jobs, but they've agreed to maintain their routines until they get the second payment. Skipper likes her job, anyway.

"I'm not doing it for the money," she says.

"That makes one of us," Carmen says, but she sounds more envious than annoyed.

With an end in sight, Carmen talks again about returning home. "I want to bring back your seeds. Think of what a difference it'll make for everyone. Isn't that the point of doing this? To help?"

For Carmen, home isn't an abstract thing. It's their small town by the sea, battered by storms and blight each year but hanging on. Nora can't imagine going back, and Carmen can't imagine not.

But Carmen is here, at least for now. Nora doesn't want her to leave, for many reasons. She wants her sisters here, like this, their walks to the park together, their morning coffee conversations, the interest they take in Hilda's life. Things are changing underfoot, and she doesn't like how little she can control it.

Since she made the deal with EarthWorks, Rafael's been less engaged. He's turned his focus back to his ongoing research. He's kind and supportive, but it's not the same. She misses their long, furtive discussions late at night, the excitement of doing something together. She would have thought he would appreciate the easier path, but even now, he thinks it was a mistake. He mutters every so often about how long it's taking EarthWorks to get back to her.

EarthWorks needs time to work through things on their side. It doesn't mean anything's wrong.

Summer lingers, with deadly heat. Years ago, the climate here was mild and temperate, but everything has shifted and continues to shift. People come up with all sorts of clever ways to make life endurable, but in Hilda's lifetime, this city will not be habitable anymore.

Carmen and Skipper weren't prepared for the weather. They buy loose-flowing clothes and floppy sun hats. Carmen works the night shift, so her commute is mostly dusk and dawn, but Nora begs Skipper to stop walking to work. Skipper concedes only somewhat, taking the light rail down to the harbor and walking along the seawall instead.

In this heat, they can't hide inside the apartment as they've been doing, so one day, Nora, Skipper, and Hilda pack up a lunch and take the train out to the beach. As they're unpacking their blankets, they get a message from Uncle Tot:

> *I don't want to worry you, but I thought you should know I received a visit from the county Renewal representative. They asked me to relay to you this message: 'If you proceed, we will be forced to take serious legal action.' They said other shit that sounded shady, and frankly, somewhat threatening toward your grandmother and her house, so I told them on my own behalf they could*

go fuck themselves. Then your grandmother got agitated and cursed them out, even though I don't think she knew what they were talking about.

"We should have warned him," says Skipper.

"It's better for him not to know." Nora watches Hilda plunge into the ocean water with a shriek.

It's concerning they haven't heard from EarthWorks. The company was supposed to get back to them a week ago confirming the deal, and Nora wonders if Uncle Tot's message is somehow related. She doesn't know what to think.

She risks sending her EarthWorks contact a note: *If we don't hear from you soon, we're going to move forward with another buyer.*

She doesn't have another buyer. She's been counting on this to work.

EarthWorks responds as they ride the train home, brains loosened by heat. EarthWorks apologizes for the delay. Business arrangements are complicated, as is product development. They need a little more time.

That's reasonable. So why does it make her queasy?

On Monday, Nora goes into work early so she can get Rafael alone before the student workers arrive. She wants to talk to him about her worries and get his perspective on what's happening. On the train, as she's scanning news headlines, a single one catches her attention:

RENEWAL CORPORATION TO ACQUIRE EARTHWORKS

She can't hear anything for a second save the thumping of her heart. She reads the entire article twice, then casts her gaze wildly about the train, wondering how everyone can sit there, when everything is collapsing. They don't know what a disaster this is.

Well, it explains the delay.

This is bad on so many levels. She should never have tried to cut a deal with EarthWorks.

She gets off the train and vomits in a trash can.

"It's fine," she tells herself, as she scrabbles around her brain for a solution. Rafael will know what to do. Maybe they really can find another buyer. Or they can revert to the original plan. Wrapped in these thoughts, she makes her way to the lab, letting the tree-lined walk calm her.

She'd planned to beat him to the lab and make him coffee, as he's done for her so many times, but the door is unlocked.

"You beat me!" she says, stepping into the lab, but Rafael isn't there.

Something crunches underfoot. Shattered glass litters the floor. The lab is wrecked.

She stares at the ruined lab, unable to process what she's seeing. Seedlings lie crushed and strewn across the floor, beakers thrown against the wall, and expensive equipment smashed to pieces. In the corner of the lab, baby heirloom plants burn in the trash. The sprinklers rain down.

Scraping her wits together, she staggers to the locked cabinet where they keep the vault material. A moan rises in her throat.

The door is open. Everything is gone.

She crouches on her knees in the glass, desperate to find something they missed.

She doesn't know what to do. Her mind is blank with shock. She should get a broom. She should do *something*. She can't.

"Oh." Rafael leans in the doorway, as dazed as she. "This is—this—" He clutches his heart.

In her desperate search for her own precious samples, she'd ignored the indiscriminate nature of the job. Renewal didn't just steal her seeds, they destroyed projects he's been working on for years.

"I'm so sorry," she says.

He focuses on her, uncomprehending.

She needs him to say something, anything, even if it's to yell at her, if he wants. She feels such regret.

But Rafael goes on standing in the doorway.

"I wish I never got you involved," Nora says.

He runs a hand through his hair and, not meeting her gaze anymore, says, "Me too."

Rafael closes the lab and tells her to take a week off. He wants time alone to assess the damage.

The good news is, they still have the vault data. After her initial panic, she'd checked. Renewal must not have realized they had it. That means with a bioprinter, they could reprint the blight samples. They could, maybe, start again with those experiments at least.

Unfortunately, the bioprinter, Rafael's most expensive equipment, lies in pieces across the floor. That, and Rafael made it clear he doesn't want anything to do with her and her mess.

This is a setback, but nothing was ever easy. Nora tries not to despair.

She'll find a new job. Except it's hard to imagine anyone will want her. Rafael only hired her because of a chance encounter, and she can't go around haunting science lectures; that wouldn't be dignified. More importantly, it wouldn't happen twice. So back to restaurant or worm factory work for now.

She always thought work was something to be suffered through, but she'd loved working for Rafael. She'd allowed herself to daydream about a career—going back to school, maybe even having her own lab someday. She doesn't know how she'll do any of that now.

And how will she keep her promise to her sisters without access to a job with proper equipment?

By the time she gets home, her mood has sunk below the mantle of the earth.

Carmen's in the kitchen making dinner. Usually she sleeps during the day, since she has to work the night shift, but she yawns like she never slept. The house is immaculate—cleaner than Nora has ever gotten it. Carmen's even scrubbed the dust from the windowsill somehow. The laundry, an eternal weight around Nora's neck, is neatly folded on her bed.

"You saw the news about EarthWorks?" Nora asks.

"It's awful," Carmen says.

"They broke into the lab."

"Oh no. Nor." Carmen sets down the knife. "Are you okay?"

"Not really."

"How fucked are we?"

"Seismically. Well. You want to tell me you were right?"

"Right?" Carmen says. "Is that the goal? I would have settled for justice myself."

Nora collapses miserably in the living room.

"So that's it?" Carmen asks.

"Give me a minute, please." Nora closes her eyes and inhales the smell of her sister's soup. She can't think beyond her brewing headache. Skipper's face rises up behind her lids, the expression on her face when Nora went off to college. How proud she was, as if she believed Nora could do anything.

"Okay, that was a minute," Carmen says, stepping into the room, and Nora can't help but smile, because this is what Carmen used to do when they were younger. Carmen sits across from her and tidies the coffee table. "Maybe it's not the end of the world. It's just . . . status quo. In fact, some have said the world already ended, and we're just living in the epilogue."

"Did I say that?"

"You were an angsty teenager."

They share a laugh, and then Nora scrubs her face. "Thank you."

Carmen takes Nora's hands, and the bottom drops out of Nora's stomach.

"I want to go home."

"What?"

"I've been thinking about it all day. I can't wait anymore. Who knows how much longer Grandma has. If I go now, I could even plant the soybeans before the season's over."

Nora stares. She forgot all about the seeds Carmen set aside. It's a bright spot in a terrible day, but Nora isn't grateful. She can't believe Carmen is leaving.

"It's another way to win, isn't it?" Carmen says.

"It's too dangerous." Nora didn't think, after everything that's happened, she had any panic left over, but she does. It rises in her like a tide. Carmen can't go.

"It's dangerous here," Carmen says. "No matter what we do, there's risk. We have to live."

Nora sizes up the table, laden with cold salads, bread, meats, and eggs.

"You decided."

Carmen nods. "When I saw the news this morning." She used her share of the money to purchase a plane ticket back to the city. "It was extravagant, but I couldn't face another long voyage."

Nora doesn't know what to say. The feast Carmen assembled revolts her. She's tearing inside. She wants Carmen to stay. She wants to know her again and be known by her. She wants her friendship into old age, her shoulder to lay her head on after a long day. She wants the moments before this one to stretch out into the rest of her life.

Skipper is devastated when Carmen tells her, "You can't."

"I miss Uncle Tot and his weird art projects and silly jokes," Carmen tries to explain. "I miss the town, the way the sun cuts over the water as it rises in the morning. The taste of Barry's apple pie. All the children walking down the street to our school in the morning. I want to be a nurse—or maybe a doctor. And—I want to see Grandma one more time before she dies. I know she wasn't an easy woman to live with, but she did raise us. She stayed when everyone else in our life left. It's not that we owe her, but I do love her."

"Will you come back?" asks Skipper, voice breaking.

Carmen sticks her hands in her pockets. "This isn't my home. You were right, Nor, when you said I shouldn't join you in the city. I'm not meant for this kind of life."

"What are you talking about? I never said that."

"You told me not to come."

"Because I was embarrassed!" Nora says. "I was struggling. I was living in a tiny apartment full of roaches and mice and three roommates and eating porridge for dinner, and I didn't want you to see me like that. To know I wasn't successful. And we didn't even have a couch for you to crash on because we had to get rid of it when we realized it had bedbugs."

Now Carmen's confused. "All this time, I thought . . ." She shakes her head. "It doesn't matter anymore. The point is, I want to go home now." She squeezes Skipper's arm. "I'll seed the beach with mussels for you, so one day, if—when you come home, the beach will be covered with them."

"But—" Nora grasps desperately for something that might change her mind. "If you wait a little longer—"

"No," says Carmen. "I'm sorry. At least this way I can make a difference, if I bring back those seeds."

Nora wonders how old they will be when they are all together again. What if it's never?

Carmen tries to hug Skipper, but Skipper says she needs some air. She pushes out the door.

After a brief hesitation, Nora goes after her. It's nighttime, and they'd agreed they'd try to avoid walking alone late since Nora's attack.

The dark is a relief. Warm air pools under lamplights, but the constriction of the heat has abated. They walk a mile without speaking.

When they reach the seawall, Skipper turns to Nora and says, "I've never not had Carmen, besides that one summer." She turns her face, distraught, to sea. "I'm going to miss her so much."

"Do you want to go with her?" Nora asks, and it feels like the hardest thing she's ever had to say. She doesn't know what she'll do if Skipper says yes. To lose both of them at once—but at least they'd be together.

Skipper shakes her head. "I hated that town." They walk, the sea breeze against their faces. Everyone is out with the same idea, and the proximity to people makes Nora feel less alone.

"That's where I work," says Skipper, pointing at a distant yard full of tall masts. This far away, they're just toothpicks glinting under a ring of security lights.

Even though they already had dinner, they stop by a vendor and buy kebabs to eat on the way home. Sorrow has hollowed them, and they are ravenous.

"When I left home," Nora says, "I didn't realize what I was doing, or how it'd impact you. I was thinking of myself, and the person I wanted to be. I was thinking I couldn't be that person if I stayed back home."

"Do you regret it?" Skipper asks.

"Yes. No. I'm realizing now how much it hurts to be on the receiving end."

"I guess that's how it is," says Skipper, licking her fingers.

They stop to study the wares of a jewelry vendor. The vendor smiles at them, revealing a mouth empty of all but two teeth. Skipper buys something cheap and gold-enameled that is not Carmen's taste: long-stemmed mushrooms growing within a circle. There are three of them.

"That's hideous," Nora tries to say, before Skipper buys it. She doesn't know what Skipper's thinking.

Skipper strokes it with her thumb. "It's perfect."

The morning Carmen leaves is overcast. She's excited about flying, and she messages them throughout the journey, but Nora continues to worry.

Her last message when she lands is cheerful. She suffered only some motion sickness, thanks to the meds she brought with her. She can't wait to get home.

Then, a day goes by, and they hear nothing. And another two days, and still nothing. Nora risks writing a message home to Uncle Tot, but he doesn't know where Carmen is. She never arrived.

Nora is corroding. She keeps thinking of Carmen, imprisoned somewhere, or worse. Something must have happened to her, and it's Nora's fault. She should never have let her go.

She remembers how she and Carmen used to walk home from school singing a never-ending song made up of lyrics they stitched together from many melodies. The way Carmen's hair curled in the humidity, and she smelled like lavender soap. How warm and dry Carmen's hand was in hers. How small.

CHAPTER FORTY-EIGHT

Not knowing is excruciating.

"I should go back," says Skipper. "Maybe I can find her."

"It's too risky," says Nora. "Unless we know what happened to her, it could happen to you. I should go." She knows that city better, after all.

Except there's Hilda. Nora can't just pick up and leave anymore.

They wait in purgatory.

Skipper buries herself in her work, and Nora misses having the same escape. The day Carmen left, she decided to spare Rafael the pain of firing her—difficult conversations shrivel him inside—and submitted her resignation.

It doesn't stop her dwelling on their last exchange. She's sorry, but she's also angry. It's not fair, she knows. They've only known each other a few months, but she thought they were friends. After all his promises, he discarded her so easily. But, also, it's her fault, because everything is always her fault, and she's tired of having that kind of power.

Where is Carmen? Why doesn't she reply?

After days of cleaning, cooking, and mending, she sits down and assembles a makeshift nursery in her bedroom. Carmen took half of the remaining seeds, but Nora has a handful left.

The chocolate-cake scent of rich earth fills the bedroom. She hangs dark curtains and jury-rigs lights. It reminds her of her container in the woods. She presses the seeds down into the soft dirt, and it feels like a small act of rebellion.

She wipes her palms on her pants and surveys the apartment. Four more hours until Hilda's home.

She grabs her jacket with the idea of going to the park to immerse herself in green and watch insects industriously construct houses that could be washed away tomorrow. She nearly runs over Rafael, coming up the stairs.

"Oh," she says.

"Yes," he says.

"I'm sorry— " she begins.

"I quit— "

"What?"

They both look at each other in confusion, unable to express what they mean.

"I was going to the park," Nora says. "If you— Do you want to . . . ?"

"All right."

They pass a few blocks in silence. When they reach the patch of green, the muscles in Nora's back loosen. The tall palm trees around the fountain remind her of home.

Rafael clears his throat. "I'm founding a private lab with a couple of colleagues. More freedom. Less bullshit. At least, that's the idea."

"That's amazing." Nora's resentment falls away in an instant, because she can see how excited he is.

"I thought it might be an opportunity."

"What do you mean?" Nora asks.

"Oh come on, are you going to make me say it?"

"I really have no idea what you're going to say."

He rolls his eyes. "Nora. I have the data. So do you want to come back and do something with it? It wouldn't be right to work on this without you."

Nora bites her lip. "I'm the worst assistant, though. I'm insubordinate."

"It's true." He grins, mischievously. "That's why you're lucky I'm a marshmallow."

"You're not," Nora says. "Well, not when it matters."

"So . . . ?"

Nora sits on the bench opposite the pond and watches a turtle slip into the cool water. "I want to. But I can't right now, not when Carmen's missing." She tells him everything that's happened since they last spoke, and it's a relief to unburden herself to someone besides Skipper.

"Are you sure it's Renewal?"

"It has to be."

"It's only been a few days. Maybe she's fine."

Nora wishes she could believe it. "We're never going to be free, are we? Not until they've won."

"So then let's figure it out," he says.

She longs for certainty.

In the pond, the turtle resurfaces and paddles back to the rock to lie in the sun again. This is what it will do every day for years until the pond must be drained and repaired, and all this time, the turtle will never know there is a park fifteen blocks away that has a lake.

Skipper comes home with a fish. "A friend of mine caught it," she tells Nora.

Skipper shows her how to clean it. As it fries in the pan, Skipper admires the trays of soil. "Carmen would love that."

They both are quiet, thinking about Carmen.

"I knew it was a bad idea," Nora says. "I should have stopped her."

Skipper returns to the kitchen and pokes the fish. "And how would you have done that? Carmen always does what she wants. And she wanted to go home. Look, Nora. Don't take this the wrong way, but you can be a little self-centered."

"Yes," she agrees, without knowing what Skipper's referring to.

"You apologize like you're responsible for everything."

But isn't she? The horrible things her sisters went through, the destruction of Rafael's lab—it all comes back to the choices she's made.

"You're not. I mean, yes, we're all responsible for our actions. We *all* are. I think your problem is you see the impact of the impact of the impact of what you've done, and you think you can control that. You discover a piece of ice, and you start to worry about all the ice in the world. It's what I've always admired about you. It's also really, really annoying."

Skipper's right, but Nora also doesn't know if she can change. She doesn't want to change. She just wants to be more successful.

"I'm sorry you feel like you need to take care of us. That must be a pain in the ass."

"It's not," says Nora.

"Okay, but you don't," Skipper says. "Or at least, focus on Hilda. Let the rest of us swim."

Nora wants to argue. There are so many things she wishes were in her control. She wants Skipper to be happy. She wants to know Carmen's okay.

"And anyway," Skipper says, "it hasn't been all bad. I'm here, aren't I?"

Her words are like a balm. Nora slides the fish onto plates. Hilda will be home from dance practice soon and hungry.

"I have an idea." Skipper hesitates, as if she expects Nora to knock it down right away. Nora realizes with a pang Skipper often assumes this. Perhaps she's right to expect that.

"What is it?"

Skipper stares at the table. "What if we talk to Renewal?"

Nora opens her mouth.

"I know. It's a bad idea."

Nora dries her hands and forces herself to keep an open mind. "Tell me more."

Skipper eyes her suspiciously, then explains. The more they talk, the more Nora begins to think it's not the worst idea. They flesh it out, until Nora can see the shape of it.

"You thought it through," Nora says, impressed.

"Well . . . yeah, I guess," says Skipper. "I talked to Carmen about it before she left. She thought it was too risky. But then today, I wondered if maybe it was worth a shot. Especially if there's a chance it could help Carmen."

"I agree," says Nora.

"You do?" Skipper blinks.

"Let's try."

They set up a virtual meeting from their apartment. Rafael joins them, along with his lawyer friend, Silvia.

It's strange to have them here, especially Rafael, pacing around her dinged-up table examining the inconsequential wall decorations. She wants to tell him to sit down, but she is also self-conscious about how frayed the armchair is.

Skipper chews her cuticles. She makes a wet sucking sound.

"Stop," Nora whispers, and Skipper drops her hand.

"Remember," Silvia says, "don't say too much. We want them to do the talking." Silvia's a no-nonsense woman with an expertise in corporate law. She's also Rafael's ex-girlfriend, but they're still friends, because of course Rafael is friends with his exes. Her presence is a condition of Rafael's help. He insisted they do things deliberately this time.

Nora nods, and Rafael hands her the egg.

"Nora Shimizu," says a gravelly voice.

She blinks and two figures appear before her, projected onto their curtains. One is the Executive Vice President for Operations. The other is the company's general counsel. They're halfway across the world, but it feels as if they're in her apartment, and she regrets doing the call here.

"You're a difficult person to find."

"Am I?" Nora says.

The executive laughs. "We were happy to hear from you."

"I'm sure. Seeing as you weren't thorough enough when you broke into Aguirre's lab." She'd said as much when she reached out, to panic them. To let them know they hadn't won yet.

There's an infinitesimal pause. "No idea what you're talking about." She didn't expect Renewal to admit to it, but she can tell they're a tiny bit on edge, wondering what Nora might have over them.

The executive clears his throat, trying to reclaim control of the conversation. "I'd like to take the opportunity to address the matter of stolen property while you were in our employ under false pretenses."

Rafael's friend flaps her arms to remind Nora not to engage in that.

Skipper goes to the windows and peers out the curtains, and Nora wishes there were more of a breeze in here. It's too warm and sweat pools inside her shirt.

"Let's cut the bullshit. Where's Carmen?" Nora says, because she wants to resolve Carmen's whereabouts before anything else.

Another beat. "Who the fuck is that?" he asks his lawyer.

The lawyer mutes the feed, then the visual.

The silence stretches out even longer.

"That's good, right?" Skipper says. "That means they don't have her."

"Let's see," says Silvia.

The feed resumes.

"We don't know what you're talking about," the man says, and Nora wishes Carmen were here to tell if his confusion is genuine. "Carmen's your sister, right? When did you last see her? If she's run off on you, we definitely weren't involved in that. In the meantime," he switches from sympathetic back to tough, "we'd like to remind you if your intention is to sell stolen property, we will bring charges."

Silvia shakes her head firmly. She doesn't think they can prove what Nora did, or they already would have—or they don't want the publicity of anything else that might come out in the process about Vault City or its contents. Vault City exists in a gray area, given its murky jurisdiction, something that up till now has been in Renewal's favor. That might not last if countries have a reason to pry.

"I understand any business arrangement with another entity would threaten your profits," Nora says. "Let's say I've developed a breed of soybeans that's completely blight proof—"

"You didn't develop shit. You stole them from our vault."

"Stole them?" Nora leans back, pretending more confidence than she feels. "You have blight-proof seeds? I don't believe it. If you did, you'd be selling them."

"When you get a business degree, let me know," he sneers. The lawyer puts a hand on his arm to stop him from saying more.

Nora laughs. "I may not know business, but I do know this: You've intentionally expanded the blight for sake of profit. You're the reason people go to bed hungry, the reason they despair over how they'll feed their children each year."

Silvia is windmilling her arms for Nora to stop, but Nora can't. Rage singes her words. This is the most dangerous thing she could have done. She's never confirmed directly how much she knows. Maybe it's a mistake, but she wants them to face their complicity.

She sees a bead of sweat trickle down the executive's temple. She picks up one of her seedlings, and their eyes widen. "So yeah, let's say I've developed blight-proof seeds. I guess I can do whatever I want with them. Give me my sister. Or I will sell them."

Her threat hangs in the air.

"We'll get back to you," the lawyer says and terminates the call.

"What do you think?" Nora says.

"You did great," Skipper tells her.

"I don't know if my nerves can take this," Rafael moans, collapsing in the uncomfortable armchair.

Silvia is the only one who maintains calm. "We have to wait. If they have her, they'll make an offer."

"And if they don't?"

"They'll offer something else."

Renewal calls back three hours later. "We don't have your sister. But we're prepared to offer you compensation for the remainder of the sample in your possession."

"I see."

Her small tower of hope collapses. If Renewal doesn't have Carmen, that's good, but she wanted an answer. The uncertainty only feeds her mounting worry.

He's still talking, and she hopes one of the others caught the terms.

"I'll have to think about it," Nora says.

"Take twenty-four hours. But while you do, tell me something. What exactly are you trying to achieve? You know we can't go back to the way things were. People can't grow crops with nothing but hope and a prayer and primitive techniques—they'll end up with nothing. That's not a threat, that's reality."

He's not wrong. Almost 95 percent of pollinators are extinct. Extreme weather wreaks havoc on crops. And if people were going to stop using Amaranthine entirely, they probably already would have.

It's impractical to believe the world can ever be what it was, even with all the seeds in the vault.

"I don't know," Nora admits. "Something different. Something better." Nora has to believe that's possible.

"I know you don't believe it, but that's what we're trying to do. We deal in reality. Mistakes were made, and it's too late now to change them. So this is it. The door has closed behind us. All we can do is focus on continuous improvement to our management techniques."

"Like the way you 'continuously improve' the blight?" Nora asks.

"We *control* the blight," he says. "And everyone is better for it."

In the corner, Rafael scoffs.

"How about the way you infect people? What's your justification for that?"

Silvia makes a noise in the back of her throat. Nora is way off script. She's talking now about something she can't prove.

The executive blinks at her. He looks at the lawyer, then back at Nora. "How do you know—"

"Don't say anything," his lawyer tells him.

"She can't—"

"We're done," the lawyer says.

Nora smiles. "See, you think you know everything. You don't. And neither do I. But I will. I'll think about your offer. But I can promise you if anything happens to my friends or family, you will not have my cooperation."

She terminates the call and collapses on the couch, body trembling.

"Okay, then," says Skipper.

"That could have gone worse," Silvia agrees.

It's disappointing to walk away without more information about Carmen, but it wasn't the only thing they were trying to achieve. There's the rest of their plan.

Nora nods at the others. "Phase two, then?"

"Phase two," Rafael agrees.

The thing Renewal doesn't understand is that Nora was raised on ruin. Sometimes it takes a fire for seeds to grow.

CHAPTER FORTY-NINE

A few hours later, when everything is in place, Nora sends a message to Renewal. *No deal. I'm going with another buyer.*

"How long do you think before they respond?" Skipper wonders.

"Soon," Nora says. Now that they know what she has, they can't afford to wait. They need to finish the job.

"They look good," Rafael says, examining the sprouts.

The door slams open, and despite herself, Nora jumps. "Hilda! Why aren't you at Maria's?"

"Come *on*," she says, throwing an arm around Skipper. "You think I was going to miss this?"

"You told her?" Nora hisses to Skipper.

"It's hard to keep secrets in a one-bedroom apartment." Skipper doesn't even look embarrassed.

"I have a right to be here," Hilda says. "Hey, Raffi." They bump fists, and Nora glares at him. She'd rather keep Hilda far away from any danger. It could all go wrong.

"What's he doing?" Skipper says.

Outside the building, Hilda's gelato man is back in place, smoking his cigarette despite the heat.

"He's a neighbor," Nora says, but suspicion grows.

The man fiddles with his egg and looks up at the window.

"I hate him," Hilda says.

A car pulls up, then another, blocking the narrow street. Eight people pile out. The gelato neighbor comes forward and talks to them. He gestures up at their window.

"Told you," says Hilda. "I can't believe you didn't believe me."

Sweat trickles down Nora's shirt. Renewal's acting even faster than she thought. They must have known where they lived all along.

"Do we have enough time?" she asks Rafael and Silvia.

"On it," Rafael says, firing off messages, but he's breathing too fast.

There's a loud *zzzzz* as they ring the apartment. The buzzer bleats a few times, then stops.

At the same time, Nora's egg buzzes. She squeezes it to load the message and nearly drops it.

It's Carmen.

Hey, sizzles. Funny story . . .

"Are you *joking*?" Skipper screams.

Carmen's lucky she isn't in the room to experience the full force of Skipper's rage.

Quickly, Carmen tells them what happened: Renewal agents were at the airport when she landed, but she managed to avoid them with the help of a new friend, one of the flight attendants. Then, in the city, her bag was stolen, along with her encrypted communicator, and she was worried about sending messages until she could find a way to do it so she wasn't tracked. Another friend of hers helped her. Carmen always has friends.

For example: She tracked down Marcus in the city—Marcus is doing great, by the way, he says hi. Carmen showed up unannounced and slept on his floor.

She's sorry if she caused any worry, knowing how it had felt when Nora was missing, and she got in touch as soon as she could figure out a safe way to do so.

She's going to spend a few more days exploring the city before catching a bus home.

Nora warns her to be careful. It worries her how flippant Carmen is about her safety. Carmen seems to think she can't be touched at home, surrounded by so many people she knows. It's foolhardy, but there's nothing Nora can do about it. Like Skipper says, it's Carmen's responsibility too.

For now, she's glad Carmen is safe, and far away from what's unfolding here.

"Rafael?" she asks.

Below the apartment, they've forced the door and entered the building.

"We should call the police," Silvia says.

"Not yet," says Nora, though her heart hammers.

A minute later, they hear footsteps thundering up the stairs.

This has to work. Is it enough? What if nobody cares?

"Dr. Aguirre, we're ready to go live," the young reporter says, coming to the door. She's a friend of Silvia's, a rising star in her field, apparently.

Rafael gets up and straightens his jacket. Nora nods.

"Good luck," says Skipper. "I'm going to keep watching this." She gestures to the feed from the apartment.

"Me too," cackles Hilda. "I can't wait until they find the dirty socks I left on the coffee table."

Weeks ago, Skipper suggested recording a conversation with Renewal executives to provoke them into providing incriminating evidence they could share with the media. Carmen thought it wasn't bold enough. As Nora had told them, it was hard to get people to care about abstract problems.

No, Carmen argued, what they needed was something salacious enough to catch the public's attention, something tangible that didn't need to be proven. If they could incite Renewal to do something out in the open, it might provoke enough titillation and outrage for people to pay attention to everything else under the rug.

Nora knew by telling Renewal she had the seeds and that she was growing the plants in her apartment, they would come, as they'd done at the lab.

But Nora and everyone weren't foolish enough to stay and wait for them to do that. After setting up cameras with a good view of the street and apartment itself, they decamped to the media studio, where Rafael had arranged an interview to be broadcast simultaneously across multiple platforms.

Rafael is the most credible messenger—not to mention, the best public speaker—and it will be good publicity for the new institute.

It was Nora's idea to simultaneously release the data of everything in the vault, including the records of the blight, the heirloom soybean they've sequenced, and the genome of every Renewal design. Nora doesn't have faith that even the most rigorous experiments could convince people, but if they release the data, people will have a chance to see the truth for themselves. They can breed their own varietals. And they can reach their own conclusions. Skipper was right. It's not about Nora.

More importantly, Renewal will understand that Nora is no longer the problem, because once the information is out there, it can't be unwound.

"How do you feel?" Silvia asks, as they watch Rafael answer the reporter's questions.

"Are people watching?"

"They will," Silvia says, "at least as long as it's entertaining. Your sister was right about that."

"And do you believe they were behind the origin of the blight?" the reporter is asking Rafael.

"No," says Rafael. "I think they saw an opportunity to capitalize, and they took it."

"Excuse me, I'm getting an update I'd like to share," the reporter says, and the media team shows the feed of Renewal's agents breaking through the door, tearing through the place in search of the seeds. "This is live footage from your friend's apartment?"

"Yes," says Rafael.

Nora winces at the destruction. They'll need to find a new couch.

"And you think they're looking for the seeds," the reporter says, with the expression of a cat cleaning her whiskers. This story will make her career.

"Absolutely."

Nora wishes she could see the faces of the Renewal leadership. They have to be watching. They must have gotten through to the agents in the apartment, because there's a rush for the exit.

Sirens blare as the police arrive below.

"See for yourself," Silvia says, offering Nora her egg, and headlines appear in her vision:

THE DEADLY SECRET RENEWAL DOESN'T WANT YOU TO KNOW

THE FATAL DISEASE RENEWAL IS ACCUSED OF SPREADING

3 WAYS RENEWAL CAUSES BLIGHT

10 ALTERNATIVES TO RENEWAL CROPS

A SECRET PLOT TO USE FAMINE TO DRIVE PROFIT

Renewal won't go quietly. They control a significant amount of agricultural and chemical products in the world. Nora knows how things have historically gone.

The evidence from the vault isn't an open-and-shut case. She wishes, for example, she could prove what she suspects about the fungus that infected Carmen. It's such an explosive allegation, even this reporter tiptoes around it.

But Nora is hopeful, at least, that there's enough to propel some change.

"It's all so unbelievable, isn't it?" the reporter says, as they conclude their interview.

Rafael turns his head to look at Nora. "I believe it."

Her blood pounds in her ears. There's so much Nora doesn't know. She might have to work on those questions for the rest of her life. But people know what she knows, that's something.

CHAPTER FIFTY

At first, it seems like the world hasn't changed.

People's views may be shifting on an individual level, but people tend to resist until something comes along to trigger a sea change.

Governments begin to clamor for the doomsday vault to be returned to public control, particularly in light of the rumors of unrest in the settlement. It'll take time, but Nora's hopeful.

One day, in the street, she overhears two people discussing their gardens. "I know a company that's selling some of those soybeans," one says.

Nora smiles and pretends she knows nothing about it.

Then, months later, one of the subsequent investigations finds concrete evidence Renewal has been experimenting with human blight, and suddenly everything ignites: There's a hasty joint-government investigation. Renewal's assets are seized, its leadership and board members charged with criminal action.

For the first time, Nora feels she can breathe.

"We're all going out to dinner!" Rafael shouts to her when the news breaks, and so they do, and the only thing Nora regrets is that Carmen isn't here to celebrate.

They've gotten used to life without Carmen. It's simpler: one fewer person bumping about the apartment, one fewer person eating, dirtying, washing clothes. One fewer voice in conversation.

Nora misses her almost as much as Skipper does.

A message arrives from Marcus. He wants to know how she is doing. He's sorry he sent her sisters off without more guidance.

Change has come to their old lab. With the takeover, new procedures are being introduced. Regulators showed up at the lab unannounced to scrutinize everything.

Their boss, John, is off on vacation having an existential crisis. He talks about quitting and starting his own farm and wants to know if Marcus is interested in joining. Marcus isn't.

Hilda's father is still stuck in Vault City, though they're working through an intermediary to buy out the remainder of his contract.

They hire a full-time caregiver for Grandma with the EarthWorks money. Carmen and Uncle Tot are repainting the house blue.

Nora works for Rafael at the new institute. Rafael also helped her get admitted to a doctorate program, and she's drowning in work between taking care of Hilda and working on problem sets and research.

Skipper goes on working at the boatyard, disappearing more and more often. Nora worries, but Skipper seems happy, so Nora doesn't press it.

That means on weekends, it's just Hilda and Nora again, which is strange, like they have to relearn the notes of a duet.

She takes Hilda shopping for clothes by way of apology for not being around enough. Neither of them knows quite how to do it. Nora grew up wearing whatever Grandma pulled from the community bin.

As an adult, unlike Carmen, Nora never took to buying new clothing, choosing instead to frequent thrift shops as a point of pride. The truth is the number of options in the city overwhelms her. She doesn't want to spend a day trying things on and having to evaluate over and over what she thinks of herself.

Hilda, though, loves it. After growing up in Vault City, where people wear the same thing most days, the idea is a novelty. She figures out what she likes: colors, soft fabrics, nothing with pants.

So Nora takes her around to different shops and tries to channel Carmen and learn the rhythm of consumption. She does her best to conceal her stress, but by the time they get home, she's spent. All day she's felt as if time is stuttering in its tracks and evening will never roll around.

The smell of smoke greets them in the foyer. Skipper is attempting to cook dinner in the kitchen, stir-frying vegetables and somehow oblivious to the rice burning in the pot. Hilda and Nora run around opening windows.

Nora turns off the pot. "You need to add more water next time." She explains the steps.

"Oh," says Skipper. "I never realized that."

"How's work?" Nora asks, setting the table.

Skipper ducks her head, but Nora's learned Skipper enjoys talking about work if she's asked. "I've been working on a new boat. It's a mishmash of whatever's discarded down at the yard."

"Sounds like the *Bumblebee*." Nora smiles.

"Yes, exactly. They let me do whatever as long as it's on my own time, and I cover the printing costs."

"You'll have to take us out for a tour of the harbor when it's done."

Skipper's eyes glitter with anticipation. She tells them all about the boat. She talks more than she has since Carmen left. "Vida says it's the ugliest boat they've ever seen, but they never saw the *Bumblebee*. It just needs a paint job. What color should I paint it?" she asks Hilda, showing her a picture.

"Pink," Hilda says, without hesitation.

"Okay," says Skipper.

Nora wants to know if Skipper's content, if Skipper will build a life for herself that's more than just four walls and a roof. She wants to know Skipper's staying.

"Everything's great," Skipper assures her. Nora relaxes a little.

She scrapes the rice that's still good from the pot and transfers it to a serving bowl.

"We should look for a new apartment next weekend," Nora tells them, picking up the old idea. "Our lease is up soon. We can afford to get a place with more space and security."

They talk about neighborhoods, and it's a kind of domesticity Nora never dreamed about. Something in her quiets. She finally has everything: work she values, a home with people she loves, an apartment in the middle of an exciting city.

"Do you ever think what your life would have been like if you hadn't left home?" Skipper asks.

"Sometimes," Nora says, but it's hard to imagine. What would she have done? Continued to experiment in the ruined container in the woods. Bred crops over and over, and wondered why they continued to die. Taken classes remotely, maybe, gotten a degree she didn't use. Lived in that house with Grandma until she died. But also: There'd have been the luxury of time with her sisters and Uncle Tot, drinking wine with them in the evening, and talking about whatever is on their mind. Exploring the world together, even if it was only their idea of the world. That, she does regret.

"You'll never know what lies down the timeline in that other multiverse," she says. "But I like where I've ended up, the things I'm learning, the chance to see the world, to be more of myself. Hilda's all right too, I guess."

"Thank you!" chirps Hilda, to show she's been listening.

"I get it," says Skipper. "I was upset when you left for college. I felt abandoned. Like me, personally. I thought maybe you left because it was too much work for you to have to take care of us, when you were young yourself, and if maybe I'd been easier, more helpful, you wouldn't have felt like you needed to go.

"Don't worry. That self-wallowing lasted only a few months. I also blamed Grandma for not being nicer. Later, when I was older, the only thing I wished was you'd taken me with you."

"I tried," Nora says, throat tight. Carmen had wanted the same thing.

"I know," says Skipper. "But I wasn't ready. I'm not sure I ever would have been."

They sit down to eat burnt rice and undercooked vegetables, and

Nora is grateful Hilda is used to eating terrible food and doesn't make a fuss about it like Carmen used to when she was a teenager.

Hilda says, "I'd like to go home someday. Not Vault City, but the place my father's from." She's not saying "we," and the idea she might go without Nora stuns her, even though if her father comes, she assumes Hilda will live with him again. She's tried to focus on the joy of having her around now.

Hilda was crushed when they escaped that place. She missed her father, and Nora's done her best to help her heal. She enrolled Hilda in school and dance classes, and she does her best with her student and lab stipend to nurture Hilda's soul. Hilda grew up with so little to stimulate her mind, so she made her own art: drawings, music, dance. She is, Nora is convinced, a genius. It thrills Nora to take her around to all the public museums here, to introduce her to new foods and styles of music. She reminds Nora in many ways of what her sisters were like. That's why she loves Hilda so easily.

That is not to say it is easy. Hilda has teenage whims and moods and succumbs to fits of depression. She misses her father but never wants to talk about him.

Nora and Hilda's relationship is so different from the relationship Nora had with her grandmother, who gave up a quarter of her life to raise them, while dealing with the heartbreak of losing a child. She wonders what it was like for Grandma, expecting the world to be a certain way all her life, and then having to watch it fall apart.

It's different, too, from Nora's relationship with her mother, who loved them but couldn't handle it all. Nora's memories of her are tainted by the way she unraveled. Mama would take anything she could get her hands on. Nora stole the bottles from her mother's room and hid them in a stump in the woods, and her mother rampaged the house looking for them. Later, Mama sat down and wept, and Grandma told her to pull herself together in front of her children for God's sake.

And Nora understood Mama needed those pills. She told Nora she was lost. The blight was back, and Mama was afraid. She didn't know how they'd eat. Life was a maze of terrible choices, and she didn't didn't think they would ever get out.

So Nora found the bottle and gave it back to her, and Mama was happier than Nora'd seen her in a long time. Mama made them dinner. She kissed them goodnight. And that night, she walked into the woods with the kitchen knife Grandma kept so sharp. She was dead, Grandma said, before the wild dogs found her.

Nora dwells on the moist imprint of the last kiss her mother gave her, and the smell of another year of blight creeping up on the woods, and all those fields of corn next door, rotting in the field.

Grandma asked Nora never to talk about it. Grandma didn't want Skipper to remember Mama that way, and it was better if Carmen never understood what had happened. It took Nora years to realize it was just that Grandma wanted to forget.

Nora carried the burden of that guilt for years. She tried to fill the void for her sisters and ensure they had all the love she cost them. It's part of the reason she didn't believe for a long time she was good at taking care of other people. It was all she could do to take care of herself.

Because of Hilda, she's learning to forgive herself. She can give Hilda something different. She can be here for her.

"We could take the train," she says to Hilda. "It's a few days' ride."

Hilda isn't paying attention. She flicks her fingers, chattering away with someone Nora can't see.

"Who are you talking to?"

"Friends," Hilda says, as if Nora doesn't have any.

Nora catches Skipper's eye and makes a face, and the two of them laugh.

Skipper stirs her rice. "I spent so much of my life learning how to make friends. But now that I'm older, I have to unlearn that. To figure out how to let go of people."

She glances at the empty chair and swallows a mouthful of charred rice.

"And you have to trust the distance doesn't undermine what you have," Nora says. "And believe someday you'll see each other again."

"Exactly." Skipper sets down her fork. Nora thinks she's going to add something more about the subject, like she's been circling a thought. But she must have changed her mind, because she just says, "I'm sorry, but this rice is inedible."

CHAPTER FIFTY-ONE

Another spring begins. The average temperature exceeds the previous year, and a massive rainstorm floods the city for days.

Nora plans her thesis on the subject of the resilience of genetically diverse agriculture and heirloom varietals.

Hilda auditions for a local dance group and isn't selected. She takes up painting instead.

Skipper finishes her boat.

She takes them for a tour of the harbor, as she'd promised. The boat, *Equilateral*, is indeed ugly, but it doesn't sink, and it cuts more quickly across the water than Nora would have thought.

It's been a decade since Nora's been in a sailboat. She's surprised by how powerful it makes her feel: the wind thrumming in the sail, the water gliding beneath her.

They circle once, twice, and then Skipper turns toward the mouth of the harbor. The water changes past the breakwater: The world expands suddenly. They are small. *Equilateral* climbs tall swells, and

Nora imagines they could glimpse the curve of the earth if they looked hard enough. Then they come down into the trough, and it is just ocean for miles.

She remembers the squall that took them by surprise in the *Bumblebee* when they were children. Everything unraveled so fast: Skipper was swept off the boat. Carmen and Nora were terrified. Nora's a slower thinker under any circumstance; she works through problems by extensive, persistent mastication, which is not ideal in an emergency, and in that moment, instinct failed her. She got to her feet, and the boom came around and smacked her in the head.

She tasted blood in her mouth: She'd bitten her tongue. She tried to steer back toward Skipper, but she was dizzy. She could barely see Skipper through the rain, and it was like she'd forgotten everything Uncle Tot ever taught her about sailing. Skipper would die because she didn't know what to do.

She doesn't know how Skipper did it. Maybe the sails were luffing so bad, Skipper was able to catch up with them. She pulled herself onboard and got the boat in order again, even freezing and sopping wet as she was. Then she went below, changed into an old sweatshirt of Uncle Tot's that hung down to her knees, and came back up to sail them home.

The whole experience was awful, but at the same time, it felt like Skipper was showing her she would be all right if Nora went away.

"Can we go back now?" asks Hilda, gripping her life jacket.

"Sure," says Skipper, but Nora sees the edges of her longing. Skipper wants to stay out here and keep sailing the sides of her triangles to some infinitely distant apex.

They eat their sandwiches on the dock and walk back home. The heat is climbing again, but it feels like they carry the cool sea breeze on their backs.

When they reach home, Skipper turns to her. "I'm going to sail around the world."

"Okay," Nora laughs, because she doesn't want to believe Skipper's serious. Skipper has always been full of dreams. This is just another.

"That's why I built the boat."

"Do you know how dangerous it would be?" Nora says. She tries to tell Skipper about storms and sickness and pirates, but Skipper knows the risks. All Nora has is the weight of her opinion, and she hurls it at Skipper. "It's a stupid thing to do alone."

Skipper lifts her chin. "I don't care. I want to do it, and it's not impossible—other people have done it. I'm sorry."

Nora watches her prepare, waiting for Skipper to lose interest or nerve. Skipper continues to contribute to household expenses, but she stops spending money on anything else. She puts all her money into the boat and this trip; she saves all summer.

Nora warns Hilda not to get excited. "This is something Skipper does. She has these grand ideas, and then she changes her mind. I don't want you to be disappointed. She'll never do it."

But Skipper continues to surprise Nora. Skipper attracts support from other sailors. They throw a party for her to raise money. An instant noodle company agrees to sponsor her, even though there's no way she can eat instant noodles for two years.

Skipper buys a chart and tacks it on the wall, and Nora complains about the holes she's made.

Skipper ignores her and continues planning.

Nora believes all the way up to the week of Skipper's departure that Skipper will abandon the idea. Then Nora has no choice but to accept it, because Hilda points out they need to throw Skipper a goodbye party.

Nora arranges crudités, the little crackers, the chips. She's organized a feast to show Skipper what she'll miss when she's eating instant noodles. It's half an hour before Skipper's friends are due to arrive, and Nora's setting out platters of food when she realizes she hasn't gotten Skipper a present.

It suddenly is urgent that she run out and find something. She doesn't have time to go far. She scurries through the aisles of the nearby shops, hunting for the perfect thing. How does she say goodbye with a plastic bobblehead? A towel? A chessboard Skipper will not be able to play by herself?

Nora collapses on a bench inside the third store she's gone to, a lingerie store, which if she were thinking rationally is an absurd place to find a gift, but she is desperate. Hilda messages her that the guests are arriving, and Nora begins to sob outright.

She has nothing to give her.

Skipper is leaving.

"Oh-oh," says the store clerk, uncertain what to do. "Sweetheart. It's not that bad."

But it is, it is. After this, Nora will be sizzleless, and all her words of wisdom about journeys and distance are shit. She can't do this, even though she has done it before, multiple times, to Skipper.

The store clerk fumbles about behind the counter. Nora wonders if she's signaling for help.

Instead, the clerk comes around with a small hard candy in a crinkly wrapper.

"Have this."

It tastes sweet and sour. It's trying to be lemon. It's singular. The solidity of the world returns to Nora.

They see Skipper off on a Tuesday morning at seven o'clock. The sky is clear blue, the wind steady. Nora hopes, secretly, the wind will die so Skipper has to wait another day, but the flags near the dock snap and ripple with satisfaction.

They help her load up the boat full of canned food and water and basic medical supplies. Skipper's wearing one of Nora's favorite shirts, and Nora decides to let her keep it.

Then Nora must hug Skipper goodbye. She holds her tight and tries to memorize the smell of her sweat and preserve in her mind all the little moments that make up the totality of her. There must be some equation that could calculate for Nora the trajectory of Skipper's future, all the people she will know and things she will say, but it's unknowable. Nora could work a lifetime and never figure it out. She has to watch it unfold in real time.

"Goodbye, Skip. Thank you for finding me. I love you." More than the ocean, more than the pink house on the hill.

"Don't worry," Skipper says. "I'll find you again."

Hilda and Nora walk to the end of the dock and watch Skipper tack back and forth in the wind. The boat grows smaller as it gets farther away. That's a matter of perspective, though.

Nora thinks about the seeds Carmen will have planted by now in the garden that might be pushing green shoots toward the sun.

Skipper enters the ocean and grows smaller still. She is just a point, disappearing into the horizon. And then Nora can't see her anymore. She's gone.

They take the long way back, delaying their return to an empty house. Nora didn't need to take off work today, she realizes. She thought this immense a goodbye would take longer. How could the moment have passed so quickly, as if there were nothing significant about it?

She should go into the lab and get things done. Work on her thesis. See if Rafael wants to go down to the café for lunch.

She asks Hilda if she wants something for breakfast, since Hilda didn't eat before they left the house. "Anything you want," Nora says. "You pick."

"Gelato," Hilda says, like she doesn't worry about all the choices she'll have to make in her life.

So that is what they eat.

ACKNOWLEDGMENTS

Some books are more work than others to write. This one was a tremendous amount of work. I ended up quitting my job after I sold it, because I knew that I wouldn't be able to do the book justice while working so many hours.

I am grateful for the support of my editor, Maxine Charles, and my agent, Mary Moore, through it all—not just for their feedback and guidance, but for their emotional fortification.

Thank you to my sisters for allowing me to write a sister-themed book. The sisters in this book are not based on them exactly, but I would sail to the other side of the world for either of them. I owe the fact that I write books at all to the enthusiasm with which my twin sister, Hana, has listened to my stories since I was young—she's read everything I've ever written, and her constructive criticism about plot and character development are equal to anyone's in the industry. And I owe my broad and deep reading appetite to my older sister, Saya, who mooches off my library accounts and keeps me fed with excellent books.

I'm grateful for the folks who beta-read this book for me. I could never write a book without beta readers. Find friends who know how to give you advice that you're excited to follow. Mine are: Sarah Starr Murphy, a writer I love, who has beta-read all three of my books and coached me through some sailing scenes, which I greatly appreciated; Tessa Yang, who, among many other things, reminded me that jellyfish can be found in arctic waters; Alison Fisher, Sara Crowley, and Barbara Barrow; and Kylie Lee Baker and Katie Wu, whom I blame for the body horror.

I did a *lot* of research for this book and used only a fraction of it, but so it goes.

We spent many summers sailing small keelboats out of my grandparents' town in Little Compton, Rhode Island, with a camp friend, Nora, but it turns out my knowledge of sailing is quite rusty.

Thank you to Tobias Buckell, for talking to me for an hour about all my sailing questions. One of his books, *Arctic Rising*, is a thriller set in the arctic, and it involves some pretty intense catamaran scenes that are more accurate than mine.

Thank you to Veronica Skotnes, for her incredibly generous responses to my questions. Veronica lives alone on a wooden sailboat in the arctic, and her photographs are stunning. Please check her out @veronicaskotnes.

Thank you, Benjamin Strong and Persphone Tan, for dealing with my random texts about sailboats.

I watched countless YouTube videos, but a shout-out especially to the folks behind these channels: Sailing Uma, Rover's Adventure, and Alluring Arctic.

I read a number of books, too, which were invaluable in informing the novel: *Maiden Voyage* by Tania Aebi; *Swell: A Sailing Surfer's Voyage of Awakening* by Liz Clark; *Reading the Glass: A Captain's View of Weather, Water, and Life on Ships* by Elliot Rappaport; *Dove* by Robin Lee Graham; *Whitewash: The Story of a Weed Killer, Cancer, and the Corruption of Science* by Carey Gillam; *Seed Money: Monsanto's Past and Our Food Future* by Bartow J. Elmore; *The Magnetic North: Notes from the Arctic Circle* by Sara Wheeler; and *Floating Coast: An Environmental History of the Bering Strait* by Bathsheba Demuth.

I'm sure you will still find errors in this book if you look for them (please don't). I took some liberties, and no doubt made a few mistakes in the service of plot. I hope it won't bother you too much.

All three of my books have stunning covers designed by the infinitely talented Jonathan Bush. I believe I owe Jonathan a lot for the decent success of my first two books, and I think the third cover is even more gorgeous. And thank you, too, to Megan Smith who designed the very different but just as striking cover for the UK edition.

When I sold the book, I knew I needed a better title. I would not have found one without the help of my retreat buddies: Killeen Hanson, Angel di Zhang, Camille Kellogg, and Katie Wu.

I remain grateful to the broader Flatiron Books team for everything they do to usher my books from start to finish: Maris Tasaka, Cat Kenney, and Bria Strothers, my marketing and publicity team; Ryan T. Jenkins and Morgan Mitchell from the production team; Megan Lynch and Zack Wagman; Kelly Gatesman, Jonathan Bush, and Jonathan Bennett for the cover and interior design; and Nicole Hall, for copyedits.

Thank you to my team at Harper Voyager UK, including my lovely editor, Chloe Gough, who has shepherded my three books through to publication across the pond with care and thoughtfulness. Thank you to Addison Duffy, my TV/film agent at UTA, for hustling my books. If you want to make this into something, please call her.

My parents have been incredibly supportive of all I do, including vacating their house so I could host a retreat in it with my friends and finish a draft of this book. I hope they know how much I appreciate them!

Thank you to Jenni Brauner, for lending me her apartment in London to work on this, and for the company of her cat, Luna. May Luna have all the hair ties her little heart desires.

Thank you to Mia Tsai and Ehigbor Okosun, for the last-mile companionship, night after night. They helped me get this one across the finish line. And thank you to Reggie Thomas and Meagan Chen—they know why.

Lastly, thank you to every friend, family member, bookseller, librarian, reviewer, and reader who has read, reviewed, told their friends, written me kind notes, and cheered me on through the release of my first two books. Your support lifts me up and encourages me to keep going on this wild journey, and I'm more grateful than I can ever properly express.

ABOUT THE AUTHOR

Yume Kitasei is the author of *Saltcrop*, *The Stardust Grail*, and *The Deep Sky*. She is Japanese and American and grew up in a space between two cultures—the same space where her stories reside. She lives in Brooklyn with two cats, Boondoggle and Filibuster.